As she stepped over the last ridge, she saw a man staring up at the steep ice flows overhead. He cried out, "Stop!"

She obeyed the fear in his voice. "Up there," he said. "Quickly." He broke into a run across snow that collapsed under his heavy step. She followed.

A massive crack! filled the air as an overhanging ledge of ice snapped off and fell to the flat where they had just been standing.

She heard the man panting next to her and turned to study him more carefully. He was unremarkable for a mountaineer.

Then she noticed the sweatband across his head. She realized he was wearing a *nection*, a headband to connect his mind with distant computers. She recoiled slightly.

"Don't be *too* upset," he said, "my headband just saved your life."

MARC STIEGLER

THE GENTLE SEDUCTION

BAEN BOOKS

THE GENTLE SEDUCTION

These stories were previously published in *Analog*.

A Baen Books Original

Baen Publishing Enterprises
260 Fifth Avenue
New York, N.Y. 10001

ISBN: 0-671-69887-7

Cover art by Corey Wolfe

First printing, July 1990

Distributed by
SIMON & SCHUSTER
1230 Avenue of the Americas
New York, N.Y. 10020

Printed in the United States of America

CONTENTS

Masters of the Mortal God

Some years ago I allowed a close friend to go through all my writings, not just the ones that I have published, but all of them, including the scribbled attempts at stories I wrote when I was in high school. When she was done, I asked her what themes, if any, were shared by all my stories. I myself had already concluded that there were no such unifying points, but I thought it at least faintly possible that a less subjective eye could spot what was invisible to me.

Well, my friend paused but for a moment before nodding her head. "All your characters are moral," she asserted. "I noticed it right off."

I started to object. After all, Gibs Stelman lies and cheats and steals. He even runs for political office. Surely he is not a moral being!

And yet, even he shares this common thread. I wonder how many of us would hold up as well as Gibs does, given the accident of his gift: the ability to grant life or death, the ability to rejuvenate the old and make them young again.

Masters Of the Mortal God

Yesterday, four more people died.

I stared at the glass in my hand, watching my splintered reflection in the crystal. The blood red liquid muted the pallor of my skin. I slouched in the cushions of my acceleration couch, just as I had the day before.

Today, four more people would die.

"Gibs, we have just entered normal space. The Forma quarantine area is just ahead," a woman's voice informed me.

I exhaled, and could barely notice the vile alcoholic stench when I breathed again.

Fortunately, there was no one aboard my impregnable hospital ship to be horrified by the smell, or to be shocked by the appearance of a once-great mindshifter. Only Safire, the ship's computer, could see me; perhaps only she cared.

I waved my left hand; the drink sloshed over, to puddle in the couch. "Thanks, Safire, let's see the place." Safire lit the overhead viewpanel. I gasped despite myself. I understood why some people thought Forma might be an artifact of an alien civilization.

The most striking characteristic was the Eye: the huge circle of permanent white clouds that stared forever back at the star Pelocampus.

The Eye existed because Forma rotated once for each revolution around Pelocampus. Beneath the Eye it was always high noon. Beneath the Eye the ocean simmered despite the protection of clouds of steam.

Theoretically, the planet should have lost its atmosphere millions of years ago. All gases should have either boiled off at the Eye, or frozen at the Pole, on the far side. Indeed, Forma *was* losing its atmosphere, but much more slowly than expected: clouds reflected much of the heat at the Eye. Fierce currents of wind and water carried heat around to the wasteland at the Pole. Even the planet's core, with a thinned mantle at the Eye and the Pole, acted as a heat exchanger.

Between the winds and the water, the weather sometimes whipped wicked. Therefore a large research expedition had come here soon after the development of the Hawking stardrive. For a long time they had been beyond even the Frontier.

Eventually civilization expanded to surround Forma. Yet Forma remained quarantined: the descendants of the researchers liked to be alone. Intruders were not welcome. The Federation respected their wishes.

"It is beautiful, is it not, Gibs?" Safire's soothing contralto interrupted my reverie.

I turned away from the scene, tossing down the rest of my drink. My head ached. "Yeah." How I hated beauty! All beauty now reminded me of beauty now gone forever.

How could I have lost her! I had been a god, giving life and death throughout the reaches of space, and still I had not been able to change one woman's fate. "Safire, another drink," I said.

"Very well." I heard the sound of a mixer humming.

I shook my head. "Wait. How long before we can set down?"

"On Forma? We can't land there. It's quarantined."

I stared at the Eye again. Did Forma have what I needed? The people were rumored to be bright, friendly, and cheerful. I needed that; I needed to surround myself with people who were happy.

But more importantly, the people of Forma had never heard of Transfer, or immortality, or Gibs Stelman. They were innocent. I needed that more than anything else.

"I don't care about the quarantine. I want to land."

"What about the warships?"

I cursed. "What warships?"

Spaceship representations grew around the image of the planet. A fleet of detector satellites sailed in a symmetric sphere. Two starship task forces hovered above the Eye and the Pole.

I squinted at the cruisers. "Earth?"

"No. Sirius and Omegar."

"What?! I thought Sirius and Omegar were at war."

"So they are, Gibs. When Sirius offered to enforce the quarantine, Omegar demanded a joint force."

"Why would either of them care about a weather research outpost?"

"I don't know."

Forma's innocence would end suddenly, it appeared. I was a little drunk. I closed my eyes to prevent the tears. I had come here to escape the troubles of Man, not to solve them! Yet, perhaps there was still time. "Do they know we're here?"

"I don't believe so," Safire replied. "We're flying dark, using only passive sensors. I only saw them because they're using active sensors."

"Good." Well, I couldn't sneak a behemoth like Safire past the cordon without being seen, but I might be able to sneak through in my sport boat. "Prep Glitter for me, Safire."

"Very well, Gibs. But from this distance I won't be able to operate her."

"What? Oh, I guess not." The relays would be a bit slow for outmaneuvering hostile warships. "I'll fly her myself."

I could feel Safire's sensors scanning me.

"What's your problem?" I continued, "I can handle her."

"Very well, Gibs." The voice was perfectly level, and Safire was a computer after all—but still I thought I heard a note of doubt.

A robot rolled in with my drink. "Thanks," I said as I leaned forward. But I faltered before gripping the glass. Reluctantly, I withdrew my hand. "Safire, is Glitter's bar well stocked?"

"All the bottles are topped off."

"Um. Well, uh, maybe you should empty them out."

"Very well, Gibs." This time, I knew I heard relief in the voice. Safire cared. It was part of her programming.

A mindshifter's skill, such as mine, can put an old man into a young body. Such skill is too rare and valuable to be purchased with money. The coin with which one purchases such Transfer is technology—the most advanced technology, often the most secret technology, of the planets.

Thus Glitter was an extraordinary vessel, almost as extraordinary as Safire herself. Her engines were built on Athens, her sensors on Cassandra, her shields on Mary Jane. Glitter could beat any one of the cruisers in the fleets around Forma. Safire could take a whole task force with ease.

But I hadn't come for fighting; I had come for surcease. All I wanted was a quiet landing. So I used minimum power, and I used a single tight beam to Safire for tracking. I almost made it through.

One of the unmanned satellites pinged me just outside the atmosphere. Vessels converged from all sides. "So much for the quiet approach," I muttered as I applied full thrust and plunged toward Forma. Two muffled ion beams lanced my hull before the atmosphere thickened enough to scatter space weapons.

I sat back in the pilot's seat, rather pleased with myself. "I told you I could get through," I told Safire through the tight comm beam.

At that moment the ship jerked to the left and started tumbling. A clap of thunder sounded in my ears, and lightning tried to turn half my cringing instruments to junk parts.

Unbelievable! Here I was, in a spaceship impregnable to the fiercest blasts of a battleship, getting whipped around by a little rough weather!

The landing still shouldn't have been difficult, but my head ached, and my body trembled from three years of fervent abuse. So Glitter tumbled and spun and hurtled into the ground at a crushing velocity. It was an ignoble ending to a life over seven lifetimes old.

Today, four more people would die.

Minutes later I realized that I was still alive. The viewplate was shattered; I skittered over the crazy-tilt floor and starboard bulkheads to the airlock and threw it open.

Powdered snow poured through the opening. The draft numbed my fingers even as I let the lock snap shut. I and Glitter lay buried beneath several hundred feet of snow.

With that information, several of the instrument readings took on meaning; they were not broken, just surprised. And the engines still worked.

An hour later, Glitter rested snug in an arctic valley. I needed a drink.

No chance, of course, since I had denied myself any sensible refreshments in a moment of Safire-induced self-retribution. I settled for a breath of fresh air.

It took me less than thirty seconds outside to realize that I'd made a mistake. Like the cat that stuck his nose through the door into the blizzard, I scurried back inside.

Dammit, I had come prepared with a *bathing suit*, not a *snow parka*. I had planned to land some thousands of miles closer to the Eye. I suppose I was lucky I landed here; the snow saved my life. Nevertheless, now that I was saved, the snow should have had the decency to evaporate.

It took me another day, with Safire's help, to fix enough of the viewplate so I could see to navigate.

I started Eyeward, taking Glitter into the air for a few minutes, skimming along for a hundred miles or so, and grounding once more to look around. On my second landing I saw the skeleton.

At least, it looked like a skeleton, floating high in the freezing air—the skeleton of an airplane, with wings of gauze. I lifted and ran Glitter as fast as I could; it was not in my plans to be found by the authorities. I left the skeleton far behind, then turned a few times at random to throw off any trackers.

When I landed again, I quickly spotted another skeleton floating in the distance.

With an oath, I roared away again. Three times I

landed before finding a place where I wasn't in line of sight of one of the damned things.

The climate was milder here; I could inhale the outside air without a burning sensation in my lungs. There were scattered clumps of pine-like trees. I parked Glitter beneath one clump and pulled a camouflage net over the top. The netting had been designed to camouflage her in the deciduous forests of Springform; it looked obscene here, but not as obscene as a flashy chrome spaceyacht.

"How long will the repairs take, Safire?" I asked as I watched robots scurry about.

"Three or four days. The damage reports are incomplete as yet."

I had no intention of being cooped up that long. "Is there anything I can do to speed things up?"

"Yes, Gibs. You could relax."

"Ha! Better yet, I'll get out of your way." I smiled. "I'll take the slipjet. When Glitter's ready, she can catch up."

There was a long pause. "Very well, Gibs."

It started as a chilly ride, which was not much of a surprise. What I had forgotten was how much colder it is to sit still in a strong wind, than it is to be throwing camouflage netting in calm air. Damn! I had coddled myself too long aboard starships and inside protected buildings. How could I have forgotten the meaning of weather, and the coldness that crept slowly into your bones?

By the time I realized I had made a grave error, I knew it was too late to get back to Glitter; my hands would be frozen before I returned.

I landed and ran in circles around the slipjet, but I couldn't get really warm again. I climbed aboard and flew a few more miles before I lost feeling in my hands and landed.

"Safire," I yelled into my wristcom; the wristcom was linked to Glitter, which was in turn linked to my beautiful starship, "I'm stuck in the middle of a wasteland." I quickly explained the situation. "Can you send Glitter after me?"

"I can fly Glitter, Gibs, but her instruments are a wreck. I can't locate your position with anything she has left."

"Well, fly her in the right general direction. I can tell if she's gone past me." At least my wristcom showed Glitter's direction. "If I see her, I'll yell."

"She's lifting now," Safire replied.

All I could do was wait. I ran in circles, and yelled, and held my hands inside my jacket. My current body was tough and healthy, but it wouldn't last long here. My teeth chattered.

Today, four more people would die.

This was my second fatal mistake in two days. Yet neither fatal mistake was as unforgiveable as the mistake I had been making for the last three years. For all the deaths in all those years, this silly ending was richly deserved.

But Death missed me again. I saw a vehicle float out of the crisp blue-blackness of the horizon. "Safire, I see her!" I cried joyfully. "Turn about 10 degrees clockward, and—" I stopped in horror.

"Gibs? What's wrong?"

"Belay that order, Safire," I replied thickly. "It's a skeleton." The machine drifted closer, turning 10 degrees clockward just as if it had heard my order.

Thunder roared behind me. I turned to see a different kind of vessel descending. As it landed I saw the emblem of Winterform on its side.

A hull section snapped down, and a uniformed woman stepped out. "You're under arrest for unlawful trespass and malicious interference with a research task," she stated in tones as crisp and cold as the winter winds.

"Great," I said with a shiver, "Throw me into confinement." I ran toward her. "And hurry."

"Freeze," she commanded, drawing a lethal-looking instrument from her belt.

"You can count on it, my lady." I stopped. She came nearer and ran a second instrument over my body. She stopped at my wrist.

"What's that device?"

"It's a wristcom, to let me communicate with my ship."

"Put out your arm, slowly."

I did, and she removed my communicator. Her fingers felt surprisingly warm as they brushed my hand.

She nodded to the ship. "Better get inside. I have medication for frostbite."

I lay on a couch not unlike an acceleration couch as she smeared excruciatingly hot cream over my arms, legs and nose. I kept my teeth clenched and winced occasionally.

"Go ahead and scream," she said gently—her voice sounded so concerned that I opened my eyes to see if it was the same person. "I know how painful this must be."

I suppressed a spasm as she rubbed my nose again. I groaned. "My body was made for sandy beaches and warm summer nights, not for arctic blues." It was true: I typically wore a tan, lean body with soulful blue eyes and an enigmatic smile. More recently my smile was grim, my eyes were bloodshot, and my body was an emaciated ghost, but I still wasn't suited to cold weather.

She snapped the medikit shut. "It looks like you'll survive. You won't even have to re-grow any toes, amazingly enough. You were lucky."

"You were my luck, my lady. Thank you." I felt very warm toward this cold savior.

"Yes." She stood up. "Now tell me what you're doing here."

I sighed. How much of the truth should I tell? "I have come seeking surcease. I require gentle harmonies and melodious laughter, to return from the edge of insanity."

The hard outline of her face did not change. "You sound like a half-baked poet. Is that what you do when you're not cavorting around the galaxy in your toy spaceyacht? Or is poetry the latest fad among the Federation's playboys?"

I winced. "Even playboys contribute more to mankind than I have of late," I whispered.

"Hmph." She started to soften; then she thought

better of it. "And you came all the way to Forma for *surcease*?"

"The Federation is such that I cannot rest, no matter where I go."

"I see." Her voice chilled so deeply that my frostbite returned. "What crimes did you commit in the Federation that forced you to flee? Besides stealing a space-yacht, that is."

My jaw dropped. "Unkind maiden!" I protested. I suppose this wasn't the time for bantering, but I couldn't help myself; I was a Shakespearean actor in my first lifetime, and the style still haunts me. "An' do thou wound most deep with thy unjust accusations!"

As it happened, my approach was precisely right. Her icy expression somehow caught the light in a new way, and her smile sparkled. "Nay, sad sir. Excuse me my distrust, but pray tell me in truth thy purpose in the lands of Winterform." Her eyes, dark and beautiful in contrast to the smooth whiteness of her skin, held me in trance. As her expression changed and changed again, I perceived depths to this person, layers like an onion, of closeness and distance, compassion and ruth-lessness, warmth and coldness.

I was in love.

Perhaps I should explain. In my first lifetime, and even my second, I sought my mates in the normal manner of mortal men. But after a few lifetimes I developed an eye for the woman who was *just right* for *this life*. In short, I became capable of recognizing love at first sight. It has never failed me since.

In my seventh lifetime, which had just ended prema-turely, I had known who my mate should be. I had never touched her. I could see her in my mind's eye now . . .

No! I shook my head; memories only serve if they are not overloaded with emotion.

I jerked as my newfound love clapped her hands in front of me.

"Are you all right?" she asked.

"At last, at last." My laughter rang with joy for the first time in a lifetime. I knelt before her, taking her hand in mine, kissing it. "My lady," I crooned, "please, please marry me."

Perhaps this was rushing things a bit, but I couldn't help it. Hope has always been my master.

Besides, I believe you should always be honest, because the truth is usually unbelievable. If the truth doesn't work, you can follow it up with a good lie and people will believe *that*.

Sadly the truth in this case was quite unbelievable. And though *I* may recognize love at first sight, my mates-to-be do not always recognize it with equal facility.

She drew back, looking stern, shaking her head, and laughing all at the same time. Clearly, she did not perceive Fate's handiwork here. "You don't even know my name!"

"It matters not, my rose who would smell as sweet. I have held a thousand names, yet I am who I am, though the river of labels flows onward."

That was the wrong thing to say; when I mentioned having held a thousand names, she became very suspicious.

She drew her gun. "You seem to have recovered some feeling in your hands. Hold them out, slowly."

"No, you don't understand," I started to explain. "I have the power to recognize love at first sight. We are destined to spend this lifetime together."

"We are, huh? I have some disappointing news for you, mister." She circled my hands with a pair of force cuffs. "Wait a minute." She moved in front of me, looking me in the eye. "You said 'this lifetime.' " Her eyes narrowed. "Have you had Transfer? Did *you* waste a mindshifter's time and ability?"

"No, you don't understand," I continued, "I *am* a mindshifter! I have saved thousands of lives! Come with me, I can give you lifetimes beyond measure as well."

She froze there, a statue of hatred. "I see. So that's why you've come to Forma, the only world where there's never been a mindshifter. You'll milk us dry before we join the Federation." Her fists clenched. "Then let me tell you something. It is a felony to try to

buy a government official. And it is . . . immoral to try
to buy a woman."

She slammed the hatch that connected her cockpit to
my compartment.

Thus ended the honest approach; she thought I sold
my services to the highest bidder. Unfortunately, there
was just enough truth in her opinion to make it hard to
disprove.

Mind transplant surgery remained a true art. Oh, it
required extraordinary engineering abilities too, in everything from complex connectivity theory to axonal
counterstimulus. But if Transfer had just been an engineering problem, Man would have programmed a computer for it. Safire could perform other kinds of surgery
more quickly and more accurately than I. Her powers
of pattern recognition and reconstruction were superb.

But beyond the facts and the formulas and even the
patterns, mindshifting required a special gift. It required the ability to *know*, for this *one unique human
being*, which neurons needed to be transplanted, which
needed to be replaced, and which needed to be recon-
nected. Each Transfer was a new challenge, a labyrin-
thine problem in both pattern recognition and learning.
Each Transfer offered the surgeon a million tiny moments of indecision, a million chances to fail. If his gift
were strong and pure, the surgeon might be able to do
four Transfers in a day.

This special gift, the oddball genius demanded for
mindshifting, belonged to a tiny handful of men. Even
on Earth, there were too few mindshifters to go around.
Even on Earth, they commanded huge prices for their
labors.

And of the handful of mindshifters in the universe,
only a spoonful of the most dedicated, adventuresome,
foolish mindshifters ventured to the Frontier. Each took
a star sector with dozens, even hundreds, of scattered
planets, and bounced from place to place in a desperate
race to save human lives. They did not necessarily
save the *wealthiest*, or the *most powerful*, but they
tried to save the *best*, and the *most needed* human
beings they encountered.

Of course, sometimes saving the *best* people is akin to saving the wealthy and powerful: the best often achieve wealth and power. And those who received Transfer inevitably became wealthy and powerful in their second or third lifetimes.

I could understand why my lady thought I had come to Forma to squeeze her people. What she didn't understand was that the price I could command on Forma would be equally great wherever I went. I offered the gift of life itself; it was beyond price.

Re-educating my loved one would have to be postponed. My current situation needed to be changed.

I contemplated the matter from every angle. I was, after all, a mortal god; I would find a way to escape.

I owned a lockpick toolkit, but it was on my slipjet. I had my laser ring, but it was powered from Glitter, and I had no way to light it since my captress removed my wristcom.

Eventually I realized I was trapped. All I had left was my guile.

"Queen of my life!" I yelled into the cockpit through the closed passage. "Please grant me the kindness to know thy name!" She did not answer. Guile would have to wait.

Eventually we landed. There was little I could do, with my wrists in the forcecuffs, except stumble into my lover-to-be as we went out the hatch.

"My name is Keara," she answered my question of hours ago.

I stumbled.

"Can't you even stand up on your own?" She propped me up and pushed me forward with a grunt.

"Keara." I smacked my lips. "Keara is a beautiful name." I had the keys to the cuffs in my right hand, plucked from the lady's clothing in our moment of ecstatic embrace. "How do you think it will look on a marriage license?"

She shook her head. "You are *impossible!*"

"Of course," I cried, slipping the cuffs from my arms. I cut her legs out from under her; she cut my legs out from under me. We wrestled in the snow. My greater size, and my black belt in modkido from 6 lifetimes earlier, gave me a great advantage.

I was deeply annoyed when she pinned me and refastened the cuffs. "Perhaps you're not impossible after all," she chuckled. "Perhaps you're just difficult."

The snow numbed my cheek. I grunted, staggering to my feet. "How'd you do that?"

"I keep fit," she muttered.

I nodded my head. I still had the reflexes and physical strength of a lush.

We walked toward a sleek, black building that stretched to the horizon. "What city is this, by the way?" I asked.

"You're in Whitepeak." Keara rolled her eyes. "You really *are* lost, aren't you?" She laughed. "Well, a jail is a jail, I imagine."

It was ridiculous, being jailed because of a bunch of aerial skeletons. "Say, what are those skeletons?" I asked.

"Skeletons?"

"Yes, my lady. The ghosts of aircraft which followed me."

"Oh." Keara laughed softly. "Those are weather sensors. Solar powered."

"Fascinating." It was also obvious, for a colony that had started as a weather research station.

A flash of sky-flooding lightning blinded me for a second. "Wow, that lightning is beyond belief!" I told her.

She pushed me into the building. "Hurry," she cried.

"What's wrong?" I asked as she rushed me down a descending corridor.

"It's a blizzarcane, you fool—" the building shook as the thunderclap arrived.

From the corner of my eye, I saw another blast of lightning tear through the ceiling to the floor. The sound deafened me. I was thrown toward a widening seam in the concrete. Hunks of roof fell all around, and Keara slid with me toward certain doom. "Keara!" I cried, though I could not hear my own voice.

She held her hands over her eyes, scrabbling against the floor. She had been looking in the direction of the bolt when it struck.

I tried to pull her aside, away from the heaving edge of the disintegrating floor, but she fought me.

I had no choice in the matter if I was going to save her life: I kicked her until she stopped moving. I couldn't pull her effectively with my hands behind my back, so I knelt beside her and used my teeth to drag her farther from the hole. More chunks of roof fell around us. I regained the cuff keys from her pocket, and released myself.

She was awfully quiet. Her eyes . . . her current body was probably permanently blinded. Her pulse fluttered. I might well have hurt her badly in my haste to save her life.

Two men in uniforms like Keara's came running down the hall; I waved frantically. "She's hurt!" I yelled, "Get a doctor!" I could almost hear what I was saying again.

One held back as they came up to me; the other pushed me aside as he stepped forward. "It's Keara," he said grimly, "the spy must have knocked her out when the attack started." He felt her pulse. "He may have killed her."

The other soldier lifted his lazegun; not coincidentally, it had been pointed at the ground beneath my feet when they arrived.

My reaction time improved with the excitement: as his weapon steadied I leaped to the side, putting the other man between myself and the gun. He fired; I smelled the smoke of burning flesh as the man who had examined Keara took the hit. With a moment's struggle, I pulled him into my arms, and his weapon into my hands. The man who had fired circled to get a clear shot, but I shot first. With a scream he went down.

Looking up, I saw four more men running down the hall.

I looked down at Keara. There was nothing I could do for her here. Angry at myself and my situation, I jumped away and headed outside.

Stepping through a breech in the wall, I quickly learned to appreciate the meaning of "blizzarcane." Gale winds blew snow in my nose and mouth so fast that the snow caked up, choking me. I stepped back toward the shelter, wondering what to do when they found me again.

Abruptly the weather cleared. The wind died, though I could see snow swirling in every direction. Dazed, I concluded we were in the eye of the storm. I raced to the shipyard with Keara's keys still clenched in my hand.

On most worlds I would have been doomed to hang around outside the locked vessels, waiting for someone to recapture me. But on Forma, retinal patterns hadn't yet replaced more primitive safeguards. One of Keara's keys opened the hatch. In seconds I was at the controls of Keara's ship. In minutes I was airborne.

Taking off might have been the stupidest decision of my life, had I not so recently made so many stupid decisions.

There was no way out of the storm's eye; at all altitudes the wind buffeted the ship back to the center, or down toward the ground. All I could do was watch the holocaust.

And holocaust it was. The blizzarcane ripped through the city, sleek, buried, and invincible though Whitepeak seemed. Nothing would have been left had the storm continued for over an hour.

But before that happened, a soft, glowing aurora settled around the blizzarcane. A last blanket of snow fell, as though the storm had collapsed to the ground. The sun appeared, throwing long shadows across the jagged pieces of the city.

Whitepeak was in trouble, and I did not even know if Keara was alive. I wanted to return, to help rebuild.

But if I returned I would probably be shot. First I would need to make some preparations on board Glitter. Keara had left my wristcom on board this ship; with some digging I finally found it. With guidance once more, I headed for Glitter again.

A skeleton wafted through the air, in my direction. I sank low, and maneuvered around it. Another one appeared.

In my efforts to keep out of view, I was herded, slowly but surely, away from my ship.

If I couldn't go back to Glitter, I figured I better at least get out of Winterform. That was easy enough since the skeletons were forcing me Eyeward. Moreover, I would feel more comfortable if I had some mountains between me and the skeletons, so I also flew clockward, toward Hayes' Rift.

I cruised low until I reached the Rightcut Mountains, which separated the Rift from the rest of the continent. I hopped over Rightcut with no skeletons in sight and breathed a sigh of relief.

Two cruisers, utterly unlike the one I commanded, popped over the mountains just behind me.

An alarm sounded as my ship shook and spun out of control.

There weren't any jumpbelts on Forman ships, I discovered; but there were glidechutes, another relic of past lifetimes. With some trepidation, I grabbed a purple one (I would have chosen something more discreet had I had time to be selective) and popped the hatch.

The ships sailed overhead. My old one left a trail of bright orange flame and dark brown smoke. It made quite a beautiful color stroke against the crisp blue sky. It crashed far down the side of Rightcut, into thick forest. The two other ships curled around, and came back for me.

I was already looking for a way down that was quick but not hard. This is always a difficult combination to find on planets that are not made of foam rubber. Still, I did well enough; as I passed over a lake I slipped from the chute harness and prayed the water was deep but not cold. The chute drifted onward, attracting attention to its graceful, confident descent.

The water was deep as I had hoped. It was also cold. I swam for the shore with enthusiasm.

I dragged myself out of the sucking mud on the bank and lay with my teeth chattering, watching the cruisers that had nailed me as they watched the glidechute. With the flick of a ship's beam, the chute turned to purple smoke. The cruisers departed.

How delightful! Now I could die of hypothermia in peace. I shook quietly, though violently. "Safire," I stammered into my wristcom, "I don't suppose you can get Glitter to me within an hour, can you?"

"No." Safire had such a way with words.

I tried to put myself into an autohypnotic state where I could be more comfortable, and failed. I opened my eyes again.

Clearly, it was autumn here: the leaves were multi-colored, red and yellow and green and auburn, and I could smell the pulp of the leaves decaying as I lay upon them.

Yet, it couldn't be a real, Earth autumn. Here in Fallform it was *always* autumn. There was no change of season, no reason for the trees to change colors. The trees had to be like this all the time.

Closer inspection showed that each tree and each type of leaf had a distinct color. They were not changing with the season; they were that color forever.

A pair of mud-spattered boots appeared before me. Looking up, I saw a reddish leather jacket and a yellow scarf. Looking higher still, I saw bright blue suspicious eyes. "Hi," I said with a smile, trying to look harmless for the lady staring down at me.

"He looks harmless enough," one of the men accompanying the brown boots said.

"At the moment, sir, I am so harmless that I may die of exposure. I hate to ask favors of strangers, but do you have dry clothes I could borrow for a day or two?"

"I don't like it," said another voice from the shadows, "He's from Winterform. He's *still* not a friend of ours. Kill him."

"Wait." The woman in brown boots knelt beside me. "What's that?" she asked, pointing at my wristcom.

Telling the truth seemed easiest. "It's a communicator that lets me talk to my ship."

"Your ship just got blown out of the sky."

Silence seemed more appropriate than *too* much truth.

She touched me. Her mouth widened. "Jurn, get a fire started, and bring a sleeping bag." She stretched out next to me and held me close, bringing me into her warmth. "You were serious about the exposure."

"I intend to survive," I muttered, still shaking, though her cheek was warm against mine.

They bundled me up and fed me hot soup, and I did in fact survive. The lady sent the others away. "Who are you?" she began the interrogation. "Why are you here?"

Never ask a person two questions simultaneously: the person will answer the question of his choice, which will be the one that gets you the least information. "I came here to escape from Winterform. I fear the authorities are eager to preside at my funeral."

"I see." She smiled. "Did you come seeking help from the authorities of Fallform?"

Her smile seemed out of place; I realized I was standing on the brink of a cliff. Calmly, very calmly, I shrugged. "Not particularly. I guess it's too late to ask, but: weren't those Fallform ships that fried my ship?"

"Every vicious bit of them." She trembled with anger, then touched her hand to the side of my head. "You must sleep. In a few hours we must travel fast, and deep, before they come looking for you."

As she touched me, I felt tired. I realized that I'd been up for . . . I didn't know how long.

"Damn these planets that don't have a decent night/ day sequence," I muttered. "How am I supposed to know when I'm supposed to sleep?"

"What?!" Alarm rang in her voice, but I hardly noticed. "What's your name?"

"Gibs. Stelman," I yawned. "What's yours?"

"Sharyn."

"Sharyn. Beautiful." With her name on my lips, I passed into oblivion.

I awoke groggy, from a nightmare.

I smelled cooking.

Rolling out of the bag, I stalked the chef. Jurn turned to me with a plate. "Here," he offered, with only a hint of hostility. It was scrambled eggs (I didn't ask what kind) and coarse bread, and it was the best meal I'd eaten in a lifetime.

"You're an outstanding cook," I commended Jurn.

He turned his head to me, scowling. "You're a leech."

I gagged. Was he right? No. Or at least, he was only almost right. "You're wrong," I said quietly. "Only recently have I been a leech." I had almost forgotten, in my joy of a moment's living.

Today, four more people would die.

I walked away from the fire.

Sharyn stole silently into the clearing. "Get packed," she commanded.

"How far do we have to go?" I asked.

Her head snapped up. "Too far," she said. She turned Eyeward. "Walk with me," she said, signaling. I hesitated for a moment out of philosophical opposition to being given orders; but in this forest she was the boss. We walked together.

Soon we came to a trail and the going became brisk. "I must thank whoever lent me these clothes for being so close to my size," I said. I waved my hands in a theatrical expression of grandeur. "And I must thank whoever designed this incredible scene for us to walk through." I pointed forward. "The sky, forever poised near sunset," I said.

Sharyn looked at me strangely. "We are near the city of Sunset," she granted, puzzled.

I bit my lip. "And the pink backlighting for curling tendrils of clouds. I've never seen anything like it before." Indeed I hadn't. It reminded me of a mackerel sky, but with long, tapered clouds.

"You've never seen a filament sky before?" The more I talked, the more I put my foot in it.

"Not for many moons," I said, then realized what a mistake *that* was: Forma had no moons, and no calendar based on them.

"Who are you?" This time she didn't make the mistake of asking a second question; this time my life hung in the balance.

"I am no one you need fear."

She laughed. "And whom do you think I fear?" she asked.

I looked across at her. She walked lightly, with the grace of one who knew her own power, her eyes up-lifted in defiance of the Universe. I had once known her feeling well, the feeling of confidence in your ability to meet your own Destiny. It was a feeling I had almost forgotten.

Suddenly I was in love. "Sharyn," I said, holding out my hand.

"What?" she replied, reaching her hand in turn toward mine.

Startled, I jerked back. "Nothing." I stared intently at the ground.

There was a pause, then curt words. "You must answer my question. You must tell me who you are."

"Yes, I must." I looked up at the filament sky, and refused to let my eyes water. "Who am I? I am the remains of the man whom once I was." I took a deep breath. "A man who was a mortal god. He was one who could save life or bring death."

"Hm." Sharyn didn't know whether to be impressed or not. "Sounds like a doctor to me."

I barked a laugh. "Yes, I was a doctor. But a normal doctor cannot save a man's life."

She looked at me, puzzled.

"The best a doctor can do is save a few more dusty hours to be appended to a man's life. A doctor cannot grant a 60 year old man more than 20 or 25 more years. He cannot grant a 40 year old man more than an equal 40 years." I held up my hands, stretching them wide before Sharyn. "But I, my lady, once I could grant eternity."

"You're the Sirian mindshifter," she said.

"What?"

"We heard that a Sirian mindshifter had landed without authorization. You really *are* a hunted man."

"I'm not Sirian!"

"Well, if you're not Sirian, then you're Omegaran."

"No."

She shook her head in exasperation. "Then why are you here?"

"I came to find a peaceful place where people were happy, yet where they had never heard of mindshifters or Transfer." My voice turned bitter. "I can see I am too late." I started to reach for her again, and stopped. I smiled. "Instead I found you."

I was deeply confused. I had first learned to recognize love at first sight near the end of my second lifetime; always since then, I had fallen in love with exactly one woman each time I mindshifted. I had never understood the pattern, but it had always run true.

Yet here, in a span of 48 hours, I had fallen in love twice! And I *did* love them both, Keara *and* Sharyn. What should I do?

"You certainly didn't find a *peaceful* place," Sharyn said with bitterness similar to mine. "Fallform and Winterform have been at war for years now. And it looks like Summerform has finally decided to unite with Fallform, since the Sirians arrived."

"What? I don't believe it. I watched Forma from space, and I haven't seen anything like an army anywhere." I thought back on the blizzarcane. "Frankly, the weather here seems more dangerous than the people."

She looked at me in disbelief. "Stelman, don't you remember who we Formans are? This was a *weather research* station! How would you *expect* us to attack each other?"

"Omigod. Of course." A number of pieces fell into place. Not only did that explain a storm so powerful it could wreck a fortified city like Whitepeak, but it explained why Glitter had been so badly crisped by a mere lightning bolt, when I first landed. "So that's why the Sirians and Omegarans are here." What an extraordinary weapon weather control would be against the rest of the Federation! Throughout history, the winners of wars had been those who had the longest-ranged weapons. But imagine using a weapon your enemy didn't even *know* was a weapon!

"The Sirians want to trade mindshifts for information on weather control. Both the Sirians and the Omegarans promise to leave a mindshifter here to keep the authorities—whichever authorities give them the best deal—immortal. Needless to say, the leaders of all four Forms are dancing as fast as they can to the Sirian tune."

I snorted. "Whoever wins Sirian support will be in for a big disappointment. The Sirians may be able to persuade a mindshifter to come to the Frontier once to make a few Transfers, but there's no way they'll persuade a surgeon to move out here permanently. The only mindshifters who'll serve Forma on a regular basis are the Frontier mindshifters—and if Forma gives all its best technology to Sirius or Omegar, no Frontier surgeon will touch Forma, because Forma won't have anything worth trading for."

"Well, the leaders of the Forms don't know that, and wouldn't believe you if you told them. The Sirians have them convinced that they'll get a Sirian mindshifter permanently stationed here." She pointed back at her handful of followers. "That's why we're here. Bardon, the President of Fallform, is the most dangerous leader: he's old, and his position is tenured. He's *desperate* to win the Transfer." She clenched her fists. "We have to unite the people of Forma, and we have to start by stopping the people like Bardon."

The scenery had changed as we spoke: the percentage of green-leaved trees increased as we dropped to lower altitudes. More interesting, I noticed a number of clumps of trees that looked suspiciously like they could conceal more technological installations.

So I wasn't surprised when Sharyn stopped. "We're here," she announced.

"You keep your ships well hidden," I commented, pointing at the three closest hiding places.

She turned sharply toward me, then smiled. "You have keen eyes after all."

"I have more than that. I have centuries of experience with societies such as Forma's. I have realigned many of them." The "realignment" of societies came with being a mortal god: at each planet I touched, I chose between life and death for the most influential minds of that planet. And a society reflects the thinking of its most influential minds. "Rather than leading a small rebel force, which is what you seem to have gathered here, why don't you let me simply assassinate the most troublesome individuals?"

She shook her head. "You don't understand. The problem is deeper than that. Even if I killed all the present leaders, the next ones would be just as bad. The whole planet is crazy with Transfer fever."

I waved her objection aside. "An experienced assassin *never* needs to kill more than twenty people to end a war or unite a planet. It just requires skillful executions. You have to make sure that the *next* twenty people, the successors to the dead, know three things: First, they must know that the first twenty were killed intentionally. Second, they must know why their predecessors were killed. Third, and most important, they be completely convinced that they are just as easy to kill as the others were."

As I was speaking, I got more and more wrapped up in my words. So I was surprised by the effect I had wrought.

Sharyn's mouth dropped open in awe. "Of course! What a brilliant idea!"

I started to disclaim any brilliance, but she continued.

"I'll get them all," she laughed, so wickedly I was surprised by her malevolence. Then her laughter ran the scales, from light amusement to near sorrow. "I'm sorry," she said.

"For what?" I asked.

"Never mind." She danced close, to kiss me on the cheek. I tried to put my arms around her, but she danced away again. "I have to go," she said, turning.

"Wait!" I cried.

She stopped. "What?"

"You can't do this alone."

"Why not? You've done it several times before, or so you said. Why would I fail where you succeeded?"

I closed my eyes. I knew what would happen: she

wouldn't believe me when I explained. Yet, I would explain anyway. "I have lived seven full lifetimes. I have had experiences beyond you imagining. There is both wisdom and power in growing older, my lady." I stood straighter, letting my stage presence fill the clump of forest around us.

"Perhaps." She nodded her head from side to side. "But I think I can handle it."

My power and the presence evaporated; I felt like an old man.

How can you explain to a first-lifer the lessons you learn the fifth or a sixth time around? How can you express the little ways you are always aware of the world around you, sensing places where things lie hidden beneath other surfaces, knowing danger in a lifting eyebrow, touching an unfamiliar surface in a careful examination before grasping it?

I had been a Frontier mindshifter, often a target of the corrupt and the fanatical. In hundreds of tests of survival I had won. To pit me, in my eighth lifetime, against a whole army of first-lifers was to seal their deaths in a sure stroke.

But Sharyn herself was a first-lifer. Though she might destroy several of her enemies with her prowess and competence, yet her advantage over any one of them was just a narrow margin. One of them would get her, before she could complete the job. "Please," I begged, "let me handle the repair of Forma."

She put her hands on her hips, and cocked her head. "Wait a minute." She walked around me, slowly, judging. "Who saved whose life yesterday?" she asked. "Who is currently the captive of whom?" Her voice held no mockery, just objective observation. "I will do this job *my* way." She turned and trotted off.

"Wait!" I yelled.

She turned long enough to blow me a kiss.

"I love you!"

She continued on, as if she hadn't heard.

I sat on a fallen tree trunk. I marshalled my arguments for my next meeting with Sharyn; I couldn't go back to Keara until I was sure Sharyn wouldn't get herself killed.

I sat for a long time. At last a bright yellow blur bounced out of the forest from my right.

"Hi," said a golden-haired girl of perhaps seventeen years. She held out her hand. "My name is Wendy."

I stood up, wiping my hand before shaking hers. "And I'm Gibs Stelman."

"I know. You're the mindshifter."

I nodded.

"I'm supposed to take care of you while Sharyn is gone."

"I see."

Wendy seemed determined to do a good job. She took my hand and dragged me down the trail. "Let me show you where everything is," she said. "At least, everything that isn't classified," she continued with a hushed whisper.

"Aren't you a bit young to be a rebel recruit?" I asked.

She frowned, but she never had the chance to answer.

The sky turned gray, and six cruisers in formation descended from the clouds belching destruction.

"Come on," Wendy cried. She dodged through the thickets and started pulling back a camouflage net.

I helped her unveil the vehicle: it was a two-man skycycle.

Under other circumstances I would have grinned broadly; four lifetimes earlier I had been a skycycle racing champion. I hadn't seen one in a couple of lifetimes, since the invention of the slipjet.

Unfortunately, with battlecruisers all around an obsolete skycycle was not my first choice vehicle. But when Wendy tilted the clear plastic bubble open, I climbed through the top and into the webbing.

Frenzied, Wendy pushed the jump throttle, and we smashed into the tree branches above us. She cried out.

"Let me run this baby," I commanded. "I know a few tricks nobody else on this planet knows when it comes to skycycles."

A skycycle is a perfectly circular, very tiny machine. The thruster is externally mounted. It is connected, not to the hull of the ship, but rather to the seat assembly inside through a gimballed fuel tank separated from the main hull by magnetic bearings. The ship literally goes the way your chair points; you spin your chair to face your destination, and zoom! you're off.

The standard commercial skycycles of centuries before were controlled by swinging your chair manually, using handholds around the rim of the hull interior; acrobatic and racing machines used hydraulic controls. This one was hydraulic.

With supreme confidence I nudged the jump throttle. The ship smashed into the tree branches above us, just as it had for Wendy.

"Whew! This baby has power, doesn't she?" I asked rhetorically. If the old skycycles had jumped like that, they might never have been replaced.

A broadsweep beam carved through a swath of trees just meters from our hiding place. With blood pumping in my ears, I pointed the cycle into the clear and let the thruster rip.

We were up a thousand meters before I could retard the thrust. One of the cruisers turned toward us. "Do we have anything to shoot with?" I asked.

"A pair of lazeguns, pointing forward from the thruster mount," Wendy's hands were clenched around the arms of her chair. She broke one hand free and flipped several switches. "Push the red button on top of the gimbal control, and they fire."

I scampered to the side as the cruiser blew apart the piece of sky we had recently occupied. We whipped down toward the beast and fired the lazeguns. "Damn," I muttered. "Why did we bother?" We had scored a direct hit, but we had merely polished the cruiser's armor.

Again they fired; again I dodged.

Down below the scene was grim, though I could see very little through the smoke. The smoke seemed to offer a hint of protection, so we plunged back down toward the thickest patch.

I spotted Sharyn.

At least I was pretty sure it was her. She was running

toward the biggest ship left, a true cruiser as big and potent as those above us.

Next I saw three of the enemy ships converge above her. "Sharyn!" I cried, and rammed the skycycle forward, into the lines of sight of the three cruisers to divert their attention, firing wildly in all directions.

They paid no attention. In unison they poured fury into the cruiser below. It disappeared in a blaze of energy.

"No!" I cried. I circled twice, but saw no sign of Sharyn.

"Look out!" Wendy yelled. We dodged another attack. I whimpered. "Sharyn."

Wendy pulled on my arm. "We have to get out of here," she pleaded, her voice cracking with sorrow.

I closed my eyes for a moment. Sharyn was gone. I wanted to die.

It would have been easy to die there; but Wendy would have died with me. She didn't deserve to die for my failures.

I felt another tug on my arm. There were tears in Wendy's eyes, tears for Sharyn.

There was no time for grief, not yet. We dived for the forest, just in time; another cruiser had run out of other things to do, and followed us enthusiastically.

We dropped through the forest canopy. Blaster fire sizzled past.

I peered through the shadows. The forest was too thick to maneuver through, for normal skycycle pilots. The cruisers should have had us trapped.

But we would be a bit more difficult to kill than that. I tilted the skycycle edge-up, and laced my way delicately through the trees. I concentrated on careful maneuvering until I and the cycle were one being, with no other thought or purpose in life.

Wendy cried for both of us.

A few hours later, I poked the cycle's bubble through the foliage. The sun was higher in the sky; we had been traveling Eyeward. We were alone.

Wendy lifted her head from her hands, shifting her head from side to side to expunge the cramp: it is not comfortable, riding sideways in a skycycle for hours on end.

I spun the ship and pointed in a new direction. "I think there's a stream over there, where we can wash our faces." I looked at my companion in sympathy. "Your eyes are bloodshot. You could use some new life."

We landed. When Wendy knelt near the stream, I splashed a wave of water at her. "Stop that," she said mournfully.

"Only if you promise to worry about what's going to happen to *you* now. It's too late to worry about the people we left behind." Ha, how ironic it was that I should play this part. I would mourn for Sharyn in my own self-destructive way, at a later time. For the moment, Wendy needed uplifting. Sorrow looked terrible on one so young.

"I don't know what will happen to me. All my friends . . ."

I hugged her. "It's all right. You and I, we'll do fine."

"We'll kill Bardon!"

Revenge is not a pretty thing; but it has kept more than one person alive when all other meaning has been stripped from them. "Yes, we'll kill Bardon. He's the man responsible for Sharyn's murder, right?"

Wendy looked puzzled. "I—I'm not sure. I would have sworn it was, until Sharyn and I talked just a few minutes before—" she looked away, "the attack."

"What? What happened then?"

"Sharyn said, she was afraid that the apparent leaders of Forma were not really the *powers* of Forma. She suspected there was someone behind the scenes: a 'Playmaster.' " Wendy looked into my eyes. "Does that mean anything to you?"

A Playmaster? I knew what it meant—or rather, what it had once meant, in the time of EarthJump, just after the hawking Stardrive was developed. Playmasters were writer/producer/director/actors, who toured with small bands of actors from planet to planet, showing the great plays of history, developing updates suitable for the times. I myself had, for a nonce, been a Playmaster.

Could there be some one person on Forma controlling all the strings? The idea wasn't testable in an important sense: you couldn't prove that there *wasn't* such a person. Yet I couldn't believe that Sharyn would just imagine something like that. "Wendy, do you know why Sharyn thought that?"

"No." Wendy plucked a tiny yellow flower from a nearby bush; I plucked another and slowly caressed it into her hair. "She had planned for us to go to Skycrest, where she'd meet us in a few days. I know she planned to go to Summerform; she thought she might find clues there to the Playmaster."

"I see. Then we'll go to Summerform." I looked at Wendy. She looked exhausted, and I know I looked worse. "But first we need a place to rest." And a place to meet Glitter, if Safire ever got her fixed. "Where's Skycrest?"

She pointed Eyeward. "It's the capitol of Springform. It's not very far. We've been traveling more or less toward it the whole time." Wendy shook her head, and almost smiled. "I have money and identification to get us in."

"Great." Why had Sharyn planned to send me to Springform? I winced. Sharyn! It no longer mattered what her plans had been. I would take Wendy to Skycrest, and then . . . I didn't know.

Wendy's finger traced a line over the ridge of mountains. "Fly over Rightcut and head Eyeward. Skycrest is close to the top of the ridge, on the far side."

"Aye aye, my lady."

We flew in slow and low, and we stopped at the city perimeter. They identified us as Gibs Alhart and his consort, Wendy Levitine, both from the city of Lily, far counterward from Skycrest. "Is your name really Levitine?" I asked.

Wendy laughed. "Is your name really Gibs? I don't believe it."

We took a suite in the most expensive hotel in the city. The bedroom had about an acre of satin-covered foamwater, which I promptly turned over to Wendy; I fell on the couch in the other room.

Lying there in the dark, I sorted through the night-mare of my life. Still there remained a bright spot: Keara! I would return to her. "Safire," I mumbled at my wristcom, half asleep, "how's Glitter coming?"

"She's ready," the machine replied. "Shall I send her after you?"

"Not yet." I would tell Wendy about the ship after she had rested. "But you better get her into my general vicinity. Be careful of the skeletons." I described a meeting place outside of Skycrest.

"Glitter will be there in sixteen hours, Gibs," Safire signed off.

I tossed and turned and could not sleep; images of burning trees and blinding lightning followed me through an endless series of contorted positions on the couch. At last I gave up.

One wall of the living room was a huge video screen. I punched buttons by the couch until video images came to life. I kept hitting buttons, watching dozens of programs go by, until one forced me to stop and back up and add volume.

It was a scene of forest burning, and cruisers scream-ing through the air. A reporter droned in the background.

"Fallform airborne troops today discovered and de-stroyed the main base of the Forma Reformation Orga-nization. Though all the installations and ships were destroyed, only one rebel body was found. That one body, however, belonged to the rebel leader, Sharyn Mirlot, and the RFO is believed by authorities to be completely broken." A picture of Sharyn appeared next, ebullient and, in my eyes, beautiful; I stifled a sob.

"The discovery of only one dead, and that one being the key to the whole organization, has sparked consid-erable speculation. There is some evidence that the Sirian mindshifter, now believed to be a Sirian assassin, had been near their encampment prior to the attack." The announcer looked up at the audience with pro-found earnestness. "Could it be that Sharyn Mirlot was *not* killed in the attack, but rather before the attack, by the assassin? There is no acknowledged reason—but it does form a pattern. The Sirian seems to be murdering all political leaders who might stand in the way of a favorable agreement between Sirius and Fallform." I gagged on the announcer's stupidity.

"No one knows for sure, but this is the possibility the experts are now considering in the light of the past two days' events. Yesterday, as you know, Keara Delgodon, the Subdirectress of Security for Winterform, was killed attempting to bring the Sirian in for deportation." Another picture of a woman I loved appeared. I ran to the screen in horror.

"Keara, wait, I love you," I whispered.

"Funeral services for the Subdirectress will be held tomorrow at one P.M."

I beat the video screen with bare hands until I could feel pain. But I did not scream. Wendy still slept.

I dressed, and slipped down to the bar. I knew I would not sleep again for a long time.

Today, four more people would die.

I had only started to admire the sparkle of the glass in my hand when a platoon of news-types, minicams and microphones in hand, spilled into the lounge. There was the abrupt sound of a lady's laughter, and in a burst of color such a lady forced her way through the reporters to a middle table, where she coiled easily into the molded chair.

The colors of her dress dazzled the eye. They were meant to distract the viewer's concentration from any betraying facial expressions: I had seen this kind of performance before, and even though I entered a drunken stupor, I was not deceived.

I looked up, into her almond-shaped eyes. They were hard eyes, swift but cynical. For a moment I felt sorry for her; she too had been scarred by encounters with a reality too terrible to be a part of a rational universe. The body she wore was older, with the skin tightening across her cheeks. Wrinkles radiated from her eyes when she smiled.

Yet when they asked her their first question, her smile made me smile. Her voice carried clearly above the din: "Of *course* I'm going to lower the people's tuitions, yet raise the funding grants. That's what every

Chairman for the past decade has promised, and a Chairman would *never* abrogate on a promise, would he?"

There was a subdued pause; the reporters weren't sure whether she was being sincere, or whether she was just joking!

For a moment, her cynical eyes lost their bitterness; she was laughing, a laughter no one in her audience could note or appreciate.

Her eyes met mine; for that moment, we shared the secret joy.

No, not again! I was in love.

I should have left the bar. When I looked at this bitter woman, I could feel myself teetering on the edge of a pit; this lady could hurt me, scar me, and walk away.

But I could not leave. I lacked the will power. I have never had the discipline that springs unaided to those who do what they should do, just because they know they should. For me, strength of character has always needed an outside crutch: always I have leaned on the woman I loved.

I don't think I was a clinging vine. Yet without the sense of love and being loved, I had always been a bit broken inside. The beginnings of lifetimes had always been painful transitions for me, for my life was always loveless then. But none of those transitions had been raw hells like *this*.

Since I lacked the discipline and wisdom to leave, I did the opposite: I approached the lady. A bodyguard-type male calmly moved to intercept me; I calmly tipped him off balance and tossed him to the side.

I fear the toss was too blatant to go unnoticed; everyone turned to look at me. I poised myself before my new love, and bowed in the Victorian manner. "We must share more moments, my lady," I offered.

Her laughter seemed a bit strained. "Heavens! I've never been propositioned so elegantly before!" She turned to a bank of minicams. "Should I have an affair with this man?" she asked. "He seems nice enough." She eyed me carefully, "Though perhaps a bit inebriated."

One of the men leaned over a radio/calculator device. In a moment he looked up and shook his head. "I think the voters prefer their leaders to be virgins," he said with a smile.

My lover-to-be sighed. "It's tragic, the frequency with which I must turn down my admirers."

Three bodyguards moved in on me this time. I could have taken them all, but it would have been noisy, and probably of no avail. My lady seemed trapped by the cameras. I accompanied her boys out of the bar, with effusive apologies (and a tip for the one I had accidentally caused to slip earlier) I asked them what was going on. "Did somebody really vote on whether or not we would have an affair?"

"Yeah, man. Don't you know who that *is* in there?" He stuck a meaty thumb over his shoulder. "That's Rainbow Dancer, the Chairman of Springform!"

"Rainbow Dancer? Sounds like a race horse," I commented.

"Huh?"

I waved my hand. "Just a joke." No one on Forma had ever seen a race horse, I realized. I stood as if stage struck. "My God, the Chairman!" I whispered.

The big man laughed. "Yeah. You're lucky she likes people, otherwise I'd've knocked your head in." His tone changed. "So long," he said with more meaning than the words denoted.

"Right." I walked back to my room with my mind spinning. The whole universe seemed to spin with it. I didn't know what sense to make of my own mind, much less what sense to make of the universe.

Was I just falling in love with every woman I saw? That couldn't be it. I hadn't fallen in love with Wendy, for example. Still, I was clearly unsane.

The planet Forma seemed equally unsane. Why would the Chairman of Springform ask for a *vote* on whether she had an affair?

I turned on the video screen again, and soon *that* question was answered: Springform was run by a full-fledged, purist videocracy. The citizens voted on everything, constantly. Politicians literally belonged to the people; they were powerless beyond their ability to persuade the people to vote their way on each individual issue; the Chairmanship could (and had, at times in the past) change on a daily, or even an hourly, basis.

I felt much saner, seeing that much raw insanity. I fell back on the couch. In a manner, I slept. I did not dream.

Soft lips brushed my cheek; "Rainbow," I murmured. Popping open one bleary eye, I saw a blurred being before me. It was Wendy.

"Rainbow, huh?" she asked. "Did you spend the night with the Chairman of Springform?" She giggled at her own joke.

"Yes, I did," I explained.

Wendy stared at me in disbelief. "Rainbow Dancer?"

"Is there another Chairman?" I asked. "The Chairman was in this motel last night."

"You're joking." She pointed a finger at me. "Stop trying to pull my leg."

"Have it your way." I shrugged.

The buzzer rang on our door. I stepped over and opened it.

"Gibs." A woman swept into my arms. She was warm and beautiful and—she was Rainbow!

I pulled back in amazement. "What are *you* doing here?"

As I stepped back, Rainbow stepped closer. My mouth was full of cotton, my chin was covered by a stubble of beard you could use to grind an axe blade, and I had slept in my clothes. She didn't seem to mind. "I came to find the only man I've ever met who could *understand* me," she explained.

Wendy peeked around the corner. "Who is it, Gibs?" she asked.

Rainbow stopped short. "Goodness. You certainly didn't lose much time finding a soft shoulder to cry on last night, did you?" Her face flushed. "Or, when you told me that we just *had* to 'share more laughter together,' did you mean a threesome?"

"Wait." I talked fast, a terrified machine gun. "This is Wendy Levitine, a friend from Fallform who—"

"Friends. Right." Rainbow turned on her heel and walked out.

"You're not being fair!" I yelled through the door. That had no effect, so I ran through the door myself. Rainbow was already rounding the corner. "I love you!"

She disappeared.

I pursed my lips. She had done it, as I had feared— she had hurt me, and walked away.

When I turned back into the room, Wendy looked at me with big wide eyes. "You really *did* spend the night with Rainbow Dancer!"

I choked back a violent reply. "Yeah." I looked at Wendy with an appraising eye. I guess I could understand why Rainbow had jumped to the wrong conclusion; Wendy certainly didn't look like the maid. "What do you want for breakfast?" I asked.

The videoscreen was lit, but I scarcely paid attention. I sipped at my orange juice, watching Wendy eat. "Wendy, tell me something. When I was talking with Sharyn," my voice faltered, "she told me that Fallform and Winterform had been at war even before the Sirians arrived. What were they fighting *over*?"

"The Howard radiation belt."

"And what is a Howard radiation belt?"

"That's the radiation belt around Forma. You need them for SEEPage."

"Seepage?"

"Yeah. Stimulated Emission of Energetic Particles. You can control the descent of charged particles into the atmosphere using Very Low Frequency radio waves. A lot of the weather manipulation techniques depend on controlling the SEEPage from the Howard belt into the atmosphere."

"Using radiation to control the weather?"

Wendy shrugged. "Sure. Radiation is an important weather factor. There're a couple of natural examples, like the Aurora Ocularis, and the Lightning Polaris."

I nodded. I had heard of the Lightning Polaris, the staggering electrical storms that flared occasionally near the Pole.

"SEEPage can be used to form and break up clouds

as well." She stopped eating. "You know those clouds that the Fallform ships dived out of? I think they were created by SEEPage."

"What about blizzarcanes?"

Wendy nodded. "Of course. A blizzarcane couldn't *possibly* occur naturally."

I suspected this discussion would fascinate the Sirians.

"Anyway, the radiation belt is not infinitely big. There're just so many particles out there to SEEP. And we don't dare use them all up, because they're part of our protection from the sun."

"How delightful." As usual, war was consuming the very resource over which the war was fought.

The videoscreen distracted me: in a stark scene of burning trees, the camera zoomed, and lo! I beheld an image in my own likeness.

The anchorman droned on, "We believe this to be the Sirian mindshifter/assassin, imaged shortly before Fallform's attack on the rebel base. Responsible authorities believe he may be somewhere in Springform."

I took Wendy by the hand. "Let's roll," I said.

"Where are we going?" she asked.

"Back to my ship, for a quick change of costume." Did the Springform authorities think they could catch me just by knowing my face? Given a few minutes aboard Glitter, I would give them the surprise of their lives.

I stepped out of the dressing room to see Wendy talking quietly to Jester, the long Vegan climbvine growing around my bar.

"I would offer you a drink," my new voice said, "but I left all the good stuff at home." I struck a pose; Oberon would have been proud.

Wendy stared for a moment, then drew back. "Who are you?"

It wasn't a standing ovation, but I had clearly been effective with my audience. I opened my arms. "It's me, Gibs. The man with whom you just dodged three police cars, the man who almost got you killed again."

She stepped forward. "Really?"

I frowned. "Really. I *told* you I wouldn't be the same person, didn't I? A disguise wouldn't be very useful if it didn't make you look different, would it?"

Wendy shook her head. "But you *sound* different, and you *walk* different. It's incredible!"

I ran my finger across my mustache. "Yes." I turned to a mirror on the wall, and for a moment let my natural vanity run wild.

For all intents and purposes, it was as if I had had Transfer to another body. Of course, I hadn't—a mindshifter can't perform his own mindshift—but he can use the finest surgical technology yet devised to perform plastic surgery. My skin was darker, my musculature heavier, my forehead a tad lower, and my nose much more aristocratic.

And my movements matched. I moved more carefully, in some ways more gracefully. I walked with long, assertive strides. Even my height seemed different. I stood straighter now all the time: My revised body begged its wearer to play heroic roles. I had played heroic roles before; today I would play one again.

"What are we going to do?" Wendy asked, almost in pain. "I thought we were going to get ready to kill the Playmaster."

I lowered my head. "We'll find the Playmaster. But first I must find my love."

Wendy just stared at me.

I blushed. "I'm not a very strong man. Or rather, I'm never any stronger than the bond I have with the woman of my life." I cupped Wendy's face in my hands. "I wish that *you* were the woman of my life. But you're not. Only Rainbow Dancer can give me that strength."

"She's *evil*, Gibs! Didn't you see how cruel she can be?" We had discussed the effect Rainbow had had on me before.

There were tears in Wendy's eyes. "She won't help you, she'll destroy you."

"Perhaps. But I have been a psychologist, too, you know. Rainbow is damaged and hurt, as I am. Perhaps I can cure her, as she cures me." I confess, I didn't understand why I loved Rainbow either. I had never before fallen in love with a woman who was, at the core, cruel and uncaring. Keara and Sharyn had threatened my life because they *did not* understand me; Rainbow would threaten me because she *did* understand. For a moment I considered the possibility that somehow the Playmaster had drugged me, to fall hopelessly in love with this most dangerous woman.

Mentally I shrugged; even if it were true, I couldn't do anything about it. I still loved Rainbow. Love was still my master.

I picked up my duffel bag. "You stay here. I'll be back as soon as I can." I smiled. "This should only take a day or two. Watch the video broadcasts; you'll love it."

I confess I felt like whistling as I left. It had been a long time since I had stalked a lover clothed in disguise, though I had done it often enough. More than once in the course of my lifetimes my lovers-to-be hadn't recognized love at first sight. More than once, I had screwed up my relationships with them so badly that I needed to start from scratch, with a new face, a new name, and a new personality. Eventually, each of my loves had learned to live with *me*, but introducing *me* in graduated doses had often been necessary to prevent disaster.

Clearly, my relationship with Rainbow needed smaller doses.

I found her near a memorial, surrounded again by the charming newscasters. "Here is a permanent monument to our children, those who died in the attacks of Bardon."

She was good. The audience was her plaything, to mold as she chose. "As you know, until recently I had believed that violence was wrong." She clenched her fist. "But our children! We must not let Bardon kill again!"

This was my chance. I leaped lightly to a stand on the base of the monument, and caressed the ascending column with my hand. "Then kill his children in turn, Rainbow Dancer, as he has killed mine." My voice almost broke as I spoke the last words, softly but with projection. The cameras turned to me.

I swept my hand about. "What will we buy with the deaths of the children of Fallform? We will buy only human misery and pain." I gazed at the cameras with confidence, yet cocked my head in puzzlement. "Have we forgotten who the true enemies are? They are not other men, those who live in other forms." Another sweep of the hand. "It is the coldness of the universe that is our enemy. That coldness is still our master."

I clenched my fist, as Rainbow had clenched hers. "Shall we follow our neighbors into a bloodbath to strip our whole world of resources, resources we need more than we need warfare? No."

"Then what do you propose, you who have no name?" Fear and anger both tainted the texture of Rainbow's voice.

"I am Fire Singer." I stepped down from the monument, to stand beside her. "I propose the creation of a united Form."

I spoke at great length about the vision of all the people of Forma working together; I suspect it made Rainbow and all the pragmatic, practical folk of Springform nauseous (it almost got to *me*), but my stage presence reigned supreme. To be a mediocre politician requires nothing beyond brilliant acting. Indeed, even to be a brilliant politician requires only two more attributes: the talent to find gifted advisors and the wisdom to listen to them.

The debate went nonstop through lunch. Points were scored, ideas were challenged. Politics in a videocracy proved more brutal than any other occupation I had encountered—except, of course, for being a mindshifter.

By dinner time the rankings in the polls had see-sawed hysterically. Rainbow Dancer's popularity plummeted from 60% to 45%. Hawk Keensight, her only serious rival in recent polls, had dropped from 40% to 35%. And I, Fire Singer, had come from nowhere to 20% of the poll.

Regardless of the consequences I *had* to escape the limelight for dinner. "Forgive me, my friends, but I must take my meals in solitude." With a parting wave, I strode away toward my skycycle.

As I escaped from the noise radius of the gathering, I heard a pair of feet, light but swift, catching up behind me. I turned. "Have dinner with me, my lady."

"Thank you," Rainbow said, still breathing hard.

We continued to walk to my cycle. "You're quite a performer," she acknowledged.

"I have been at it for a long time."

"Funny, I've never heard of you." Her voice chilled. "Who are you, anyway?"

It is hard to come down from a theatrical performance, to return to a semblance of normal humanity. Thus I continued, still feeling my lifetimes behind me, still feeling the stage beneath, "I am one who has lost more to wars and human stupidity than you could imagine."

"I see." We walked in silence for a bit.

"And what, my lady, have you lost?"

"What?" Her almond eyes widened, looking at me. Then she laughed, bitterly. "It's not what I have lost; it's what I've gained."

We reached the skycycle. My voice finally came out of stage projection; at last I could be gentle. "Then what have you gained?"

"Guilt."

We stood within inches of each other. My heart jumped, because of her nearness, because of her deadliness, and because *guilt* was something with which I was infinitely familiar.

Today, four more people would die.

"What is the nature of your guilt, Rainbow? Let me take some of your burden."

She shook her head. "I know you. You're the Sirian assassin, aren't you? But you've changed. . . . We met yesterday, didn't we?"

I was stunned. How had I given it away? Perhaps, almost certainly, it was my speech. *My lady*—how many people say that any more? How sloppy I had been!

"Yes, my lady, 'tis I. I came for the one I love. You."

She looked away. "My guilt. I'm sorry." She stepped away. "It's as I said—" she said loudly, though only I was near, "—*he's* the assassin!"

Cameramen ran from all directions. A police cruiser soared out of the sun, and from somewhere a megaphone blared "This is the police. Hold your hands up. Step away from the skycycle and Ms. Dancer."

I did not pay proper attention to the police warning: I tossed Rainbow into the cycle and jumped in behind her. A lazegun burned to the bone in my left arm. We were aloft before I felt the pain. "Safire," I howled into my wristcom, "send Glitter to meet me at the edge of the city, by the clockward entrance."

A police cruiser motored up beside me, and I flipped the cycle on its side before they could draw a bead. They couldn't just knock the ship down, with Rainbow on board. They would have to have a perfect shot at me through the clear cycle bubble.

They would have a tough job. I set the the seats (and thus the thrusters) spinning, carefully controlling the thrust so that our overall motion continued clockward. Spinning, Rainbow and I switched positions constantly, eluding outside sharpshooters. We were safe, as long as I didn't get so dizzy I crashed it. Rainbow turned ghostly white; her eyes squeezed shut.

Some smart guy put a lazegun blast through the engine compartment. The cycle slowed, and we dropped to the ground. I flipped her upside down on the way.

Rainbow hadn't been strapped in; she was spreadeagled across the clear bubble. "Safire, I can't make it; have Glitter come get me." I had hoped to get clear of the city, to reduce the risk of police sharpshooters; now, I would just have to let them shoot me.

Before we grounded, I popped the bubble. Rainbow fell to the ground. Disengaging the webbing carefully, I rolled out beside her. The police megaphone blared once more as a cruiser floated down toward us. Rainbow groaned.

Another lazegun blast ripped into my skull; had I been a mortal man, I would have died then. I grabbed Rainbow and dragged her over my shoulders, covering myself with her body.

The police cruiser split open with a roar and crashed to the ground. Looking to my left I saw Glitter descending nearby. Several rocks and trees disappeared as Glitter eliminated hidden marksmen.

My arm hurt. I took a moment to get calm, to achieve some autohypnotic anesthesia. The trance level wasn't adequate to eliminate the pain, but I felt better.

With a deep breath, I crept from underneath the cycle and hurried toward my ship, still carrying Rainbow on my back. Another marksman opened up, cutting out my left leg. As I spun to the ground, another marksman, presumably one who had had a line on me before the first one hit, fired. I felt Rainbow's body change shape as heat seared a line across my back. I didn't have to look to see what had happened.

Rainbow had been sliced in two.

Glitter picked off the marksmen who had fired. I pulled myself with my one good arm toward the ship. "Glitter, better send out a robot to collect me," I ordered. An airlock opened.

Wendy came running out.

"Get back!" I yelled, too late. There was another marksman. She fell.

I reached her seconds later. "You beautiful fool," I whispered. "I wasn't worth risking your life for." My eyes blurred. "I wasn't even in danger." I had lost Rainbow my love, and Wendy my friend, and somehow the loss of Wendy hurt more. In all my lifetimes no one had ever lost her life to save mine.

One last marksman sneaked into range before Glitter's robots could get me inside. He put a bolt through one lung and both ventricles of my heart. Had I been a mortal man, again I would have died.

But though I was mortal, I was a mortal god, one who granted life and enforced death.

Frontier mindshifters lived in a universe crowded with rich and powerful men—men who, despite all their power, were doomed to die without our special friendship.

We did not befriend them all. And too often, they believed that if *they* couldn't live forever, neither should anyone else. We were their targets, first for bribery, then for blackmail.

So virtually all the Frontier mindshifters took extraordinary precautions. From first Transfer, mindshifters endowed one another with enhancements, enhancements to protect the brain—for that was the part of the body that *had to* survive. A typical mindshifter had a skull of tungstalloy composite, with a tiny ten-minute oxygenating pump at its base. In many circumstances, that pump was enough to keep the mindshifter alive until he could get into surgery.

I was also lucky that lazeguns made lousy weapons: unlike the bullets of earlier centuries that made goo of all the organs they touched, a lazegun bolt produced a self-cauterizing, clean incision.

So Safire and Glitter were able to save my life. With stitches and glue they knit together enough of my system so that I could heal. It would be months before the injuries disappeared, but I could breath and move normally, if not swiftly. While lying quiet, I planned, ever more feverishly, my revenge against the Playmaster.

Glitter lay in shallow water off the coast of Flame. Flame was the city of Summerform closest to the Eye, at the tip of a peninsula. I was ready to begin my search in earnest.

Somewhere on Forma was a Playmaster, and as I thought about him my bones chilled. The enemy had been *too good*. He *must* have lived multiple lives, as I had.

But up to now, the Master had been hidden, almost unsuspected. He had played games with the lives of first lifers with ease. I would not be so simple an opponent.

He had arranged Sharyn's death, I knew it.

He was also responsible for Keara's death, and for Rainbow's. How could the sharpshooters have failed to warn each other about interlocking fire? Rainbow had not been killed by accident. And I had *not* struck Keara so hard as to jeopardize her life.

Please, immortal gods wherever you might be, please tell me I had not killed Keara.

Sharyn had believed that the Playmaster was in

Summerform, though Bardon of Fallform had been her enemy. Very well, I would start in Summerform.

At least I was properly equipped for this trip from Glitter to shore. I had come to Forma with a bathing suit and scuba gear. I swam the two miles to shore through bathtub-warm water.

I stepped out of the surf onto the beach; even with flippers on, I could feel the burning sand against my feet, and I hurried toward a huddle of shade canopies protecting assorted scientists and tourists from the sun.

I reached shade and flopped down. I tried not to breathe too hard; even the air here burned if taken in too swiftly.

I unpacked my waterproof duffel bag and slipped into some clothes. The scuba gear went into the bag. In another minute, I would ask someone how to get to downtown Flame. But for my first minute, I watched the heat shimmer through the air.

Out of the corner of my eye, I became aware of the fluid motion of the shimmer, and the waves, and the brown sand; finally I realized that the fluid motion was more than these.

The fluid motion was a woman, walking casually, nude, across the burning sands. The shimmer was her hair, hanging to her waist. The movement of her sand-brown body was languid, like syrup, against the backdrop of the ocean waves.

My heart jumped in my mouth; I couldn't be in love again, not without even talking to her.

She looked at me. I wanted to melt, but I was too tense; instead, I splintered. She smiled. She walked toward me.

I wanted to scream to her, to get away from me, that she would surely die if she didn't run, but I couldn't speak.

"You just came from the sea," she said, laughter in her eyes. "There is a spaceship there, hidden beneath the waves. Did you see it?"

I shook my head. "A spaceship in the *water*? What would it be doing there?"

Now she laughed from deep within her throat. "Trying

to hide." She shrugged. "It's a logical place to try to hide, for a person who isn't native to Forma and who doesn't know how closely the status of the ocean is monitored."

Of course it was monitored, dummy! I cursed myself. Just as the skeletons of Winterform flew for meteorology, so must there be an aquarian counterpart.

She held out her hand. "Let us be friends, in the time that is left."

I followed her. "The time that is left?"

"Of course. Is there not an end to time in each life, regardless of life's duration?"

I pursed my lips; I would not tell her how I had cheated the end to time, again and again.

We walked to a deserted canopy. She lay in the sun; I sat in the shadows. Her movements were hypnotic. This scene, with the ocean and the sand and the clear skies above, was a standard first image for focussing a patient for hypnosis. And the lady, whoever she was, rocked her leg in a gentle hypnotic rhythm. I trusted her completely, for no reason I could see; I felt the beginnings of trance coming on, and did not fight it.

"Why do you travel the stars?" she asked; I was past being surprised by her knowledge.

"To bring life." I closed my eyes. "Though not for a long time."

"Tell me."

I told her of the lady I'd lost a lifetime ago; I told her of the good friend who had died in Transfer while I grieved over lost love when I should have been concentrating on his life.

I told her of the four people who died, every day.

"Do you blame yourself because men age? Do you think that it's reasonable to blame yourself?"

"Of course not. But I could save the lives of four people every day, if I could still make Transfers." I trembled. "But I can't. I'm afraid."

"If you died today, those people would still die. Would you hold yourself responsible then?"

"No."

"You must think, not of the people who will die, but

of the people who can live. You're wrong when you say that 'today, four more people will die.' Instead, you must remember that, perhaps tomorrow, four more people will *live*."

I shook my head. "If you were one of the people who would die waiting for tomorrow, would you feel the same way?"

"Yes." Her eyes met mine. I believed her.

"Perhaps."

We continued.

She was a masterful therapist; I do not know when the trance ended, but when I looked at her and saw her as a human being, I was far back up the rode toward sanity. We crossed the sands to a limousine, to take us into town. I raised my eyebrows. "A limo?"

"Of course. What else would the heiress to the Grantship of Summerform travel in?"

"The heiress!" In horror, I grabbed her by the shoulders. "You're the next target! We have to find you a safe place!" I raised my arm. "Safire, send Glitter as fast as she'll fly." I started searching the skies for cruisers, and blizzards, and anything else the mind of an evil Master might conceive.

She slipped from my touch. "Of course I'm your next target, silly." She looked puzzled for a moment. "Why would you seek a place of safety for me? You know it's too late."

"What?!"

"The poison. I know I'm dying." She brushed her hand through my hair. "I was hoping you'd consider giving me the antidote. I love the people of Forma. I believe you do, too." She looked away for a moment. "Why then are you killing?"

"I'm not!" I tried to scream, but the air scorched my lungs. "It's a set up!"

She seemed puzzled. "I believe I know you now. You are here to help the people of Forma. You are a good man. If my death will help, I accept it."

"Have you been poisoned?" I tried to get some sense out of this conversation. "I'll run every test I know. We'll find an antidote." I was talking nonsense, of course;

there are billions of poisons in the universe that cannot be counteracted, poisons that strike the brain so that even Transfer cannot help. Death was still my master.

She knew it, too. Her expression became even more peaceful. "Then you *aren't* the assassin."

"NO! NO!" I held my head in my hands.

She touched me. "You have to promise me something."

I looked at her. "What?"

"I know you will destroy the person who's behind this. But you must promise me that first, you'll get even by *saving Forma*. You have the tools, and the talent, and now again you have the sanity. Promise me that you'll *save Forma* before killing my killer."

At the time, numb as I was, it seemed a tiny thing. "I promise."

"Thank you." She jerked, a broken motion that was not her own. I held her close. "A three day poison," she mused, taking a shuddering breath. "Just long enough . . . the enemy . . . how did he know?"

An ambulance slid to a stop beside us, and two men leaped out to carry her away. I stared in amazed horror. "We've been on call," the medic explained as they pulled her from me and put her in the back. They left me alone.

Glitter came into sight; I boarded her.

On my first sip of Aldebarone wine I choked. Furious at my weakness, I forced the whole glassful down in one gulp and refilled it.

On my next sip I choked again. In helpless fury I hurled the glass against the wall. The glass didn't even give me the satisfaction of breaking. A robot scurried in to clean up; in minutes, all sign of my anger had disappeared into time's passage.

Karmel, the heiress to the Grantship of Summerform, had ruined my one path to ruination. I couldn't even escape into a drunken stupor any more. I was trapped with my memories.

With a deep breath I swore revenge, again. And again I remembered the promise I had made, to save Forma first.

I laughed, maliciously. It would be ridiculously easy to save Forma. The Playmaster had made a terrible mistake setting me up as the murderer, because he had also set me up as the invincible power behind the murders. The whole planet trembled at my touch, the touch of the *assassin*.

When I had announced from Glitter that I was departing, but that I would return the following day, all of Forma jumped to clear airspace; they knew I would only announce my plans if I could not be stopped.

They had seen me die on stage, under the eyes of their own cameras, in Springform. Yet I had lived to kill again in Summer. They thought I was an immortal god. They were fools.

Today, four more people would die.

But perhaps other people's lives, or at least some of the time of their lives, would be saved.

"Safire?"

"Yes, Gibs."

"Call the heads of state of Forma."

"All at once?"

"Oh, start with the Directress of Winterform."

One by one Safire and I went through the names, telling them to meet me in sixteen hours at Skycrest for a brief trip to the radiation belt.

The Sirians and Omegarans were furious, I was sure; but they could only attack me if they attacked *together*, in mutual trust. I pointed out to the Sirian commander that the Omegaran commander looked the right age to need a mindshift; I made a reciprocal comment to the Omegaran. Fearful that I had made a deal with their enemy, each fumed in silence. Each held his fleet idle.

At the appointed time, I ferried the Forman leaders in Glitter up to the Safire. They were impressed, which was why I took them aloft: Safire is a *big* ship. She carries a cargo of 2000 clone bodies, with the facilities to manufacture more, plus two entire Transfer systems (in case one breaks down), enough room for a twenty man crew (though I live alone most of the time), and a composite arsenal of all the deadliest weapons devised by the most advanced planets in the reaches of Man.

I looked at my guests from the head of the conference table. There was the Grantsman of Summerform with his wife; they seemed more concerned with their own lives than with the death of their daughter Karmel. That concern explained why I had met with Karmel on the beach and had been touched by her with impunity: the Grantsman had been afraid to interfere. I could understand their concern; I could not appreciate it. Karmel had been far more worthy than her parents.

There was Hawk Keensight of Springform. I smiled at him; he sweated. I suspected he might know more about the Playmaster. In time he would tell me everything he knew. People talk a great deal when their lives are at stake.

There was President Bardon of Fallform. He was my only current suspect for Playmaster, though Safire had already told me he lacked the tungstalloy skull of one with many Transfers. Also, he was terrified that he would not receive Transfer, a puzzling level of fear for the one I sought. It mattered little; he too would speak to me when his time came to lie beneath my knife.

And there was the Directress of Winterform. Her hair was silver, and she needed Transfer soon, or it would be too late. Yet she did not flinch under my steady gaze. She was a truly regal lady.

"So far, I have killed only secondary leaders in your governments," I began. "But as you now see, the execution of those who don't measure up is the least of my tools. I am a mindshifter first, and an assassin second.

"I have bad news for you," I continued. "The Sirians and the Omegarans are powerless, here on the Frontier." I stood erect, hands behind my back. It had been long since I projected not merely presence, but power; yet I remembered. "Power on Forma lies with the Frontier mindshifter in whose jurisdiction you lie." I smiled. "*My* jurisdiction."

I explained to them the nature of the system. They believed. I explained to them what would have to happen, if any of them hoped for a second lifetime. They understood. I appointed a council of respected scientists from each form, to mediate the use of the radiation belt. They accepted.

The war ended.

I returned the leaders to their respective peoples. The Directress of Winterform stayed long enough to have a private chat. She was a good person. I would arrange her Transfer.

I shuddered; I still didn't know if I could shift a mind. I didn't want to find out.

The Playmaster seemed somehow far from my mind; I basked for a moment in knowing that I had done a good thing, that with the end of the feud between the forms, thousands of people would live better lives.

I took Glitter back into the Rift, where I had met Sharyn. As I stepped into the burned-out clearing I could smell the trees and the plants, growing fast to heal the wound. The sun sat in its low throne, frozen between the mountain ridges, staring at the Eye of Forma. I walked through the quiet rustle of the leaves.

When I returned, I heard a woman's voice singing, from inside Glitter. It was not Safire's voice.

With a burst of speed I jumped through the hatch to surprise the intruder.

She turned from her inspection of my paintings. "Have you found the Master yet?"

"No." I studied her; she didn't appear to be armed. "Get out of my ship."

She laughed; it came from inside, through many layers, as had Keara's laughter.

"Do you still seek the Master?" she asked.

"Yes."

She shook her head lightly, with a knowledge of her own power that reminded me of Sharyn. "You must stop your search," she whispered. "You will not find what you seek." She stared at me, with the harsh gaze only Rainbow could bestow.

I stood speechless.

She moved forward, flowing like water, flowing like Karmel.

"They're dead!" I cried, images of the past cascading through my head.

"They're gone," she continued so softly.

We stood locked in tableau. "You have lived many lives," I accused her.

"Yes." She closed her eyes in pain. "Even on this one planet, I have worn many bodies." She opened her eyes. "In other lives I have been an actress. And a mindshifter. Lately, I have been a teacher."

I choked. "Why did you do this?"

"I didn't want to kill anyone, yet I had to make them understand how easily they *could* be killed. The Sirians had completely brainwashed them by the time we investigated." She smiled. "I had started working my way through the power structures, without a real plan, when *you* arrived. Then, you gave me your idea for assassinations. I only wish I had trusted you more, to let you know."

"Don't apologize." Another thought struck me. "Wendy?"

The woman looked away. "I told her to let you protect yourself. I told her you could survive in ways she'd never dreamed. She didn't believe me."

"You, too, are only a mortal god."

She seemed amused. "No. I am only a mortal woman." She looked at me again, almost afraid. "I have used you."

I thought about it. Today, for the first time in a lifetime, I had a clear mind. "You gave me purpose."

"I hurt you."

"You gave me hope."

"You should hate me."

"I must love you." I took her in my arms. We stood embraced for a long moment.

"Safire," I commanded, "dim the lights." The sharp edges of the room faded.

"Safire," the woman said, "gentle music." A waltz began to play.

I softened my hold on my lady. "What is your name?" I asked.

She laughed. "I have held a thousand names. Yet I am who I am. Name me." We began to dance.

Tomorrow, four more people would live.

Too Loving A Touch

Too many cash prizes, offered by skeptics investigating psychic powers, have gone unclaimed for the rational mind to take claims of extrasensory perception too seriously.

And yet I still remember an incident from my adolescence, when I desperately needed a young woman's phone number (well, it seemed desperate at the time: if I did not get her number in the next 48 hours, I knew my life would be ruined). I remember lying in bed, feverish with my horror that my last opportunity for happiness would pass me by. I remember how loud and fast my heartbeat grew, how dry my mouth became, how totally my reasoning power left me.

So I lay there unable to think or sleep. Then suddenly I was calm. My heart stopped racing, and I was happy. For no clear or compelling reason, I was quite sure that a particular friend of mine would call, and that he would have the magic number even though he had no more access to the person or the number than I.

Then the phone rang.

The psychologists of today have a boxful of explanations for such events. I myself prefer any one of a dozen of their explanations to the mystical alternative. Still, it is most important to remember the incidents in your life that violate your expectations. Psychologists have also proved that the surprising, disconcerting incidents are the ones we are most likely to forget. This is perhaps the ultimate tragedy—for these incidents are the only ones that point out the flaws in our views, that would enable us to fix and improve the models of the world we use to mold our expectations.

And let's face it—no matter how many times we prove that ESP does not exist, we will never be able to disprove it entirely. Just as the experiments in physics that endlessly seek a proton decay can only increase the number of billions of protons needed to detect one, so we can only restrict the probability of psychic events to increasingly smaller odds. We can never reach zero.

And for anyone who believes in psychic phenomenon, I have good news as well: I have every faith that, if someone were to prove the existence of ESP one day, the physicists and the psychologists would have plausible explanations for it the day after. Goodness, the people who brought us outrageously counterintuitive explanations of the universe like quantum chromodynamics and Heisenberg uncertainty should surely be able to explain a simple thing like telepathy!

Too Loving A Touch

Veddin's eyes closed as his warship skipped into normal space. His concentration focussed on his ship's sensors. Images poured through the shiplink embedded in his cerebellum. He had expected to find yet another Squishy ambush, but he floated safe and easy amidst his own robot fleet.

He opened his eyes, to see the beauty of normal space himself. The hard points of starlight and the brilliant sun of the Hydra system blazed with cheer.

Veddin's vision merged again with the images from the *DareDrop's* sensors. The scene telescoped. The sun brightened, then dimmed as the *DareDrop's* computer screened its rays. Soon Hydra floated just beyond Veddin's nose. It was a lustrous blue and white jewel, unlike anything in the FreeFed. His own home planet, Kaylanx, was perhaps more colorful with its violent swirls of red, green, and violet, but Kaylanx was not *warm*, as was Hydra.

He nudged his ship towards the planet. A small contingent of the main fleet followed. Senships scattered into early-warning array around the system.

This was foolish, Veddin realized—using standard military tactics just outside the one invincible planet in the galaxy. He almost ordered the senships back to the main fleet. But with a shrug he let them go. What else could he do with them, after all? For the first time, he understood why the Directorate had let him bring his fleet; now that FreeFed had been found by the larger human civilization, the Directorate had less use for the fleet than Veddin now had for the senships.

Something about Hydra disturbed Veddin. A troubled frown formed, then faded as he realized what was missing: There were neither moons nor battle-stations around the planet. His sensors backed off a bit and caught a single space station glinting in the sun. It was surrounded by gigantic freighters from the rest of human space. They were beautiful, and Veddin felt awed by the builders of these craft that dwarfed the *DareDrop*.

He also felt an unreasonable surge of joy, being here. It was different from anything he'd ever felt before, a joy that filled parts of his soul that until now had been empty.

Alerted by the sensation, almost alarmed, Veddin searched for an explanation. Meanwhile the joy grew stronger.

"Commander of the unidentified war fleet, this is maneuver control. Please identify yourself." The voice came not through any of the *DareDrop*'s communications channels, but through his mind itself. It reminded him of his first contact with a Hydran Couple, as the savage Battle of Kaylanx Moons climaxed. That had been just before the Hydrans drove the Squishy fleet terror-stricken back into their own territory.

"This is Colonel Veddin Zhukpokrovsk, from the planet of Kaylanx, requesting permission to dock," Veddin thought for the controller.

The sternness of the controller's first thought dissolved. "Veddin Zhukpokrovsk! We've been worried about you!"

Veddin must have transmitted his bafflement, because the controller went on. "The Seekers told us to expect you several days ago. When you didn't show up on schedule, Tarn and Tara Westfall became concerned—and when Tarn gets concerned, *everybody* gets concerned!"

Veddin was still baffled. He had come here to Touch Autumn Westfall, but . . .

"Tarn is her father, you ninny. Tarn and Tara are the commissioners of Hydra."

"They're what!?"

"Didn't anybody tell you that you have a psi-resonant pair bond to the commissioners' daughter?" The controller chuckled. "Probably not. The Seekers wouldn't consider it a proper thing to mention."

Veddin was still dazed; the controller's thought pattern changed, and changed subjects as well. "Dear Colonel, why'd you bring a fleet with you? You certainly don't need it, and I suspect there's a rule against it somewhere."

Veddin was still trying to understand why the speaker's "voice" had changed. There were two chuckles this time, one in each "voice." "We're a Couple, silly," they said in unison.

Veddin shook his head; of course there were two of them, forming a single psi-resonance.

"Are you going to answer our question, or are you going to try to blast us out of space?" the controllers jested.

He tried to remember their question, and answered just as they were about to repeat it. "I brought my fleet in case I was ambushed."

Loud giggles threaded through his mind. Veddin felt aggravated anger. "Thank the Lords I did, too. I would've been killed if it hadn't been for my robots."

"What?!" The laughter stopped; Veddin thought he could sense a trace of horror mixed with their shock.

He waited till the shock wore off, then told them about the ambush that occurred shortly after he left Kaylanx. Disbelief colored the controllers' thoughts so much that Veddin finally linked them with the *DareDrop*, so they could see and feel the giant hole gouged in her side by an enemy missile. If the warhead hadn't been a dud . . . well, Veddin never would have known about it.

When he finished, the controllers were grim. "We'll have to tell the commissioners. I've never heard of an attack on humans from a species that knew about us."

The Couple vanished from his mind. The unexplained joy he had felt earlier returned, even stronger now than before.

Another Couple Touched his mind. "Veddin?"

"That's me," Veddin acknowledged, still contemplating the joy.

The new Couple saw his contemplation and shared his joy. "You're getting closer to your touched-one. Autumn feels the same thing." An image of a young woman appeared in his mind, sent by Tarn and Tara Westfall—for the Westfalls were the Couple who now contacted him. Another mind touched his, and he could see through Autumn's eyes a pair of delicate woman's hands, and he could look out the cockpit of a hoverplane at the oceans below. He knew that Autumn could see the *DareDrop*'s control room in much the same manner, through the link her parents provided.

"I am coming," was the message Autumn and Veddin exchanged before the contact dissolved.

"It will be better, of course, when you touch one another," the Westfalls explained to him. "For now, however, you'd better concentrate on docking. Or can your ship enter the atmosphere?"

"I can land anywhere," Veddin replied.

"Excellent. I'll put you in touch with spaceport control."

"Isn't there some kind of Customs inspection?"

"Ah, yes. Customs. Are you carrying anything dangerous—firearms, drugs, or potentially diseased foods, animals, or plants?"

"Nothing except a few gigaton-equivalents in weaponry."

"Are there safety devices to prevent misfiring?"

"Yes."

"Are you planning to use these weapons against us?"

"No."

"That's what the folks at the space station thought. Customs inspection ended."

"What?"

"Customs is much easier when you can just see what's in a person's mind. One thing, though." The thought was wryly amused.

"What's that?"

"Leave your war robots in orbit. There's really no need to land them."

"Sure." Veddin blushed an apology, but the Westfalls were already gone.

*   *   *

The landing was unlike any other. In the FreeFed, all ship-to-shore communication was handled via the ship's communication channels. Here, there were all the normal communication and detection electroptics, but in addition there was a mental link with the ground controller. Veddin found himself acting as a passive relay between the ship and the port.

At least he wasn't alone in being upset by the arrangement; the port controller had never dealt with a pilot who was in direct mental communication with his ship, either. "All in all, I'm glad it's over," the controller admitted to Veddin as the ship touched down. "It takes a bit to adjust to that kind of arrangement." His thoughts turned sympathetic. "I fear that for *you*, though, the adjusting is just about to begin."

Veddin grimaced. The Seekers, when they first told him that he was half of a Couple, warned him that Hydra was different from Kaylanx. "Less sex, more laughter," was their capsule description. It had been funny, at the time: the Seekers had been so *grave*, while discussing sex and laughter, of all things! Here, their warning took on new meaning. Veddin had had trouble just finding a traffic controller who didn't giggle incessantly. The Seekers' warning had been true, despite its irony.

And there would be other problems, Veddin realized as he looked outside at the damaged hovacar coming to meet him. Veddin knew it was damaged, because there was just an open cockpit where the sealed capsule should have been. With an effort, Veddin accepted that the hovacar was not damaged at all. Lords of Tarantell! The people on board wore no spacesuits, nor even breathing masks! They were *outside*, on the surface of a *planet*, without any protection whatever! It made Veddin very queasy indeed. He tried to think of the phenomenon in a different way: Here was a planet where, instead of sealing small cities, they'd simply sealed the whole planet from outside disturbances.

He still felt queasy. Well, the people were wearing more clothing than people normally wore around Kaylanx;

perhaps Veddin could think of the full-length pants, shirts, and boots as a sort of very light spacesuit. A *very* light spacesuit.

He pulled on the clothes the Seekers had given him on Kaylanx. They were a bit small—even the Seekers had been unprepared for a 230-centimeter-tall ex-wrestler—but Veddin was thankful for them. He would have felt terribly exposed, standing outside on a planet with only a pair of shorts, sandals, and a utility harness.

At last he stepped out of the airlock. As Veddin came down the ship ramp, he recognized one of the three Couples waiting for him: Tarn and Tara Westfall. Each Couple stood hand in hand, fingers lightly interlaced. Meanwhile, the song of joy in Veddin's soul—Autumn's song, he realized—grew stronger.

Veddin stumbled as the world ended.

At least, it seemed like the world ended. Autumn's song just . . . stopped. For a moment Veddin was too stunned by his own loss to notice events around him.

One of the Couples screamed. Another Couple dropped to the ground, and the third Couple grabbed each other desperately.

A supply truck nearing his ship veered, coughed across the white armalloy skirt of the spaceport and crashed into a derrick. Thick smoke billowed around it.

Veddin regained partial awareness. The lost song was still his most immediate reality. When he saw the truck burning he gasped, "Autumn!" She must be in the wreckage.

Now fully aware, he ran for the truck. It was hopeless, he thought; Autumn must have died, or he would still feel *something*. Nevertheless he ran, and pulled at the crushed door. It came off easily in his hands.

There was another Couple in the truck. They seemed unhurt, yet they clawed at each other and wept, oblivious to the danger around them. "Autumn!" Veddin cried, peering through the smoke. She wasn't there. New fire belched from the truck's belly. He turned back to the hysterical Couple. "Get out!" Veddin screamed. "You'll be killed!"

They didn't respond. There wasn't time to coax. Veddin

grabbed the man and hurled him from the wreckage. He took the woman's arm and dragged her away from the flames. The truck exploded. The Couple was still too close to the flames, but they seemed vaguely aware now, and they struggled away from the disaster.

Veddin wiped his brow. Where was Autumn? His eyes bulged as he saw a hoverplane slide over the horizon, canting to one side. Autumn's hoverplane! Still breathing hard, he ran for his ship.

His shiplink hadn't been affected by whatever calamity had struck the Couples; the *DareDrop* responded calmly to his commands. "Lock onto that plane," his urgent thought rang out. Through his ship's sensors, he watched the craft come down at a crazy angle toward the port. "Tractors on—hold the plane off the ground" —but as he gave the order his ship's computer told him the plane was too far away, and the angle was wrong. Veddin cursed; he'd have to launch to catch her.

But Autumn's parents were right next to his ship; they'd be crisped if the *DareDrop* took off now. He turned away from the airlock. One half of his mind watched the plane through his ship's eyes, one half sorted out the pathetic humans there by the landing struts. Pair by pair he dragged them onto their hovacar.

He coaxed Tarn Westfall into pressing the accelerator. As the hovacar rocked away, Veddin rushed back to his ship.

Only the fact that the hoverplane started high in the sky had spared it from crashing; its rate of descent had increased dramatically. The plane was slowing down now, but it wasn't slowing down fast enough.

Veddin fell into his chair as the boosters blazed. He still shook with exertion, but he had to get into the air *now*.

The *DareDrop* lurched into position. As the tractors locked on, the plane actually fought against their guidance; but despite the plane's most furious counterthrusts Veddin landed it with a feather touch. He landed close by and jumped out.

Autumn leaped lightly from the plane. She looked

awfully young in person. But, Lords of Tarantell, she was beautiful! Her deep blue one-piece jumpsuit held flickering threads of silver that outlined her long, supple body; the ocean wind whipped through her strawberry blonde hair, to set it shimmering in the sunlight. Her golden eyes blazed with angry fire.

Veddin paused as he realized she was angry.

"What the hell do you think you're doing?" she yelled at him. She had a thick accent, a more distorted form of Standard than even the language of Kaylanx. She stamped her foot. "I have to get to the space port. I don't have time for idiots."

"I'm sorry," Veddin muttered, blushing. With a start, he realized how unjust her attack on him was. "Wait a minute. Your plane was about to crash. I just saved your life."

She stared at him. "Man, what planet're you from? Haven't you ever ridden a plane before? That's the way they always fly. Computer controlled. Multiple redundancy. Nothing can go wrong." She muttered something under her breath.

This time Veddin turned bright red. "I'm sorry. It's just that, I'm from Kaylanx, and I've never—"

"You're from *where*?" Autumn had started to turn away, but now she turned back. "Veddin!" Her voice softened; indeed, Veddin wouldn't have guessed it was the same person speaking. "Are you, are you Veddin Zhukpokrovsk?"

Veddin nodded. "Yes, I'm, uh . . ." He was lost in her eyes. She approached him slowly, held out her hand, and his hand was there. When they touched, Veddin could feel a hint of that earlier joy.

Now Autumn blushed. "I'm sorry. When the feeling . . . stopped, I just *had* to get to the port as soon as possible, to find out what happened."

Veddin nodded. "Yes." He frowned. "I think there's something terribly wrong here. Your parents are, uh . . ."

"What? What about them?"

Veddin's voice caught on the words. "I'll show you." He took her into the ship and they hopped across the last kilometer to the port, with the hoverplane in tow.

As they flew, Veddin considered the mistake he'd made. "I guess I was hasty to assume your plane was falling out of control, but I thought it was manually operated, like the supply truck that crashed on its way out to my ship." He frowned. "Why are the planes automated and not the supply trucks?"

He realized it was a dumb question; how would Autumn know about spaceport supply trucks?

But she looked around the tiny compartment of his control room, and Veddin could almost see her picturing the outside of his vessel; a tight little gray teardrop, battered and scarred from too many encounters with too many enemies. She answered, somehow sad. "I've never seen a ship like this before. Probably the automated trucks wouldn't know what to do with it. They keep a couple of manual loaders just for unusual ships."

They arrived at the spaceport. Veddin landed a safe distance from the Couples and led Autumn into the open. He had been watching the Couples through his ship's sensors, but when Autumn saw her parents, she gasped and ran to them. "Mom, Dad, what's wrong?"

All three of the Couples had stripped of clothing. They clung to each other in grim caricatures of love's embrace. But there was no love there, only desperation, fear, and horror. Autumn made an effort to cover the three pairs with the discarded clothes, failed, gave up.

She swung toward Veddin. "Don't stand there *staring*," she said, "we have to cover them up or something."

Veddin knew this wasn't a funny situation, but for just a moment he was taken by the absurdity of it all. He gave an explosive laugh, shook his head. "I'm sorry, my dear, but they pulled their clothes off of their own volition. It hardly seems like my responsibility to clothe them." A new expression spread over Autumn's face; he wasn't sure what it was, but he knew he wouldn't like the results. He continued hastily, "Actually, I think I may have some blankets on board my ship; I know I have some tarps, anyway." He led the way back into the ship. There was a narrow vertical tube just outside the control room, in the thick part of the teardrop. He knelt there and pointed down the ladder rungs. "There are towels and such in the bathroom, on that side."

She peered over his shoulder. "Okay, I'll see what I can find. What else do you have?"

He rose and unlatched a compartment above them, which crashed with a resounding ring against the rear bulkhead. "Sorry," he muttered, "I usually don't do this in gravity."

Autumn hung on to him, rather shaken. "Yeah, I'll bet."

"Anyway, the tarps are up there, if you can find 'em."

"Okay. Can you give me a boost?"

"Sure." He lifted her up into the compartment. "Meanwhile, I have work to do." He retreated into the control room before Autumn's wrath could catch him.

"Where are you going?" she screamed through the walls at him.

"I'm gonna try to raise somebody on the radio," he yelled back.

"Who?"

"Just anyone at all on this peculiar planet of yours."

"Oh." Something clattered over head, but Veddin forced himself to disregard it and work with the ship's various receivers and transmitters. First he tried contacting the port control tower, using the frequencies they'd used to guide him in. All he could get was muffled whimperings in the background. A thump outside announced the return of Autumn from the overhead compartment.

"What does anyone at all say?" she asked.

Veddin shook his head.

"Oh." She disappeared again.

Veddin was lost in his efforts for some time thereafter, growing more grim as each effort produced fewer results. At last he yelled, "I can't find anything!"

There was a gentle tap on his shoulder. "You don't have to yell," was the dry rejoinder.

He looked up; her nose was within inches of his. He was astonished at how beautiful Autumn's eyes were.

He swallowed hard. "Did you get your parents all bundled up?"

"Yeah. They're, uh, all right I guess." She shook her head. "Faresh and Hella are almost catatonic, but at least they're still breathing."

"Um." Veddin shook his head, returning to the communication problem. "I get lots of inter-robot traffic, but there don't seem to be any people out there, sending or receiving anything."

"I'm not surprised—even if this is just a local problem, you're not likely to find *people* talking by radio."

Veddin stared at her. "Why not?"

She pursed her lips. "They're all psychic, you numbskull. What do they need radios for? Some of the more powerful transmitting couples run a sort of broadcasting system for news of general interest. There are some Couples that can't find a resonant psiband in common with some other Couples, but it's easy enough to get an intermediary if you've really got something to say."

"I see." Veddin bit his lip; he wished she'd told him that earlier. Well, she was concerned with her parents.

"Can we bring them on board?"

"Who?"

"My parents and the others. Can we bring them on board?"

Veddin opened his mouth, shut it. "Sure, we can stuff 'em in the empty supply holds."

Autumn's voice took on a dangerous edge. "It's either that or carry them to the control tower. The ship's closer."

Veddin felt his neck muscles tense. "Don't you think we should find out what else is happening around here? At least your parents are safe. Others may not be."

She gritted her teeth, then the defiance disappeared. "You're right, of course."

Veddin nodded solemnly. "We all have our moments."

Autumn harrumphed. "Only a moment, now and then."

Veddin rose from his chair, ducked out of the control room. "Where's the nearest town?"

As they stepped out of the airlock, Autumn pointed

south. "I remember seeing a cluster of buildings that way as I was coming in."

"Okay. The next question is, how should we get there: Your plane or my ship? If you don't mind, I think we should take your plane. I doubt they'd appreciate me obliterating a couple of buildings with backwash."

Autumn put her hands on her hips. "Of *course* we're taking my plane. You think I'd trust *your* driving?"

They were standing next to the plane's door before Veddin realized that, for a long time, the two of them had been holding hands.

As the plane took off, Veddin turned to Autumn. She was turned away from him, and her shoulders were shaking. He touched her. "It'll be all right. All we have to do is find out what's causing this, and we'll fix it."

She turned forward. "I just don't understand why it's *destroyed* everybody. As nearly as I can tell, they're all all right except that they've lost their Touch."

Veddin nodded. "What penalties are involved in becoming a Couple?"

"What do you mean?"

"Do you lose anything in exchange for the wholeness of finding your touched-one?"

She shook her head violently. "Of course not."

Veddin decided not to pursue it, but Autumn continued. "They've just lost their loved ones, that's all, in a way we can't even understand."

"Not even the loss of your loved ones should destroy your ability to act."

"Well, maybe it shouldn't, but it does. It would probably happen to you too if you lost your family."

Veddin looked away. "No, it wouldn't."

"How do you know?"

"Because my younger sister was on Moon Leiea when the Squishies destroyed it." He tried to swallow but could not. "Leiea was in my defense sector. When Laurain died, I knew." His voice took a note of determination. "But I couldn't stop fighting because of that. There were other moons, and Kaylanx itself. They would have destroyed the whole system, just the way they destroyed Colander, if we stopped fighting."

Autumn seemed slightly chastised. "I'm sorry."

"So am I." His hands roamed over the deep rips in the arms of his chair, the internal scars that matched the scars on the *DareDrop*'s hull. "I'm just glad the Hydrans felt the disturbance in the psifields and found us. Without you, we would have lost everything."

Her shoulders sagged, and for a moment she did not look adolescent. "Why do they all *hate* us so much? I can see why normal species think we're deformed mutants, with our occasional super-resonant Couple, and our billions of people with no psi resonance at all, but why can't they just leave us be? Isn't the terrible isolation we suffer punishment enough?"

Veddin watched the planet slip underneath. A cluster of unnatural shapes approached. "Look," he said.

She peered over his shoulder. "It's the city."

Veddin never would have recognized it as a city. On Kaylanx, a city was a tight crush of warrens. Here the buildings were only one or two stories, and they were scattered across a grassy plain, completely exposed to the elements. To the northwest there were three stadium-sized buildings, and when Veddin scrutinized them he could make out the shapes of robots scurrying about.

Autumn saw the direction of his gaze. "Those are factories," she explained. "Mostly run by robots, though they're supervised by us. These factories make space-ship parts; the tallest roof encloses a final assembly area for small ships." As she described Hydra's shipbuilding industry, Veddin was again amazed by Autumn's technical expertise.

He made no comments.

She pointed back at the city proper. "Normally, you'd see Couples here and there sunning themselves." She bit her lip. "And there would be hovacars coming and going, and laughter—" She stopped on a sob. "It's happened here, too."

Veddin reached over to hold her by the shoulders, then gasped. "Look!" He pointed at a Couple near the edge of town, directing a motley collection of robots to cart another Couple indoors. Even as Veddin watched, the Couple stopped supervising the robots. They reached out to hold each other tightly for a moment, then returned to their work.

Autumn redirected the ship's computer to steer them toward the Couple. "Thank the Lords there's someone left!"

The Couple on the ground was equally glad to see Veddin and Autumn step out of the hoverplane under their own power. The dark-skinned, dark-haired man clasped each of them by the hand. "Shea and Fanth Ostrit," he introduced his wife and himself. "I thought we were the only survivors," he said. "We need all the help we can get."

Veddin nodded. "What are you doing?"

"Getting people inside before they blister in the sun, trying to get them to eat." He shook his head. "Not much success with the second. We fixed up the first Couples with intravenous feeders and robot attendants, but we ran out of equipment." Even as he spoke he reached for his touched-one, who reached for him as well. The conversation ended while the two revitalized each other.

A baby cried on the second floor of the building to their right. Shea and Fanth broke out of their trance at the sound. "I'll go see if there's anything wrong," Shea said. She trotted into the house.

Veddin asked Fanth, "What *is* it that's happened to everybody?"

Fanth shrugged. "Somebody's jamming all our resonances."

"Fanth!" Shea came to the balcony of the house, cradling a child in her arms. "Hurry up here. The mother is turning blue. I don't know what's wrong with her."

"Right." Fanth dashed toward the house. He turned before entering and waved at one of the robots. "Peter! Follow me."

Veddin came up behind Peter, and Autumn followed him. "Why aren't you and Shea affected?" Veddin asked as they climbed the steps.

"We are. But I guess we're getting along better than most because we're sort of new here. The Seekers just brought us together about a year ago, and we haven't developed as close a bond as the others." He looked puzzled. "Don't you feel the jamming? Are you multiply resonant psimates, who're strong enough to overcome it? You don't seem to be affected at all."

They reached the second-floor landing; the door to one bedroom hung open. "No, we're not multiply resonant," Veddin said. He felt a warning tug on his arm from Autumn, but he disregarded it. "We're isolates."

Fanth took a reflexive step away. "Oh."

Autumn stepped around Peter. "That's not quite true. We *are* a Couple, but the Seekers just found Veddin recently. I was going to meet him at the spaceport when, when," she started to lose control, and Veddin held her tight.

Veddin finished explaining. "Her parents were at the port. They weren't in very good shape."

Shea poked her head out from the bedroom. "Fanth?"

Fanth went in, took one look at the woman on the bed, and swore. "Ciquestan's deficiency. Peter! Tell Chipper to bring my medkit!" Fanth smiled wryly at Veddin and Autumn as they walked in. "I was a doctor on Eridani III, before the Seekers found me. I never thought I'd use my training again."

Autumn knelt by the bed. The woman was young, hardly older than Autumn herself, and almost as beautiful. Autumn spoke. "What can can we do to help?"

Fanth looked grim. "Not much here, I'm afraid. You could start down the street where we left off, to see if there are others like this."

Veddin looked out over the balcony at the horizon. "What about the other towns? Are you sure the jamming is just here, on the spaceport island?"

Chipper whirred into the room. Fanth grabbed the bag and started to work.

Shea turned to Veddin. "How would *we* know how widespread the problem is?"

Fanth looked up from inserting a tube in the woman's arm. "It's probably the whole planet, Shea." His voice held little hope. "A psi-resonant field keeps its strength no matter how far away you go. The jamming has surely spread all over Hydra."

For a long moment the four of them pondered the scope of the disaster. At length, Fanth stood up. "Well, we won't do any of them any good standing here. Let's go."

Veddin shook his head. "What are you going to do?"

Shea look tired. "We'll go on down the street. What else *can* we do?"

Autumn stomped her foot. "You can't help the whole planet like that!"

Fanth started shaking with stress. "We can't do anything about the whole planet. We have to do what we can. Maybe there are other Couples like us and—" he paused, "couples like you, who can help the people on the other islands."

Autumn leaned forward to say something cutting, but Veddin spoke first. "What happened to this woman, anyway? Is this a reaction to the jamming?"

"In a sense. She has Ciquestan's deficiency, which has nothing to do with the jamming, but she and her touched one probably kept the chemical imbalance under control using their psi powers." Fanth paused.

In the midst of the stillness, the sound of someone's breathing stopped.

Fanth turned back to the bed. "No!" He ripped at the sleeve of the woman's gown, and pushed another needle in. A mottle of darker blue spread across her features. "Damn!" Fanth clenched and unclenched his hands, not knowing what to do.

Shea took him by the arm. "Come on," she whispered. "We'll save the next one." She looked at Autumn. "We'll be down the street if you need us." They shuffled out of the room.

Veddin turned away from the dead woman. "We have to find the jammer." He didn't know what to do in this house. He hurried to leave. "Isn't there some way to track down the source of a psi field?"

Autumn didn't answer till they were out of the house again. "Some of the most sensitive receptor Couples, and the telekinetics, can home in on a sender's location in space. But . . ."

"But all the receptor Couples and telekinetics are probably in bad shape, and even if they aren't, if they tried to find the jammer they'd probably get broken up and then they'd *really* be in rough shape," Veddin completed her sentence.

She looked down. "Probably."

"Isn't there some mechanical way to locate them? On Kaylanx, we developed the ability to at least detect resonant psi fields, after we met the Squishies. We were even able to shield ourselves somewhat by the time they attacked Kaylanx. Surely Hydra has a far better psi technology than the FreeFed."

"Not really. There's never been a need to understand psi here; all they've ever had to do is use it." Autumn looked up at him. "There have been some experiments, at a couple of the universities. In fact, I seem to remember hearing about Couple Berrens, on Pyrta, making some breakthroughs recently." Her voice perked up. "The Berrenses have an especially powerful resonance, too; they might've been strong enough to survive the jammer, especially since Pyrta is on the other side of the planet." Autumn's features tensed with hatred. "When we find out who's responsible, we'll kill them."

"First we have to find them. How can we contact the Berrens Couple?"

Until that moment, Veddin hadn't noticed that the sun was sinking. The city lights had been slowly brightening, taking up the slack. Now Veddin noticed the lights, because they went out.

Earlier, the city had been too quiet. Now the stillness was deathly.

Autumn's hand came to her mouth. "Oh no."

"What happened now?" Veddin tried to force himself to grasp the kaleidoscope of disasters the last few hours had brought. He didn't succeed.

"The fusion reactor for this island chain must've failed. The reactors are monitored by psikinetics, who tune the reactors by controlling the cold catalyston flux. The flux density must've dropped below the critical region. There's no power, probably anywhere in this whole ocean."

Veddin rolled his eyes. "Joy. Don't you people do anything without using psi powers?"

Autumn's eyes were flashing again. Veddin decided that that was their natural state. "Of course we do things without psi! Why do you think we have fusion reactors in the first place? For the most part the machines do the work. Couples only do the important work, like keeping the machines from going berserk." She paused. "People only do a handful of the most important jobs. It's just that the important jobs are, uh . . ."

"Important," Veddin said dryly. "So now it's only the important jobs that aren't getting done." Looking around, he saw a robot frozen in the middle of the grassy land; undoubtedly it was externally powered, by transmission lines from the reactor. "It looks like none of the unimportant work is going to get done around here anymore, either." He pointed at the robot.

"It could be worse, you know. If the flux had gone up instead of down, the reactor could have exploded."

It was Veddin who exploded. "Surely you've got fail-safe systems!"

"Well, we do, but . . ."

"Lords of Tarantell! Even your hoverplane had multiple redundancy!"

"Yes, you're right, of course. But hoverplanes are usually flown by people who'd be helpless if the plane failed. The reactors are run by psikinetics who specialize in probability manipulation." She paused. "We import our reactors, and the reactors come equipped to be operated by isolates. But since there's *always* at least one psicouple, probably two, watching a reactor, I'm afraid we don't maintain the systems the way we ought to. I've mentioned it to my father a couple of times, but I don't think he ever did anything about it."

Veddin wanted to scream. "We've got to fly back to my ship right away. I'll pull in some of my senships from system orbit, put them around the planet. At least then we'll have warning if one of Hydra's reactors blows up." He headed for the hoverplane.

Autumn pulled on his arm. "Wait, Veddin. We can't fly back." There was a hysterical note in her voice.

He turned toward her, jerking quickly; his nerves were also frayed. "Why not?"

"The plane—it's beam-powered. It won't fly."

Veddin was stupefied for only a moment. "Then we walk." He turned back to the grassy lane, turned left, turned right, threw his hands up. "Which way do we go?"

Autumn bit her lip. "I don't know."

"Wonderful. Do you have any maps on your hover-plane?"

She shook her head. "We don't use maps here."

Veddin just stared at her, the question on his face.

She answered. "When a Couple wants to know how to get someplace, they just think with another Couple in the right area, someone who knows their way around that island."

"I see." Veddin felt weak. "And you, milady, how do you navigate?"

"Sometimes I have friends put me in contact with the right Couple." She shrugged. "Actually, I usually ask the robots how to get where I'm going."

Veddin stared at the frozen robot in front of him. It stared back. Finally Veddin burst out laughing; it seemed a more reasonable reaction than crying. "Do they shoot looters here? I'd guess not. Come on, lady." He held out his hand. "We'd better eat something before we leave. It could be a long journey."

Together, they headed into the nearest house.

While Autumn rattled through the kitchen, Veddin stepped outside and looked for a convenient roof to climb. Seeing none, he loped to the tree behind the house, and sped to the top: it was a lot different to climb a live tree than a jungle gym, he discovered, but not enough to stop him. Peering around in the fading light, he spotted what looked like a starship's needle prow. It was more or less back in the direction he thought they'd come from. Satisfied, he returned to Autumn.

Through the door into the living room Veddin could see two pairs of eyes staring at him. The room was gloomy, but Veddin thought the eyes belonged to two children. He felt certain that they were holding hands. "Hi," he waved at the kids, and stepped toward them.

They vanished before he could reach the doorway.

"There's no need to be frightened," Veddin shouted out. "Are you hungry? We're fixing things to eat." He became aware of scuffling behind him and turned to Autumn.

"It's no use," she said, "they don't speak Standard yet."

"They don't? They look like they're nine or ten. Surely they've learned the language by now."

Autumn shook her head as she searched the cabinets. "It's the last thing they teach in the schools." She smiled at him. "You keep forgetting that this is Hydra. Those children are touched-ones, with the same telepathic powers everybody else has."

"Don't they learn a little before they come here?"

"Those two you just saw were born on Hydra."

"Really? That's some coincidence, isn't it, for both members of a Couple to be born on the same planet?"

"Not on Hydra." Autumn snapped down a knife on a wedge of cheese. "Couples don't necessarily fall in love, get married, and have children, you know. Sometimes they even hate each other. Many of them have other lovers. When someone wants to have a child, the Seekers try to find matings that will produce children with resonant bonds."

"I didn't know they knew enough about Coupling to do that."

Autumn snicked some sort of taff roll in half with a loud bang. "They don't. They make a lot of mistakes."

Veddin came up behind her and wrapped his arms around her waist. "I'm very thankful for one of those mistakes."

He glimpsed a smile playing across Autumn's lips.

Veddin stepped away. "What's for dinner?"

Autumn turned to the table. "I'm sorry I couldn't do better," she said, waving her hand at a collection of pale vegetables. "But most of the food here requires cooking, and of course we don't have any power."

"Quite all right," Veddin replied, taking a healthy bite out of a lime-colored, but otherwise carrot-like thing. He made a face. "On second thought . . ."

Autumn looked away, and Veddin was mad at himself. "Wait, I didn't mean it. Here, eat something with me. We have to hurry. I think I know where we're going, but I'd rather get started while there's still some daylight." He went back to munching on the green carrot, and Autumn joined him. "In fact," he started stuffing his pockets with food, "I think we can probably carry this stuff with us."

"Stop!" Autumn ordered as he grabbed a plump blob. "You'll crush the ograns. I thought I saw a knapsack in the living room; we can find a better way to carry stuff than in your pockets."

"Fine." Veddin watched with both humor and joy as she gathered up the food; she was beautiful, and durable, and spoiled, and he feared he was quite in love.

Disregarding Veddin's offer of help, Autumn whipped the pack to her back. They headed off past the hoverplane, in the general direction of the starship prow Veddin had seen. "How old are you, Autumn?" Veddin asked.

"Almost nineteen. Why?"

"Just curious." Veddin was almost thirty, himself.

"Were you hoping for a respectable old dowager? If so, that's tough. I like me as I am."

"I see. I guess I can live with that."

"Yeah?" She flashed him a smile with the same energy her eyes held when she was angry.

"Yeah." He considered her for a moment. "You know, all through this trip I've been surprised at how much you know about the machines here: the spaceport, the factories, and the fusion reactors."

She shrugged. "I talk to the robots a lot. And I've spent a lot of time working with equipment all over Hydra. Most of the Couples don't like machines. They'd probably get rid of them if they could. But not everybody is a multiply-resonant telekinetic/psikinetic/receptor/broadcaster. Most of them need the machines as much as people from Earth or Kaylanx." She hesitated. "Sometimes I think I have more in common with machines than with people. The robots don't have any touched-ones either." She smiled shyly at him. "At least, I *used* to think I was like the machines. Until you came."

They trudged silently along for a time. The neatly cut lawn of the city turned wild and ragged as the buildings disappeared in the distance. It started to get cooler, and darker; far darker than Veddin had ever seen it get on a planet. He moaned when he realized why. "Lords of Tarantell! You don't have any moons here!"

It took Autumn a moment to understand his meaning. "No, of course not. Hydra doesn't have any moons. Why?"

"Because we're trapped out here, that's why. In a few minutes it'll be too dark to see." He glanced back the way they'd come. "There's not a building close enough to get to, either."

Autumn laughed. "Don't worry, the wild animals won't hurt you. We don't have any wild animals."

"No, but we'll get damn cold, at this latitude." He considered it for a moment. "Though I was sort of surprised at how warm it was during the day."

Autumn laughed again. "Of course it's warm, silly. The psikinetics control the weather, taking the edge off the . . ." She stopped laughing. "Lords of Tarantell. No."

"Well, let's hope the loss of weather control doesn't catch up with us for a couple of days. I think we'll make it through tonight, and tomorrow we'll be back on the ship."

"Yes, but—" she shook her head. "The main purpose of the weather control is to stop the tornadoes and hurricanes that're constantly starting up around the equator. If we don't stop them, they'll destroy most of the islands. And all the people who live there." She paused. "Including Couple Berrens and the university."

Veddin picked up the pace.

And stopped when Autumn stumbled in the dark and cried out in pain.

"You all right?" he asked, kneeling next to her.

"Yes. I stepped into a rut, I guess." She reached down to touch her left ankle.

Veddin gently squeezed both her ankles; she seemed to be all right. "We're stopping here for the night."

"We can't."

"We are." They did. Veddin lay down beside Autumn, reached out to hold her.

She squirmed away. "I don't think we should, uh . . ."

Veddin rolled his eyes in disbelief. What had the Seekers *told* her about him? Did they think he was a sex maniac? "Child, I've had more than my share of women. I don't need to add you to the collection. But it's getting cold out here, and I'm damn well going to hold you warm until morning. Now, if you want to kick and thrash with a man who just plans to conserve your energy, that's fine by me, because it'll surely keep you warm enough. But you don't have to."

She snuggled up next to him. "Okay."

She was a warm glow in his arms. Veddin chuckled. "On the other hand, if you want to be added to the collection, that'll keep you warm, too, and—" Veddin swallowed hard as Autumn jabbed him in the stomach.

They eventually dozed into fitful slumber.

As he rolled away from the sunshine, he choked on a dew-laden clump of grass. With a moan, Veddin extricated himself from Autumn's death grip. He stretched.

It was a mistake. He was cold, damp, and very very stiff. His stomach was hungry. And his brain was dead tired.

He turned to his companion, shook her gently. "Hm?" she mumbled. Veddin pulled her to her feet, ran his hand through her hair in a futile attempt to remove the worst tangles. Still she was beautiful in the morning light.

"Leave me alone," she yawned.

Chuckling, Veddin shook her.

"Cretin. I've committed mass murder on a dozen planets for lesser offences," Autumn mumbled, her eyes closed. "It's unhealthy to get up when you're asleep."

"Arise, arise," Veddin told her as he slung her right arm over his shoulders and half guided, half carried her down the road. "Kill me later. At the moment, we have a planet to save."

Her mumblings subsided. The sun rose, the people warmed, and soon Veddin could again see the spires of spacecraft in the distance. "Hail the miracle! We've been going in the right direction!"

"Great. When do we eat?"

"As soon as we arrive. As soon as we get within shiplink range of the *DareDrop*, I'll tell her to start cooking breakfast. I suppose there'll be enough food for two. Of course, the ship's awfully small, so you'll have to eat outside." Veddin wisely told her this from an adequate distance; when Autumn lunged at him, he dodged easily.

"You're an evil man," she told him, though it was her joy that flashed, not her anger.

As they came within broadcast range of Veddin's shiplink, Veddin told Autumn what news the ship had to offer. "Nothing's changed, Autumn. Your parents are still half way to the control tower, out of control."

"Have they eaten yet?"

"No."

"Let's get them aboard your ship and take them with us."

Veddin pursed his lips. "There isn't room."

"Well, it would be kinda crowded, but—"

"No! If we have to fight, they'd die without acceleration couches."

"What fighting?! Who could you possibly wind up fighting?"

He looked at her quizzically. "Don't you remember? You were going to kill the jammer."

"I was joking."

"You may think so now, but you were serious then.

Think, lady. How did this happen? It's sure not a natural phenomenon. You said yourself that plenty of species hate us."

"Nobody'd dare attack us!"

"The Squishies dared to attack me, even though I was on my way here."

"What?!"

Veddin told her about the ambush. "This jamming would be a brilliant *coup de grace* for them. I'd swear this was their doing, if I knew how they could have done it." He shrugged. "I don't know how anybody else could have done it, either. I still bet it's the Squishies."

Autumn was silent.

The *DareDrop* was clearly visible now. "I'll race you to the ship," Veddin offered as he began trotting. Autumn passed him in a flurry of blonde hair, and he was surprised to find himself gasping for breath when he caught up with her. "Men are so weak," she sniffed as they climbed aboard.

As Veddin plunked down into his chair, he glanced up at Autumn. "I'll bet we don't know how to get to your research island, do we?"

Autumn groaned. "No, you're right."

"Um. Fortunately I have given this matter some thought. You say the machines here know how to get around?"

"Yes, but they all use transmitted power. They're all shut down."

Veddin laughed. "Not all. Just the ones in this island cluster, that are powered by the deactivated reactor. Which reminds me." He closed his eyes for a few seconds. "There. I've called some of my senships into planet orbit, to watch for exploding reactors. And I've sent a message shuttle back to Kaylanx, to tell them that the Couples of Hydra are out of commission, and they'd better get the warfleet back in shape before the Squishies show up." He closed his eyes again, to concentrate on the *DareDrop*. "Back to current events. What's the name of the island we're looking for?"

"Pyrta."

Veddin relaxed in his chair, working with his ship to

communicate with Hydra's network of automatons. "Strap yourself in. We're gonna make this a short ride."

The blastoff was less than gentle. Veddin had pangs of sympathy for Autumn, listening to her gasp for breath, but he could no longer suppress the sense of urgency he'd felt since they were stranded in the city. Pyrta was near the equator; he could just see the two of them arriving in time to watch a hurricane smash whatever useful equipment there might be to bits.

Once in free fall, Veddin asked more questions about Hydrans. "Autumn, *why* are humans so different from other species? What makes human psis so much more powerful—and so much more rare?"

Autumn looked a bit wan from the acceleration and now the weightlessness, but she answered nevertheless. "There are a lot of arguments about that; it may be the hottest question the biologists have." She untangled her arms from the webbing, tried to get comfortable. "One part of the answer is pretty straightforward. As the . . . complexity, I guess, of an organism increases, the probability of resonant psibond formation decreases: There are so many more links required to form the resonance. The flip side of that, though, is once those linkages form, the resonance is much more powerful." Her expression turned perplexed. "What we don't really understand yet is how we could have evolved so far before developing psychic powers. Everywhere else, psi develops before intelligence does. Psychic ability usually serves as the bridge from muscle-oriented evolution to intelligence-oriented evolution. 'Course, the evolution of intelligence doesn't go too far. It always plateaus before the beings get too complex for near-one-hundred-percent pair formation. An average alien Couple isn't quite as smart as an average human in isolation."

Veddin nodded. "How related are complexity and intelligence? Are more intelligent Couples more powerful as well?"

"Not necessarily. Psi power and intelligence are related statistically, but not directly. My parents, for example, have a normal, single-resonance bond. But they're very intelligent, or they wouldn't be the Commissioners." She shook her head. "On the other hand, there are some really *dumb* Couples out there that are awfully powerful."

Veddin chuckled. "I see." He thought for a moment. "But you still haven't told me why man developed so much intelligence without developing any psychic powers along the way."

"Nobody knows. We think early man must have had psychic abilities; marginal pre-men wouldn't stand a chance without it." She shrugged. "But then the psychic abilities disappeared, somehow. The pre-men had developed just enough so that continued evolution of intelligence worked better than reverting to animals."

Veddin closed his eyes as the *DareDrop* interrupted. "Get ready. We're going back down." Just before the acceleration hit, he wondered, "You know, maybe the same thing happened to those pre-men that's happening here."

"What?"

"Wouldn't that explain it? Suppose somebody started jamming the psifields on Earth, way back when?"

Before Autumn could reply, the breath was squeezed from their bodies.

They stepped out of the *DareDrop* into a large circle of scorched earth. The stench from the crisped wildlife caused them both to gag.

"You practically destroyed the place we were coming to visit," Autumn complained. "Even our biggest ships don't wreck the landscape this way."

They hurried from the area. "The *DareDrop* is a warship, woman. It is not a sightseeing bus. You need power in a warship, not pretty baffling." They were out of the ring of destruction, and the air was laden with the smell of flowers of all kinds. Veddin sneezed, powerfully, and stifled a second attempt by his nose to protect itself.

"Are you all right?"

He straightened up, gritted his teeth. "Sure." He was allergic to flowers, but he'd survive. "I just hope the buildings are air conditioned."

The heart of the university was six six-story buildings hexagonally arranged. Veddin remained in contact with the *DareDrop* via a portable shiplink amplifier. And the *DareDrop*, in turn, stayed in contact with Hydra's automaton network. The ship told him which building contained the Berrens office; he led Autumn at a brisk pace through the doors.

There were two people in the outer hall, one clinging to the left wall, one to the right, dying. Autumn hugged herself closer to Veddin. "What can we do?" she whispered.

"Stop the jammer," Veddin replied, walking past them.

They stopped as they reached the center well of the building. "Great," Veddin muttered, "now what?" They looked around together. "Don't they have a directory or something on the wall, to tell you how to get to different offices?"

Autumn pointed at a booth with two chairs. "Usually, there's a receptionist who—"

"Who puts you in Touch with the people you're looking for. I should have guessed." Veddin snorted. "Why is nothing ever easy here?"

Just then, a Couple came to the rail on the second floor. "Who are you?" the man croaked. He had obviously not used language for years.

"We're looking for Couple Berrens," Veddin called out. He saw a staircase and, grabbing Autumn's hand, hurried for the second floor. "Don't go away, we'll be up in a second."

"Where is there worth going?" the woman said with cold amusement. "There is, of course, our office, which is at least comfortable. Follow us."

Cursing under his breath, Veddin reached the second floor just in time to watch the Couple disappear down a corridor. He and Autumn caught up as they turned right through a glasscene door with the inscription *Couple Shayloh* above it.

Still holding hands, the Couple wrenched the curtains apart to let in some light. "Who are you? What did you come here for?" the man asked.

"I'm Autumn Westfall, and this is Veddin Zhukpokrovsk."

Veddin gave them a Kaylanxian salute.

"We're here to see Drs. Berrens, to see if they have any machines we can use to track down the jammer."

"Really," the woman said, with the same cold amusement she'd shown earlier. The Couple took a couch in one corner of the room; Autumn led Veddin to a couch across from them.

The woman continued. "I'm intrigued. Imagine using a *machine* to locate a source of psi power."

The man chuckled; at least, that's what Veddin took his gagging sound to mean. "Yes, my dear, a machine." He looked at Autumn. "Unfortunately, Drs. Berrens are dead. The shock of separation was too much for them."

Veddin had seen too much death to be shocked; he was more intrigued by the Shaylohs. "What about you two? Why haven't *you* died?"

"Because we are class 9 resonants," the woman began haughtily.

"Not even the most powerful jamming could possibly break our bond," the man ended.

"Can you locate the jammer for us?" Veddin demanded.

"No." The man wheezed. "We can't even transmit to you across the room." His wheeze turned into a sigh. "It hardly seems worth living."

The woman spoke again. "You're isolates, aren't you? That's why you're not affected."

Autumn blushed. "No, we're a Couple, but we had just met each other when the jamming started, so we really didn't get a chance to, well . . ."

"We haven't lost our souls, like everybody else on this planet," Veddin said in disgust.

The Couple stared at Veddin long and hard. "Don't mock us, isolate," the man said.

"You have no idea how great the gift of psi resonance is," the woman said.

Veddin started to lose control of his temper. "But I do know how great the price is, half-creature. Are you

even now too blind to see how much you've lost?"
Veddin shook his head. "No matter. Tell us, how do we
find the Berrens laboratory?"

"I don't know how to explain in words," the man said
in anger.

"Then lead us," Veddin demanded.

The man just glared at him. Suddenly Veddin was
aware of the time ticking by, while people all over the
planet drew closer to death in many hideous ways, and
his patience disappeared. With two swift strides he was
between the paired ones, and he wrenched them apart.
"Tell us," he spat.

The man shrieked; the woman whimpered. "Please,"
they begged as one.

Autumn started to speak, but Veddin broke her off.
"Tell me," he repeated.

"Hemten!" the man choked out. A wide slab of metal
rolled around the corner. "Our research robot will show
you," he explained.

Still Veddin held the Couple apart while the robot
whirred into the room, until they had explained to the
robot what was wanted.

"Release them," Autumn begged.

"Of course," Veddin replied, doing so.

Huddled in each other's arms, the Shaylohs glared at
Veddin. "On another day, we would have destroyed a
barbaric creature who dared to keep us apart," the
woman said.

Veddin turned to them with a hot reply, but he took
a deep breath and willed himself to remember the
warm welcome he'd received in approaching Hydra,
and the gentle power of those who had come to Kaylanx
to stop the war. "On another day, you would be a
noble and generous Couple, and we would be friends."

As they followed the robot down the hall, Veddin
noticed Autumn pondering him reflectively. "You were
barbaric in there," she said, "but you were right. And,
at the end . . . You're not a barbarian." She held out
her hand, and they moved together into the room
through which the robot disappeared.

The walls were studded with readouts and mechanical arms; the central workbench was littered with parts and patching. Veddin saw movement out of the corner of his eye. He turned and gasped. "Squishies!" With a vicious tug he pulled Autumn behind him, and from the bench he grabbed the longest tool he could reach. "Get down!" he ordered Autumn, then leaped at the two purplish, jelly-soft humanoids who stared at him with unreadable expressions.

"Wait!" Autumn screamed in his ear, then grabbed at his drawn-back arm. Veddin, surprised and off balance, tumbled to the floor. "They're not Diorecians!" Autumn cried. "They're our friends!"

Veddin rolled catlike to his feet. He paused just long enough to see that indeed these were not quite like the Squishies he'd fought at Kaylanx. The noses were flatter, the arms longer, and the faces held flecks of green.

Autumn blocked his path. "It's all right. This is a Couple from Tarca. The Tarcans are on our side: though they think we're deformed mutants, they're more amazed than horrified. Hydra is crawling with Tarcan scientists who're studying us like crazy. We're the most interesting puzzle to come along in millennia."

As Autumn spoke, the aliens moved very slowly, their outside hands raised in weaponless greeting, their inner hands clasped together. When they were close, one hand reached out to Veddin. His muscles writhed in horror, but he let the alien touch him.

He came into direct mental contact with the Couple. Since they had also touched Autumn, he had indirect contact with her as well.

"Aha," the aliens thought. "Another powerful resonance broken asunder." The mind held a moment of puzzlement, then expressed understanding. "No—two isolates who would be Coupled, but not yet. Am I right?"

Autumn and Veddin agreed, as two separate voices. The two alien personalities were for all practical purposes just one being, but Veddin could tell Autumn's thoughts very distinctly.

Veddin's foremost thought was astonishment that this alien Couple was still able to transmit.

"Yes, though human pairings come apart, our bond is unharmed," the Couple continued, amused. "Obviously."

Again, Veddin and Autumn thought the same thought, though again they were distinct thoughts. "How can that be? Only the most multiply resonant of the human bonds have even a scrap of Coupling left."

Again the Tarcans were amused. "Yes, this seems quite a puzzle. Human Couples are so powerful, yet so . . . fragile. We believe the difference must be evolutionary. In our species, the bonds were tested for millions of years under harsh conditions: other species on our planet also had psi, and any Couplings that could be broken were, during that time."

Veddin saw an image of Autumn's parents, and Autumn thought at the aliens, "Can you find the source of the interference?"

"No," was the sad response. "But we see you came seeking machines to do such seeking. We have no direction-finding mechanisms, but we do have several units that can detect psifields and measure their local strength."

"What good will that do? If psifields don't lose strength with distance, how could we even tell if we were getting close?"

The aliens projected no thoughts for a moment. "It is true that psifields attenuate very slowly, but they do attenuate."

"We'll use my ship," Veddin realized. "Would interplanetary distances be enough to detect changes?"

The aliens assented.

"Then we should at least be able to tell whether the source is on Hydra or not."

"Yes." The Tarcans looked at an instrument on the bench; as Veddin saw it through their eyes they explained its operation to him. "It's strictly experimental, so treat it gently," they warned.

"Like a kitten," Veddin promised as he reached to pick up the gadget. He pointed at another piece of equipment. "That looks like another model of the same thing."

The Tarcans agreed. "But don't try to move it; that was the first one, and it's tuning is not adjustable. Even a tiny jar could break it."

"That's all right." Veddin turned his thoughts to Autumn. "I want you to stay here and use the old one. We need a detector permanently stationed to watch in case the jammer moves. Somehow, I suspect that when he sees my warship dropping on him, he may try to get away, or something silly like that."

Autumn raised her eyebrows. "No way. I'm going with you. These people can watch the detector."

Veddin snorted. "Great. How will I talk to them? I can talk to you via Hemten"—he nodded at the robot, now sitting quietly in the corner—"but not with the Tarcans. They don't even have vocal cords, do they?"

"They know how to read and write. They can communicate with the robot just fine—better than most of the native Hydrans," Autumn retorted.

Veddin shook his head. "Besides, things may get nasty after I find the jammer. I *still* think it's the Squishies. And whoever it is, he's bound to be armed to the teeth."

Even under normal circumstances Autumn's anger was hard to bear; but now, through the Tarcan linkage, Veddin could *feel* her anger in his mind. It was a palpable, relentless force. Veddin started to succumb when an alarm went off in his brain.

It took him a second to realize that the alarm was from the *DareDrop*, rather than from one of the people in mental linkage. "My Lords," was his last oath before breaking contact with the Tarcans.

With a bound he was at the door. "A Squishy fleet just skipped in," he explained rapidly, though Autumn had seen the images in his mind as well as he had. "They'll destroy the whole system if we don't stop them." He took a deep breath. "It's a big fleet." Numbers and descriptions were already pouring into his brain, and every second the prospects turned bleaker; the Squishies must have stripped their worlds raw to bring these fleets here. Lords, how Veddin hated fanatics! "I can't hold them for long. We have to find the jammer and destroy him, so your people can deal with the Squishies. I'll still take readings on the jammer's strength; I'll just do it while I'm shooting missiles and commanding a fleet." With that, he was running down the hall as fast as he could go. "Tell the robot to link to the *DareDrop!*" he shouted over his shoulder.

He was being crushed to death by the fury of his own acceleration when he got the first message from Autumn. "Veddin, my detector reads 7.9."

Veddin scowled at his own detector, sitting on his copilot couch. He remembered the Tarcans warning to treat it gently. "Gently," he muttered. He eased up on the acceleration enough to reach over and switch the thing on. "Mine reads 8.8," he radioed back to Autumn. "Obviously, our detectors aren't calibrated with each other. I guess it was silly to hope this would be easy." If his own detector was even still working correctly.

Once out of the atmosphere he started warming up his shields and beamers. The ships in his robot fleet did the same even as they sailed into position to met the titanic swarm of enemy. For a moment he considered telling Autumn to peek out a window, to see the most incredible light show in the universe, then shrugged the idea aside. She probably wouldn't be impressed; or worse, she would be scared for his own safety in the hell that would soon evolve.

Veddin pulled a tight orbit around Hydra and headed for the fleets.

Autumn's voice came through again. "I'm sorry, Veddin. More news. Veddin, my reading has changed. It's dropped to 7.7. The jammer's moving."

Veddin didn't have the time to be upset; the battle had already been joined. The Squishies were blasting into the system at an acceleration much too great for them to stand for long. Fanaticism was at work again. Veddin's fleet was only partly gathered, and they were retreating as fast as they could, waiting for reinforcements.

Fortunately the robot ships could maneuver rings around the Squishies; but if they couldn't slow the Squishies down soon, there wouldn't be room to fight before Hydra was overwhelmed. Veddin inched his acceleration up another notch, and started skipping in and out of normal space like a drunk star racer; he was too far away, the lag time for his communications was crippling his fleet.

And then he decelerated as viciously as he had accelerated: the Squishies had already launched a salvo of planetbreakers! Veddin's own ships were strewn too thinly to catch them all; he would have to get them himself. The Squishies must have had planetbreakers to waste, to start shooting them already. Well, they'd keep Veddin tied down by Hydra, anyway.

"My detector is still reading 8.8," he told Autumn. "I'm gonna veer off now and get a third reading from another direction." He didn't tell her that he was heading that way primarily to stop the Squishy missiles.

There was something funny about the missiles; some of them didn't generate the radiation trace of planetbreakers. One of the senships he'd left in orbit around Hydra scanned them quickly; they were full of electroptics, but there was no warhead. Damn! "Autumn, the Squishies are shooting some strange missiles. I'll bet they're full of psi-jamming equipment." If he were right, the whole nightmare on Hydra *was* a Squishy plot. The ramifications were endless, but he didn't have time to think about them now. With several brief sweeps of his weapons this first flock of missiles disappeared, far in front of his own ship, very very far from their target. Veddin headed back out toward the battle.

And another volley of planetbreakers screamed toward Hydra.

Even as he turned his ship to intercept them, he received an image from one of the senships he'd put around Hydra. The image was of hellfire rising from the ocean. One of the fusion reactors had just blown sky high. Even as he watched, the senship's computers analyzed the tidal wave and calculated its future path;

Pyrta, the island where Autumn waited, would be destroyed within minutes.

Veddin screamed in primeval rage, as he had when his sister died. "Autumn! Is there a plane around? There's a tidal wave coming toward you. You have to get off the island!"

"My detector reading has dropped to 7.6," she said. Obviously, she wasn't going to budge until they found the jammer.

Hardly coherent as a thinking entity, Veddin directed his ship to destroy the second wave of missiles. As he calmed, he looked back at the glowing readout on the psi detector. "It's still 8.8," he almost howled.

They now had six readings from two machines at three locations, at roughly three times. He shifted the numbers to the *DareDrop*'s computer, but without much hope of a fix on the jammer. There were too many imponderables; and the jammer was moving! They might never get enough readings! Where could the jammer be?

Even as he realized where the jammer had to be, Autumn came to the same realization. "Veddin! The jammer is you!"

Of course! How else would the Squishies get something close enough to Hydra? Somehow they'd planted one aboard his own ship in that last battle.

Wait, there was another explanation. "Unless my detector's broken," he countered in misery. "I wouldn't be surprised if it's just junk now, after all that acceleration." To check, he'd have to go back to the island, to see if Autumn's readings went back up. Or scan the *DareDrop* in minute detail.

There was no time. Before he could get back to Pyrta he'd have lost them all: The island, the detector, and Autumn would all be gone.

A third salvo of planetbreakers came flashing toward Hydra.

A swarm of Squishy ships blasted their way through the screen of Veddin's fleet at last, and plunged toward the planet only seconds slower than the missiles.

Veddin cut power and unsnapped his webbing. "Autumn, listen carefully." He stepped free from his couch, and ducked out of the control room. "Go get the Shaylohs; you know, the Couple down the hall. Tell them that if we're lucky they're gonna get their powers back suddenly—but *tell them* that they don't have a moment to waste celebrating. First, they have to stop that tidal wave before it kills them and you."

"Okay."

"I'm not through yet." Veddin pulled down his space-suit. "Next, there's a bunch of missiles loaded with jammers, and if the jammers get close enough, you're dead. You have to stop those." He struggled the last inches into his spacesuit. He wondered how great the range of those jammers was; if it was as great as the jammer on board the *DareDrop*, Hydra was sunk. Fortunately, there wasn't enough room on each missile for a big power plant. Probably the one on the *DareDrop* had tapped into the *DareDrop*'s engines.

"Okay."

"Wait. There's a bunch of planetbreakers coming with the jammers. If any of those get to your planet, there'll be nothing left but a dozen small moons." He plunged through the narrow passage to the airlock.

"Okay."

"Shush. There's a fleet right behind them, loaded to the gills with more of the same. And the rest of the fleets are breaking through now." The outer port opened up, and Veddin poised at the opening. "And Autumn, I love you," he sobbed.

"Veddin!" He heard her cry before he leaped from the ship.

He pointed his retrojet at the ship and pushed himself away as fast as he could accelerate; minutes before, when he first knew what he had to do, he'd had his fleet fire a dozen missiles at the *DareDrop*. Even one hit would obliterate the ship and any jammers that she might carry.

He didn't really have a chance of getting far enough away; the missiles were just seconds from contact when he jumped through the portal. One after another, twelve explosions sent blinding pulses of light that his helmet filters could only partially block off.

It had been stupid to try to escape, Veddin now realized. His radiation meters leaped to frenzied peaks. At least on board the ship his death would have been quick and painless. He sighed.

With faint curiosity, he turned toward the planet. There was no way he could see from here whether the tidal wave had struck.

He turned back toward the fleets and the volleys of missiles, glowing brightly as they needled toward Hydra. They were beautiful needles, quite hypnotic in their movements as they slowly bunched together.

The widespread points of light came together, and dissolved in a titanic explosion of brightness that excelled even the brilliance of the *DareDrop*'s demise.

The planetbreakers had blown the jammers to smithereens, Veddin realized. Then he noticed Autumn's song in his heart, so soft now, yet so unforgettable. He felt like rejoicing, until he felt the guts of his radiation-torn body coming up his throat, looking for someplace else to go. He remembered he was dying.

Then he was gone from there, no longer a part of his dying body. Now he was trapped in a multiple mind.

He was dimly aware that the Shaylohs were a part of that mind. "We are sorry," the mind said, "we would request your assistance, but there is no time, and we know you would volunteer, if time permitted," With that the mind swept, not merely around him, but *through* him. Everything he knew of space, of war, and of alien beings, was theirs. There followed a contemplation too brief and too intense for Veddin to understand. The mind opened a window on a brightly lit scene filled with warships. On board the ships were points of light; points that were somehow more like the mind himself than they were like the flares of the engines, and as he watched, those points of light dimmed and disappeared by the thousands. Other forces, yet again different in their appearance, grasped the ships and twisted them into the distance. The battle was over.

But the mind was growing; more and more Hydrans were finding themselves and joining the attack. With them they brought power, and hate. Soon the hate grew stronger than any of the other forces there, a lust for revenge that exploded as the members of that mind remembered and thought and searched, to see that other minds, the minds of friends and lovers, were missing, were gone forever. Wild with pain and hate, the mind shifted, passing thousands of stars to a planet covered with bright points like those once carried by the ships in the alien fleet. In a single shuddering pass through that planet, the mind snuffed out every last point of light.

The mind shifted again, to another system. Here there floated several planets covered with light. For a moment the mind paused. It considered which to destroy next.

Till now everything had moved too fast for Veddin to comprehend. But he understood the half-planned genocide that that mind would commit and, though Veddin too had reason to hate the Squishies, he was appalled at the totality of the coming annihilation. "Wait!" he cried into the agonized consciousness. "You can't just kill them all!"

The mind was well shielded. It fully expected some type of attack from the Squishies; it relished the thought of destroying the attackers. But the mind was not prepared for an attack from within. "You must stop!" Veddin cried with all his resolve and determination.

The mind stopped. And the people who composed that mind stopped, and thought, and saw what they had done, and were horrified.

The separate minds (for they were one no longer) turned to Veddin. "Thank you."

Veddin relaxed. The minds shifted away again, back to Hydra.

And Veddin found himself in a spacesuit filled with vomit and blood. His stomach still heaved to drive more forth. He had forgotten that he was dying.

*   *   *

Pain, blinding pain, fire screaming through every cubic centimeter of his soul. He tried to twist and turn, but couldn't even tell if he succeeded; he could feel nothing beyond the pain. He wondered if this was what it felt like to die of radiation. No, that couldn't be; he should already be dead. Could it be that the ancient religions had told the truth after all: Could this be Hell?

Somewhere amidst the pain there came a chuckle; certainly it was the Devil. "No," the voice said, regretting its earlier amusement. "Fear not. This is not Hell, and I am not the Devil, though I can surely understand why you might think that. Hold on to your sanity for just a few moments, and you'll be fine."

The pain subsided. A gentle rolling motion replaced the agony; he must be in a flotation tank. Ungluing his eyelids, Veddin looked up through the transparent case. A couple stood there holding hands, smiling at him. He rolled in the tank, reveling in his release from pain.

"We're sorry about the pain," the Couple told him, "but we haven't found a method to prevent it. It's a pretty wracking experience, for a human brain to have psikinetic Couples and receptor Couples stomp around, rebuilding each individual cell." The man shook his head. "It was pretty horrible for us, too."

"Sounds like it." Veddin marveled again at the powers these people had. He forced himself to remember their weaknesses as well.

He tensed as he felt the song in his heart growing stronger. "Autumn," he cried. "I have to get out!" As he beat against the tank lid, the Couple unlatched it. Veddin jumped out of the tank into the cool air, and became acutely aware of his nakedness.

The woman handed him a towel. The man turned to a closet and pulled out some clothes. "Autumn will be here in a few minutes," they thought soothingly, completely misunderstanding his panic. "We've found it unwise to let touched-ones be present during cell-rebuilding operations; often the pain damages them even more than it damages the person being worked on."

Veddin's thoughts were incoherent. Finally he considered his ship, and was horrified. "The *DareDrop*," he thought in anguish, "she's gone." He looked wildly at the Couple, his mind filled with need.

"We think they've rebuilt one of the alien vessels for you, a replacement for the *DareDrop*." They were puzzled by his interest. "It's not the same, but it should serve most of the functions. Frankly, it'll be more comfortable, if the images of the *DareDrop* in your mind are any indication." The Couple smiled. Veddin received from them an image of the hall outside. He saw himself walking down the hall to a door, through which the landing field could be seen. "It's just outside."

With a final tug at the sleeve of the ill-fitting shirt they'd given him, Veddin dashed from the room. "Thanks," he thought over his shoulder.

As he broke from the building, he could feel the gentle pressure from his embedded shiplink. He turned left as the *DareDrop II* told him which way to go. He ran with increasing terror. A different kind of shudder formed inside of him; Autumn knew something was wrong.

Suddenly he was fighting his way through molasses. He worked harder with each step he took. At last he could go no farther.

"Stop," a mind projected at him. He was trapped.

"Let me go," Veddin begged. Autumn's song was pure with love now, and it grew closer. He turned to see Autumn approach, concern on her face. She jogged toward him as she saw his agony. "No!" Veddin screamed in voice and thought.

Now Autumn slowed to a stop. Her muscles strained as Veddin's had. "What's wrong?" she asked. Her parents were coming up behind her; they too looked concerned.

"Don't touch me!" Veddin said.

Autumn choked. "Why?" her voice wavered.

"Surely you know why! Do you want to wind up like the rest of the creatures here?"

"Calm yourself," the Westfalls commanded, "Your thoughts are chaotic."

They were right. Veddin forced himself to breathe deeply, slowly. He had panicked back in the flotation tank, and the panic was irrational. Touching Autumn would not turn him into a vegetable. He remembered that Couple they had met near the spaceport, helping people get indoors. They had been together almost a year, and they had still been able to act in the crisis.

Perhaps he could Touch Autumn, to try to explain . . .

No, he couldn't. Emotionally, he *wanted* to Touch her, to become a Couple with her. She could fulfill needs that he'd never admitted needed fulfilling. If he Touched her, he would never let go. Better not to even try.

Why did he have to love the woman whose touch would leave him crippled?

"What a foolish thought," Tarn and Tara Westfall interjected. "Our reliance on psi is no more crippling than your reliance on electroptics, Kaylanxian. What if Kaylanx's central power generators disintegrated? We, the psis, would have to save you, as you saved us. The difference is minimal."

"No!" It wasn't the same, but it took Veddin a moment to put it into an organized thought. "There is a difference. If Kaylanx lost her generators, I'll grant that she would probably die. But I would have *tried* to save her." They had freed his arms; he swept them over all Hydra. "*You didn't even try!*"

The Westfalls withdrew in embarrassment for a moment; another Couple, the pair who controlled Veddin's bonds, came in. "That is not an indictment against us either, Veddin Zhukpokrovsk. That is a tribute to you as an individual. Do you really believe all Kaylanxians share your will to succeed? How many of *them* would work with you if the lights went out on Kaylanx? How many would stare in horror and amazement, waiting for salvation, as we did?"

Veddin had no answer.

The Westfalls returned. "We're all a bit overwrought from the past two days' nightmare. It's difficult to discuss this unemotionally. Wouldn't it be better to postpone decisions for a few days, to let the light of objectivity begin to return?"

If he stayed long enough, Veddin knew he would lose. Touching Autumn would be so *easy*.

Pity flowed from the Westfalls. "How deep your conflict runs, Veddin Zhukpokrovsk. One part of you feels you must stay, and another part thinks you must leave." They paused. "Stay, Veddin. The emptiness that holds you is ancient, born in Man's beginning, before Nature stole from us the right to Touch. Few men ever get the chance to share the joy once meant for us. You would search forever for the answers you can find here with ease. Without Autumn you will never be free."

"And with her, I will never be free." Veddin turned away, not even noticing that the molasses that bound him was gone.

"Don't go!" Autumn begged. "Come with me. Please. See Hydra through my eyes. It's beautiful here." She stretched her arms toward him. "I love you."

"And I love you." He shook his head. "But there *must* be another answer, a better answer. Don't you see—it's us, the isolates, that makes Couples strong! To forego our isolation is to make us just like the Squishies. Is that a worthy goal? The children who grow up here, Coupled from birth, are they lucky never to know what it's like to be men? The answers that Hydra offers are no better than the isolation most humans suffer."

There was the mental equivalent of a polite cough in Veddin's mind, and the Couple that had bound him spoke. With a start, Veddin recognized them: they were the Shaylohs. "We don't pretend to have any answers," they began, "but we do have an alternative for you to consider."

Everyone was alert to the new thought. "Yes?"

"We have studied the psi-resonance jamming technology in depth since the battle. We could give Veddin a small implant that would locally jam psi-resonances. That way, he could touch Autumn, without Touching."

"Ingenious!" the Westfalls thought.

"Marvelous!" Veddin replied.

"Not on your life!" Autumn shrieked.

The Shaylohs focussed their attention on Autumn. "Would you rather lose him completely? We will design the device so that, if you ever succeed in convincing your touched-one that it is unnecessary, he may deactivate it."

A long moment passed while Autumn considered the compromise. "All right," she muttered.

A twinge of pressure formed under Veddin's left temple, then disappeared. Autumn broke free of the restraining psiforces and ran into his arms. Again Veddin felt the dim echo of a true Touch. It would be so easy to complete the sensation . . . yet, he believed, it would be so wrong. There must be more to mankind's destiny than just being like the others. He was convinced of that, though he couldn't say why.

He heard Tarn Westfall's hoarse voice—apparently the jammer blocked mental transmissions as well. "Good luck to both of you. Veddin, may your compromise bear new and interesting fruit." Tarn looked at Autumn and almost laughed out loud. "And you, my daughter, may you be successful in ending the compromise to your advantage." Now he did laugh. "I don't know which one of you to bet on."

Veddin hugged Autumn. She responded in kind. He whispered, "Do you have anything you want to take with you? We're leaving for Kaylanx, you know, at least for a short time. I can't stay here, not now. The next destination after Kaylanx, I leave to you."

She shook her head. "I suspect the Shaylohs have already put my things on your ship. That's just the sort of thing they'd do."

"Very well. We'll go see."

They turned toward the waiting starship. Hand in hand they went, still alone, but now at least together.

Petals Of Rose

Stan Schmidt observes that the best science fiction often arises from attempts to answer really hard questions—questions so hard that most people would not even try to answer them. *Petals* was one of my first, and deepest, encounters with a problem of seemingly insurmountable difficulty.

Suppose the mayfly, which only lives 24 hours, were intelligent. Could such a short life have meaning? Could beings in such a straitened circumstance build a civilization? And could humans work with such beings despite the terrible distance in understanding that must necessarily separate us?

The answers to all these questions is yes. Ahh, but at what cost?

Petals Of Rose

Look to the Rose that blows about us—"Lo,
Laughing," she says, "Into the World I blow,
At once the Silken Petals of my Being
Tear, and my Treasure to the Great Winds throw."
—Rosan translation of the Lazarine translation of the
English translation of the *Rubaiyat* by Omar Khayyám

Sorrel Everwood felt his ears slowly being ampu-
tated; he reached up to adjust the damn strap on his
infrared goggles a tenth time. While he was there, he
adjusted the coloration control as well.

At last the Rosan he faced looked like the Rosans in
xenoanthropological films. Hundreds of delicate cooling
fins, the Rosan equivalent of scales or feathers, covered
his body. He seemed to be wearing flower petals, petals of deep red laced with a fine network of pink veins.
His wide, gentle eyes were violet with flecks of gold.
The gold in his eyes matched the gold in his medallion,
the medallion of the ruling Bloodbond.

Some of his petals were curled, and turned green
toward the edges. *Or Sae Hi Tor must be old for a
Rosan*, Sorrell decided before concentrating again on
the Bloodbond's words.

"I assure you we'll give you all the help, the highest
priorities, available." Or Sae spoke slowly in logitalk for
the humans. "Obviously we stand to gain even more
from a translight communicator than you do. And I
hope that—"

Or Sae rose suddenly from his chair, heading for the
exit passage. "I'm sorry," he murmured. "May you die
by a . . . rising . . ." He crumpled to the floor.

Sorrel was already moving toward Or Sae. Wandra
screamed. The screaming made Sorrel turn, and as he
turned he realized what was happening. Thus, when he
turned back to Or Sae, he was not surprised to see a
pool of green brainblood seeping from Or Sae's head,
solidifying into jelly. Nor was he surprised when a
sweet, gentle scent, disturbingly like honeysuckle, filled
the air.

*Sorrel hadn't known he still had it in him to hate; he
had been so long so tired and so resigned. But sitting
there with the Lazarine, the hate came back to him,
along with fear and defiance.* "Why me?" *he asked
harshly, or at least as harshly as he could manage with
the fear in his throat.*

Balcyrak Kretkyen Niopay blinked slowly. "Because
you are the most qualified being in the universe. Isn't
that obvious?"

Sorrel said nothing; yes, in some ways it was obvious.

*The Lazarine laughed—a resounding sound, which
faded slowly.* "I'm sorry—I know that for you it's not a
laughing matter." *A robutler entered; Balcyrak pointed
to the serving tray.* "Refreshment?"

"Thanks." *Sorrel took the warmed liquor glass, containing . . . well, he wasn't sure what it contained, but
it was probably costly, certainly good, and hopefully
soothing to a dry throat. As he sipped, Balcyrak changed
the subject.*

"We know how much you hate us."

Sorrel coughed, inhaled sharply.

"And also why. I am sorry about your wife. We are
sorry for all who die too soon, regardless of how many
Lazarines those sentients may have killed, regardless of
how involved we may have been in killing them in
return."

*Sorrel's wife had been an officer on board a human
flagship when Man chose to fight Lazaran, before Man
overcame his brooding jealousy. So long ago . . .*

"But the work is, in our opinion, too important for
historical phenomena, however recent, to interfere. You
are the galaxy's foremost authority on Rosans, knowing

them even better than they know themselves—in fact, you are the only sentient ever to have transformed an alien culture without force of weapons. That is quite an achievement; it may be said that you are the only successful xenopsychologist ever born."

"Without force of weapons?" Sorrel felt fiery horror. "Millions of Rosans died in the revolution."

Balcyrak waved it away. "But they were killed by other Rosans, the Rosans who could understand the superior regenerative society you offered them. Have you ever read Darwin?"

Sorrel snorted. "I don't have time for reading ancient history."

"Of course; I am sorry to mention it. No matter. The deaths were just a manifestation of the fittest surviving. Because the six-parent religion was superior, it destroyed the four-parent religion. After all, the superiority of six-parenthood inspired you to write your dissertation in the first place. The people of Khayyam are lucky that Prim Sol Mem Brite read it."

"Yeah. But not so lucky he killed so many of his own people because of it," Sorrel frowned. He wanted to argue, but this was neither the time nor the place. "Look. Why don't you go to Khayyam yourself? Why do you need a human as your local overlord?"

The Lazarine frilled his mane in distress. "You will not be an overlord; you will be an associate. Humans are the only beings who can be effective as interfaces between the ideas that originate here and the applied engineering that will originate there. We cannot do it ourselves. It is too . . . painful. For them as well as us." He paused, watching Sorrel, speaking softly. "You've never been to Khayyam, have you?"

Sorrel shook his head. It was an intolerable irony that he should never have visited the planet of the people whose lives he had transformed. He had never met a Rosan in his entire life; he had merely written a dissertation about them, in school, shortly after his wife's death.

And with the dissertation he had caused so many new deaths.

Balcyrak interrupted his thoughts. "Fear not, Man Everwood. You will understand why we can't go ourselves after you've been there a while. After you've become like a Lazarine unto them."

"What?!" Sorrel wrenched forward in his chair.

The Lazarine smiled; he seemed languid, almost uncaring, but then all Lazarine activity seemed languid by human standards. "When you are Lazarine-like, you will understand."

Sorrel realized that Balcyrak was assuming he would take the job, assuming that he would go to Khayyam as Balcyrak's proxy. Even more infuriating, Sorrel realized that Balcyrak was right.

"You'll see," the Lazarine promised.

Wandra took a large gulp from the glass Sorrel had given her; she was still shaken from the death of the Bloodbond. The three humans were back on the ship, though they hadn't yet taken off their coolsuits. The coolsuits made them look like pale, ragged Rosans, as far as Sorrel could tell.

Wandra spoke. "I just don't believe it. I know, I know; everything I had read about the Rosans before coming here warned me about their deaths, and I should've realized that it'd be a casual occurrence." She took another gulp. "But dammit, I still don't believe it. How could somebody be that way?"

"It's simple enough," Cal started with his cool, sarcastic voice. "You'd be that way too if you only had thirty-six hours to live. You don't have time to pay too much attention to somebody else dying."

Sorrel sighed. Cal was going to be a problem; already he was building a shield of cynicism to insulate himself from the wounds this planet could leave. But then, Wandra's hysteria boded ill as well. "It's not quite that simple, Cal. Though the adult phase of the Rosan life cycle lasts only thirty-six hours, they pack a lot more life into those thirty-six hours than most humans pack into a hundred years. The main reason death isn't a cause for grief is that it's so necessary for the children; a Rosan can't, after all, have children in our sense of the word unless his brainblood is preserved for the larval bloodfeast." Sorrel shrugged. "For that matter, the bloodfeast confers a bit of immortality to every Rosan; the bloodchild starts adult life with many of the memories of the bloodparents, and much of the knowledge of the brainparents."

Cal snorted. "Yeah. Immortality. The kids remember everything. Only problem is, you're still dead. Hell, you might as well write a book—that's about as immortal as a Rosan can get."

"And that's probably a lot more immortal than any of us will get," Sorrel said, and immediately regretted its saying; Sorrel, after all, already had that kind of immortality.

Cal stalked from the cabin.

Sorrel watched Wandra pace across the deck, watched her wring her hands in agony. "Yes, Wandra, what do you want to tell me about Cal?" he asked at last.

Wandra paused in mid-stride. "I, uh . . ."

Sorrel nodded his head. "I'm supposed to say that since I'm a psychologist I analyzed you and already know what you want to say. Unfortunately, it would hardly take a psychologist to see that you're disturbed— more disturbed now than you were before Cal left."

She sighed, sat back down. "I suppose you're right. Look, Dr. Everwood—"

"Sorrel," he said, "My name is Sorrel."

"Right. Sorry. Do you know how Cal happened to become a part of this expedition?"

"Not really. I confess I've wondered about it. He doesn't seem like the type to volunteer for a job like this."

"He didn't—not exactly, anyway. He's a flunk. Blew his postdoc thesis at U. of New Terra. Since he couldn't make it as a theoretician, they consigned him to engineering. Apparently that's a big loss of prestige where he comes from."

Sorrel nodded. "Yes, on Narchia it would be. So he came out here to get as far as possible from the embarrassment."

"Yeah."

Sorrel shrugged. "Well, at least he should be successful at getting far enough away. Lord knows, there's nobody here to bother him." Except for Sorrel himself, he realized; his "success" would be a continual insult to Cal. He looked at Wandra; she looked back, knowing his thoughts as he had just known hers. "So who's the psychologist now?" he murmured.

She laughed, the first time since planetfall.

Sorrel stood up. "Let's go back and meet the new Bloodbond. He should be settled in by now; we have lots of business to discuss."

The office had changed little; the Bloodkeepers had taken the remains of Or Sae Hi Tor to the larval gateway, so the next returning larva could take him in bloodfeast. The stacks of papers in the out-slot of the desk seemed larger; those in the in-slot seemed smaller. Tri Bel Heer Te was a member of the current dayspinner ruling bloodline. They directed the MoonBender cavern works during the thirty-six-hour daylight half of Khayyam's cycle, as Or Sae's bloodline ruled during the nightspin half of the planet's revolution.

Tri Bel rose to greet him with a touching of petals along the forearm. The gold, silver, and green medallion of the Bloodbond glinted with splendor. "My children will remember this meeting forever," she said, giving the traditional greeting. With Sorrel, the greeting might well be true; Tri Bel looked upon Sorrel in raptured awe. Her wide, bright, Rosan eyes were wider than usual, and Sorrel had the uncomfortable feeling that this was how she might look upon a god.

"We will remember you in our books," Sorrel said, using the closest human counterpart of a racial memory. "And even the Lazarines shall sing our songs, should we of Earth and you of Khayyam succeed in our plans."

The awe surrendered to the press of business in just a few seconds—still a long time in Rosan terms. "I wouldn't be surprised. Let's talk," Tri Bel said. The Rosan gestured for Sorrel to take the resting incline at the head of the conference table; Sorrel uncomfortably sidled to one of the others. He wasn't a god, dammit! Why did they have to treat him like one?

Sorrel spoke, as fast as he could, in Ancient Rosan (Ancient Rosan being several years, or hundreds of generations, old); he didn't want to waste any more of Tri Bel's time than necessary. "Do you know what we were discussing with your predecessor?"

"No, I haven't had time to read his lifescription yet."

"The significant information we bring is this," Sorrel ticked off. "The Lazarines have developed a universe-gestalt incorporating methods of faster-than-light communication, methods much faster than sending messages on starships. Cal Minov and Wandra Furenz, the other two humans with me, have translated the Lazarine gestalt into a practical theory. Now all we need is a massive engineering effort, to find a workable implementation of the theories. The Rosans, of course, are the fastest, most efficient engineers in the universe, and the project is so large it'd take any other beings decades of effort. Here on Khayyam we hope to cut that time to less than a hundred generations." Sorrel scratched on his goggles. "When we're done, your descendants will be able to talk to beings on other worlds and receive answers within their own lifetimes."

The Rosan should have been bored with this slow aimless speech—but because this was Sorrel Everwood, the One Parent of the Faith of Six Parents, she was not. Besides, the merits in FTL communication were truly awesome. The merits were especially great for the Rosans, who were isolated on Khayyam by lifespan as well as by distance. Tri Bel's tragic smile seemed a bit human, yet a bit elfin as well. "Man Everwood, again you bring us salvation. How can we repay such a debt?" She shook her head. "Have you spoken with our scientists and engineers? Have they seen the plans?"

"No, we've been waiting for a Bloodbond's authorization."

"You've waited hours, just for a Bloodbond?" Tri Bel's eyes filled with puzzlement, then cleared. "We must arrange for the work to begin. Send Man Minov and Man Furenz to the Bel Dom laboratories at once."

She shook herself. "I can't believe you waited hours for authorization!" She moved to her desk. "Your project has Priority 1A, the pick of the engineering pool and all material resources, as well as the right of bloodfeast selections, with higher bloodfeast priority only for Executive Bonds. Further, your techs have fully expanded egg-laying rights. The orders shall be ready within the hour."

Sorrel's head spun; the FTLcom was being backed with resources far beyond his wildest expectations. Bloodfeast selection would permit them to mix and match the brainbloods of the best FTLcom workers in each generation, to selectively shape the chemogenetic skills and blood memories of the next generation even further. And fully expanded egg-laying rights would make positions in the project extremely valuable, since FTLcom workers would be permitted to have more than two replacement eggs, as well as multiple brainchildren and bloodchildren. "Thank you," he said to the Rosan, who was already speaking into the room's transceivers. He listened for a moment, but couldn't understand a word; both because it was modern Rosan, and because Tri Bel spoke impossibly fast. Sorrel left immediately; though Tri Bel never would have dismissed him, Sorrel knew she couldn't work effectively with a god in the room.

There were almost 200 quiet, expectant Rosans listening there in the stone hall. Sorrel cleared his throat. "I want to apologize for the crowding. It looks like our cavern is a bit small for our task. However, a new cavenet is nearing completion, and we've been assured that it'll be ours once it's ready." Sorrel realized it wouldn't make any difference to these students, who would pass into bloodfeast long before the new accommodations were complete. "Anyway, this is Calvin Minov, a spacetime physicist, and this is Wandra Furenz, a topocurve mathematician. Since I know absolutely nothing about faster-than-light communication, or spacetime, or anything that has to do with engineering, I'll give the floor to them."

Cal climbed the low step stiffly, followed by a smiling Wandra.

Sorrel looked at Cal. "Cal, why don't you start off, give them an idea of where we're going, how, and why?"

"Yeah, sure, uh," he turned to the class and froze. Sorrel pressed a copy of the manuscript explaining the theories into his hand—a manuscript that Cal had written. "Just tell them what you know, Cal," he whispered in Anglic.

Cal looked down at the book, seemed to remember where he was, and turned to the lightboard, calling up the first diagram. Sorrel stepped down and examined the roomful of FTLcom students.

They were the best, chosen by Sorrel in consultation with the Chief Geneticist and the Assistant Coordinator of the Bloodkeep; each student had six good parents with backgrounds in science, engineering, or mathematics behind him. The students were young as well, with fat still in their cheeks, not only because young ones would have more time to assimilate more material, but also because only a youth would sit still for the slow ambling ways of humans.

Sorrel turned his attention back to the teacher. Cal, cool and aloof though he might be, was warming to his subject. He talked faster as he went along, and he talked still faster as he realized that no matter how fast he talked his students would keep up with him. In fact, Sorrel knew, the worst mistake Cal could make would be to talk too slowly, for then his students would lose concentration.

Ooops—one of them asked him a question, with such swift sentences he couldn't follow . . . there would be a great deal of adjusting to do. Not to mention the problems it would pose if the humans got too attached to any of the Rosans they taught. . . . At least Cal might be immune to that, but Sorrel could see long, terrible times with Wandra. He'd have to take a very close look at her ego chart. For the first time Sorrel felt that he belonged on this trip, not just because he would awe the natives and make things move swiftly, but because he would be useful as well.

A right arm wrapped itself around his left, and Wandra whispered in his ear. "Well, I think Cal's going to do all right without us. We're planning to take two-hour shifts in the teaching with one-hour breaks after each pair of lectures, so the students'll have a chance once in a while to behave like normal Rosans. How does that sound?"

Sorrel nodded. "We're playing this all by ear, so your suggestion sounds as good as any. We'll see how it goes with this group, and readjust later. I've got a feeling that two or four hours of humans talking is too much at a shot, but we'll see."

Wandra had been gently tugging him out of the room while he talked. Two Rosans in an electric wagon whooshed by with a load of tunneling equipment. Wandra plopped onto the cool stone floor and Sorrel followed, awkwardly falling over her as she dragged him down. She laughed, beautifully, and he laughed as well. She shook her head. "I was getting so tired standing there in the lecture hall, I couldn't wait for a chance to sit down," Wandra said.

Sorrel nodded. "Yes, I've got the feeling all my blood went into my legs. I think we'll have to install a few chairs here and there in strategic locations around Khayyam. Either that, or do some genetic engineering on the Rosans so they need chairs, too—that way we can invent the chair for them and make a huge profit, selling cushions."

Wandra laughed again, a wonderful human sound. Rosans knew laughter, too, but it was a swift, chirping sound, the laughter of hummingbirds. There was no time for rich melodies here on Khayyam.

Wandra's laughter cut just a bit short. "Were you watching the engineers while you were speaking?"

Sorrel sighed. "Yes, I was."

"They worship you."

"I know."

The silence hung heavy in the still, dry air. Wandra spoke again. "I know you did something special for these people once, but frankly I'm amazed by how they remember you. That was hundreds of generations ago, wasn't it, whatever you did?"

Sorrel sighed. "Yeah, but the Rosan memory is long and fickle."

Wandra just stared at him.

He exhaled slowly. "Especially, they remember their gods."

She nodded. "Brek Dar El Kind said something like that."

"Brek Dar El Kind?"

"One of the students."

"Um." Long pause. "Did he tell you of the Faith of Six Parents?" She shook her head. "Well, it's the main religion of Khayyam. In fact, it's the only religion here in the MoonBenders Cavernwork. The followers of the earlier religion were wiped out here in a war some years ago. Shortly after I finished my dissertation on Rosan culture, as it happens."

"Um. Coincidence?"

Sorrel clutched his head in his hands. "I'm afraid not. You see, I invented the Faith of Six Parents." He shrugged. "Oh, it wasn't a religion when I invented it, it was just an idea—but when my idea got mixed with real beings on a real planet with real problems, it became a religion." He took a deep breath.

Just then they heard someone—or something—skitter around the corner. The something made sharp clicking steps, much different from the Rosans. "Freeze," Sorrel ordered Wandra.

He turned toward the sound. Sure enough, a krat hunched there, eyeing them hungrily.

The man and the krat looked at each other for a long time, there in the tunnel. The krat's petals were more ragged than Rosan petals, and a vicious scar gouged the length of his left side. The small but tough creature approached.

An electric cart whirred down the passage toward them, and the krat vanished.

Sorrel noticed his hands were shaking, and his brow was damp despite the dustiness. "They really aren't

very dangerous," he said, as much to himself as to
Wandra. "Usually the krat don't bother adult Rosans.
But the Rosans recently started another big extermina-
tion push on the krat, and hunger makes them bolder."

Wandra squeezed his arm. "Thanks," she said, before
looking him in the eye with some amusement. "You
were telling me about your dissertation."

"Ah yes." Sorrel took a deep breath. "I guess I'll give
you the whole spiel."

He exhaled slowly. "I'll start with the Rosan lifecycle.
Rosans have two sexes, pretty much like humans, except they get along better." Wandra hit Sorrel in the
arm, and he laughed. "Anyway, each pair of genetic
parents produce several eggs. The eggs hatch in about a
year, and the larvae take off into the deserts. These
larval Rosans are tough beasts, tough enough to survive
repeated exposure to Khayyam's sun. The larvae grow
and fight for about two years before returning to the
place of hatching. At that time they metamorphose into
adults." Sorrel felt Wandra's breath upon his cheek,
and enjoyed the warmth of having a woman near him
again. It had been a long time. "The last act of meta-
morphosis is the bloodfeast, in which the larva consumes the bulk of the brainblood of its bloodparents.
From the bloodparents the larva gets many memories,
opinions, and attitudes—foremost are the memories associated with the parents', uh . . ." What was a human
equivalent? Sorrel winced. "Their *purpose*, I suppose.
Except the *purpose* is also transmitted in brainblood,
and it takes generations to change the direction of the
brainblood's purpose, even if one of the individuals in
the bloodline is fanatically dedicated to a different purpose." Sorrel shrugged. "Anyway, the larva also feasts
on a part of the brainblood of the brainparents and
receives some of their memories as well—though the
brainparent memories are stripped of emotional associa-
tions. You could think of the brainparent memories as
being collections of highlighted *facts*, and the bloodparent
memories as being both facts and *beliefs*." Sorrel chuckled. "Actually, there are theorists who think that *all*
memories are passed, even though only a part of the

bloodmemories are remembered. But it'd be hard to prove—no Rosan could live long enough to remember that many memories anyway. Especially since the individual Rosan has a photographic memory, as far as his own life is concerned. Just remembering one parent's whole life would be a lifetime affair."

Sorrel stood up, dragging Wandra with him as she had earlier dragged him. "Let's walk." Their direction led away from that of the krat's departure. "Since the larvae always return to their hatch-place for the blood-feast, genetic parents tended to be the bloodparents as well. Thus there were four parents.

"But after the invention of the shovel, civilization developed inside the caverns, where Rosans could live both day and night. In this new environment the identity of genetic and bloodparents was no longer necessary; in fact, it was a severe hindrance to progress. Since the egg and larval stages last three years, the memories of the great scientists and philosophers missed a hundred generations of civilization between incarnations." Sorrel's voice turned bitter. "That's where my distant, objective eye came into play. I saw something better. You see, if they used a different larva—a larva that reached maturity just as a person died—the person's memories wouldn't have to wait for three years. No, that person's memories could be incarnated the next day." Sorrel shrugged. "The Rosans themselves never saw this possibility. I wouldn't be surprised if there's an instinct for having genetic parents as bloodparents. Not that an instinct was needed anymore—the correspondence of genetic parents with bloodparents was institutionalized in the Faith of Four Parents. The religious leaders, of course, vehemently opposed the six-parent concept."

"So there was a war."

Sorrel nodded. "War isn't common among Rosans—it takes too many generations to make a change that way. Assassination and brainblood-burning are more common. But when they have a war, it's a total war in the finest human tradition." *Like the kind we waged against the Lazarines*, he thought. "The Faith of Six won, of course; no one in the universe can beat the speed with which a six-parent Rosan culture can make advances in experimental sciences like weaponry, because no one else could conduct so many experiments so fast as a series of determined generations of Rosans."

"Which is why we brought the FTLcom here, to be done swiftly."

"Yes." Sorrel looked at his watch. "You know, if you hurry, you'll *still* be late for your part of today's lecture."

Wandra stared at his timepiece, turned and rushed down the tunnel. Sorrel laughed, watching.

Cal never learned their names.

Their faces and their names changed, but their minds stayed the same—as each tech on the FTLcom project died, the Bloodkeepers fed his brainblood to the next, best returning larva. There was one class for the dayspinners and one for the nightspinners. The minds were constant within those two groups.

Too constant. Day after day Cal would answer the same questions—sharp, insightful questions, but still the same questions. Oh, the Rosans always knew all the facts before they came to class: they read all the textbooks beforehand. With photographic memories it was a breeze. Yes, they knew the facts—but to *understand* and *manipulate* those facts was another matter, and facts without understanding simply wouldn't transmit through brainblood. The brainblood absorbed abstruse mathematics in tiny increments; to produce a clear imprint would require generations of effort.

Sorrel and the Bloodkeepers told him that soon their determined screening and selection of bloodlines would produce engineers who remembered FTL hyperspace mechanics with facility, for whom the brainblood's *purpose* was directed toward this kind of learning. But for now there was a slow, painful learning process.

So Cal would teach. Incredibly swiftly they would learn, and then the new faces would come the next day, having forgotten. So Cal would teach.

Until one nightspin he met Dor Laff To Lin. She was delicate and graceful, even for a Rosan. Her mouth quirked into a laughing smile at the slightest provocation. Better yet, she asked new questions.

New questions! Her brain- and blood-parents had passed their knowledge and their understanding in brainblood, and Dor Laff knew it all. She knew, perhaps, as much as Cal himself, and when she reached midnight age Cal no longer knew answers to her questions. He blustered and flushed at her; she laughed and worked with him. She taught the rest of the class to help him find the answers to her new questions, digging ever deeper into the vitals of the Universe.

Cal had never known a woman with whom he could laugh and work, nor had he ever been a member of a team, a leading member at that: though Dor Laff controlled the discussions, it was Cal's mind that was central; it was Cal's mind that was tapped for knowledge and insights. They pushed him beyond the seeming limits of his creativity, to see new truths, and then they took his truth and ran with it farther and faster, in many directions, than a human mind could go.

But Cal didn't have time to be disturbed by their superiority—for as one group ran off with a new idea, Dor Laff would bring him back to work another track, another direction, to send another group racing in another new direction. Never had he loved so deeply someone who had given him so much.

Dawn approached; the brightness in Dor Laff's eyes was fading, but Cal was too flushed with victory to notice. He half-sat, half-fell to the edge of the lecture platform. Waves of exhaustion caught up with him. "Dor Laff, you're a miracle," he told her in ecstasy.

She knelt beside him and touched his cheek. The gentle petals of her hand brushed across his forehead. "Will you remember me?" she asked.

He looked into her eyes. "Of course I will."

She hugged him. "Thank you, thank you for letting me touch your immortality." She turned. "Good-bye."

He called to her, but she was gone for the moment. The fatigue of thirty hours of concentration took him; he slept.

When he woke, she was gone forever.

*   *   *

". . . and things are going remarkably smoothly, all in all," Sorrel was saying into his dictalog when Wandra's call came through.

"Sorrel, we've got a problem here," Wandra yelled above the background sound of an angry crowd. "Cal's lost his cool, with a vengeance. We'll be lucky if they don't lynch us."

"Stay calm," he urged on his way out the door. "Be with you in a flash."

The FTLcom cavern had changed a great deal since the last time Sorrel had seen it; corners here and there contained the beginnings of pieces of equipment that would've given Euclid headaches; some were shrouded to prevent glances into the gravwarps being generated. There were nearly 400 Rosans there now, all murmuring to one another. Cal stood before them, cursing and pleading in anguish. "Why don't you remember? Why are you asking me the same thing again? Why do you question me? Listen to me, please!" Several of the Rosans had left their inclines and gathered near the front platform.

A dozen Rosans saw Sorrel enter the room and hurried to him. "Man Everwood, what should we do?" they asked, with reverence in their eyes.

"Nothing," he replied grimly. "Don't let any Rosans touch him. I'm gonna have enough trouble with him as it is." He turned to Wandra. "How tough are you in a fistfight?" Sorrel asked in Anglic.

"Brown belt in modkido. How 'bout you?" She barked a short, tense laugh.

He shook his head. "I'm too old, I'm afraid. I'll distract him; you grab him. Wish we had more manpower, but if the Rosans tried to touch him, he'd really go wild."

"They'd only get hurt, anyway—too fragile," she commented as they moved in on the podium.

"Cal," Sorrel yelled above the noise, "A shuttle just arrived from New Terra! There's a message for you!"

Cal stopped cold. "What?"

Wandra rushed him. He flailed, and Sorrel ran up to

assist Wandra. A few minutes' struggle left Cal tired and sobbing.

"Take him back to his cave?" Wandra asked.

Sorrel shook his head. "The ship. Let's surround him with as much humanness as we can. He's suffering classic culture shock."

They picked him up, started him moving out of the cavern. "Classic culture shock? I never heard of anybody frothing gibberish because of culture shock before."

"Well, almost classic culture shock," Sorrel grunted. "You've gotta admit, this culture has a lot of shock in it." He bit his lip, and together they dragged Cal's limp body back to the ship.

Sorrel had never been a practicing psychologist, at least not to the extent of hanging out a shingle and looking for lost psyches. But it seemed to be his main function on this trip; perhaps Balcyrak had known all along that this would happen.

The psychologist took a deep breath, but otherwise retained a professional calm. Apparently this episode had been triggered by the death of a Rosan woman. Sorrel cursed himself for thinking Cal's aloofness would protect him; the aloofness had made him all the more vulnerable, once someone broke through the shell.

At the moment Sorrel was sitting quietly next to Cal, who lay on an accelerator couch pouring forth his soul. Freud would have loved it. Sorrel did not. It had taken great effort even to get Dor Laff's name, and Cal still didn't acknowledge her as his source of pain. "Is that the only problem with the Rosans, Cal? Are you sure?"

Cal nodded. "I can't stand it. Every day I teach the same thing, again and again, and the faces are *different*." The last ended in a howl of horror. "Every day different, never the same person twice." He whimpered, "Please, let me have just one student twice."

Sorrel shook his head. "Don't they remember, Cal? Don't they ever, from one day to the next? Just one thing. Can you remember?"

"Well . . . just a couple of things. Not much. Always the same questions . . ."

Wandra knocked at the open door of the cabin; Sorrel waved her in. "How's he doin', Doc?" she asked, attempting to be light and cheery.

"Cal's as fine as ever, of course. I think we'll spend the rest of the afternoon here, though. Can you manage the courses by yourself?"

She nodded. "You bet, Doc. Stimpills and me, we've got what it takes."

"Yeah, I'll bet. Next Cal will have to take the whole show for two days, while you recuperate.'"

"Faith, Doc, faith. Catch ya later." She was gone before Sorrel could speak again.

He turned back to Cal. "You were telling me what else bothers you about the Rosans, besides the fact that they forget every day."

"I was?" Cal twisted his head to Sorrel. "I, uh, I guess there is something else. They don't remember too well, but . . ." Cal's shoulders shook as he sobbed. "They're, they're smarter than we are. I just don't believe how much smarter they are. So fast, so sharp. Every day I say the same things over again, but every day they learn it again in just a matter of minutes." He rolled over, away from Sorrel, and mumbled into the couch, "God, what I'd give to be able to think as fast as they can."

"Would you give your life for it, Cal? They do."

"I know, I know, but . . ." He rolled back over, smiled through the tears. "My old quant prof, Durbrig, used to tell me my problem was that I wanted it all. I guess I still do."

"I guess so, too. I envy you that, Cal. I wish I still had enough hope to dare to want it all." Sorrel stood up. "Stay here until, oh, maybe 5100 hours, and come on back to the cavernwork. Think you'll be all right?"

"Yeah." He smiled, crossed his arms as Wandra would. "Sure thing, Doc."

The new nightspin Bloodbond was different from the earlier Bonds; this Sorrel could tell already, and he hadn't even met the being yet. But so far three other Rosans had gone in to see the Bond, leaving Sorrel to cool his heels for upwards of two minutes—a short but significant wait. Earlier, Sorrel had received immediate service, regardless of how important the other callers were and how precious their time was. It had always made Sorrel uncomfortable before, but now its absence left a trace of anxiety nibbling his mind.

As the third Rosan left, Kik Nee Mord Deth beckoned him. "What, Man, want you?" he asked in peremptory Rosan.

"Equipment," Sorrel replied as smoothly as he could manage. "FTLcom tech bloodmemories firm now. Prototype construction begins. Trouble develops acquiring these items." He held out a list to Kik Nee, who snatched it, skimmed it, and thrust it back to Sorrel.

"Precious items," he commented. "Needed elsewhere."

"Priority 1A on FTLcom," Sorrel replied almost haughtily. That internal haughtiness surprised Sorrel himself. He'd never imagined himself pushing for the prerogatives the first Bloodbond had granted him, but Kik Nee rubbed him the wrong way. "Impediment intentional?"

The Rosan exhaled sharply. "Much work waits," he almost pleaded. "Let it progress. You need not speed, you have time."

And that, Sorrel knew, told the whole story. *You have time*, the Bloodbond knew, and hated. Jealousy haunted the Rosans at last. Sorrel cleared his throat. "I'm sorry. I've not treated you justly." Sorrel moved forward, took an incline. "But that equipment is needed. Without it the project halts. Though I can wait, engineers cannot. I waste not their lives." Sorrel remembered an old analogy, from the Rosan past. "There's an old bit of Rosan poetry—have you read Gesh Lok Tel Hor?"

The Rosan's lips drew back in disgust. "No time for ancient history."

Sorrel shook his head, blushed. "Of course not," he mumbled. "I'm sorry, again."

Kik Nee turned to the next waiting Rosan, who rushed into rapidfire discussion—again Sorrel was embarrassed at how much the Rosans had to slow down to talk to humans. But Sorrel wasn't done here yet. "Equipment?"

he demanded in a loud, human voice, over the hummingbird sounds of the Rosans.

Kik Nee turned to him, head slumped ever so slightly. "Yours," he acquiesced.

Sorrel left with much food for thought.

Balcyrak stood with his back to Sorrel, watching the darkening sea, while the wind whipped his fur. Sorrel shivered, though the air was warm—on old Earth, the feeling in this evening air would have meant a storm coming.

Balcyrak turned as Sorrel approached. "You must see a sunrise while you are on Khayyam, Man Everwood. Do you know of them?"

Sorrel nodded. "I am, after all, the expert on the planet, right?"

Balcyrak chuckled. "Then tell me this, expert. From whence did the planet get its name?"

Sorrel tilted his head in thought. "You've got me there. I know it was discovered by a Lazarine, but Khayyam doesn't sound like a Lazarine name."

"It is not. The leader of the Lazarine expedition that landed on Khayyam was an expert, if you will, on Man. Omar Khayyam was one of your own poets. The Lazarine explorer named the planet for the human author who wrote so eloquently of a species similar to the people of Khayyam." *He paused, looking again to the sea.*

"Yes, look—a thousand Blossoms with the Day

Woke—and a Thousand scattered in the Clay

And this first Summer Month that brings the Rose

Shall leave Another's gentle Petals, once blown, to lay."

Sorrel cleared his throat. "It does seem apropos, at that."

Balcyrak turned back to the human. "Yes. And now I have a warning for you."

"Oh?"

"Watch out while you are on Khayyam, my friend-to-be. When you arrive, you will be honored, but it will not last. You will prove too alien to them, and a love/hate bond will form. It will prove cyclic. First they will *love, then they will hate, then they will love again." The Lazarine's hand clenched and unclenched as he spoke. "Much as Man loves and hates Lazaran," he whispered to the wind.*

Sorrel squinted at him. "I see." Sorrel moved to stand shoulder to shoulder with Balcyrak, at the edge of the precipice. "Why is it so important to you that the FTL communicator be ready so soon? Granted, it'll prove valuable beyond price, but why the rush? Why do you need to send people hurtling halfway across known space to get it done so quickly?"

Now it seemed that Balcyrak shivered under his thick coat of hair. "I suppose you should know. I suppose it might help motivate you, as well." He paused. "There will be another war between our peoples, Man Everwood."

Sorrel nodded; though currently the peacefulness of Man's relationship with the Lazarines was sickeningly sweet, he knew there was an undercurrent of hatred, a slowly growing group of people who disliked the Lazarines as much as Sorrel himself did. "Who will win?"

"Does it matter? Someone will lose. Someone, Man Everwood, will lose everything. The next war will be a war of genocide. Our wisest consuls have studied carefully, and they know not who will be destroyed, but all agree that one or the other of our species is doomed."

Sorrel paled; he hadn't realized it would go that far.

"We need better communications, Man Everwood. The time it takes for even the starships to carry messages is too great for your people. Given better communications, and hence swifter understanding, we believe we can avert the war."

Sharp cynicism left a sour taste in Sorrel's mouth. "Communications will avert a war, huh? Just like that." He snapped his fingers. He'd heard that sort of thing before, but only from human dreamers who thought that words had substance. He hadn't expected it from a calm, realistic Lazarine.

"I don't blame you for doubting. Certainly, talk has rarely helped your species avert internal warfare. But this is considerably different." For the first time, the Lazarine's eyes refused to meet Sorrel's. "There is

*a . . . molding of directions involved. It is difficult to
explain." Balcyrak's eyes regained their penetrating intensity. "But I am telling you the truth; communication
is the answer." Now his amusement returned as well.
"This also is something you'll understand better after
working with the people of Khayyam."*

Sorrel pursed his lips; Balcyrak's sincerity made a
believer of him. "I confess, the urgency of the project
seems somewhat greater now than it did a few minutes
ago."

"I thought it might. Yes." A particularly strong gust
of wind pushed them back from the cliff just as the sun
sank beyond the horizon. They turned back to the path.
"And remember to see a sunrise while you are there,
Man Everwood. It is special indeed."

Sorrel squeezed through the narrow passage into the
fresh-cut cavenet. "Whew!" he exclaimed, "what a small
entrance. I didn't even see it at first. You'll have to
enlarge it."

The tunneling chief looked upset. "Of course, Man
Everwood. The entranceway is always widened as the
last step, so our noise and dust disturb the rest of the
cavernwork as little as possible."

"Oh. I understand." Sorrel toured the new FTLcom
lab facilities with some pleasure. "Well, it all looks
pretty good to me, though I don't know anything about
the arrangements you need for hyperspace experiments.
I suppose we should have Cal and Wandra take a look."

They squeezed back out of the cavenet. Sorrel looked
again at the narrow entrance. "Wait a minute. What if
we *don't* open it up now?" He pondered for a moment.

The tunneling chief looked upset again. "Why wouldn't
you open it?"

"Just in case of emergencies, that's all." He nodded
his head. "Chief, these labs are ours to do with as we
please, right?"

"Of course."

An evil gleam entered Sorrel's eyes. "Cal and Wandra
will probably shoot me for this—the lecture hall is

horribly overcrowded, and they need this space now—but I think we'll leave it as is."

The chief's petals fluttered rebelliously.

"Don't widen the entrance," Sorrel said, to make his orders explicit. "We'll open it later. When we want it, I'll have one of your bloodchildren do it for us."

The chief looked like he'd collapse with sorrow. Still he managed to stutter, "Yes, Man Everwood."

Sorrel touched his forearm. "And thanks. You've done a wonderful job. We'll remember you forever."

"Thank you, Man Everwood." The chief's eyes shone brightly again.

All the Rosans are bright, Wandra thought, *but this Sor Lai Don Shee is something special, even among Rosans.*

In fact, he and his descendants could be the key to turning the FTLcom problem into a trivial task. Sor Lai's bloodfeast memories were impossibly crisp, leaving him a perfect understanding of everything his four FTLcom engineering parents had understood.

That was exceptional enough—but then Sor Lai went beyond that. He also learned new things faster than anyone else, he asked the most insightful questions, and he brought new points of view to bear on every problem. In just a few weeks he could have resolved every remaining problem in the final design, Wandra was sure.

But he didn't have a few weeks, and when the second instruction session was over, Wandra didn't want to let him go; she wanted to keep teaching him, to pack as much of her mind into his as fast as she could. She hurried from the platform, worried she wouldn't catch him before he burst from the room in normal Rosan fashion.

But he was not hurrying off with his peers; rather, he was hurrying toward Wandra, and only swift Rosan reflexes kept them from colliding in mid-step.

Wandra gurgled with laughter. "Two minds with one thought," she said. "Would you like to continue our discussions?"

Sor Lai smiled as only a Rosan could smile, with the cheeks lifting gaily and petals fluttering as though in a breeze. "Very much, Man Furenz. I would appreciate it beyond your knowing."

She crossed her fingers at him. "My name is Wandra, Sor Lai. I hate formality."

She had to admit, she liked Sor Lai for more than merely his superior performance. She liked the naive optimism he'd shown early in the day, and she enjoyed watching that optimism develop by midnight age into a mature confidence. He knew that the eccentricities of the Universe could impede progress, or even reverse progress, but never, in the long run, stop progress.

They turned to the cavern passage. "Come with me," Wandra bubbled. "We'll go to my . . ." Wandra bit her lip; there was no word for "home" in Rosan. "We'll go to my place-of-work."

Sor Lai looked puzzled. "Isn't the lecture hall your place-of-work?"

She threw up her hands. "I have many places-of-work. This is a special one."

"I see. I think I understand."

She took him by the arm. "I see a free speedcart up ahead. Race ya!"

Sor Lai won the race, of course, laughing all the way.

They survived Sor Lai's driving, somewhat to Wandra's surprise, and stopped before the small fountain at the entrance to Wandra's cavern. "Beautiful!" Sor Lai exclaimed. "How many people worked upon this? And what does it do?"

Wandra shook her head. "I built it myself; I'm a sometimes-sculptor. It's not very good, I'm afraid. And all it does is shoot water in the air, from the fairy's fingertips, and collect it again among the green rocks beneath her feet." She turned to flick the pump switch. A thin stream danced up, spiraled down again. Sor Lai bent to touch the smooth stone, amazed. "This is the work of many lifetimes. Joyous." He rose up. "What else do Men do in their immortality?"

Wandra stammered in horror.

"Do not answer. I'm sorry." He came and took her arm. "I must see the rest of your place-of-work." They entered Wandra's home together.

Sor Lai pointed at the walls. "The pictures. Of what are the pictures?" he demanded.

Wandra looked at the scenes of Karly for the first time in weeks. "Pictures of my—" again, there was no word for home— "birth world. I had our ship computer make these up specially—they appear through my infrared goggles to look the way the originals look in normal light—normal light, that is, for a Man. So you're seeing my planet as I see it, more or less."

"These are all pictures of the surface!"

Wandra nodded. "It is gentler on my world than on Khayyam." She looked at the dry-ice-capped mountain towering above the capital and chuckled. "Though not too gentle, I suppose."

Sor Lai looked at another scene, where the sun set over a pink, powdery beach. "Those aren't Men, are they? They're too small."

Wandra followed his pointing finger. "They are almost Men, Sor Lai. They are my children. Humans metamorphose slowly, gradually becoming more Manlike."

"Your children!" He scrutinized the picture. "They laugh with grace. Have you met them? You could have met them, couldn't you?"

Wandra laughed. "Yes, Sor Lai, I lived with them for a long time."

Sor Lai turned back to Wandra. "Do they know your memories well?"

Wandra pondered that. "I suppose you could say they do, at least as Men go. They're more like me than their father, that's for sure. They'll be great mathematicians, someday, not housekeepers like my ex-husband." She shook her head.

Sor Lai turned slowly through the room. "And a love couch right here, in your place-of-work!"

Wandra blushed, though she wasn't sure why; she'd never thought of herself as the innocent type. "Not for a long time, my friend. I use it for, uh . . . You've noticed that Men tire faster than Rosans, haven't you? I rest there. We are unconscious for almost a third of our lives, resting."

"And still you get so many things done." Sor Lai's admiration continued.

By now Wandra's face was burning. "We do our best," she muttered. She turned to her kitchen. "Now, I have to eat something, or I'll die of starvation."

Sor Lai's admiration turned to amazement. "Eat! Like a larva?" he gasped.

"You bet," she agreed. "We don't store enough fat before adulthood to last for the rest of our lives, though sometimes it seems like my body's trying to."

At last Sor Lai was speechless. Wandra cooked, set the table, and started to eat. She talked mathematics continually, until she noticed the horror on Sor Lai's face. She felt uncomfortable. "Listen, do you want me to eat another time?"

"No, not at all," Sor Lai said. To Wandra, he seemed to be shuddering. "It's . . . intriguing."

She looked at him a while, then continued her meal.

"I remember my bloodfeast," he said, petals waving ecstatically. "It is a joy beyond imagining."

"I believe it," Wandra replied. "When we eat, though, it's nothing like that." She had heard of Rosans with keen memories of the bloodfeast ecstasy actually stealing someone's brainblood, to try to eat it—even though the adult Rosan's digestive tract is atrophied. And the ecstasy had to be strong indeed, to risk the consequences—for the stealing of another Rosan's brainblood was punishable by brainblood cremation.

They talked. Wandra finished her meal at last, and the two of them sat upon her bed, still talking. Suddenly Sor Lai clapped his hands and jumped to his feet. "You know, this hyperspace link with sound and video is all right, but the properties of the four-space beg you to generate three-dimensional pictures. Do you have a computer terminal here?"

Wandra was on her feet as well. "It begs you, huh? Well, it never begged me, but if you say so, here—" She marched to her desk and pulled out a keyboard.

The wall in front of her lit up, and with quick keystrokes she logged into the Rosan central computer system.

Sor Lai crossed the room to join her. His fingers flew across the keys, and he spoke in machine-gun Rosan as the ideas developed and the machines to implement them took shape. Wandra could only stand and stare. "There," he proclaimed at last. "It's even better than I thought. When the FTLcom is ready, you won't even have to send a ship to deliver the construction plans to people on other planets. We'll be able to project and receive 3-D images all with one transceiver, without any equipment at the other end. Unless they throw a blast screen around your target location or some such thing."

Wandra continued to stare at him. "That's incredible."

He smiled broadly. "Yes, it is, isn't it?"

She laughed. "Even more incredible than a Man who eats even after she becomes an adult."

His smile turned quiet. "No, not as incredible as that."

They hugged each other, artificial coolsuit petals touching honest, living, roselike petals.

For the first time, Wandra became aware of how much thinner Sor Lai was now than when they'd left for her home. She looked at her watch; six hours had passed—the equivalent, in Rosan terms, of almost ten years.

Wandra jerked away. "Sor Lai!" she almost screamed. "We have to get you back!"

"I guess we should, at that," he conceded.

They speeded through the cavenets, as fast as they'd gone before, yet it was too slow for Wandra's concern. She had used up an awesome part of Sor Lai's life, just bringing him home.

Wandra tried to counter her guilt with logic. After all, the time had been productive, hadn't it? And yes, it had been worth it, hadn't it? She hurt nevertheless.

They returned to the conference cavern, where Cal was lecturing. Sor Lai took his place among his fellows, but Wandra couldn't bear to leave. She listened to Cal's lecture absently, looking among the now dawning-aged nightspinners, seeing them for the first time, watching them grow old.

The lecture ended, and a break was taken—a break to work on the two prototypes nearing completion. Wandra hovered by Sor Lai's team. Work ended, and Wandra lectured, and work continued, until dawn.

Wandra fought the tears gathering in her eyes. The curled, green-tinged petals spread inexorably across Sor Lai's body. He smiled at her sadly. "You should leave me now," he whispered. "It's time for me to go, to let my children remember."

"No, let us not waste a minute of life," Wandra choked.

The laughter in his eyes calmed. "I am tired," he said. He settled to the ground. "I'm sorry."

Wandra knelt beside him.

The air turned sweet with honeysuckle, and the flowing blood mingled with a woman's tears.

Sorrel peeked around the corner, into the interior of Wandra's home. "Anybody home?" he asked, watching her lie upon her bed.

She turned to him, tired and distraught. "Hi," she smiled wanly. "I'm sorry I haven't made it in yet. The students are probably better off without me, anyway."

Sorrel slipped in, moved to sit on the edge of her bed. "Are you sick? Did you finally find a bacterium on this planet that knows what to do with our proteins?"

She shook her head.

He nodded. "I understand there was an exceptional student during nightspin."

She nodded.

"I also hear . . . you were rather fond of him."

She rolled away. "God, yes. He was kind, he was beautiful, he was . . ."

"He was all good things. I know. It seems to be a common trait among the Rosans." He rolled her gently over to face him.

"Why do they have to die so soon?" she yelled at him. "Why can't they live like we do, and laugh and love and talk with their children and . . ." She was crying.

Sorrel raised her by her shoulders, held her close. "They can't live like we do because Nature didn't design them to live like we do. Because at the time of their evolving, death at dawn was certain. Why would Nature spend such an effort, giving long life to one doomed to die anyway?"

Wandra started rocking, bringing her legs up into a foetal position. Sorrel stroked her hair. "You remember that krat we saw a while ago, outside the conference hall?"

She nodded.

"I saw it again yesterday."

She looked up. "What? The same one?"

Sorrel shrugged. "It had the same ragged scar on its side."

Wandra's mouth hung open, forming the obvious question.

"The krats have been luckier than the Rosans. When the Rosans moved into the caverns, they found a place free of evolutionary pressures, where they could prosper without menace. But when the krats came, they found the Rosans already here, determined to keep their caves and destroy the invaders. Thus the krats still had evolutionary pressures. Only the strong survived. Nature discovered that longevity would be useful for krats; and the krats earned longer lives through generations of bloodletting.

"But Nature doesn't choose for long life among Rosans, because there is no need—and only need causes Nature to care. Nature doesn't care whether the Rosans survive with grace or joy—Nature only cares that they survive, one way or another. The Rosans can never develop longevity, because they are too good at surviving without it." Sorrel was surprised at the bitterness creeping into his voice. "The characteristics that make them so wonderful and worth saving are the same characteristics that damn them to mere instants of time for all eternity."

"It's not fair," Wandra wailed.

"Fairness and justice have nothing to do with it."

Sorrel continued, and this time the bitterness was undeniable. The vision of his children dying on a radiation-burned planet burned his mind. "Nature knows nothing of justice. Only Men think of justice; it is a concept we invented and it exists only when we can create it."

They were both quiet for a long time; finally Wandra spoke. "Isn't there something we can do? Intravenous feeding or something?"

Sorrel shook his head. "That's done under special conditions, but the basic lifetime of the Rosan is built into the cells. Even with plenty of nutrients, the cells just stop metabolizing. It's as if they knew they were supposed to die."

"What about slowing down their metabolisms?"

Sorrel looked her in the eye. "If you could extend your life by a tenth, but to do it you had to cut your ability to live each moment of that life in half, would you do it?"

Wandra sobbed. Sorrel stroked her hair again. "I wish I could say something more soothing." His voice turned gentle again.

Wandra's arms tightened around Sorrel's chest. "Would you . . . stay with me? Till tomorrow?"

Sorrel drew a ragged breath; suddenly, he felt like the old man he sometimes knew himself to be. "I would," he said softly, "if I really believed that, in your heart, you wanted me to." He kissed her on the forehead, disengaged slowly. "I'll see you in a few hours. If you have trouble sleeping, call me." He looked down at her a last time. "Dream well," he whispered as he left.

Kir Bay played with his FTLcom medallion as he spoke. "Well, at least we still have plenty of time left. It'll be hours before the Bloodbond election. It's a shame, though, that the Supremi candidate is certain to win."

Sorrel gasped in horror. "What?!" It had been several days since Sorrel last listened to the Rosan news broadcasts. Now he cursed himself under his breath for not keeping better track; less than a week ago, the Supremi had been just another religious splinter group, with a half-sentence mention in the course of a full spin's broadcasts.

"Is it that important?" the engineer was puzzled. "It's not as if it'll kill the project."

Sorrel rolled his eyes to the ceiling. "Politicians, unfortunately, are even crazier than they seem, Kir Bay. If the Supremi get control of the government, not only will they destroy the project, they'll also destroy you—and I mean burning your brainblood, not just arranging an early death."

It was Kir Bay's turn to gasp in horror. "Are you serious?"

"How closely have you listened to the Supremi plans? They hate humans and everything associated with them. As chief engineer on our project, you're a public enemy in their eyes."

Kir Bay's petals tensed against his body. "I just can't believe it."

"Then come with me." Sorrel consulted Daisy, the starship's computer, on his radcom and found a place where they could hear a prominent Supremi politician speak.

They arrived to find a large crowd mesmerized by the fiery words of a fanatic. Few people saw Sorrel and Kir Bay arrive; those who did drew away from them in contempt, and some of them hissed in fury.

Soon Kir Bay had had enough. "You were right. We're in great danger."

Sorrel pulled him out of the Supremi cavern. "Fortunately I've made some preparations for this, though not as many as I'd planned. Damn! You people move too fast." He sighed. "Listen. Long ago, a special set of laboratories was prepared for the FTLcom project. Just as they were getting finished, I put a damper on the job, and now I'm the only one who knows where they are." He told Kir Bay how to find the narrow entrance-way. "Get everybody down there you can—but do it quietly!"

"What about you?"

"I've got an appointment with a Bloodkeeper. I'll catch up with you later." Sorrel shoved him toward the cart, then ran off in the other direction, toward the Bloodkeep.

There was one Bloodkeeper left who still believed in the FTLcom project, one Bloodkeeper whose bloodline Sorrel had nurtured and protected from the Man-hatred that now exploded through the Rosan culture. Sorrel had talked with the current member of that bloodline earlier that nightspin, though he hadn't talked with him about the dangers of Supremi leadership. Sorrel hoped the two of them could work something out to protect the bloodlines they had so painfully constructed.

As he ran, Sorrel listened on his radio to Daisy's translation of the Rosan newscasts. With a sinking heart, he found that Kir Bay had been wrong; they didn't even have hours before the Supremi took control. There was a revolution in progress, and the elections were being pushed ahead of schedule to select the new Bloodbond.

Sorrel leaned against the wall of the tunnel, panting, wishing he'd learned how to drive the Rosan vehicles even though it was crazy for a human to try to drive down the tunnels—men just didn't have fast enough reflexes for Rosan traffic.

Soon he realized that he wasn't going to make it to the Bloodkeep in time, and he interrupted Daisy's incessant reports on the radcom. "Daisy, is there anything you can hook me with to get through to the Bloodkeep? I need to talk to Mai Toam Let Call."

Sorrel listened as Daisy tried various patches into the Rosan communication systems. Finally they linked to the Bloodkeep, and Mai Toam answered. "Thank God you're there!" Sorrel exclaimed. "Have you been listening to the news?"

"Yes." The Rosan's voice sounded grave. "We face trouble, I fear."

"By the galaxyful," Sorrel muttered. "Listen . . . is it possible to, uh . . . jimmy the labels on people's brainblood?"

Mai Toam coughed politely. "It is flagrantly illegal, Man Everwood." His cough gurgled into a chuckle. "It is not, however, unheard of."

"I see."

Daisy's voice filled the line. "I don't wish to interrupt you, gentlemen, but I've heard some news I believe to be important. The selections are over. The Supremi have given orders to capture everyone involved with the FTLcom project."

It had all happened so swiftly! Sorrel held down the fear in his stomach. "Call Kir Bay and warn him. Tell him I'll meet him at the new labs."

Sorrel rushed down the cavernwork tunnels toward the hidden cavenet, giving orders over his radcom all the way. "Mai Toam, quickly! Switch brainblood name-tags on the cannisters for Dor Kat, Tey Fin, and Dor Lee with the nametags for other Rosans—Rosans who're supposed to be loyal to the Supremi. Can your blood-memories transmit the switches?"

"Probably, Man Everwood, but I'll give you a list for safety. High chance says they destroy my brainblood when ledgers show tampered feast labels."

"Oh my god." Sorell stopped his running, trying to think of an alternative to losing the Keeper's descendants.

"No fear, Man Everwood. Hope is, to switch my brainblood also. You need remember, whereto I'm switched. Prai Kan Tor Loov will be me renewed."

"Good. I'll remember," Sorrel promised, praying he told the truth. He'd have to write that name down at first opportunity. "Kir Bay, have you stashed the equipment?"

"Yes. All's set."

"Great. I'll be there in—" Sorrel leaped to the landing one level lower, turned right, and ran into four younger Rosans. *The Supremi got me*, was Sorrel's first panicky thought.

"Man Everwood, Kir Bay sent us. We return you to your ship swiftly."

"But—"

The radcom spoke; it was Kir Bay again. "All's controlled here, Man Everwood; your advance planning let us prepare with thoroughness and speed. Thank you. Now, you must return to your ship, where you'll be safe for a few generations."

"But—"

The four Rosans were already herding him back the way he had come.

"Where are Cal and Wandra?" Sorrel demanded.

"Good luck, Man Everwood," the radcom answered obliquely. "May you die by a rising star."

One of the four shepherds answered more directly. "Man Minov and man Furenz return to the ship. You'll see soon." As they rounded another corner, the lead Rosan jumped back, hitting Sorrel in the chest. "Feign death," he commanded.

Sorrel performed as ordered, slumping into their arms. They carried him around the corner, shouted several rapid sentences at someone. More hands grabbed Sorrel, more words, and he heard many people going with him for interminable distances. His arm was being slowly, agonizingly, dislocated from his shoulder by one of his carriers; but he had no time to worry about that; his concentration was focussed on trying not to breathe. He was not very successful.

At last there was a scuffle. "Run!" someone yelled in his ear, and Sorrel twisted to his feet and ran, following the Rosan leader, not daring to look around to see what was happening. The two of them continued to run till they reached the entrance to the outercave, where the ship lay. Five more Rosans pressed there against a long outcropping of stone, along with Cal and Wandra. Wandra held her finger to her lips, gesturing Sorrel to silence. She whispered, "Guards," and pointed over the outcropping. Sorrel nodded.

The six Rosans held a quiet but rapidfire conference, lasting almost a minute, then split in four directions. There was noise from beyond the outcropping, and a portable sonic pulverizer—designed for crushing rocks during excavation—screamed. "Run for the ship!" Sorrel's Rosan yelled above the din. "Good luck!" He ran in front of the three humans into the open stretch by the slagged landing area.

The weapons there could've killed fully armored Rosan larvae, to say nothing of killing delicate humans, but fortunately the guards were busy. Again Sorrel didn't have time to see how they were being distracted—his goggles obstructed his peripheral vision—but the FTLcom team was doing a good job, and only one guard saw the three humans coming. The Rosan leader leaped at him and knocked him down, but in leaping the leader took the tip of a larva-prod in the chest and started to writhe uncontrollably. Wandra screamed; Sorrel pushed her toward the ship's lock as it swept to ground level. Another sonic blaster wailed, and the three humans dived into the lock, which now swept back up into the body of the ship.

All three were shaking and panting. "We've gotta lift off," Cal gasped, heading for the pilot room.

"No," Sorrel said, "don't. Nothing out there will hurt our asteroid armor. It'd take them generations to haul a main tunnel beamer up here from the bottom levels—and if they did that we'd have plenty of warning." Sorrel was still panting, thinking he talked too much. "Daisy," he breathed at the computer, "show us the cavernwork entrance."

"Yes, sir."

Cal and Wandra followed Sorrel into the rec bay; everyone collapsed onto his or her favorite recliner, then looked at the vidscreen's view of the entrance. Several Rosans lay in pools of green jelly, including four of the people who had helped them escape.

"Damn," Cal muttered.

Another party of solemn Rosans, wearing the medallions of the Supremi Elders, came into view, to pour smouldering acid on the brainblood of the traitors, the friends-to-humans.

Wandra clenched her fists in horror. "You bastards!" she screamed into the unhearing viewer.

"Viewer off, Daisy," Sorrel commanded.

"I'll kill 'em," Cal swore, heading for the weapons locker with renewed strength.

Sorrel leaped up, blocking his path. "You'll only get yourself killed."

"Get out of my way," Cal warned, pushing Sorrel hard.

"Stop, you idiot," Sorrel said in exasperation, then

hit Cal three times, twice in the stomach, once in the eye.

Caught by surprise, Cal dropped to the floor. By the time he struggled back to his feet Sorrel was snapping a sleep hypo out of his med kit. Cal tried to dodge, but Sorrel winged him with the hypo. "Moron," Cal muttered as his eyeballs rolled up. Sorrel caught him as he fell. "I'll kill the fiends anyway. Wait till I get up."

But by the time Cal returned to consciousness, the fiends, and the followers, and the vanquished friends, had all already died.

Two days later Sorrel called a council of war. They were sitting in the rec bay, weighing possibilities. "Bring in a battleship," was Cal's first, half-serious suggestion.

Sorrel shuddered. "Right. I'm sure the Rosans work every bit as well under compulsion as Men do."

Wandra bit her nails. "Isn't there some way we can talk with the new leaders?"

Sorrel shrugged. "They know how to reach us—the radcom's in perfect shape. I'm afraid, though, that they're not interested. If I didn't know better, I'd guess they'd forgotten us."

Cal sneered. "What? Forget their God?"

Daisy rang an alert bell. "We have visitors."

Sorrel looked up. "Are they armed?"

"No."

"Then let's see 'em."

The vidscreen brightened, to show a small party of Rosans. The two leaders, carefully facing away from the cavernworks, proudly bore the medallions of FTLcom techs. "Connect us to the external two-way, Daisy," Sorrel said as he rose. "Hello," he waved to the Rosans. "Glad to see somebody finally came around."

Several of the followers looked away, muttering, touching their shoulders with their hands, then sweeping a half-circle, as in the prayers of the Faith of Six Parents. Even the leaders averted their eyes.

One of them spoke. "Men of Earth, my children will remember this moment forever. We apologize for disturbing you."

"Nonsense, my friends." Sorrel smiled, then whispered to Daisy. "Are you sure they're unarmed?"

Yes, Daisy printed on the vidscreen, invisible to the visitors.

"Why don't you two come in?" Sorrel continued.

They swept the prayerful half-circle. "We'd be honored, Man Everwood."

The lock descended to them, and Sorrel sighed. "It's so comfortable in here, those guys would freeze to death. Daisy, you'd better turn up the heat—" Sorrel turned to his companions "—and we'd better check out our coolsuits again."

They were older Rosans, Sorrel realized when they had come inside the ship. "What time is it out there?" he asked.

"Close to dawn, Man Everwood."

Sorrel nodded.

"As you can see, the blood of the FTLcom is weak, yet still lives."

"I hope that that'll soon change?" Sorrel asked. "Else you shouldn't have risked coming here."

"Yes. During nightspin there's still much danger. But the dayspinners never turned as fanatical, though Supremi attitudes abound. We think you could return to MoonBender during dayspin with little risk."

Cal banged the table. "Great. So we can get the project underway again."

The Rosans' petals drooped. "Not quite so easy. Without at least neutrality from nightspin leaders, any dayspin work would be regularly sabotaged. Further, dayspin leaders wouldn't make a commitment without nightspin assent—the nightspin Bloodbond is more powerful, since more people live in nightspin time."

Sorrel muttered. "So we have to get nightspin authority."

"Yes."

Sorrel got up, started pacing around the room. "Tell me. Would they kill me on sight, if I returned during nightspin?"

The two Rosans spoke briefly, then the one replied. "No, we don't think so—the Supremi religion is still rooted, after all, in the Faith of Six Parents, and they must revere you for that. Now that all's calmer, you might be safe. But Man Furenz and Man Minov concern us; their danger would be great."

"Good enough. I'll go convince the Supremi leader—what's his name?"

"Kip Sur Tel Yan."

"Ah. Take me to him, and we'll have priority 1A again before his bloodfeast."

The Rosans gawked. "How?"

Sorrel pursed his lips. "I shall be like a Lazarine unto him," he said grimly. No one understood, and he waved his hands. "Fear not. Kip Sur is putty for my molding. Soon he'll know the FTLcom is the most magnificent weapon the Supremi ever dreamed of." *And Balcyrak will be proud of me*, he thought sourly. He strapped his infrared goggles back into place and departed with the Rosans.

The Bond was old, very old; it was a state Sorrel had seen too many times. But this time that was a good sign. "I have a proposition for you," Sorrel told the Supremi leader.

Rosan facial muscles aren't designed for sneering. Kip Sur gave Sorrel a good imitation. "A weakling from an inferior race brings me a proposition?"

Sorrel drew himself up in anger. "May I remind you that this particular weakling brought the Faith of Six from Beyond, to make possible your successes of today?"

The Bond's wide, bright eyes radiated anger. Sorrel continued.

"May I remind you that, though you go soon to meet a rising star, I will remain, to make or break the plans you design today."

That got Kip Sur where it hurt; but Sorrel had to move fast, before Kip Sur's agony turned into even more burning jealousy. "Fear not. You have a chance here to touch eternity, for I can protect and assure your plans, if we come to an agreement."

The agony and depression turned to slyness. "What is your proposition?"

"I intend to help you expand into the Universe, to

spread the glory and power of the Supremi across the stars."

"You want me to authorize the continuation of the FTLcom project."

Sorrel was again surprised at the speed of Rosan thought. "I don't think you appreciate the values the FTLcom has to offer the Supremi. There are billions of planets out there, hundreds of intelligent species, and the FTLcom will open them all up for you. Think of it! Always before your people have been trapped on this planet, unable to touch any part of the Universe that didn't reach out to touch you."

The Bond was swept up in a vision of his own. "Of course! Fleets of robot battleships, that we could control from here no matter how far they traveled! At last, to achieve our destiny as conquerors!"

It wasn't exactly the vision Sorrel planned, but it would do. "There's more. With all those conquered species, you'll have plenty of manpower to build colonization ships—ships large enough and stout enough to contain full generations of Rosans, adults and larvae and eggs, so the Supremi could build cities on gentler planets, where growth would not be so slow and painful. Whereas today you can at best fill a handful of cavernworks, tomorrow you could fill hundreds of worlds."

The Bond's slyness now turned to suspicion. "Why would you help us conquer your own people?"

Sorrel frowned. Since he didn't know what kind of a lie to tell, he settled reluctantly on the truth. "The FTLcom will enrich your people's lives, Kip Sur, but I don't think it'll do so in the manner you foresee; I believe the desire to conquer will pass, and Man will benefit almost as much as Rosan from our development."

"You doubt that we, with our superior ability, will one day conquer you? Is not victory of the strong inevitable?"

Sorrel shrugged. "We have a testing here, of your future vision against mine—but in both those futures the FTLcom is crucial. I can accept the dangers in your vision, if you can accept the dangers in mine."

The old Bond relaxed on his incline. "Let the visions

compete," he said, and rushed to his desk to prepare orders. "Congratulations, Man Everwood; your FTLcom is now a top priority, even higher than before."

Of course, there couldn't be a higher priority than the old FTLcom priority, but Sorrel thanked the Bond anyway; naturally a prioritization made generations ago wouldn't be remembered in the brainblood.

The Bond turned back to Sorrel, teeth bared in a look of pure evil. "But only the visions shall compete, and neither of us will ever know who was right. Guards!"

The adrenalin surged through Sorrel's bloodstream; his heart nearly exploded as he saw his soon-to-be executioners coming. But despite his rising panic, his brain surged with thought as swift as a Rosan's. He searched the room for a means of escape; he saw the Bond with a clarity given only to those walking the edge of death.

Even as Sorrel watched, the Bond seemed to age. Sorrel had known countless Rosans as they aged—far more than any Rosan had ever known—and in his need, Sorrel foresaw to within seconds how long the Bond would live; it was not much. Sorrel waved for help. "Guards!" he echoed the Bond's request, but with much urgency. He jumped half across the desk, grabbing the surprised Bond in a steely grip; the Rosan struggled, but was no match for Sorrel's strength.

Kip Sur shouted orders to the guards, but Sorrel shouted louder and longer. "The Bond's been poisoned! Send for a doctor immediately! Someone get over here and help me get him to the floor—he's writhing, and I'm afraid he'll hurt himself." Just then the Bond did writhe again, and both he and Sorrel crashed to the floor.

The Bond took a deep breath. "Hate," he spat in Sorrel's face, exhaling hard.

His breath was sweet with honeysuckle.

A guard stood uncertainly over them. "What kind of poison?" he asked.

Sorrel struggled to his feet, shaking his head. "I was wrong; call off the medics." Brainblood spread on the floor. "It was just . . . old age."

*   *   *

"You wish me to feast a larva with the blood of Prai Kan Tor Loov?" The Bloodkeeper scowled at Sorrel. "He is a Supremi Keeper, not an FTLcom tech. Why would you want him?"

"Do we have a 1A priority or not?" Sorrel snapped; he'd already bungled this operation, and he feared that soon the Keeper would deduce the truth. "The FTLcom tech bloodlines have all been destroyed—your ancestors already took care of that. We're searching for the closest derivatives of those lines. There are only a few bloods with even brainparent histories of FTLcom blood. The computer searches show Prai Kan to be one such."

The scowl did not ease. "You have no jurisdiction over the blood of Keepers."

Sorrel crossed his arms. "Do I have to go to the Bond and embarrass you? Does our priority not tell you the importance of my presence here?"

The Rosan ground his teeth, then at last signed the papers. "He shall join us in the next generation. May you die by a rising star, Sacred One."

The next day Sorrel returned to the Bloodkeep. He found that a smiling face had replaced the scowling one. "My children will remember this moment, Man Everwood," the new Keeper began. "My name is Col Salm Keer Prai."

"Descendant of Mai Toam Let Call?"

The Rosan's eyes danced with laughter. "Are you a member of the Supremi ruling family? If so, then I am not. If not, then I am so."

Sorrel laughed with the Keeper. "How is your bloodmemory?"

"Keen. I have taken the liberty of arranging a number of bloodfeasts for you already. I trust you'll be surprised at how swiftly my bloodmixes bear techs with good memories for FTLcom work."

"I trust also. But there's other blood even more important that you don't know about." Sorrel told him of the secret FTLcom cavern. "The brainbloods of all the techs who died in the labs should still be there.

We'll truly have a Renaissance, if you can somehow return their bloods to the system."

Col Salm pondered a moment. "Difficult, but worthy. It shall be done." He looked at Sorrel with the too-common awe of a child. "You've performed a miracle, saving so many of our people."

"Umph," Sorrel still chastised himself for not having done better, but then, it was also true that no Rosan could have done as well. "Yes, the techs have been saved. I just wish I knew what to do about the Supremi, whom I would like not to see saved."

Col Salm's petals waved in agreement. "How sad there are no more politicians or theologians like Prim Sol Mem Brite."

Sorrel looked away. "Yes. Or even like Or Sae Hi Tor." A puzzled thought overtook him. "That reminds me of something I've wondered about for a long time. What ever happened to the brainblood of Prim Sol Mem Brite? I would have expected all the political bloodlines to trace back to the First Disciple of the Faith of Six."

"Didn't you know the fate of the first carrier of your Gospel?" The Rosan must have been stunned by such ignorance; Sorrel blushed furiously. "I'm sorry to be the bearer of these age-old tidings. There was much turmoil in the wake of Prim Sol's revelations. The labels in the bloodkeeps were all either destroyed or switched, by either supporters of the Great Faith or by the traitors who still supported the Faith of Four. The Disciple's brainblood was lost amid the chaos, as were all other people's."

"Couldn't you trace his lineage after the fact? Surely anyone who had him as a blood- or brainparent would remember, at least for a few generations."

"Oh yes, many people claimed him as ancestor—far more than any being's brainblood could give feast for." He waved his petals in futility. "They say our newer computers could trace back to him, and then back again to modern times, but it would be the work of generations. Several efforts have been made in the past. They failed, long before it even could be determined whether success was possible." His petals pulsed in sorrow. "And if found, what value would it produce? His memories are ages too remote to be found again—even the best memories could not bring him back."

"They couldn't, huh?" Sorrel clapped his hands in joy. "My friend, I think you've just ended our troubles. Thank you." He was quite sure he left the good Keeper quite mystified.

Sorrel was whistling when he barged into Wandra's room on board the ship. "I'm canceling all your lectures for the next few days," he said.

"What?" Wandra whirled away from her dresser to face him. "Who would I be lecturing anyway?"

Sorrel told her about the techs who would soon receive incarnations. "But that's not the best news, and that's why you won't start teaching yet."

"What could be better?"

Sorrel pulled out a grease pencil and scribbled on the wall.

"Hey! Stop that!" Wandra tried to pull him away, but he laughed and finished his writing. PRIM SOL MEM BRITE RETURNS, the scribble said.

"I've started putting a few inscriptions like this here and there throughout MoonBender. So the natives can get used to the idea."

"Have you completely lost your mind? What are you doing?"

"I'm bringing the Faith back to Khayyam. And you and me, lady, we're gonna bring the Disciple himself back to do it!" Sorrel told her about the great politician/theologian who so many years ago first translated Sorrel's dissertation into the Faith of Six Parents. "So your task, my lady, is to hop onto that computer and find his descendants."

She shook her head, dazed. "Would you calm down? You're still moving too fast for me. What good will it do to find his descendants? They don't remember anything about him, do they? To say nothing of being like him."

Sorrel rubbed his hands together. "True, my lady, true. And even the best Rosan memorists can't bring

back memories more than a handful of generations old."
He pointed to himself. "But this ain't no Rosan memorist
here." His voice turned grim. "No, I'm no Rosan. I'm
almost an immortal. And just this once, that 'almost' will
be enough."

It took many days to find a bloodline with a high
probability of tracing from the Disciple; and that was just
the beginning. "So we believe you are his descendant,"
Sorrel told the Rosan who had been chosen by fate and
technology. "We want to hypnotize you and do a complete memorist retrogression to find his memories."

The Rosan puffed up with pride in his heritage. "I'd
love to have his memories," he said dreamily. "Can you
do it? I didn't know you could retromemorize that far."

Sorrel grimaced. "Well, you've hit on the problem.
You see, we can do it—but you'll never know. If you
agree to memorist hypnosis, you'll spend the rest of
your life here in trance. Then we'll do the same with
your children, and their children, and finally some generation we will find out whether the computers were
right, whether the Disciple is the founder of your family."

The dreamy look fell from the Rosan's face for a
moment. "It must be very important."

"More so than I can explain."

The Rosan sighed. "What nobler cause could there
be, than to give one's life to reunite the Writer of the
Gospel with his Disciple, the Parent with his Child?
Let us begin."

So they began. Layer after layer of Rosan personalities peeled back before Sorrel's patient yet relentless
questing. But each peeling brought him to two bloodparents, two predecessors, and two more possible paths
to Prim Sol. Soon Sorrel could no longer peel back
through all the parents; he and Wandra were reduced
to eking out clues from the Rosan computers and the
Rosan minds. With those clues, they fought and considered and guessed and, finally, selected the paths to
search.

And the helpful Rosan's children came to them, and
stayed, and grew old, and died. Though the Rosans

came freely, and rarely complained of their loss, yet with each child and with each child's child the burden of Sorrel's guilt grew. Each day Sorrel cursed himself for a fool; had he known truly the price of the search before beginning, he would not have started, he would say, and Wandra would tap her foot and tell him he was full of it, and soothe him and convince him that it was too late to turn back, that they should not waste the lives of the Rosans who volunteered to help.

And finally they reached back into the time of the Revelation, and a dying Rosan opened his eyes with surprise to tell them, "I remember."

Sorrel paced back and forth in front of the larval Keep.

"You look like an expectant father," Wandra chastised him.

"I suppose in a sense I *am* a father," he replied. "In some sense, he is my creation—both in that earlier time when he rose because of my work, and now because this Rosan remembers his memories because of my efforts." He stopped his pacing. He muttered, "Perhaps together we can do enough good to compensate these people for the wrongs we caused separately."

Wandra snorted. "He certainly ought to be able to do something—with the blood of Or Sae Hi Tor, Dor Laff Toa Linn, Prim Sol Mem Brite, and Sor Lai Don Shee in his mind. Sor Hi Laf Brite should have a medallion with the emblem of Superman on it."

The gate opened, and a newborn Rosan stepped out. Sorrel looked at him with concern; he seemed thin for a Rosan just out of bloodfeast. Would his life be even shorter than normal?"

"Sor Hi?" Wandra stepped up to the young being.

"Yes," he said. "You must be Man Furenz." He turned to Sorrel. His voice turned reverent. "And you must be Man Everwood." He stepped forward hesitantly. "Prim Sol always hoped that one day one of his descendants would meet you; I remember, and his memory knows great joy this day." He held out his hand, and the petals of his forearm caressed Sorrel's forearm.

Sorrel choked. "So do I. I'm glad you're here."

Abruptly Sor Hi stepped back, saw people waiting for him. "I must go; the dusking teachers wait for me." He strode off. "I'll see you again soon."

"We should be teaching him," Sorrel grumbled as he and Wandra walked off.

"Like hell. You want to slow him down that much?" Sorrel didn't say anything.

Wandra giggled. "I think we should doublecheck our arrangements with the prophecies and legends, to make sure everybody finds out that Sor Hi is the one who's been promised." She threw her head back in laughter. From time to time, in the moments when they most needed release from grief over the retromemory treatments of Prim Sol's family, Wandra and Sorrel had traveled through the cavernwork sowing legends. They would tell Rosans of the visions their ancestors had had of the Disciple's return, and speak of omens and portents. Later they found new stories spreading, stories that they hadn't started, and when asked for verification they would give it, thus expanding on someone else's fabrication. The populace was ripe for a Return.

Sorrel chuckled. "Don't worry about people finding out that Sor Hi's the one—the techs have found some advertisers who're just delighted to sell this product. The advertisers, you see, are Believers."

"Wonderful." Wandra rested her head on Sorrel's shoulder.

A group of Rosans hurried by, and Sor Hi was among them. "How's it going?" Sorrel yelled to him.

Sor Hi paused. "It's wonderful. Prim Sol's memories are of the sorrow and hatred between the bloodlines who fought during the Revelation. He knew only of the anger and obstinacy that opposed him. But for me it's different—this time, I am as much a hero as the Disciple was a villain." He breathed deep, then looked at Sorrel. "It is a wonderful world that you and he created," he ended.

Wandra agreed. "Yes, it is."

Sorrel watched him disappear into another passage. "I wish there were something we could do for him."

"There is."

Sorrel looked down at her. "What?"

"Get some sleep, so we can be available later, if he needs us." She snuggled against his arm. "Or maybe do something else. I think we should celebrate. Can I seduce you?"

Sorrel smiled at her. "I'm afraid you may." They headed for the ship. "Let's find out."

Sorrel and Wandra found the FTLcom laboratories almost vacant; what few Rosans were there were busy at communication consoles, not FTL prototypes. Cal sat in the one chair in the room—specifically provided for the humans—with a look of bewilderment.

"I don't know whether to laugh or cry," he sighed. "Sor Hi was here for about six hours, studying our problems. Wandra, did you know we were ditching the hyperspace rotational method because nobody could figure out how to control the timing?"

Wandra nodded.

"Well, at the end of six hours, Sor Hi just looked at it and asked why we couldn't do it one way rather than another, and the solution was obvious." Cal turned to Sorrel. "What this means to you is that we should have an operational FTLcom in just a few days."

Sorrel's jaw dropped open; Wandra jumped up and down and clapped, and hugged both Cal and Sorrel. "Congratulations to all of us!" she exclaimed.

"Yeah," Cal said sourly. "That is, we should have one operational if anyone ever goes back to work. Unfortunately, everybody here's gone bonkers. They can't think of anything except the upcoming Bloodbond election."

Wandra clapped some more. "That's fine, Cal. Who's winning?"

"Who else? The finest mathematical physicist in the universe. The Supremi incumbent doesn't have a chance, unless he can stall the election until Sor Hi is dead."

From his coolsuit Sorrel unhitched his comlink to Daisy. "Well, since everybody else is caught up in the election, we might as well be, too."

They listened to the reports. This time it was with

more pleasure than Sorrel had felt the last time politics
interfered with work, when the Supremi ascended to
leadership.

From time to time Sor Hi would return, say polite
words to Sorrel and the rest of the humans, then launch
into vibrant discussions with his advisors. Each time he
returned he was more confident, more mature, more
capable. Once the broadcasts told of an assassination
attempt on him, but even as Sorrel's hands grew clammy,
Sor Hi came bursting into the cavern, reassuring them
he was all right. "If nobody tries to kill you, then
nobody's taking you seriously," he explained cheerfully.
"At least I know that people are interested."

"I want to help him," Sorrel muttered as Sor Hi
burst off again in a whirlwind of activity.

"I know. You've said it before. Nobody's going to pay
any attention to you," Wandra replied.

Four hours later, Sor Hi returned again. He dismissed his advisors to talk to the humans. "Would you
like to be with me in the Hall of Choosing? I would be
honored by your presence when the vote is taken."

No offworlder, Sorrel knew, had ever attended a
Rosan election. "Thank you," Sorrel said. "We'd be
honored as well."

Two two-story platforms rose out of the sea of Rosan
faces there in the Hall—an awesome cavern, with as
much space as the largest of human spacedomes. On
the lower level of each platform the most important
advisors of each candidate stood, answering detailed
questions for the media, and on the high level stood
each candidate himself, describing his plans, hopes,
and dreams, pulling his audience into those dreams and
making those dreams their own. The room was filled
with talking, listening, reading, and watching, all of
which had an intensity that Sorrel had never imagined.
Wandra leaned over to him. "You know, you can almost
see the information in this room; you can see the knowledge being transmitted in wave after wave."

Sorrel nodded.

Suddenly a hush fell; the voting began at counting
booths scattered throughout the Hall.

Then it was over; the loudspeakers announced Sor Hi's victory. An awesome cheer began and ended; Sor Hi gave his inauguration address. It lasted a full minute and a half. A second cheer began—but the noise of a violent explosion shattered the joy. The vibration threw Sorrel to the floor, but he leaped up again even as he realized he was falling. He ran to catch the tumbling body of the new Bloodbond, Sor Hi.

Muscles tore and his back wrenched as Sorrel caught Sor Hi in his arms. Together they fell back to the platform, with Sorrel twisting to protect Sor Hi as much as possible.

Sorrel groaned and rolled over. A Rosan with the medic's medallion leaned over Sor Hi. "He's alive," the medic announced, Sorrel sighed, rolled over again, winced at the new pain in his back, and fell into unconsciousness.

When he rolled over again, he found himself in a comfortable bed, his own bed on the ship. He heard the high-pitched, hummingbird sound of a Rosan chuckling, and opened his eyes to look toward the sound.

Sor Hi lay propped in a cot, looking back at him. "Thank you, Parent. And congratulations. We have won."

"What happened?"

"Another assassination attempt. This one succeeded, but not well enough. I have lived long enough. The Supremi bloodlines have been ordered diluted. And they have no immortal beings to protect their dreams from my orders, as I have you to protect mine."

Sorrel looked at the wounds and bandages covering Sor Hi's body. Yes, the assassins had succeeded all too truly. A wounded Rosan had little time left—his body would burn its layers of stored nutrient in a furious attempt to repair the damage, leading to swift death by starvation.

Sorrel rose slowly and painfully from the bed. "Can I get you anything?"

Sor Hi's eyes drifted absently around the room. "No. I am happy here."

Sorrel searched Sor Hi's face with growing acuteness; the thickness was lifting from Sorrel's mind. Sor Hi's skin was drawn tight against his cheeks; death approached.

" 'May you die by a rising star,' " Sor Hi muttered. "Isn't it funny? Ever since we went into the caves, no one has ever died by a rising star. I wonder what it would be like."

With a horrified sense of awe and wonder, Sorrel looked at his watch. He found what he had somehow already known: the sunrise was coming. "Follow me," he told Sor Hi, "I have something to show you."

The top of the ship peeked out from the cavernworks; there Sorrel and Sor Hi found a view of Khayyam in the morning. Now the sun too peeked out from the horizon, and touched the shallow pools of water dotting Khayyam's surface. In that fiery touch the warm water quivered, and bubbled, and broke into boiling. Clouds of steam rose into the purplish sky, condensing into rain as it rose, falling, and boiling again into steam as it neared the surface. Frenzied rainbows danced across those spinning almost-rainstorms, only to disappear as the rains evaporated until the next sunrise.

Sor Hi exhaled sharply. "It is incomparable," he whispered in awe. "My children must remember this beauty for me." He looked at Sorrel. "And they must remember you, too." He drew a last hard breath. "I . . ." The surprise of sudden insight entered his eyes. "It's even harder for you," he said. "You . . . must keep on living."

Sorrel sobbed. "Yes, my son." The honeysuckle overtook them, each in its own way.

They found Sorrel there in the nose of the ship, and moved him gently to his own room. For three days he lay there, not speaking, not eating, not moving. He was aware of people when they came to him, he heard them when they spoke, he felt them as they hooked the feeder to him, but he did not care. Deep in its own quiet his mind waited, waited for something to trigger it back to life. Sorrel didn't know what he waited for, and about that, too, he did not care.

On the fourth day they told him the FTLcom was

ready. Now they could project a three-dimensional image to Lazara and get one back in return. They told him they were about to make contact with Balcyrak.

It was the trigger his mind awaited. He looked up at them, then rose and followed them to the FTL lab.

Balcyrak studied him quietly, smiling gently. "Do you still hate us, Man Everwood?"

Sorrel looked down, shook his head, "No. I have walked in your shoes."

"Yes. It is not easy, to be a Lazarine."

Sorrel started to speak, choked, shook his head.

Balcyrak continued. "I want to thank you for all you have done for us. My whole race thanks you, and our civilization shall sing of you, our savior."

Sorrel stared at Balcyrak for a moment, then realized what he meant. Balcyrak had lied earlier. There had been no question of who would win the next Lazaran/Man war, had one occurred. Sorrel had saved the beings who had killed his wife; he did not mind. "I'm glad." He felt weary. "By the way, Balcyrak, there's something I'm curious about—how old are you?"

Balcyrak relaxed in his chair. "Nearly fourteen millennia, I would reckon, by your measure."

Sorrel pondered that. "Just about entering middle age, for someone who lives 25,000 years."

"Yes."

Sorrel sighed. "It would be wonderful, to be almost immortal like you."

Balcyrak sat up, looked sharply at him and through him, as Sorrel started to smile. Balcyrak saw the smile and chuckled. "Yes, almost immortal."

Together they started to laugh, a rich powerful laughter that even the dark universe could not deny.

The Bully and the Crazy Boy

"The Bully and the Crazy Boy" was the first story I ever sold. Before Stan Schmidt at Analog accepted this one, I had written and submitted about 50 stories, over a six year period, to a variety of editors and magazines. For anyone who has tried to sell a story and failed, I think the story of the writing of this story has an important lesson.

In the days before "Bully," I treasured each of my story ideas as a priceless gem. Each gem, I thought, deserved its own setting, its own story. I acted as the original Scrooge, dribbling out ideas one at a time.

Finally I noticed that, in the time it took me to write one or two stories, I easily came up with a dozen new ideas. There was no good reason to parcel out my best thoughts in such a parsimonius manner. The perspiration, not the inspiration, was the sticky point in my writing efforts.

So with "The Bully and the Crazy Boy" I combined two of my ideas: an idea for a one-time-only military maneuver, and an idea for an alien species (indeed, an entire galaxy of alien species) who are both smarter and more technologically advanced than we are. I put them together in one clashing whole. Earlier, I had written long stories based around each of these ideas; "Bully" is roughly half as long as either of the originals, giving "Bully" an "idea density" about four times as great as either of the earlier pieces.

What is science fiction about if not ideas? Give the reader what he wants. Give him lots of what he wants. And don't worry—the fount of ideas shall not run dry.

152

The Bully And The Crazy Boy

Weightless, Fleet Admiral Encrai launched himself off the wall of the C-Cubed room, arched, snapped against the far wall on his front paws, twisted, and sprang back across the room. Ordinarily the lithe power of his body would have pleased him; but now he paced in fury, trying to regain his feline poise.

Damn! Damn! How could he have expected the stupid primates to be insane? Why hadn't the psychologists warned him? Granted, they'd told him the species hadn't completed its evolution to a communal hunting animal. Granted, they'd warned him to expect strange behavior. But this! How could he predict that, after crushing the puny defenses around Uranus, the primates' orbital city would accept his ships, then blow itself up? Unbelievable! Not rational! What kind of creatures *were* these?

Again Encrai questioned the wisdom of taking this solar system now; certainly it'd be more sensible to let this species ripen a bit, let them gain a measure of non-primitiveness (he hated to call it sophistication—certainly no *primate* could achieve *that*) so they'd be useful slaves.

His pacing slowed; at last he shrugged. The High Command's decision was made, their orders given. Encrai's full F class fleet would knock off the primates quickly, before the retrenchment wars began.

"Admiral—an enemy fleet just broke towards us from a planetoid fragment." Captain Taress spoke crisply from across the room.

Touching the controls on his magnetic harness, Encrai curved through the air to his command station. Floating

153

between his webcradle and his console, he looked up at the holoscreen, which covered the whole front wall of the room. Part of that wall teemed with statistics and gauges, changing endlessly as the Flagship staff and the Command/Control/Communication staff requested new data.

But Encrai barely noticed these. His attention centered on the 3-D display of fleet dispositions. Part of that display now detached itself, to expand for detailed analysis in the tactical viewer. A dense handful of numbered ellipses, the primate fleet, approached the dispersed center of Encrai's fleet—approached Encrai's flagship itself! Unbelievable!

Chief Assistant Mrech, a bright young strategist, glanced back at him. "Looks to me like Jirbri's in position to pick them off fastest. Shall I punch it out?"

Encrai hissed. "No, it could be another pack of suicidal idiots. I'd better take care of them myself." Besides, he needed something fun to do; the disaster at the primate Outbase still rankled.

As he punched out commands on his console, a handful of ships on the tactical screen broke from the Kalixi formation to swirl around the opposing clay pigeons. But the swirling was careful—no Kalixi ship approached the pigeons closely enough to be destroyed by the explosion of a primate's main thrust chamber.

The battle was over at its beginning. A final blasting pass cooked the two biggest enemy ships; a handful of life boats scattered from them. Kalixi ships turned to mop up the lifeboats, but Encrai forbade it.

The Chief Assistant cocked his head. "You're going to pick them up?"

Encrai swished his tail in acknowledgment. "Only if they agree to leave the lifeboats and get picked up in spacesuits. I don't think a primate can be very dangerous with just the weapons he carries in his spacesuit, do you? And I need the information." In particular, he needed to know why the stupid creatures were so eager to blow themselves up.

The Admiral yawned. "Have Jirbri question them. When he's done, buzz." The assistant mrowed understanding; Encrai stretched forward from his console, and floated out of the room.

A burrstinger buzzed close to him, spinning around him, waiting for him to stop trying to track it, so it could land. His nose, his nose was the stinger's target.

But his eyes were closed, and when he opened them he saw it was the intercom buzzing at him, and he himself was doing the spinning, tethered in the center of his room. Encrai touched his harness. "Yes?" he yawned.

"We found something interesting when we took the prisoners, Admiral." The assistant's voice almost purred.

"Something interesting with the *primates*?"

"One of the prisoners is special." Encrai could almost see Mrech sniffing the high air.

"Very funny, Colonel. A special primate, indeed."

"It's true—apparently one of our guests is the creature that developed the primate defense strategy. He's an Admiral, of sorts. He seems quite eager to help us defeat him, since we pointed out how unpleasant his alternatives are."

Encrai opened his mouth, then closed it. With a furious swish of his tail he bounded into the hall.

Soaring gracefully back into the Command/Control/Communications room, Encrai watched Marine guards manacle a primate to the prison chair, next to the Admiral's control station. Encrai frowned for a moment; the chair had been designed to immobilize all kinds of intelligent beings—but all kinds of intelligent beings generally meant felines, canines, and low-gravity arachnoids. The chair didn't fit on the primate very well.

But then, these primates were weak little creatures, according to the precampaign analyses. The chair wouldn't have to fit to hold him. Encrai smiled. Besides, what could a primate do, even if he got free, amidst full-grown, full-clawed Kalixi? The Admiral turned to the psychmed accompanying the Marines. "Is this the primate," he curled his lips, "who calls himself an Admiral?"

The psychmed swished his tail. "Yes, sir. He seems

to be the originator of the primate battle plans. The other prisoners support his statements under all forms of extraction." The psychmed ruffled his fur. "Naturally, when we found out that this," he tapped the primate with his tail, "was supposed to be an Admiral, we examined his mind, such as it is, a bit more carefully. He has a number of implanted psychoblocks, presumably protecting important information."

Encrai smiled. "No doubt he's protecting top secret technological details."

The psychmed laughed. "I wouldn't be surprised. Anyway, his blocks are sophisticated enough so that he might be damaged if I try to penetrate them hastily. Whatever is inside those blocks will stay there 'til after the campaign. Unless he tells us willingly."

Encrai raised an eyebrow. "Willingly?"

"Yes, we gave him a drug that stimulates verbosity. He'll probably be telling you a lot more than you ask for. I'm not sure it was necessary—*all* these creatures like to talk, it seems—but if you don't ask a question just the right way, you'll probably get the information you want anyway. Remember, though, it still won't register on the lie-sniffer if he just answers the poorly worded question truthfully."

"As if he had any secrets that could hurt us."

"Indeed."

Encrai's lips pulled back in a ferocious grin, exposing a vast collection of murderous teeth. "This is great! I've never planned a battle with the enemy Admiral giving me advice before. Such a shame it couldn't have happened in the battle with Valesh and his damned Crusairs."

The psychmed saluted. "Maybe next time, sir." He turned to leave, then turned back again. "Oh, one last thing. Two of the primate's teeth are filled with a chemical—a stimulant of some kind, leaking slowly into his mouth. The primate said the chemical keeps him alive, so we left it. It seems harmless enough."

"Fine. Let's hope he lives long enough to be useful."

The psychmed pushed toward the doorway.

Floating in his webcradle, Encrai examined the prisoner. He seemed small, even for a primate; Black hair and ashen skin seemed his dominate features. Frail was the best one-word descriptor. But the jaw was set in determination, even though the eyes stayed downcast. For a moment the primate reminded Encrai of a pouting kitten.

The Kalixi Admiral tapped his webcradle and drifted towards the prisoner, into the gentle breeze from behind the prison chair that made it possible for the great cat to be downwind of the primate. He closed his eyes to focus on the primate's scents: the bitter organic staleness of its soft body wrapping, the sweet saltiness of its perspiration, the flavor of its most recent meal—an almost fruity flavor it was, mixed with acidic digestive juices. How strange that fruitiness was! Encrai had never met an intelligent omnivore before. Not even a semi-intelligent one.

He tapped the pad on the translator. "I understand you're the Admiral of the primate fleet," Encrai said. The translator repeated the words in the local barbarism of a language.

The creature just nodded its head up and down.

Encrai swished his tail. "Well, are you or are you not the Admiral of the primate fleet?"

The primate looked at him with big eyes, then broke into laughter. "When I nod my head that means 'yes' in our language. Yes, my name is Craig Thearsporn, and I'm the Campaign Admiral for the Fleet of Interplanetary Alliance." He looked Admiral Encrai over. "Are you the Admiral for the Kalixi fleet?"

"Who do you think is doing the questioning here?"

The prisoner shrugged his shoulders. Gestures and expressions seemed to be important methods of communication with the creatures; Encrai decided to watch more closely. It wouldn't be difficult to infer the meanings; Encrai had a knack for such empathic intuitions.

The Admiral touched the lock button on his harness, to prevent any drifting while he questioned the primate. "What were you doing out here?"

The prisoner shrugged again. "The Kalixi we captured from your exploratory fleet told us that an Admiral always hangs far back, if possible. So we came to get you."

"Did you really expect to destroy me and my flagship?"

The primate turned his eyes down again, heaved a sob. "No, not really."

Encrai swished his tail. "And why'd you let us take you alive?"

The primate smiled. "For one thing, I wanted to live."

Encrai mrowed understanding.

The liesniffer's requirements were fulfilled, but the primate went on. "Besides, I wanted to meet you." He shook his head back and forth. "Ever since that first exploratory hunting party slaughtered every person on the first space city it found, I've known something's terribly wrong with the universe. So *wrong*. Why are you so vicious, so cruel, so determined to destroy and conquer? Why not come as traders, benefiting us both?"

Encrai snorted, then laughed. He shouldn't have bothered to answer, but he was vain about his species, and proud of his vanity. "Why don't we trade? Because, primate, the Kalixi are conquerors, not traders." His claws extended, retracted, extended. "For a thousand years we were slaves, as you'll be. We were declawed. We, the Kalixi!" The claws extended one last time. "But we were patient, learning in secret, as our masters weakened and waned and were replaced by other masters." His paw raked through the air, tearing the throat from an ephemeral opponent. "And under the terrible oppression, those of us who were weak died, and those of us who were strong gained strength. Now our enemies know us in our power and glory."

"You've defeated them?"

Encrai hissed. "We've destroyed them. The species who subjugated us are extinct, by our claws. Now we are the masters, and others are the slaves."

"So you're continuing the system you despised."

"It's a good system—the strong live and conquer, the weak serve and die." Encrai smiled. "You're lucky to be conquered by the Kalixi. We're the Destined Ones, fated to conquer the galaxy. Already we have over 600 solar systems and 150 slave species. No other single species has subjugated that many others for millions of years."

The primate seemed shaken. "Don't you have any allies? What about your enemies? Why don't *they* form an alliance? I can't believe the universe is so devoid of cooperation. Even among us, at least hate is powerful enough to mold friendships."

Encrai laughed. "Poor naive omnivore. I guess that with your background, it's understandable." Encrai looked the creature in the eye. "The universe is the domain of the carnivores, primate. Planetary evolution dictates it. With few, few exceptions, the carnivores develop intelligence first—and once a carnivore develops intelligence, no other species has a chance." He smiled; had he not become an Admiral, Encrai might well have been a university professor. "But regardless of how much our intelligence expands, still we retain our ancient instincts. We know the love of the good hunt, and the joy of the final kill." He spoke the words with relish. "And as we hunt and are hunted, our intelligence and instincts develop apace."

The primate shook its head; water gathered in its eyes. "Dear God, no! Are all the other species really like yours?"

Encrai swished his tail. "Of course not; they are much less sophisticated. From your point of view, though, they're similar." He rolled his eyes. "Actually, I've heard rumors of a group of omnivorous species that've united to protect themselves from the carnivores. But I doubt the rumors. How could omnivores survive long enough to find each other?"

A funny expression spread over the primate's face; for some reason, it made the Admiral uneasy. "Perhaps they survive by being just a little bit insane."

What did *that* mean? Encrai slitted his eyes. Oh well—at least it brought them to the topic of insanity; and that was the thing that interested Encrai. "Perhaps they have. Though it certainly didn't help the primates at the Uranus Outbase. Tell me, primate—why did that Outbase destroy itself?"

The primate wrestled with the chair, trying to get more comfortable. "That's a long story. Have you ever heard the story of the Bully and the Crazy Boy?"

The verbosity drug had definitely taken effect. "No, nor do I want to hear it now. Just tell me why they blew themselves up."

The primate shrugged. "We struck at you through the only weakness we could find."

Encrai turned bright eyes to his captive. "Indeed!"

The primate nodded.

"Well, goodness! Don't keep me in suspense, primate, tell me. I'm always trying to correct my defects." He wondered if primates were able to recognize sarcasm.

"Your flaw is that you're too rational."

What a stupid thing to say! Faagh! Yet the Admiral's spine tingled.

"Yes, that was the only flaw we could find," the primate continued, "aside from a tendency to overconfidence. I fear you never let your overconfidence influence important decisions."

"Um. And, ah—just how did you figure out that we are, um, too rational?"

"Well, that's a good story, too. I'm the one who realized you had this flaw—not because I'm the smartest Admiral we have, but because I've fought this fight before." He looked down at himself, then continued, "I'm a sort of small man, as you may have noticed, and—"

Encrai saw a complete autobiography coming, which he wished to avoid. "From all this I gather that the rest of your ships will behave as suicidally and insanely as the Outbase did?"

The shadow of a snarl passed over the primate's face. "With a vengeance, Admiral, with a vengeance."

"I see." The Admiral adjusted his harness, and returned to his control station. The central battlescreen brightened to full vigor as he touched the pads. Two disjoint sections appeared, the left one filled with the shape of the Kalixi fleet, the right one containing Saturn and its many moons. To the far left of the right section, two tiny dots represented the advanced scouts recording the Saturn scene; to the right of Saturn, on the sunward side, a small group of large objects approached the planet and its system.

"Tell me, primate, what are those clumsy objects moving toward Saturn?" A pointer appeared on the screen and drew the skeleton of a sphere around the spots of light.

"They're the battle stations from Earth, I imagine. Admiral Springrain deduced that you'd come from this direction. It's the obvious line of approach, if you plan to take the planets one at a time. When we realized that we'd have to meet you at Titan, the Terran Federate sent its battle stations to help defend Titan." The primate smiled. "Actually, I should thank you, after a manner. You're the first thing that's united mankind since the beginning of history."

"That's right, I'd forgotten. Your species wars against itself, doesn't it?" Amazing. At least they'd make a fascinating study for the xenologists. Evolution had been short-circuited here. Lessons could be learned.

Another thought struck Encrai. "So you anticipated our coming this way. I'm impressed."

"We assumed you'd take the simplest route. That destroys the element of surprise, but you can beat us without surprise. Your technology and tactics should beat us regardless."

Encrai appreciated that; it was exactly the conclusion *he'd* come to, of course. "You admit we'll win?"

Water collected in the primate's eyes. "How can you lose! You have more people, more resources, better technology. You're certainly more vicious, and . . . if the handful of prisoners we took from your exploratory group are any indication, you're even, . . . you're even," the primate's voice choked on a sob. "You're even smarter than we are." The primate's face contorted with bright dogged anger. "And we intend to beat your damned tails down your throats, and stomp you into pulp and spit on you when we're done."

The Admiral smiled broadly. "Good for you." So they were realistic—but spunky. "Tell me, where are your fleets, and where are they going to be, in order to carry out this commendable operation?"

The primate told him, expansively. He described the details of the designs of the ships in each fleet. He explained their tactical theory upon entering the conflict.

Returning to his console, Encrai set up a new scene on the display, a close-up of Titan and its neighbors, and started the games. Fleets entered the 3-D playing area and splintered into ships. The ships in turn branched into sets of potentialities, vectors for their possible action. Then, one by one, inferior potentiality branches dissolved, and optimal ones solidified. The scene commanded all of Encrai's attention; this was one of the parts of war he enjoyed most.

The battle's dance slowed as primate ships winked out of existence in the midst of their optimal paths; none escaped the Kalixi guns. "You know, it's almost a shame your species hasn't learned to compensate for acceleration without locking everybody in a stasis box. This could be a pleasant battle, if your ships could maneuver."

The primate just floated in his chair.

Encrai took careful note of a flaw in the design of the primate strategy, and played out a second scenario. The new game ran quickly to completion, as Encrai had predicted. "Why commit your fleets in such a loosely coupled fashion? There're large gaps in the pattern."

The primate nodded. "Yeah, we left some openings for the research ships to watch through."

"Research ships?"

Again the primate nodded. "Assuming we survive this time, we'll have to know a lot more to survive again. The Martian Republic donated its research fleet. We hope to get detailed pictures of your ships in the instants before they explode, after our missiles strike. By putting enough of those fragments together, along with the remains of the destroyed ships, maybe the next time you come to the solar system, you'll be facing ships just like your own."

Encrai snorted. "Fools! You think you can understand *our* technology? Just by taking pictures and collecting debris?" He searched his memory for an analogy, something out of the alien's own history. "Could a medieval primate build an airplane just by looking at the construction diagrams? It's absurd."

The primate winced. "I don't know. Certainly no ordinary medieval man could have done it. But a medieval man who knew the scientific method might be able to, given time. The scientific method is our greatest strength. It's the best method for learning there is." A look of—horror? Yes, a look of horror passed over the primate's face. "Unless you've found something better than the scientific method. If you've learned a better way to learn, we're lost." His eyes held a plea. "You don't have anything better than science, do you?"

The great cat hissed; Captain Taress turned to look at him with puzzlement.

The alien was right. Science was the key, and the Kalixi had nothing better. For the first time, a chill of fear ran along his spine—a chill he very quickly suppressed.

Encrai punched in a new set of orders for his fleet, modifying their battle plan. "You shall pay dearly for the opportunity to learn from the Kalixi," he muttered grimly. The new orders detailed a massive incursion into the gaps between the alien fleets, breaking their flanks and splintering them in chaos.

Encrai yawned, and stretched. He turned to Chief Assistant Mrech. "Colonel, watch after things, will you?" With a look at the timetable, he turned to the alien. "I'll be back in about six hours. We'll watch the battle together." He smiled. "May the best minds win."

The burrstinger closed, closed, and—Encrai opened his eyes with a start; his whole body was bent with tension, ready to pounce.

It was wrong—something was wrong in this campaign, but he didn't know what it was. And his hunches seldom erred.

But until his hunch blossomed into understanding, he could do nothing. And soon it would be irrelevant, anyway. The battle was starting. It was time to go see the show.

Encrai hurtled through the air at terrifying velocity, snagging the edge of his webcradle with outstretched claws as he passed. Back at his console, he created a new display upon the holoscreen; now the two scenes, one of Titan and the other of his fleet, coalesced. Saturn lay dead center, straddled by two opposing armadas. The humans far outnumbered the Kalixi. They looked quite imposing on the screen, but it was only an illusion. In the first conflict, between a Kalixi Class J fleet and the Martian Second Fleet, twenty-five Kalixi vessels knocked off one hundred and eighty primate ships before the primates pegged their first Kalixi ship; even after that, the Kalixi lost only three more ships, while the humans lost another forty-six. Armor alloy and fusion missiles just couldn't contest the clean power of gammaxers and gravshields. For the upcoming battle, the High Command anticipated the destruction of eleven human ships for every Kalixi; considering the weakness Encrai had found in the alien strategy, newer figures suggested a ratio of seventeen to one. And the human's suicidal tendency made no difference—insanity worked once, but only once.

Then why did Encrai's intuition disagree?

Encrai turned to the prisoner. "I wish to compliment you on the accuracy of your reporting. The fleets are indeed arriving just as you said they would, in just the disposition you described. Thank you."

"Yeah." Shadows hung under the prisoner's eyes, and stubble darkened his chin. The Kalixi Admiral chose not to notice.

Instead he turned back to the holoscreen. It was all so beautiful. Simple and elegant. There was, he told himself, nothing to fear.

Then the outer edge broke away from the battlescreen, forming a set of new displays far removed from the battle. These new sections held no fleets, just scattered ships—but the ships were moving at incredible speeds. The Kalixi advance scouts had just detected them. And though they were far away, they were unquestionably heading for the battle zone, and they were accelerating at the fastest pace that the best of the alien stasis boxes could handle and still keep the occupants alive. Encrai played with the controls, and potentialities expanded from those ships in narrow, senseless patterns.

To get to the battle in time, they'd have to continue to accelerate, and when they arrived they'd be going so fast they'd only be in the battle for a few seconds before they flashed past, hopelessly out of control, to speed beyond the limits of the solar system and die—for the aliens had no interstellar jumpdrive, nothing that could get those ships home again. It was truly suicidal, and in that sense at least it seemed typical of these primates.

"Where did those ships come from?" Encrai asked in tense bewilderment. "Where are they *going*?"

Somehow, the prisoner's silence seemed ominous. Encrai turned to the alien, and saw that he was no longer haggard and tired. His eyes were bright with a new emotion—was it pride? Could a primate feel pride? "Tell me, primate Admiral, what are those ships doing out there?"

The man smiled broadly, and Encrai's gnawing tension leaped in his throat. Instantly he swung over the human, claws extended, ready for the killing stroke. "Tell me," he spat.

The man leaned back, squirming away from the claws. "Where'd they come from? They came from the far side of the sun, beyond the bounds of the solar system. They've been accelerating since we figured out your timetable." He paused, and Encrai came closer with his claws. "They're on their way to the battle, obviously. They're on their way to *win*."

"How? They'll only be *in* the battle for a few seconds before they leave again, as swiftly as they came. They'll hardly have time to fire, much less time to aim."

The prisoner raised an eyebrow. "Well, in one sense you're even more right than you realize—many won't get to fire at all. By the time they get to the battle, they'll be traveling at almost a third of the speed of light. Many of those ships'll be dead hulls even before they get *to* the battle."

Encrai cocked his head, questioning.

"Don't you see? At one-third the speed of light, every dust particle in the solar system is their enemy—because in *their* reference frame, those particles are traveling at a third of the speed of light. Those dust particles, then, are slow—but incredibly massive—cosmic rays."

Encrai's eyes widened in dawning horror as he leaped to the console. He trembled as he composed the fleet's evacuation orders.

And as he worked, the prisoner's words taunted him, telling him what he already knew. "Of course, that works both ways. Those ships, those ships, *Admiral*, are the biggest damn cosmic rays in the universe right now. They won't *have* to aim their missiles—they aren't even going to try. Their warheads are just hunks of lead, with enough deuterium to vaporize. They'll explode way in front of your ships, leaving clouds of lead nuclei cosmic rays to blast through your damn gravshields. How long can your gravshields take *that*, Admiral?"

The evacuation orders sped from the Admiral's console. He finished, looked at an instrument display, and sagged in his cradle in agony. "Too late," he sobbed in a cracked voice. "I'm too far away. My beam'll take half an hour to get to Saturn from here. The suiciders will arrive before my message does."

The man broke into hysterical laughter. "We didn't have a chance, not a chance in the world. But we tried, goddammit, we *had* to try, and we *won!*"

Encrai was too numb to respond. He looked dully at the display, saw a small mystery resolved. "Those gaps between your fleets—they're for the suiciders, aren't they?" The gaps into which Encrai had sent so many Kalixi ships.

The human Admiral nodded. "They're really for the research ships, but they're tunnels for the suiciders as well."

Burning, paralyzing terror fought with cold, penetrating thought in Encrai's mind; but he was Kalixi, and thought won over terror. He set his teeth in determination. "That still won't destroy my fleet, Admiral. You'll hurt us, terribly, but we'll win anyway. We're warriors, Admiral. Even this can't bring you victory."

The human Admiral shook his head again. "You've missed the most important part of the attack. We aren't counting on a single pass to destroy you—because those ships won't ever get to pass. Look at the trajectories and the timings on those ships. Go ahead and look, Admiral."

Encrai turned to the holoscreen. Under his direction, the senseless patterns branched again—then, far faster than anything he'd ever seen before, the branches fell away and a handful of single solid certainties locked into place. The certainties emanated from a single point in the center of the Kalixi formation, radiating out in a cone to the suiciders' ships. Encrai gasped. "Spiders in web! They're going to collide with each other!"

The human—what was his name! Thearsporn? Thearsporn nodded again—an awful custom, this nodding was. "We hope to get ten to fifteen of them to ram together within five nanoseconds of each other. The explosion won't be as bright as a star, but it'll be pretty close."

New waves of shock washed through Encrai's brain, waning as his mind froze, waxing each time a coherent thought tried to form. "My fleet. The center of my fleet." He shuddered. "But your own ships! That star will destroy your own ships as well!"

Thearsporn turned sober. "Yes, it will. Only the farthest research vessels will survive."

Encrai ripped deep tears in his web, unbelieving, incapable of believing. "Why? How?"

The Admiral's voice answered gently. "Let me tell you the story of the Bully and the Crazy Boy."

Encrai had no answer.

"Once there was a crazy boy who always walked home from school. One day a bully confronted him, and dared the boy to get around him. The boy tried to cajole the bully, but failed. So they fought. And the bully beat the boy unmercifully. But in the course of the fighting the boy got in one good blow, and bloodied the bully's nose."

The voice through the translator was soft, soothing; by concentrating on the voice, Encrai could think again.

"The next day, the bully and the crazy boy met and fought again, and the boy was brutally beaten, but again he got in one good blow, kicking the bully in the knee."

Encrai noticed Thearsporn's face; it became increasingly contorted as he spoke. The words were heated now, and Thearsporn's eyes, which were bright before, now burned.

"And they continued to meet and fight for a week. By then the crazy boy was a bruised mass of ruptured flesh. But despite all the bruises he wasn't defeated. In fact, he looked up at the bully and pleaded, 'Please, please don't make me hurt you again.' The bully laughed at him, knowing he was a crazy, stupid boy—but he stopped laughing because laughing hurt, because the boy'd split his lip the day before, and the bully put his hand to his lips, and felt the swelling from his eye that still hadn't subsided, and felt the pain in his knee as he shifted his weight. And the bully looked at the crazy boy with horror, and turned and hurried away."

Encrai felt bile rise in his throat. Insanity, insanity was what this man was about. Why couldn't Thearsporn and his kind just accept the idea of slavery, like rational beings, when the alternative was death?

Encrai's numbness was gone; rational thought replaced the emptiness.

And with new thoughts came a new wave of horror. He formed new orders on his console; orders for his flagship and personal guard.

Captain Taress gasped as he read the orders. "25g's! The compensators won't be able to handle it all."

"I know that, Captain," Encrai growled. "Do it anyway!" Encrai turned back to the human Admiral. "Are any of those suicidal ships headed for *us*?"

Thearsporn shook his head. "Nope, 'fraid not."

A stench from the liesniffer assailed Encrai's senses; his snarl was cut off as a hammer of acceleration nailed him in his webcradle. The human snapped sideways in his chair, awkwardly positioned to survive such force.

"Where are they?" Encrai demanded of his prisoner. "How soon will the suiciders get here?"

Thearsporn twisted into the acceleration, trying to get away from the even more terrible agony assaulting him from the pain transmitters in the chair. "They're, they're off to one side, away from the scouts. Coming from an off angle. Should be here any minute."

Even as Thearsporn spoke, Encrai saw a dozen cosmic rays blossom into existence on his flagship's own scanners. With a strangled cry, Encrai screamed interception orders for his ships, orders they had only seconds to execute.

But Encrai's officers were the best in the universe, and they made it. The guardships lurched forward, spraying death even as the guards themselves died. The flagship's acceleration rotated 90 degrees and doubled. And the dead crews of the suicide ships couldn't retarget on the dodging flagship.

"We made it," Encrai muttered, then shouted in joy, "we made it!"

His thoughts turned to the future even as his happiness swept away his horrors. They would have to send another fleet to this system, he realized. His personal career was destroyed, of course, but there was something more important here. These crazy primates had to be subdued.

It would be difficult to convince the High Command to send another fleet now, with the retrenchment wars coming, but Encrai would convince them. And it wouldn't take much; even a class H fleet, hardly bigger than the original exploratory group, could beat the remains of the human defenses. Yes, a class H fleet . . . and a single Planetburster, just in case the fleet failed to conquer. Yes. Encrai turned cheerfully to his prisoner.

The prisoner was clamping his jaw, swallowing hard. Encrai remembered the psychmed talking about a stimulant in the primate's teeth.

"What . . ." Encrai started, then slapped his hand down on the alarm button. The man's complexion darkened, perspiration erupted from his face, and Encrai could smell the man's anger as he tore himself from the ill-fitting prison chair in the 5 g gravity.

With a powerful lunge Encrai was upon the beast—for beast Thearsporn was, with the light of insanity in his eyes. Closing swiftly, Encrai delivered a lethal stroke of his claws.

But Thearsporn snapped away, and the lethal stroke merely raked across his side, drawing a swath of skin and blood. Thearsporn extended his fist with impossible strength, and bones snapped in Encrai's side as he crashed through the air.

Disregarding his pain, Encrai followed as Thearsporn dodged down the corridors. A Marine appeared and fired a lasegun through Thearsporn's abdomen, but it didn't diminish his speed. He disappeared around the corner.

Encrai realized that he was heading for the fusion pool at ship's center.

The creature was insane, no doubt about it. Worse, he was dying—he was already dead, if he would just realize it; no doubt about it. But he would not realize it, and he would get to the fusion pool; there was no doubt about that either. Encrai wondered briefly how the Admiral knew where to go and how to get there.

Not that it mattered. Encrai started to take a deep breath, found it was a terrible mistake. The broken bones in his chest must have punctured a lung. And an artery. Moist warmth collected near his throat. He was dying.

Not that it mattered. In a few moments he would become part of another, even smaller, star. Admiral Thearsporn's star.

Encrai sighed. He felt a certain sense of guilt, failing his people like this, but the guilt seemed remote. Poor, poor Kalixi. He wished he could tell them; he wished he could tell them how much they still had to learn before they could conquer.

But for now the learning was too late; and soon the fury of atoms in bondage conquered all.

Evolution Of Entropic Error

Have you ever served on a jury? Have you listened to the careful framing of the statements, watched the little rituals which subdue the emotions that would otherwise interfere with reason, obscuring the correct analysis of evidence? For all the faults of our judicial system, you simply can't doubt the superiority of this system to two forms of justice that preceded it: the will of the powerful, and the whim of the lynch mob.

Technologies, like nuclear power and genetic engineering, are still judged by the traditional methods of two centuries ago. Wealthy lobbies maneuver behind the scenes to ensure that their products receive subsidies, while also working to assure that competing technologies are abolished by fiat and or crippled by regulation—the will of the powerful.

Meanwhile protesters sally forth to destroy their favorite enemies, armed with more anger than knowledge, while the news media magnify the loss of sanity, focusing on the emotions of the contestants, treating the subtleties of serious issues like homely wallflowers at the high school dance—the whim of the lynch mob.

Hopefully we will invent—and learn to live by—a variant of trial by jury for technology. We need to hurry, however, because our technologies grow more potent every day; every day, it becomes easier for the lobbies and the lynch mobs to cripple us so badly that we cannot recover.

Goodness! This is a terribly serious introduction for such a lighthearted bit of research as "The Conservation of Error in Closed Conservative Systems." How is it connected?

171

Well, regardless of what means one uses to make decisions on the use and abuse of technology, there are clearly dangerous technologies. I have here an update on the latest research in one such technology. You may not have heard of it before—but as you can see from this article, the potentialities are beyond any mortal grasp. Indeed, I would like to take this opportunity to demand a total, outright ban on work in this field, to go into effect immediately.

There are just some things that we weren't meant to know.

Evolution Of Entropic Error
In Closed Conservative Systems

Ever since the successful quantization of universal error by our statistical mechanics group here at Oxford,[1] Dr. Zachariah Marnel's mathematicians in the U.S. have denounced us.[2] Yet every experiment we conduct lends more support to our Theory of Error Conservation.[3] Dr. Marnel's dogmatic clinging to his own theory of entropic error has become absurd.

I am sure the basic difference between our two theories is familiar to all readers; Error Conservation states that the total error of a closed system remains constant. The theory of entropic error, on the other hand, claims that the total error of any system is constantly increasing, just as the entropy of the universe increases. Thus, according to Dr. Marnel, every time an error is neutralized (or "corrected" in the terminology of the specialists) this neutralization causes the creation of two or more new errors.[4] One could express it in this manner: Although two wrongs don't make a right, two rights do make a wrong. This, on the face of it, is absurd.

But let us settle the matter with an examination of our most recent experiments. The first experiment was an attempt to determine the factors and formulae relating different types of error. Three types of error were investigated: 1) scientific error, 2) legislative error, and 3) administrative error. The experimental design was straightforward: A government research project was analyzed in terms of a) the inaccuracies of the conclusions of the scientists, b) the injustices written into the laws based on these conclusions, and c) the misinterpretations of these laws by the officials in charge of enforcement. We chose to study these three types of error because Error Conservation applies only to closed systems. Although no real system is truly closed, all three of these groups work in vacuums divorced from reality. They approach the idea very closely.

We discovered a linear relationship between scientific error (S) and legislative error (L):

$$L = K(S) + L_1$$

where K is the conversion coefficient and L_1 is the natural error of the legislative body in the absence of scientific input. L_1 varied from legislative body to legislative body; it seemed to be roughly proportional to the number of representatives in the given legislature, but we did not explore this in any depth. The conversion coefficient was found to be approximately 2.7×10^4 legislative error/scientific error. This K was constant to within the limits of our measurement accuracy over a wide array of scientific research projects.

The administrative error (A) was a somewhat more complicated function of the scientific error:

$$A = A_0 e^{GS}$$

Where A_0 is the natural error of the administration in the absence of scientific input, and G is the conversion factor. Here, the conversion factor G is approximately 4.5×10^7/scientific error. As is obvious from both the function and the factor, administrative error rises much faster than legislative error as the system increases in size. We postulate the difference to be caused by the following phenomenon: Whereas a group of legislators must ultimately resolve their errors into a single unified statement, administrators are free to act independently in their misinterpretation and generate individual errors at will.

In any event, this relationship remained constant over many cycles of research-leads-to-laws-leads-to-enforcement-leads-to-new-research as the enforcement failed to give the desired results. Error was always conserved when expressed in constant units—we converted to scientific error for all comparisons. Even when research groups were broken into smaller groups or lumped into larger ones, the total error of the original bureaucracies always equalled the sum of the errors of the new bureaucracies.

One of the most striking predictions in Dr. Marnel's theory of entropic error is the existence of error-generating (i.e. "accident-prone") persons.[5] Obviously our Theory of Error Conservation leaves no place in the universe for such error-generators. In a diligent search we were able to locate three individuals with some of the theoretical characteristics of the accident-prone as described by Dr. Marnel. Unfortunately, two of them met with untimely deaths before we could contact them, and the third was hospitalized the day experimentation was to begin. So we have not yet verified or contradicted the existence of error-generators, although we are still trying.

We have, however, explored the so-called Theoretician's Dilemma.[6] This is the common superstition that when a theoretician enters the laboratory, everything goes wrong (i.e., if the theoretician observes an experiment, errors are made that invalidate the experiment).

Our initial results in this area were dismaying: scientific error did in fact increase when a theoretician received access to the lab. We were baffled for some time by this phenomenon. But then we noticed a curious subtlety in the effect. As the theoretician observed for longer periods of time, he caused less increase in error.

From this we deduced the existence of both potential and kinetic error. Kinetic error is directly observable, whereas potential error is "stored." Potential error must be reconverted into kinetic error to become observable.

This concept fitted our observations neatly. The theoreticians we studied worked mostly with mathematics, which made it difficult for them to commit real errors. Yet error was constantly being pumped into them by experimental results. This caused a buildup of potential error which had little chance to escape. When the theoretician observed an experiment, this potential leaked off and showed up as kinetic error in the laboratory. As the potential error was exhausted, the Theoretician's Dilemma disappeared.

There have been several articles hotly debating what

happens to a theoretician's potential error when he dies. We are now filling out paperwork to acquire a theoretician with which we can experiment. In light of the large numbers of Ph.Ds currently on the welfare roles, our only fear is that the government will release more theoreticians to our research than we could hope to exterminate and analyze in a timely fashion.

It should be noted in passing that our work has many practical uses. We now see that important research should involve as few people as possible. This holds down the total error. The theoreticians for important research should always be observing extraneous experiments, so that the error they absorb from the team's real experiments can be channeled off into other fields (some groups have always had their theoreticians involved in pointless experiments, which shows the power of human intuition). And although our government has chosen to overlook the military applications, others have not. The United States, with guidance from Dr. Marnel's group, is working on a method to parachute theoreticians into enemy territory.[7] It is estimated that a single high-yield physicist (i.e., a physicist who has done voluminous work with no experimentally verifiable results— such a man would have a large potential error buildup) could incapacitate the Kremlin for a decade, if the potential error were released properly. And it is rumored that Russia is working on a technique for storing administrative potential error.[8] This would be a major strategic breakthrough; administrators are more numerous, more expendable, and easier to plant in high-security areas. Once again, the weapons of tomorrow are being developed by the superpowers of today.

But I have digressed. My main purpose here is to reply to the ridiculous accusations of Dr. Marnel. He has repeatedly vilified the research which my group has done. Our experimental results consistently confirm our claims for error conservation. Other groups throughout England have verified our results. Yet Dr. Marnel has not turned his attention to the flaws of his theory. Nor has he attacked our results or our methods. Rather, he has attacked myself and my colleagues personally: he claims that our research has failed to find growth in error because we ourselves have made errors in our measurements—and that, when we add these errors in, the total error has increased at every step.

Now, my coworkers are careful, objective men, and I am appalled that a reputable scientist such as Dr. Marnel would lower himself to personal attacks when he is unable to find flaw in a rival's theory. I can only hope the scientific community will censure him as long as he continues in his ungentlemanly—and unscientific—conduct.

REFERENCES
1. Marc Stiegler and Hal O. Caust, "A New Mechanism for Quantization in Error Bound Environments," *Association for Statistical Studies of Erroneous Systems*, Vol. 5, No. 3, Nov. 1980, pp. 13–1313.

2. Z. Marnel, "Error Reporting in Conservative Theories," *Journal of Mistaken Engineering*, Vol. 2, No. 18, March 1981, pp. 13–14.

3. Manfred Reasons, "Conservation of Error: Validation and Verification," *Fault-Intolerant Research Methodologies*, Vol. 0, No. 0, May 1981, pp. 0–13.

4. Skip N. Slide, "Entropic Rise of Error Power in Industrial Settings," *Applications for the Error Engineer*, Vol. 8, No. 16, July 1981, pp. 17–23.

5. Cat A. Strophe and Gibs G. Stelman, "Prevention of Accident Cascade in the Individual," *Journal of Accident Research*, Vol. 3, No. 6, Nov. 1981, pp. 1129–1138.

6. Abe Stractions, "Max's Demon, Schrod's Cat, and Our Dilemma," *Theories of Theorizing*, Vol. 9, No. 11, Aug. 1981, pp. 33–37.

7. Gen. G. Pyle, "Survivable High-Yield Nonlethal Weaponry in Commercial Non-Ruggedized Containers," *Military Means Quarterly*, Vol. 11, No. 12, Feb. 1981, pp. 118–121.

8. Steep Throatski, "Bureaucracy Holding Its Own in Foreign Powers," *Aviation Secrets Weekly*, Vol. 84, No. 9, March 1981, pp. 1970–1982.

A Simple Case Of Suicide

If morality is the underlying characteristic that unites all my characters, then Maxwell Palmer in "A Simple Case of Suicide" is surely the archetype of my writing career.

Maxwell Palmer may also have been the most difficult character to present. Certainly, if we measure by the number of rewrites needed to publish his story, he proved to be most difficult indeed. I wrote "Suicide," from scratch, five times over a seven year period. Each time the horror grew; only the main character, and the fateful ending, remained the same.

This story takes place in one of those futures that the Club of Rome and other doomsayers from Malthus to Jeremy Rifkin seem so fond of. On most days, I find it difficult to believe in such futures. We already know how to avoid it, given an ecologist's understanding of the Tragedy of the Commons, an economist's understanding of the statistical genius of free markets, and some creativity in relating the two. Still, too few people understand all three.

The Club of Rome study assumed that there would be no technological progress; if we give control of the planet's resources to people who believe that only massive government enforced conservation can save the planet, there will indeed be no technological progress. Then the Club of Rome will be proven "right."

Sometimes it seems that many people want such a centralised control of our lives. For this reason I can't entirely write off this future as a mere horror story.

Let us hope we never need a President with the strength of honor described here.

A Simple Case Of Suicide

It was hot in Washington, and muggy, as usual. Why did the air conditioning have to break down today, of all days?

It did not matter. With a last deep breath—and a brief, hacking cough—Max nodded to the Secret Service agent.

The agent opened the door, and Max stepped swiftly through the crowded rows and rows of seats. He paused as he came to the podium, to look once more at the Presidential Seal affixed to the lectern. *Will I ever get over the awe of looking at these symbols of power?* he wondered. He smiled, grimly. *No: if I haven't gotten over them yet, I never will.* Determination renewed, he climbed the two short steps and turned to survey his audience.

One of the camera crews was waving frantically to tell him to wait. He nodded to them. His eye wandered over his prepared notes. They were pointless, of course. He had spent the night dreaming of the words he would say today; over and over they haunted him. He shuffled the papers, putting them aside on the lectern, except for one. The important one.

He gazed at it, and was pleased that his hand held it steadily. *I must convey a sense of importance and destiny as no man before,* he realized again. *For the message I give must ring in their ears for decades.*

It will be, he realized again, *my last, my greatest, act—of betrayal.*

He made no excuses for it in his own mind; he would betray millions of people today, as he had already betrayed everyone whose life had ever come too close to his. His wife, his son, his mother, his father, his best friend, his only hero—he had betrayed them all, sooner or later. They were gone now except, perhaps, for their ghosts.

Yes, he could feel their ghosts there now, looking over his shoulder at the paper, watching him watch the crowd . . .

"You've got to be *crazy* to keep on going back to school every year," Max's younger cousin said. She seemed quite childlike to Max; Max, after all, was already twenty-five.

Max shrugged, lying on the couch, deep in the middle of a well-worn spy novel. "There are worse things in the world than going to grad school."

"Oh yeah?"

"Sure. Getting a job, for example."

The squeaking from his father's room subsided. A loud "Whew" sounded from the same direction.

"He's done with his exercise bicycle," Janet mumbled ominously.

The sound of an elephant stampede thundered down the hall and broke into the living room. "I just went three miles farther than ever before," Max's father bellowed triumphantly.

"Um-hm," Max replied.

Max caught a glimpse of a falling object, and he heard a loud thump as his father slipped suddenly and fell down. Max looked up from his book with a slight smirk. "You all right?"

His father was spread-eagled on the floor, gasping, sputtering, and gulping air. His eyes bulged.

"Dad?" It took Max and Janet several seconds to realize that something was really wrong. Max reacted first. "Dad!" He jumped to his father's side. Janet screamed.

Max knelt over his father. Still he gasped for air, yet his face was turning blue at the same time. "What's wrong?"

His father didn't respond.

Janet yelled again. "What's wrong?"

Max didn't look up. "Call the ambulance."

The gasping was dying down. Max brought his hands up, moved them toward his father's chest; he had had CPR training two years before, he had learned what to do.

But that CPR had been two years ago. He had forgotten what to do. His hands were shaking; he couldn't believe this was really happening; his blood was pounding in his head, screaming *Do something! Do something!*

He put his hands on his father's chest—*but he couldn't remember what to do.*

The bluish tinge in his father's face deepened, turning grayish.

He died as Max knelt there, trying to remember how to save his life.

A few days later, an old friend called him; an old friend who was now a psychologist.

". . . It's really not too surprising that I couldn't remember what to do," Max explained. "I just didn't expect it, for one thing, right out of the blue like that. And CPR training only lasts a year—you've got to take a refresher every year to stay qualified."

"But still you blame yourself." Joe was probably a terrific psychologist, Max realized. He was so calm and steady as he directed the therapy: that was what Joe had called to give him, though Max was sure Joe would never admit it.

Max considered the matter for a moment: did he blame himself for his father's death? His first instinct was to just deny any guilt feelings because he didn't believe in feeling guilty. But he realized that he wouldn't be kidding anybody, not even himself. "Yes, I blame myself."

"But surely you see that there's no reason to blame yourself."

"You're right, Joe. But . . ." and his voice started to tremble. *"Joe, I was so close. I almost could have saved his life."* He shrugged, though Joe could not see. "Don't worry, Joe. I'm not suicidal or obsessed by it. I'm just guilt-ridden. I probably always will be."

* * *

Yes, the ghosts were there, looking over his shoulder at the millions and billions of lives that Max held in the paper in his hands. Max was so *close* to saving their lives. But he didn't dare.

The cameraman nodded to him.

Dry as his throat had been, now it was drier still. He smiled nevertheless. *Dry throat? Tough. This speech is gonna get a lot harder before it gets easier*. He breathed deeply.

"People of America," his voice rang with pride. "People of the World," he said more softly. Max hadn't been sure whether he should include them or not, but finally he decided he had to. After all, they listened today, too; they knew his decision had profound consequences for them as well as for America.

It was so important, that today even Tina would be watching. Even Steve.

It was dry, sunny, and not too hot for once, standing on the edge of the lake. No doubt the coolness was caused by the breeze that now blew sand in his face. Max turned away from the glare and the sand. Steve strolled toward him, holding hands with a skinny girl in white shorts and a red halter. Steve waved at him; Max waved back.

Steve released her hand. "Tina, this is the guy who's been my roommate for the last six years, Maxwell Palmer. Max, this is Tina, the most beautiful woman in the world."

Max shook her hand. Close up, she no longer looked skinny, and her eyes were bright emerald green. Max was mesmerized. "The most beautiful girl in the world," he muttered. "I can well believe it," he said more clearly, with a touch of envy.

Tina frowned, smiled, blushed, and shook her head. "Not hardly. You're both crazy."

"Yeah," Steve said, "that's one of our problems. We're too much alike." Steve's eyes met Max's, and they shared a silent chuckle. "Where's Holly?" he asked Max.

Max sighed. "I dunno. Looks like she stood me up

again." It hurt, inside, but it wasn't the first time. Max could stand it.

"Oh, well." Steve shook his head. "Crud. Another one of my problems is that I can't remember a damn thing. Lunch is still in the car." He trotted back the way they'd come. "Be back in a flash," he yelled.

Max looked over at Tina, looked down at his feet, looked at Tina again. "Steve's a great guy."

"Yeah." After a long pause, Tina said, "So you're the other half of the grad student team that's gonna change the world."

Max laughed. "At least we're gonna try. You can't change it if you don't make the attempt, can you?"

Tina shrugged. "I guess not." For the first time, they looked each other in the eye. Both looked away.

Tina brushed back her hair nervously; it fell limply around her shoulders. "What's your family constellation?"

"My what?" Max asked.

"Your family constellation. I just read a book about that. You know, are you the oldest, youngest, or middle child in your family, things like that."

"Oh. Am I oldest or youngest? The answer is yes." So much for being infatuated with Steve's new girl friend. She was beautiful, but if she believed in dumb stuff like that. . . . It was just as well that she wasn't too perfect. Steve's and Max's tastes in women ran too close together most of the time, anyway. "I am the oldest, and the youngest, and the middle."

"What?" She frowned, not understanding the joke. "Oh—you're an only child. That's a shame. You'll have a lot of trouble when you get married, then."

Max snorted.

"No, it's true."

"Even the claims like that that *are* true are only *statistically* true, though. I'll bet they say eldest children shouldn't marry each other, right?"

"Right. They'll both try to dominate the marriage."

"Aha. But my mother and father were both eldest children, and their marriage worked perfectly."

"I see." She'd caught the use of the past tense, but misinterpreted it. "*Worked* perfectly?"

Max looked away. "They died."

"Oh. I'm sorry." She blushed, then hurried on. "Goodness. An only child reared by two eldest children. Tell me, do you feel, uh, *parental* feelings a lot? A need to help people?" Max looked puzzled, and Tina continued. "You grew up as the focus of a lot of intense caring, right?"

Max nodded. "I suppose so." He gave a short, loud laugh. "Actually, it was even worse than that. My father's father ran out when Dad was seventeen, so Dad had been surrogate father for his brothers before getting married. And my mother's mother died when Mom was eighteen, so Mom was surrogate mother for her sister. I suppose I'm the quintessence of Parenthood, the distillation of a super-mother and a super-father."

"Yes." Tina raised her eyebrow. "If you're really the quintessence of Parenthood, then who is your Child?"

Max thought about it, and was disturbed to see the whole silly constellation business making sense. His voice held just a hint of awe. He quoted from a sign in his office, " 'The human race is a child, who must be protected until he is old enough not to hurt himself.' "

"What?"

"That's a sign on my office wall. It's one of my pet phrases, when I'm talking about war, and bombs, and starvation, and such. I've always been at least half-serious when I said it, too. I guess Mankind is my child."

"I see." Her words held deep understanding. At least Tina seemed to be trying to suggest that they held deep understanding.

Their eyes met, and held.

"Hey, would one of you statues help me with this stuff?" Steve Felman yelled across the sand.

"As you know, we are here to discuss life—and death." Max frowned slightly; his timing was a bit off in the delivery. Jason would have done it better. "As you know, our researchers have made a breakthrough in the integration of microprocessor technology and microbiology. A breakthrough that would permit us to cure all

disease—not only the common cold, but cancer also—
not only the common cancers, but the mutant II cancers as well." He looked confidently across the reporters and congressmen in his audience.

"No one ever need die of disease again." He knew it
was true, with a certainty that few presidents ever feel.
He knew it was true despite the screams of *hoax* by
some grant-hungry researchers.

The cure was sure and clean. Maxwell Palmer knew
it was good. Maxwell Palmer, after all, had conceived
it.

Max tossed himself into the beanbag chair. "Barkeep,
I need another drink." He waved his arm in the air at
Steve Felman, his new roommate. Well, relatively new;
they'd been sharing an apartment for two months now,
and it was the best friendship Max had ever had, better
than he'd ever thought possible. They could sense each
other's mood without a word; sometimes Steve would
come into the room while Max was stretched on the
floor in deep depression, and put on an old record—
and it was exactly the one song that Max needed to hear
to shake the sorrow. Could he ever find a woman who
understood his needs so perfectly? He suspected not.

Steve chuckled. "So you need another drink, huh?
Man, those robotics majors are real lushes."

"Ha! A biochemistry major should talk about lush.
Who is it that consumes the most pure alcohol in the
world? The biochemists. Not the robots, buster."

"Of course. Robots don't consume mass alcohol. Robots, like robotics majors, are much too prissy and
sterile for that kind of thing."

"Ha! At least robots work for a living. What do
biochemistry majors do? Collect unemployment and
Social Security." Max coughed.

"Sounds to me like you need a biochem major right
now, joker, to cure your flu."

"Ha! You guys can't even cure the common cold.
What can we expect from you with *real* diseases?"

"Maybe I can't cure the common cold *yet*. But no
robot *ever* will."

"Hold on there." Max thought about it for a minute. "You know, I'll bet we *could* use robots to cure the cold."

"Oh no. You've *already* had too much to drink."

"Wait a minute." Max sat up in the beanbag, not too successfully. "I can see it now: a robot the size of a germ, gobbling up viruses as fast as it can move."

"Great idea. Did you bring a few robots like that home with you?" Steve walked away from the bar, jumped headlong onto the couch.

"I'm serious."

Steve believed him. He rubbed his nose, staring at the ceiling. "How's the robot gonna recognize the viruses? You might, one of these centuries, make a robot the size of a germ, but where are you gonna put the brain power inside it to make it smart enough to recognize invaders?"

"We could datalink them to a big computer on the outside, let the number-cruncher do the thinking."

"I see. Okay, then, how're you gonna make enough of these things to make a difference? I mean, you're gonna have to have enough in your bloodstream so that you can destroy the viruses faster than they can reproduce, unless you're gonna make the robots reproduce, too."

Max frowned. "That is a problem, I guess. You can't really make a robot reproduce inside your body. Not enough silicon."

"Among other things."

Max shrugged. "So, it'll be expensive." Steve looked at him with big, doubtful eyes. "Okay, it'll be *very* expensive. That's no sweat here in America, right? And we're the only ones likely to develop a robot that's that tiny anyway, anytime this century."

Steve rolled over and sat up. "Finally, smarty, even if your computer had the brains to figure out which were the good cells and which were bad, where would it get the education?"

Max snapped his fingers. "No sweat, man. That's where *you* come in. You biochem types teach it what it needs to know."

"I see. So there's a use for us biochem types after all." Steve mellowed at that admission. "Hmmmm. And haaaa. You know, that's not such a bad half-baked idea."

Max stood up; he was starting to get excited about the whole thing. "You know, I'll bet we could do it. The two of us." As he thought about it, his confidence grew. "They couldn't stop us!"

Steve stood up, too. "You might be right. We could do this after we get our bachelor's degrees, when we go to grad school. It could be sort of a combined dissertation for robotics and biochemistry." He nodded his head. "I like it. You know, we could cure more than just the common cold."

"That's right. Nobody'd ever have to get sick again. From anything."

Steve walked over to the bar. "We might even be able to cure old age—I don't know how, maybe by having the robots clean up the free radicals or something. It might be worth investigating, anyway."

Max coughed again. "Right. *After* we cure the common cold."

Steve poured two short glasses of Glen Livet. "Are we gonna do this half-baked thing?"

"Yes."

"Swear to it?"

"Yes."

They solemnly shook hands on the pact. "A toast, then," Steve said, taking a glass.

Max raised the other glass. "To our dissertation!"

"To our dissertation!"

"What you may not know is that only American technology and American financing can bring the cure from a laboratory experiment to a product that saves lives."

He raised the piece of paper that Congress had put through the legislative process in just three short weeks, desperately rushing to complete the bill before the Congress recessed today. It had been an extraordinary effort, a master thrust, for they knew that this was the only chance they would ever have of getting it past the president who had fought it for so long.

Max waved the paper for the cameras. "I hold here the largest single procurement bill in the history of Man. I hold the key to the creation of paradise, the salvation of millions of people." He brought the piece of paper down between clenched fists. "I hold here the slaughter of billions of innocent victims, and the extinction of life on Earth." His hands trembled briefly; he was committed now.

"Have you ever seen someone die of cancer? I have. It is not a pretty thing, to die slowly, painfully."

Max walked very softly into the room, the sound of his steps masked by the moaning and occasional thrashing of the gaunt woman lying on the bed. "Mom?" he started.

She moaned and turned his way. She opened her sleepless eyes, that lay sunken in pits of shadow. "Max." She held out her hand—and screamed. "Sorry," she whimpered.

The cancer was eating her alive. For a time the pain killers had been quite effective, and she lived a normal life, at least as normal a life as one could live in a hospital bed.

But now the cancer had invaded her spinal cord, slowly working its way to her brain. It was no longer the pain sensors in her body that screamed in dying agony, but rather the central nerves themselves. The pain killers could no longer kill the pain; dosages strong enough to kill the pain would kill her, too. Though perhaps that wasn't a bad idea.

He talked to her. He told her about his summer job, and his preparations to start college in the fall. She listened, and moaned, and changed positions, and screamed. She screamed when she lay still, and she screamed when she moved, no matter where she moved, for the cancer followed her to each new position.

Finally it was time to go. Max stood up uncertainly. "I'll be seeing ya, Mom." He started automatically to say "Keep smiling"—it was Max's way of saying farewell—but he choked it off.

His mother smiled at him—it was a hideous caricature of a smile, for the lines of pain stamped her face with indelible creases—but it was her best effort nevertheless. "Keep smiling," she said.

Max stood there in agony, seeing her pain. "You too," he blurted as he hurried out of the room.

He never told anyone to keep smiling again.

"Cancer is a hideous disease, more terrible than any other disease we have ever known." He looked down, then looked up again. His voice turned soft, and terrifying in its gentle pressure. "Have you ever seen a city die of radiation poisoning? It is not a pretty thing, to die slowly, painfully."

Max felt flustered as he considered the number of times he had tried to make people see that these two, death by disease and death by radiation, were related. God, how he wished he were Jason! His voice rose involuntarily; he couldn't control it.

"Can't you see what's wrong with saving millions of lives? Billions may die! Can't you see that we have too many people already trying to share this planet?"

"Politicians!" Max exploded. "What disgusting kinds of creatures. You say this guy is a *friend* of yours?"

"Come on." Tina tugged him down the sidewalk until they were by the gate of a low stone wall. Behind the wall elms drooped in the summer heat, though it was cooler now that the sun was sinking. "He's a neat person despite his occupation." Her eyes twinkled. "And he's sharp, too. I'll bet that before the evening's over, you'll have a different opinion."

"About a *politician*? Not hardly."

"You'll have a different opinion about something. I don't know what, but Jason always . . . People are always just a little bit different after talking to him."

"No doubt he uses mind drugs."

"What an excellent idea!" a voice from somewhere among the elms cried. "Mind drugs! Tell me, do you have any recommendations? I've always believed in softening people up first, particularly if they hate—" and now the voice changed to mimic Max's "—*politicians*."

Max peered into the shadows, and saw nothing until somebody tapped him on the shoulder. He jumped around.

"Hi. I'm Jason. Jay to my friends, except when they're angry at me." A small, pale man with dark eyes and black hair offered his hand.

"I'm Max." They shook hands.

"Hi, Jay." Tina hugged him, and Max felt a twinge of jealously. Not that *he* had any right to be jealous. Tina was Steve's girl; at least she had been when Steve left for the summer. Though now, Max wasn't so sure. Whom did she love: Steve? Or Max? Max was uncomfortable with the question; he knew he wanted her himself, desperately; but Steve had met her first. In Max's code of ethics, she belonged to Steve.

Tina had him by the arm again. "Come on, dopey. Didn't you hear what he said?"

Max blinked.

"If we don't get inside soon, the bugs will climb out of the trees and eat us alive." She pulled him along.

They sat down at the kitchen table: a long, beautifully carved table steeped in the smells of food and the echoes of loud laughter and deep discussions. It was a place of home.

Max sat at the corner, with Jason at the head of the table next to him, leaning forward, his dark eyes alive with energy, somehow not conflicting with his soft smile. "So you don't like politicians."

"Well," Max suppressed a blush, then decided he might as well be honest, "not really. Not at all."

"Why?" His tone was sharp, though friendly.

Max shrugged. "Look at all the stupid things they do." He sat forward himself. "Like wars, and arms races, and burglary—"

"Burglary?"

"Yeah, stealing money from one person to give it to another—usually to give it to another bureaucrat."

"Like in the social safety net system."

"Yeah."

Jason nodded. "It's not an easy problem. Surely you can see that it's hard for a politician to fight Social

Security—there are a lot of people who want it kept alive, no matter how much it costs, because it's benefitting them. And every year there are more people it benefits, and more voters who would hang anybody who tried to stop it."

"And there's fewer people to pay for it." Max had been furious that summer when he got his first pay check, to find that almost half his pay had been taken out before he even got it. "Everybody knows it'll destroy us eventually. Even the politicians. And they *know* that the longer they wait the harder it'll be to stop. If they were any good, they'd risk their jobs *now*, before it's too late."

Jason stroked his chin. "Ah. What *you* want isn't a politician. What you want is a statesman."

Max stared at him blankly.

"A politician is a man who can get voted into office. A statesman is somebody who, once into office, can make wise decisions. The two have very little in common."

"Then which one are you?" Max smiled wickedly.

Jason looked away from Max's face. "I'm not quite sure. Right now I'm running for the House. I suppose I'm a politician." He looked back at Max, and his smile returned. "Of course, I *plan* to be a statesman once I get there."

"Ha! Not a chance." Max loved to be cynical, particularly when he was justified.

"That is unjustified cynicism," Jason countered, as if he were a mind reader. "Being expedient from time to time doesn't prove you're completely immoral all the time. Haven't you ever done something you knew was stupid, just to please your advisor, in effect buying his vote?"

"Well . . ." Dammit! Of course he had. But—

"Besides, there have been some who became statesmen, you know—or do you think Thomas Jefferson and Abe Lincoln were men without principles, the way you seem to think all politicans are?" He raised an eyebrow. "Actually, there's no way you can tell whether I can do it until I've actually been tested. Or don't you believe in the experimental method?"

Max almost choked. "Of course I believe in it."

"Then how can you make such silly claims?" Jason's smile broadened. "Better yet, what are *you* doing that is so much more meaningful and worthwhile than what *I'm* doing?" His eyes picked up the laughter in his smile. "I hear you're supposed to be protecting the human race while it's growing up."

Max ran his hands down the arms of the chair. "Oh, not quite." His voice turned a bit smug. "I *am* working on saving millions of lives, which is almost as good. We might even achieve immortality."

"Oh, really? Are you sure that saving lives and making them immortal is the right thing to do for humanity right now?"

Max stared blankly at Jason yet again. "What do you mean?"

Jason seemed surprised by Max's incomprehension. "Isn't it obvious? There are eight billion people crowded together here already. You're talking about increasing the number of people, increasing the burden on the planet's resources, reducing the amount of resources per person." He slapped his hand palm up on the table. "Man, some of the people you'll be saving are going to burn gasoline that *you* could have burned, put smog in the air *you'll* have to breathe, and increase the price of the food *you* buy. For some people, it'll make the difference between buying enough, and not enough."

"Wait a minute."

"In fact, the group you'll have the most impact on is the older, more disease-prone part of the population— the ones using the safety net—the ones you were just moaning about. What'll it do to your taxes if they keep on living?" Jason shrugged his shoulders. "Course, *you'll* be rich and famous, after inventing the cure. It won't be a problem for you—you'll be a member of the rich, protected class. It'll just be a problem for people like me, who're trying to stop the problem."

Max found his jaw hanging open; slowly he closed it.

There was a science magazine lying to one side; Jason stretched for it, couldn't reach it. "Tina, could you get that for me?"

Tina retrieved the magazine for him.

"Thank you, my dear," Jason said. Again Max felt groundless jealousy.

Jason flicked rapidly through the pages. "What about the new cancers they just isolated—or rather, the ones they just recognized as being different?"

"We'll be able to cure those, too, I'm pretty sure." Max was still dizzy from the rate at which the topic changed.

Jason stopped on a page. "There it is. 'Though they have the same symptoms as the usual cancers, like lung cancer and melanoma, these mutant II cancers have three distinctive features: they are much more prevalent in the post-industrial societies, even considering lifespan biases; they have a peculiar binodal distribution, striking primarily young adults ages eighteen to twenty-five, and people just past the midlife crisis, ages forty-five to fifty-five; and they have a 99.9% mortality rate, being virtually immune to traditional therapies." Jason looked up at Max. "This disease just might save the world."

"What?" Max felt dizzy. Where'd this guy come from? Where was his mind going?

"Don't you see? By wiping out people when they hit retirement age, we can reduce the strain on our society caused by retirement. Better yet, by killing off the ones just getting out of high school and college, when they're entering their best breeding years, we can reduce the overall population."

"We don't have to reduce the population. The population is going down anyway."

Jason waved the objection away breezily. "Just a temporary fad, with this new-woman identity. In five years the population will start zooming up again. I just hope it doesn't grow so fast that it makes up for all the slow-growth years instantly."

"You can't be serious."

"Sure I can. Don't you see the danger? As the population grows, so does the probability that someone will pull the trigger on a nuclear holocaust. To go around curing all the diseases—to say *nothing* of passing out

immortality like candy—would be crazy. It's a simple
case of suicide."

"You're not serious." Max just couldn't believe him.

Jason leaned forward, looking Max steadily in the
eye, still smiling. "Am I? Does it make a difference
whether I'm serious or not?"

Did it make a difference? If his arguments were
correct, shouldn't Max take them seriously, regardless
of whether Jason took them seriously?

Tina pressed his hand. "I *told* you Jason would change
your opinions."

Jason looked over at her. "And *you*, Tina, what have
you been doing lately that you shouldn't have?"

The three of them argued long into the night, about
many things. Somehow, Jason seemed invincible. Max
had never seen anything like it; Max or Tina would box
him into a corner with his newest, crazy opinion. But
then he'd rush them with a flurry of new ideas, new
points of view, and suddenly *they* were the ones caught
in a corner.

Max *still* didn't know whether to take him seriously
or not. But he started reading the papers, looking for
proofs and justifications for his conviction that saving
lives was still an honorable enterprise.

Unfortunately, hideously, he found that Jason had
been wrong: it wouldn't take five years for the trend of
falling population to reverse itself. By the end of the
summer, the census takers were giving the sociologists
shocking information that destroyed all the pet theories.

The population was rising again. The only things
growing as fast as the population were poverty and
mutant II cancers.

"And we Americans 'share,' " he lingered over the
euphemism with careful but heavy sarcasm, "more of
this planet than most other people put together—a
single American consumes as many resources as hundreds of people in Norafrica.

"*And everyone in the world knows it!* How many
more cities like San Diego must we lose? How many

more notable Americans must be stalked by terrorists before we see the connection?"

"My God. Have you told Tina yet?" Max sat motionless in the chair."

"No, Mr. President."

Max squirmed; he wasn't used to the title, though he had borne it for a year now.

"We left it for you to tell her."

"Of course." Max turned in his chair, then looked back at the Secret Service agent. "I would like to speak to the wives of the four men who died, Bill," he said to the Secret Service agent.

"Very well, Mr. President." The Secret Service agent bowed and left.

Max held his head in his hands and screamed softly. His son—*their* son—had been kidnapped in a bloody struggle. Why did people do these inhuman things?

The story was already breaking in the newspapers; it was hard to stop a leak when half the people in Washington heard or saw the fighting. Max didn't want to tell Tina until he found out why it had happened.

He didn't have to wait too long. Within the hour they received a package at the White House. And the package contained . . . He went to tell Tina.

He held her and he told her; she was rigid as a statue. "It's a normal list of demands: two million dollars cash, the release of the five SALO prisoners we took in September, a planeful of guns and ammunition."

"Can't we give it to them?" She pleaded, but she knew the answer.

"If we do, they'll never let an American president alone again. Hideous as this is, it'll only get worse if we don't stop them now. You know that, don't you?"

Tina sobbed; her whole body shook. "Do we know these are really the people who kidnapped him—the same ones who blew up San Diego?"

Max's stomach rose in his throat. "Oh God. Yes, we know it's them, Tina." He couldn't open his mouth, much less talk, but he had to tell her. He had to tell her. "They included proof in the package. They . . . they sent back . . . Mike's right index finger."

Her eyes bulged; she screamed; Max held her as tightly as he could.

"I can't help him, Tina." He was crying. "But we'll kill them for it, if I have to do it myself. I'll resign when it's over, we'll get a house in the Rockies. I'm sorry."

Max tried to keep his promise; he did keep the first part. He gave the terrorists their five comrades, and their money, and a planeful of ammunition, and the SALO terrorists took Mike on board and headed for Bolivia, and Max signed the strike orders that sent three Firechargers to intercept, and they obliterated the plane and burned the money and killed the five freed prisoners and the twelve terrorists.

And killed Mike. At least, that was a possibility; no one knew for sure whether Mike was still alive by then.

Max did not keep the second half of his promise. He did not resign. In fact, the incident gave him a power in international politics unmatched in modern times: only a madman would order his own son killed. Oddly enough, the world respected madmen.

Max read the note Tina had left for the hundredth time.

Dear Max,

I know you believe you did the right thing. Perhaps I do too. I don't know. But . . . I just can't bear to live with the man who killed our son. I'm sorry. I love you.

He couldn't blame her. He couldn't live with the man who had killed their son either, but he had less choice.

Had he killed their son? Part of his psyche railed against the notion: it was the SALO terrorists who were responsible, dammit!

What does it mean to be responsible for something? Max could remember Jay asking. Max remembered his conclusion on the matter after Jason had forced him to think deeply about it years ago. *Responsibility is shared by all those who have the knowledge and the power to prevent an event, but who let it—or make it— happen anyway.* The SALO terrorists were responsible, even more responsible than he was, because it would have been easier for them to make decisions that saved his son's life. But Max was responsible, too. He accepted it.

He found he could not resign, to leave the world to forge its own solutions to its problems; he was responsible for that, too, now. He accepted it.

"We, the people of America, are consuming this planet!" He was starting to shake; he slowly straightened his shoulders, as Jason had taught him. He stepped back to the lectern (he had stepped away toward the audience at some point in his speech) and was calm. "Each day there are incidents that could lead to the holocaust. Each month we escape Final Confrontation by even narrower margins."

"Mr. President, they're heading for Vladivostok. We won't be able to reach them in time. They're only minutes from Russian waters, and it looks like half the Soviet Air Force is loitering around the area, just in case they need help."

"Very well, General. Keep me posted."

Max leaned back in his chair and shuddered. It was just another ordinary crisis. Another ordinary chance for the world to end.

He could order a GHOL strike now. The enemy commandoes would be dead, and the world would once again receive notice that murder of the innocent leads to murder of the murderers as well.

But it would set a new and terrible precedent, the precedent Max had fought against setting since his first inauguration. He couldn't use the GHOL, the Ground-attack Heavy Orbital gamma ray Laser, to settle ordinary crises. Otherwise it would be used each time a crisis arose, each time with a little bit less circumspection, until . . .

He knew what he had to do. His stomach flip-flopped as he thought about it, but he knew he had to do it.

He turned to the hot line. He called Kiril Perstev.

The premier appeared on the visiphone. "Good day,

Mr. President," he said in perfect English. He smiled. "I presume you think you have a problem."

Max's heart pounded in fear. Kiril was too good; he was the closest match to Jason he had ever met, fluent in many languages, with many points of view that he could shift into and out of with lightning speed. He was for Russia what Jason should have been for America.

But Kiril's motivations were different. God, how Max wished he understood what motivated Kiril Perstev. "I don't have a problem, Premier. You do."

Kiril raised an eyebrow.

"Three hours ago, terrorists attacked Japan's two largest ocean harvesters. The terrorists slaughtered the crews and raced for safety. We, of course, have interceptors in hot pursuit."

"In what way is this a problem for me, Mr. President? To be sure, the Soviet Union regrets the loss of life, but we support the liberation movements throughout the world as well."

"These pirates seem to be heading for Vladivostok. It's as if they expected to find safe harbor there. Naturally, if they make it, it will be more difficult to punish them. We would probably have to use the GHOL to saturate the entire city with lethal radiation levels, to make sure that justice was served."

Kiril studied Max through the visiphone. "That would, of course, lead to the holocaust."

Of course it would. Though Kiril was currently the strongest member of the ruling troika, many issues had not yet been settled. For Kiril, a show of weakness, particularly because of a mistake, would be fatal. Kiril's only alternative would be massive retaliation.

Max clenched his fist under the table. The fear tasted bitter in his mouth. Yet he stared coolly back at Kiril. "Premier, the pirates are dead men. How many others shall die with them?"

Kiril leaned back, bringing his fingers together in a steeple. "You would not do it. It is not in your nature. You are philosophically incapable of ending the world." He smiled wolfishly. "In fact, I believe that if I pressed the buttons and destroyed the United States, you would decide not to retaliate, in order to protect the human race."

Max's heart leaped in his throat; still he smiled back at Kiril. "You have an interesting point. I concede. It is against my philosophy to destroy you, or to destroy humanity." He leaned forward, and whispered into the visiphone. "But, Kiril, it is also against my philosophy to bluff. I'm not the kind of person who would bluff—someone might call it, and I would lose." His look hardened further. "No, Kiril, I would not bluff. You face a contradiction: my philosophy permits me neither to threaten nor to carry out the threat. Yet I *have* threatened. Where have you erred in your reasoning, Kiril? Don't guess wrong here, Kiril: for if you guess wrong, you will lose everything."

Kiril laughed, a loud belly laugh; but as the laughter faded, and Max remained immobile, Kiril's smile went away. For a moment doubt flickered in his eyes, before his mask returned. "Any pirates who attempt to use our territorial waters as a sanctuary will naturally be disappointed. Such an incursion into our security would be dealt with instantly by our Navy and air forces: such pirates would have their ships destroyed, and survivors would be executed," he said tonelessly as he broke the connection.

Max sank back in his chair, completely drained. *How many more times will I get away with it,* he wondered.

His bluff had worked.

"Don't you see how dangerous it would be to let our population grow untempered?" A ghost whispered in Max's ear. "It would be a simple case of suicide."

Max shook his head, and for a moment he felt the burden he had carried so long dragging him down. "Lord knows I have tried to make the world ready for this cancer cure."

"You're wrong, Jason. There *is* a way mankind can survive!"

"Goodness, *you* certainly are certain of yourself. For a change," Jason responded with a smile. "Would you

care to sit down before you destroy all my most cher-
ished pessimistic theories?" Since becoming a member
of Congress, Jason had mellowed just a bit. Actually,
Max wasn't sure "mellowed" was the right word: Jason
just didn't talk as fast as he once had. That might be put
down to weariness. But Jay's eyes still held a feverish
brightness: perhaps the slowing of his verbal attacks
was a part of converting himself from a *politician* to a
statesman.

Once he had Max seated at the kitchen table, Jason
leaned forward in the old style, and his words speeded
up. "So tell me about the solution to all our woes. How
are we going to prevent the holocaust?"

"By reducing the population."

"Sounds wonderful, but not very implementable. Or
do you come equipped with a mechanism for perform-
ing this miracle as well?"

"Sure. We'll start a birthright lottery, conducted by
the UN. Every country will get so many 'places' in the
lottery, and the particular couples who get to bear
children will be chosen at random."

"A beautiful idea that has absolutely no chance of
success. Right off the bat, I can see a problem—naturally,
the leaders of all the countries will want preferential
treatment. They want children, too, after all, and they
have the power." He stared at Max, puzzled. "Besides,
why would any country be interested in paying attention to a lottery, anyway?"

"You mean, what carrot would I hold out to them?"

"Exactly."

"We'd offer medical assistance, education, and food
to the countries that went along with it."

"Um. What incentive could we give Americans? The
safety net already gives them those things."

Max felt exasperated; why was Jason *always against*
ideas, never *for* them? "Actually, I was hoping you
would supply some of the ideas for making this thing
work yourself."

Jason shook his head. "No matter how neat or clever
a solution may be, Max, no matter how effective the
idea might be if it could be put into action, you have to

remember that a workable solution to a problem not only has to function within the physical laws of the universe, it also has to function within the social laws of dealing with people. Any kind of a birthright lottery will have to get *everyone* to agree to it. That just won't happen. What would we do with people who had illegal babies—what would we do with the illegal babies themselves? Do you figure on shooting them?" Jason waved his hand. "To be implementable, you have to have a solution that requires as few people as possible, and to make the people you want to use exchangeable, so that if the particular person you want to help you won't, you can go find somebody else to fulfill his part in the project."

Max took a deep breath. "Yeah, I knew all that, sort of. I just hoped that *you* might be able to fill in some of the gaps."

"I wish I could, Max." Jay shrugged. "But I don't know how. I'm not a superman." He smiled. "Not yet, anyway."

"Well, I have another idea." It still left a bad taste in his mouth, but the second idea would work. "We could start up a few conventional wars, and commit enough atrocities and slaughter enough people to bring the population back down again."

"Now that sounds more promising—you don't need anywhere near as many people to help you start a war as you need to end one. There is, of course, a problem— how do you guarantee the conventional war won't escalate into a holocaust?"

"By neutralizing the missiles. We'll build an ABM system."

Jason coughed politely. "I can't help thinking somebody's already working on that."

"I'm sure they are. But I wonder if they're aware of all the new stuff going on with lasers and molecular computers these days." He described the new generation of x-ray lasers being used in the labs, what they were used for, and how they might be used for other purposes. "Anyway, if we could put a few megawatt x-ray lasers—with the kind of precision we're getting in the labs—in the sky, we ought to be able to make nuclear attack pretty unlikely to succeed, don't you think?"

Jason looked at him strangely. "Perhaps you're right. They could very well have overlooked this possibility. I'll investigate it." He sat back in his chair and clasped his hands. For a moment the fever subsided from his expression; he was strictly serious. "You know, I'm currently holding discussions with the members of the House and the Senate on putting together a new group to . . . well, a group to be a think tank, more or less, but with no party biases, with only the congress to be loyal to. I know that that probably sounds as unimplementable as anything else we've discussed here, but I think I can do it." He nodded to himself, as if finally reaching a decision. "How would you like to be the boss?"

"Me?"

"Is there anyone else in the room? I'm going to need all the good people I can get."

"But my work—"

"Your medical research is more dangerous to humanity's survival than any other work in the world today. All those weapon makers out there aren't anywhere near as dangerous as you and Steve are. We *already have* the weapons we need to destroy ourselves. It's people like *you* who'll create a reason for us to *use* them."

He lurched forward to the edge of his chair; his intensity was greater than ever before. "Come with me, Max, and help me make a world that will be ready for your cancer cure when it's finished. I'll warn you right now—I don't think we can do it. But I know for sure that it can't be done at all if nobody tries. I want us to try."

Max shook his head slowly. "I don't know. I'll think about it." He smiled. "Maybe, if you promise to try to make the birthright lottery idea work."

Jason smiled back. "I don't know. I'll think about it. Maybe, if you promise to come to work for me."

CLASSIFICATION:
   TOP SECRET
AUTHORIZATION KEY:
   SILENT CAMPER
ACCESS SUBKEY:
   STEEPLE
NOTE TO GENERAL MAVERY ON THE DEVELOP-
MENT OF THE HIGH-ENERGY XRAY PLATFORM
(HEXPLAT)
   Work is progressing swiftly toward launch of a pro-
totype platform. Current estimates suggest we will be
able to identify, acquire, and kill individual missiles
with 95% confidence at a rate of five targets per second
per platform. This is equivalent to wiping out the entire
Soviet ballistic force in three minutes with two HEXPLAT
platforms.

"I have known for many years that this day would
come, when the cure for mutant II cancers would be
uncovered." Yes, he had known it would come, for he
had known Steve would bring it, even without Max's
help.

"We have to tell him, Max," Tina chided. "He's a
good man; he can take it."

Max squeezed her hand. "I know he can. But, God,
how I hate to do this to him. His whole world will be
wiped out."

They came at last to the door of Max and Steve's
apartment. They entered. Steve sat upon the couch, a
guitar in his hands, softly singing melancholy songs. He
glanced up as they opened the door. "Howdy," he said,
interrupting himself.

"Hi, Steve." Max cleared his throat.

Steve looked back and forth between the two of
them. "Is something wrong?"

Tina started forward, unlocking her hand from Max's;
somehow, it was uncomfortable to hold hands in Steve's
presence. "We've got a couple of announcements, Steve."

"I see." He put the guitar aside, and sat up, cross-
legged. "So?"

Max took a deep breath. "First off, I'm moving out of the apartment." He took Tina in his arms. "We're getting married."

Steve turned away. "I see," he choked out. He turned back, blinking his eyes. "Well, I sorta knew this was coming anyway. It would be sorta hard to miss it, wouldn't it?"

Max didn't say anything. Sure, Steve had known, academically, that Max had won the girl they both loved, but only now did Steve feel it in his gut. *I almost wish it were the other way around,* Max thought. *I'd rather suffer myself than to have you, my best friend, suffer.*

"Well, at least I'll still see you every day on the project," Steve said, making a half-hearted effort at a joke. But both Max and Tina turned away when he said it. Steve's voice turned panicky. "We *will* still see each other on the project, won't we?"

Max covered his face with his hands. "No," he mumbled.

Steve stood up. "What did you say, Max?"

"I said . . . we won't see you on the project." He forced himself to speak clearly. "Steve, Jason offered me a job, a while ago. I—"

"Jason! That creep!" Steve stomped across the room. "You're not letting him tell you how to run your life, are you? Did you let his goddam willies infect you, about mankind's survival and all that bilge?" He held up his hands. "Not that we aren't in a lot of trouble, don't get me wrong. But Jason's so sure he knows *exactly* what the problems are and *exactly* what to do to solve them, and he's full of it! You see that, don't you?"

Max started to step back, then held his ground. "He's *not* full of it, and you know it."

"So you're just gonna walk out on *six years* of our lives, all the plans we made, all the *promises* we made?"

Max stared stonily into the distance. "I'm sorry, Steve. Yes. I'm just going to walk out."

Steve stepped back, too shocked to be angry. But the anger came back, a burning anger that flushed his whole complexion. "Then get out," he spat. "You think our project is dead, just because you're a traitor, but it's not. I don't care what you and Jason think of it. *Our idea is a good one.* I'll complete the work we started. I'll show you." He walked to the door. "I wish you'd never met Jason." He sobbed. "I wish I'd never introduced you to Tina."

"But people have shouted down every effort to make the world safer. The whole world ranted against the birthright lottery. All of America turned its back on the space program." Max choked with rage. "And the space program was the only program in the world that might have put people safely beyond the reach of the GHOL. But we destroyed it in the name of the safety net— never admitting that mankind's only true safety net is continued progress."

"Surely you can see that, over the long haul, the space program is the only thing that can save us." Max wanted to make it a plea, but he dared not show weakness in front of Senator Kelvane; that would be fatal.

Though it might be fatal just to have to talk to the senator; Kelvane *knew* that he had won, if Max asked to see him personally.

Kelvane snorted. "You fellahs an' your long hauls," he said with the Southern drawl he was so proud of. "I've got enough trouble with today an' tomorrow." He jabbed a slim finger at Max; Max couldn't help thinking it ought to be a fat cigar with smoke pouring off, to match the classical image of a politician.

But it wasn't. Kelvane was a classical politician—not a statesman—but he was smooth, like fine bourbon.

"Y'all have a long haul of time to pay for your long-haul solutions. Now my constituency needs things they can see in their lifetimes."

"Senator, the space program budget is so trivial compared to the Social Security budget—destroying the space program will have absolutely no impact on the current budgetary problems."

Kelvane just shook his head. "Boy, it don't matter one bit whether it helps or not. It's the signal it makes that's important. Cutting off all the silly games lets the people see that we are making all the sacrifices we can to correct the problems."

Max had already lost; he let his fury take control. "You're killing the whole human race for the sake of a few voters!"

The senator smiled; it was still a smooth smile, but it was ugly. "Why, no, son. I'm killing *you* for the sake of *me*. Big difference there." The senator rose to go. "If you were Jason Masino, things might be different." Kelvane's eyes filled with a strange combination of feelings: a bit of fear, a deep awe, and a profound, even compassionate, concern. Somewhere, sometime, Jason had touched him.

But the touch was too long ago; the look faded, and the senator went for the throat. "But you aren't him. Not by a long shot."

Max hated him for a time, but that feeling faded, too; there were so many others like him it wasn't worth wasting the energy.

Eventually, of course, the future became the present, more swiftly for Senator Kelvane than for many. Kelvane was in San Diego when the SALO completed their crude, hand-made nuclear device. They lit it off in the hotel adjacent to the auditorium where Kelvane was speaking to the assembled governors. Kelvane's last moments were spent a hundred meters from ground zero of a twenty-four-kiloton explosion.

"The world is not yet ready for American medical technology; not even America is ready for the banishment of disease.

"But some day we will be ready. Some day we will have a defense against the GHOL. When it's impossible for us to kill ourselves on impulse, we will be able to save lives impulsively. But until then we must discipline ourselves, and hold the technology of even longer life in abeyance." Was that concept too sophisticated to be pitched to the American public—the idea that sometimes one technology dare not be brought to life until after some other technology arrived to solve the problems of the first? He prayed it was not; but he heard Jason's ghost laughing nevertheless.

Jason sipped a cup of coffee; as Jason said, coffee was his only vice, except for sugar cookies. "Tell me, Max, is there anything you would not do, anything you would not sacrifice, to guarantee Man's survival?"

Max finished buttering his toast and glanced at Jason. He knew he should think carefully before answering, but he thought he already *had* thought carefully. "I don't think so."

"I see. I asked, because we have a new problem."

Max's stomach tightened.

"They're building a new weapon, Max, that's impervious to the HEXPLAT."

"Who? How?"

Jason shook his head "I don't know, Max. But somebody is."

"How do you know?"

"Because that's the way people are. There are millions of men employed in the world for the purpose of finding better ways to kill people. One of them will succeed."

Jason had fallen off the deep end this time. Max threw up his hands in exasperation. "So what are we supposed to do about it? We'll have to deal with it when the time comes."

"Can we afford to wait until the time comes, Max? How likely is it that Steve will complete his research?"

Max swelled with pride. "He'll do it, Jason. Just a few more years: he's licked all the hard problems. The work he won the Nobel Prize for answered most of our toughest biological questions. There are still difficulties, technology-wise, but he'll beat them all."

"That reminds me, Max. Have you talked to Steve lately?"

Max looked away. "No. I wrote him a letter, congratulating him on his Nobel, but . . ." He choked.

Jason returned to the main topic. "Let me propose a hypothetical dilemma." Jason put his empty cup to one side. "Suppose someone were working on an invention that was wonderful and would help people a great deal, but that was sure to start a war as soon as the invention was completed. The war would naturally be a bad thing, but the invention would benefit people more than hurt them, over all." He banged his finger on the table. "But now suppose you also knew that other people were developing weapons that guaranteed that, if such a war started, it would end all civilization."

"I would arrange for the quiet executions of all the people who were developing weapons," Max interrupted.

"Suppose you didn't know who they were, or that there were so many of them you couldn't hope to kill them all before they found out what you were doing and killed you instead."

This hypothetical dilemma wasn't hypothetical enough for Max's taste. He had a terrible feeling he knew where Jason was heading.

Jason continued. "What would you propose that we do, in such a situation?"

Max ran his hand through his thinning hair, desperate for a better idea than the one Jason was sure to propose. "I don't know. I suppose we could start a war immediately, while we had the chance, before the new weapons were developed." Max spoke in a light, jesting tone.

"We could do that easily enough. Even a minority party leader like myself, just by whispering the wrong words in the right ears, could start a fire in any of a dozen countries that would spread to a world-encompassing conflagration. The planet is ready for it." Jason wasn't jesting at all, it seemed. "We could slaughter enough people to make enough room for all the survivors for centuries. Even an immortality drug would pose no threat." He stared into the coffee cup. "But that would involve the murder of billions. I have an alternative suggestion."

"What?"

"Let us further hypothesize that the war-starting invention is being developed by one individual who is unlikely to be replaced, an individual we know." Jason raised his hands helplessly. "Why sacrifice billions when sacrificing one will do the task?"

Max felt cold. "What do you mean?"

"In these times of scarce resources, high prices, and few jobs, it would be easy to find someone who would, for modest remuneration, eliminate a single troublesome individual."

"You mean kill Steve?" Max couldn't believe his ears.

"Why not?"

"Because . . ." Why not indeed? "Because Steve is a *good* person. He's dedicated his life to saving lives."

"Are there not people like that among the billions you'd rather slaughter?"

Of course there were.

Jason continued. "Shall I start the war?"

"No."

"Why not?"

"Because . . . because people like Steve are the reason why Man is worth saving. If, in order to save Man we have to kill the people like Steve, then Man isn't worth saving; what we would have salvaged with his murder would no longer *be* Man, but something less wonderful, something hideous."

"I was wondering," Jason said reflectively, "if you would ever come to that conclusion."

CLASSIFICATION:
  TOP SECRET
AUTHORIZATION KEY:
  LAND SPIRIT
ACCESS KEY:
  BARBARA
NOTE TO GENERAL STOEHRMAN ON DEVELOPMENT OF THE GROUND-ATTACK HEAVY ORBITAL LASER (GHOL):
  There are considerable technical problems that arise in upgrading a HEXPLAT for attacking ground sites, but we believe these problems can be resolved. For one thing, the emission frequency must be lifted into the gamma ray range for effective penetration of shielded targets.

But the long-term outlook looks fabulous. Current estimates suggest that we will be able to focus the beam narrowly enough to destroy individual ships and aircraft, though perhaps not individual trucks and tanks. At the same time, between the direct effects of the ray and the residual radiation consequences, we should be able to "shotgun" and deposit 90% lethality levels against lightly protected targets in a 5,000-square kilometer area in six seconds. This is equivalent to incinerating all of Germany in three minutes with only two GHOL platforms.

"Some will not believe me when I say that we stand daily on the edge of the holocaust. What has saved us, they ask. And why won't it continue in the future, they demand." Max looked around the room at some of the prime offenders.

"Humanity is doomed because its vision is impaired." Jason started another diatribe.

"Do you really believe that, Jay?" Max really wasn't up to a battle this early in the morning. He looked at Jason: was even Jason really up to it? His smile was the same, the feverish energy still shone in his eyes. But he had become more pale in his three years as a senator. He was thinner. And the darkness that circled his eyes was deeper now, heavier with sorrow.

"Yes, Max, I really believe it."

Max was stunned; for the first time, Jason answered that question without frivolity. This was serious. Max spoke softly. "What's wrong with humanity's vision, Jay?"

"We have a planetful of people, many of whom are individually capable of planning carefully for twenty- and thirty-year periods—at least long enough to pay off a house mortgage—yet when they act as a group they can't plan for consequences just one year away. It's a classic case of two heads being half as good as one." He slapped his hand on the table, got up and paced back and forth across the kitchen. It was a different kitchen from the kitchen at which they first argued so many years ago. The table was less elegant, and the atmosphere was less homey; but it was home here in Washington nonetheless. It was gray outside, and the grayness leaked in through the window.

Max cleared his throat. "Is there some way we can beat that, to make people as smart collectively as they are individually?"

"I don't know!" For the first time, Jason seemed afraid and without an answer. "Our species is no better than the evolutionary forces that made it. Evolution too is shortsighted: every step that evolution takes must be an *immediate* improvement, standing on its own. Neither Man nor evolution could compete against even a mediocre chess player: neither Man nor evolution could make a bishop sacrifice, even if they *knew*, beforehand, that the sacrifice led to mate in two moves."

"As in the safety net program."

"Exactly." Jason shook his head. "Investment in new research is down to one ten-thousandth of a percent of gross national product. There were fewer new patents issued this year than any year since the nineteenth century. Ask any individual, and he'll tell you that without investment in new and better ways, our growing population will live deteriorating lives until, in desperate grabs for each other's wealth, someone starts the war that leads to the Final Confrontation. Any individual will tell you that there's no money for investment because ninety percent of all wealth goes into the maintenance programs of the social safety net." He threw his hands in the air. "But when that man goes to vote, he says, 'Yeah, but I want to get *my* share of the safety net before you get rid of it.'" Jason shook his head.

Max leaned forward. "But the Final Confrontation may not be too final, if we can hold off until we can get to the other planets. If we can spread mankind far enough, someone will survive."

Jason sat down on the edge of the seat. "Will they, Max? I've been thinking about this lately. It's so much harder to *create* than it is to *destroy*. That's the basic law of nature, you know: entropy. The total quantity of disorder in the universe always rises, any time you do anything. Entropy always sides with the man who wants to destroy beautiful things, as long as he doesn't try to put anything in its place. It's *always* easier to destroy; and as technology advances, the technology of destruction will continue to advance faster than the technology of creation, because entropy will help the destruction. Any technology powerful enough to transport a man to a safe place can produce weapons powerful enough to destroy him after he's arrived." He hit the table even as Max opened his mouth to contradict him. "Sure, sometimes there've been time lags, but the weapons always caught up, and as time goes by the speed with which they catch up will speed up. We can't outrun our own technology, Max."

"If we can hold out long enough, eventually we're bound to find a way to prevent war: a sociological solution. Then it won't make any *difference* how powerful our weapons are."

"But how long will it take us to get there, Max? Where are we going to get the time to wait?" Jason's hand slapped the table. "How do we persuade a society to take near-term action to solve long-term problems? *That* is our short-term problem."

CLASSIFICATION:
  TOP SECRET
AUTHORIZATION KEY:
  TAR BELL
ACCESS KEY:
  SERENDIPITY
  MEMORANDUM TO GENERAL BRADLEY ON DEVELOPMENT OF THE GRAVSHIELD ANTI-LASER DEFENSE
  Though theoretically feasible, the practicality of gravshield defenses for cities against GHOL platforms is nil. Several technological revolutions will be required to permit a shield generator to cope with the concentration of energy that a GHOL can achieve. We continue to investigate; the technology will certainly evolve, but it will probably be decades in development.
                    * * *

In his mind, Max answered the laughing ghost, who knew that this roomful of people could never make a decision to save tomorrow.

Jason, I know the answer. I know how to make people find a solution that will take years and years to implement. But God, Jason, it's hideous. Isn't there a better way?

The ghost did not answer.

"We have survived, sometimes because of skill, and sometimes because of luck. But more importantly, we have survived because some people have given their lives to guarantee our survival."

Jason's campaign speech ended. They hustled Jason off the platform toward the waiting helicopter, leaving Max to field the endless questions.

"Then tell us, Mr. Palmer, do you really think Jason Masino has a chance at the presidency?"

The questions came at Max from all sides of the throng that was mostly reporters. Max turned in the general direction of the question and chuckled. "Does he have a chance?! I pity his competition! And I urge them not to trap themselves into a debate with Jay on TV. If they do, Jason will rip them to shreds."

"Can we quote you?"

Max shrugged. That statement probably wasn't the most politic thing he had ever said, but one of the wonders of watching Jay run for president was that you didn't *have* to worry about every little word. Jason was the first candidate in decades who *was*, clearly, better than his opponents. "Go ahead and quote me. Why not?"

A different voice rose above the din from a different direction. "Mr. Palmer, as Jason Masino's foremost advisor, what role would you expect to play in the executive branch? Do you see yourself in a cabinet position?"

Of course, you still had to be a *little* politic, in any democracy. "That is entirely Jason's decision. I am an advisor only: I certainly wouldn't presume to second-guess his future decisions."

Max could see the helicopter's rotors whirling to takeoff speed; Jason was safely aboard. Max excused himself and headed for the landing platform, where another helicopter would arrive shortly to pick him up.

As he progressed through the crowd, his eyes were drawn to a large, curiously dressed young man, with a great overcoat too long even for him, the overcoat whipping in the wind. As Max watched, the man reached into his coat and pulled forth a short rocket launcher.

"No!" Max screamed, tossing people out of his way to reach the man.

The man calmly adjusted the sights, and Max could see him muttering to himself as he squinted to track the helicopter.

Didn't anybody else see what was happening? Where were the Secret Service people? Was this real?

The man nodded, leaning back a little deeper in preparation for the launch. "Stop!" Max yelled hysterically.

The man opened his other eye, startled, but as Max leaped for him he squeezed the trigger.

With a snarl Max chopped the man in the throat. As the man gurgled for breath, Max brought a rigid index finger up into the man's eyeball, thrusting his finger as deep as he could reach. The man thrashed raggedly, hanging from Max's finger. He fell away.

Max looked up to see a trail of whistling smoke reach the helicopter. A bright jet of fuel burst from its side. The helicopter lurched, then spun end over end until it reached the ground. A brighter jet of exploding pieces burst from the wreckage. Max ran toward it.

Some newspaper reporter, much too swift on his feet, ran up to parallel Max's running. "What if Jason Masino is dead, Mr. Palmer?" the man yelled. "What will you do?"

"I don't know," Max yelled back. "He can't be dead."

"But if he is . . ."

Max struck the man in the face and continued toward the wreckage.

What could he do? What could he do? The question pounded in his brain. The world: it was dying. Jason had seen it in all its details. Jason had understood the dangers as no other man ever had, and Jason had been afraid. Jason had been afraid that even he, Jason, would fail to save mankind. If even Jason had been afraid of failure, what other man could possibly succeed?

Yet somebody had to. And to have any chance at all of succeeding, somebody had to try.

Max held a press conference one week later. "There has never been a man as great or dedicated as Jason Masino, and perhaps there never will be again." He paused to get control of his voice, which still got away from him at times. "But the greatness of Jason Masino should not be allowed to perish just because the man himself is gone. It was his *spirit* that held his greatness, and that cannot be killed. His dreams, his hopes, his visions are *ours* now. We can still build a future as great as his greatest imaginings." He looked around the audience with a slow, determined gaze that would one day be famous. "Therefore, I hereby announce my candidacy for president. I can never be Jason Masino, but I can, with your help, be the implementor of his dream."

"But do we dare depend on skill and luck, and the sacrifices of a few rare men, forever?"

FROM: Carl Stroud, Chief of Simulations, Global Resource Analysis Center
Dear Max, Max read in the memorandum the day before he was to present his speech on the cancer cure. *I've been running scenarios frantically for the last three weeks. I guess you'd guess that.*

As you predicted, we cannot create a scenario for survival that includes a cure for mutant II cancers. Of course, you'd guessed that, too.

But in an effort to retune the simulation, hoping to find a technical flaw in our approach, I ran scenarios across the last decade, using real-world history as my input. Max, in fifty simulation runs, Man never survived our most recent ten years!

So I cursed and fumed, because of course we did survive (we did, didn't we? Sometimes I wonder) and I made debug dumps.

The simulation is good, Max—I knew that there had to be something wrong in the data. So I tweaked and calibrated.

I only found one adjustment that let mankind survive consistently: I inserted a leader-actor for America who was superhuman. It worked. The outputs stabilized on what the world's last ten years of history actually look like.

Max—that leader-actor was you!

We can survive, with you as president! Please, Max, sign that bill!

Max's eyes watered. *I wish I could, Carl.*

Perhaps Jason could have done it. Max could imagine Jason repealing the two-term presidency constitutional amendment. Max could imagine an immortal Jason, using the next generation of viral robotoids to keep himself young, successfully balancing, checking, and countering all the forces that tried to destroy Earth, for years without end.

But Jason wasn't available. And Max was running short on tools to use in the fight. Someday, he knew, Kiril would call Max's bluff—even if Max could retain power, which he could not. In two years his second term would end.

Who would be the next president? Max knew the leading contenders, perhaps better than they knew themselves. Most of them were honest, sincere men; but none of them met the requirements for world-savior.

Even Jason might have failed; even Jason never found a solution to the general problem: how do you make a society make a sacrifice today, when the benefit won't be seen for decades?

But Max had been given the answer—*a gift of the gods*, Max thought with near reverence, though he had long since lost faith in gods. But it was a gift so perfectly timed, it almost had to be supernatural. *Jason, did you somehow reach out of the tomb to give me this answer?*

Certainly not. Jason would have rejected an answer like this; it was a hideous answer. It was as if the answer really had been designed by darker powers. It was so hideous Max feared it even more than he feared the Final Confrontation.

"Are we such fools that we are willing to play games with the survival of the whole human race?!"

Max could give the foolish, impetuous, men-children of the world a message that even Jason couldn't deliver. Max could give them a message that would last decades; not because of his indisputable logic, or his silver words, but because of the last tool he had left with which to touch them, because of the last gift he could give them. It was a rare gift, that which he could give them, perhaps unique among gifts in being respected everywhere among the peoples of Man.

He could give them a martyr.

Max looked out at the throng of congressmen, now utterly silent, and looked out at the cameras, and the people all over the world, and raised the procurement bill once again into the spotlight. He ripped it to tiny, tiny pieces, there in the burning brilliance. "You have a great task to do, Men of Earth." For a moment Max felt the ghosts gather round him—to augment his strength this time, not steal it. "You have many problems to solve. You must build a defense against the current generation of hideous weapons, for weapons are dangerous as long as the unsane may obtain power. You must begin the birthright lottery in earnest, so that the unsane will find few followers unsane enough to follow. You must destroy the social safety net that has given you the security it promised, but has taken away the growth that was the original promise of America and the only true security available for Man. You must rebuild the space program, and its ships, and you must establish people in places of safety." He lifted his hands, and the shreds of paper scattered from the podium. "And you must never, never, think of saving lives today, when tomorrow is so far away." He bowed his head. "I thank you."

There was clapping, but it was perfunctory: the audience, the congress, was stunned into rare speechlessness. Max saw that even his fiercest enemies now looked at him with respect, transfixed as Jason might have transfixed them.

Max smiled bravely, shaking hands with a few as he proceeded to the door. Still his weakness didn't show. He climbed into the presidential limousine surrounded by well-wishers and flash-popping cameras. He pulled the curtains as the car swung into motion.

The trembling began. *"No, no,"* he moaned, curling into a foetal position, all alone with the ghosts. *"No!"* He coughed, the same hacking cough that had sent him to the doctor just three short weeks ago.

"What's the verdict, Dr. McFarley? Will I survive my cough?" Max asked playfully. He rebuttoned his shirt. It was cold in the doctor's office; but then, it's always cold in a doctor's office.

Dr. McFarley looked back at Max grimly.

The chill in the room deepened. "Is it bad?" Max asked, no longer playfully.

Dr. McFarley sat down next to him. "It's lung cancer, Max. Mutant II lung cancer."

Max's heart skipped, skipped, skipped. "It *can't* be!"

There was a long pause. The doctor cleared his throat. "You have nine months. Maybe a year." The doctor looked away. After a moment of meticulous study of his fingernails, he continued, still not looking at Max. "Only Steve Felman can help you now. I'm sorry."

A tear squeezed from his closed eyes. *"I want to live! Please,* let me live!"

The ghosts had no answer save silence.

The Gentle Seduction

In February of 1988, I held a quiet but nonetheless remarkable conversation with a close friend. She had many questions about nanotechnology, and I had many answers—answers that I had not even known I had, before she asked the questions.

What made the conversation remarkable, however, was my realization of the place our discussion held in human history. I saw how our casual exchange, still not complete when last I saw her, would unfold over the years. I witnessed the last words I hope she will one day speak, words that will at last draw our dialogue to its proper close. Those words, her final remark, are meant to be spoken ten thousand years from tomorrow.

For a month after our discussion a white-hot image of the future consumed me, growing inside, forcing me to let it out. Twice while driving down freeways I had to pull to the shoulder, stop my car, and copy down the passages that gripped my mind. Whole pages came out in photocopy quality. I hardly existed as a person; often I felt I was merely the instrument used by the story to create itself. I came to understand how a writer in earlier times might have believed that he was under a geas, that he was inhabited by another's spirit.

"The Gentle Seduction" itself has been accused of being a fantasy, so full of hope for man's future that any modern person (at least, any modern cynic) must surely reject it out of hand. But what man, two centuries ago, would have believed that one day we would totally eradicate smallpox from the earth? What man, just a few months ago, would have believed that common wisdom would be upended and that the Berlin Wall

*would come down? Perhaps at this moment more than
any other moment in history, people have the clearest
reasons to believe in a hopeful future.*

*The scientific underpinnings of the future described
in "The Gentle Seduction" are quite real. Astonishing
and unbelievable as that future is, the main reason we
may fail is if we fail to try.*

The Gentle Seduction

He worked with computers; she worked with trees, and the flowers that took hold on the sides of the Mountain.

She was surprised that he was interested in her. He was so smart; she was so . . . normal. But he was interesting; he always had said something new and different to say; he was nice.

She was twenty-five. He was older, almost thirty-three; sometimes, Jack seemed very old indeed.

One day they walked through the mist of a gray day by the Mountain. The forest here on the edge of Rainier glowed in the mist, bright with lush greens. On this day he told her about the future, the future he was building.

Other times when he had spoken of the future, a wild look had entered his eyes. But now his eyes were sharply focused as he talked, as if, this time, he could see it all very clearly. He spoke as if he were describing something as real and obvious as the veins of a leaf hanging down before them on the path.

"Have you ever heard of Singularity?" he asked.

She shook her head. "What is it?"

"Singularity is a time in the future as envisioned by Vernor Vinge. It'll occur when the rate of change of technology is very great—so great that the effort to keep up with the change will overwhelm us. People will face a whole new set of problems that we can't even imagine." A look of great tranquility smoothed the ridges around his eyes. "On the other hand, all our normal, day to day problems will be trivial. For example, you'll be immortal."

221

She shook her head with distaste. "I don't want to live forever," she said.

He smiled, his eyes twinkling. "Of course you do, you just don't know it yet."

She shuddered. "The future scares me."

"There's no reason to fear it. You'll love it." He looked away from her. His next words were bitter, but his tone was resigned. "It pisses me off that you'll live to see it and I won't."

Speaking to the sorrow in his voice, she tried to cheer him. "You'll live to see it, too," she replied.

He shook his head. "No. I have a bad heart. My father died young from a heart attack, and so did my father's father. If I'm lucky, I have maybe thirty more years. It'll take at least a hundred years for us to get to Singularity."

"Then I'll be dead before it happens, too. Good," she said.

He chuckled. "No. You'll live long enough, so that they'll figure out how to make you live long enough so that you can live longer."

"You're still only seven years older than I am."

"Ah, but you have your mother's genes. She looks very young."

She smiled, and changed the subject. "I'll have to tell her you said that. She'll like it."

There was a long pause. Then she confessed, "My grandfather is ninety-two, and he still cuts the grass every week."

Jack smiled triumphantly. "See?"

She was adamant. "I'll live to be eighty or ninety. I don't want to live longer than that."

"Not if you're crippled, of course not. But they'll find ways of rejuvenating you." He laughed knowingly. "You'll look older when you're sixty than when you're one-hundred-twenty," he said.

She just shook her head.

Another time, as they walked in the sun along the beach of Fox Island, he told her more about the future. "You'll have a headband." He ran his fingers across his forehead; he squinted as the wind blew sand in his eyes. "It'll allow you to talk right to your computer."

She frowned. "I don't want to talk to a computer."

"Sure you do. At least, you will. Your computer will watch your baby all night long. If it sees something wrong, it'll wake you." Wicked delight widened his smile, and she knew he would now tell her something outrageous. "While you're lying in bed with your eyes closed, you'll look at your baby through your computer's TV camera to see if it's something serious."

"Ugh."

"Of course, there's a tiny chance, really tiny, that an accident could scramble your memories."

The thought made her dizzy with horror. "I would rather die." She grabbed his arm and pulled him under the bridge, out of the wind. She shuddered, though unsure whether her chill came from the wind or the fear.

He changed his tack. Pointing at a scattering of elaborate seaside mansions across the water, he asked, "Would you like to live in one of those?"

She studied them. "Maybe that one," she said, pointing at a beautiful old Victorian home. "Or that one." She pointed at another, very different from the first, a series of diagonal slashes with huge windows.

"Have you ever heard of nanotechnology?" he asked.

"Uh-uh."

"Well, with nanotechnology they'll build these tiny little machines—machines the size of molecules." He pointed at the drink in her hand. "They'll put a billion of them in a spaceship the size of a Coke can, and shoot it off to an asteroid. The Coke can will rebuild the asteroid into mansions and palaces. You'll have an asteroid all to yourself, if you want one."

"I don't want an asteroid. I don't want to go into space."

He shook his head. "Don't you want to see Mars? You liked the Grand Canyon; I remember how you told me about it. Mars has huge gorges—they make the Grand Canyon look tiny. Don't you want to see them? Don't you want to hike across them?"

It took her a long time to reply. "I guess so," she admitted.

"I won't tell you all the things I expect to happen," he smiled mischievously, "I'm afraid I'd *really* scare you. But you'll see it all. And you'll remember that I told you." His voice grew intense. "And you'll remember that I knew you'd remember."

She shook her head. Sometimes Jack was just silly.

They fell asleep in each other's arms often, though they never made love. Sometimes she wondered why not; she wondered if he also wondered why not. Somehow it just didn't seem important.

He seemed so at home in the deep forest, he so clearly belonged on the Mountain, she first thought they might stay together forever. But one day she went with him to his office. She watched as he worked with computers, as he worked with other people. He was as natural a part of their computer world as he was a part of her Mountain world.

Working in that alien world, he was a different person. In the woods, he was a calm source of sustaining strength. Here, he was a feverish instructor. His heart belonged to the forest, but his mind, she realized, belonged to the machines that would build his vision.

One day he received a call. A distant company gave him an offer he could not refuse. So he went to California, to build great computers, to hurry his vision to fruition.

She stayed by the Mountain. She walked the snows, and watched the birds fly overhead. Yet no bird flew so high that she could not climb the slopes of Rainier until she stood above it.

He would come to visit on weekends sometimes, and they would backpack, or ski cross-country. But his visits became less frequent. He would write, instead. That too decreased in regularity. One letter was the last, though neither of them knew it at the time.

A year passed. And by then, it just didn't seem to matter.

*　　*　　*

She married a forest ranger, a bright, quiet man with dark eyes and a rugged face. They had three small children and two large dogs, friendly dogs with thick soft fur. She loved all the members of her family, almost all the time; it was the theme that never changed though she thought about different things at different times.

Her children grew up and moved away.

Erich, the beautiful red chow, went to sleep one night and never awakened.

A terrible avalanche, from a seemingly safe slope, fell down the Mountain and buried a climbing team, her husband among them.

Haikku, her mighty and faithful akita, whimpered in his old age. He crooned his apology for leaving her alone, and that night he joined Erich and her husband.

She was eighty-two. She had lived a long and happy life. She was not afraid to die. But she stood outside in the snow and faced a terrible decision.

Overnight, a thick blanket of new white powder had fallen, burying her sidewalk. Standing in the snow, she stared at a mechanical beast her children had given her years before. It represented one possible choice.

In one hand she held a shovel. In the other hand she held a small capsule. The capsule was another gift her children had given her. They had begged her to take it. Until now, she had refused. The capsule represented another choice.

Her back was aching. It was an ache that sometimes expanded, shooting spikes of pain down her legs. Today the pain was great; she could not shovel the sidewalk.

The mechanical beast was a robot, a fully automatic snow remover. She could just flip a switch and it would hurl the snow away, but that seemed grotesque; the noise would be terrible, the mounds of thoughtlessly discarded snow would remain as an unseemly scar until late spring.

She opened her hand and looked at the capsule. It was not a pill to make her younger; that much her children had promised her. They knew she would reject such a thing out of hand. But the millions of tiny

machines tucked inside the capsule would disperse
throughout her body and repair every trace of damage
to her bones. They would also rebuild her sagging
muscle tissue. In short, the pill would cure her back
and make the pain go away.

The thought of all those little machines inside her
made her shudder. But the thought of the automatic
snow remover made her sick.

She went back inside the house to get a glass of
water.

In a few days her back felt fine; her healthy muscles
gave her a feeling of new vigor, and the vigor gave rise
to a yearning to go out and do things that she had not
considered for many years. She started to climb the
Mountain, but it was too much for her: she huffed and
puffed and had to go home. Annoyed, she went to the
drug store and bought another capsule, one that re-
stored her circulatory system and her lungs. Her next
assault on the Mountain carried her as far as she dared,
and the steady beat of her heart urged her to go on
despite the crumbling snow.

But she was getting increasingly forgetful. Things
that had happened years earlier were clear in her mind,
but she could not remember what she needed at the
store. One day she forgot her daughter's telephone
number, and found that she had forgotten where she
had misplaced the phone book. The store had another
capsule that tightened up her neural circuitry. After
taking it, she discovered a side effect no one had bothered to mention. The pill did not merely make her
memory effective again; rather, it made her memory
perfect. With a brief glance through the pages of the
phone book, she found she no longer needed it. She
shrugged and continued on with her life.

One day as she skied across the slopes, a stranger
passed her going the other way. He was tall and rugged, and he reminded her of her husband. She was
annoyed that he did not even look at her, though she
had smiled at him; when she looked in the mirror upon
returning home, she understood why. She was ninety-

five years old; she looked like an old woman. It was ridiculous; fortunately it was easily fixed.

When she turned one-hundred-fifteen she stabilized her physical appearance. Thereafter, she always appeared to be about the age of thirty-two.

She still owned the snug little house she thought of as home. But she slept more often in the tent she carried in her pack. Built with nanomachined equipment, the pack was lighter than any other she had ever owned, yet it was impossibly strong. All her tools performed feats she would once have thought miraculous, and none weighed more than a pound. She lived in great comfort despite the inherent rigors of the glacier-crusted slopes.

One day, she was climbing along the ancient trail from Camp Muir toward the summit, crossing the ridges to reach Disappointment Cleaver. As she stepped over the last ridge to the broad flat in front of the Cleaver, she saw a man standing alone. He was staring up the steep ice flows overhead. He stepped backward, and backward, and turned to walk briskly in her direction. She continued forward to pass him, but he cried out, "Stop!"

She obeyed the fear in his voice. He paused, and his eyes came unfocused for a moment. He pointed to the right of the ridge she had just crossed, a fin of rock rising rapidly along the Mountain's edge. "Up there," he said. "Quickly." He broke into a hobbling run across snow that sometimes collapsed under his heavy step. She followed, her adrenalin rising with her bewilderment.

A massive *Crack!* filled the air. Far above the Cleaver, an overhanging ledge of ice snapped off and fell with an acrobat's graceful tumbling motion to the flat where they had just been standing. The mass qualified as a large hill in its own right. When it landed it broke into a thousand huge pieces. Some of the pieces ground each other to powder, while others bounced off the flat, down another precipice of several thousand feet, to crash again in a duller explosion of sound.

The ice fall was an extraordinary event to witness

under any circumstance; the narrowness of escape from death that accompanied it overlaid the experience with a religious awe.

She heard the man panting next to her. She turned to study him more carefully.

He was unremarkable for a mountaineer; his lean form supported long straps of hard muscle, and the reflected sun from the glaciers had given him a coffee-colored tan. Then she noticed the sweatband across his head. It was not just a sweatband: she could see from the stretch marks that a series of thin disks ran across within the cotton layers. She realized he was wearing a *nection*, a headband to connect his mind with distant computers.

She recoiled slightly; he smiled and touched his forehead. "Don't be too upset," he said, "my headband just saved your life."

She stuttered. "I wasn't upset," she said, though she knew that he knew she was lying. "I've just never seen one up close before."

It was true. Her grandchildren told her that nections were quite common in space, but on Earth they were almost illegal. It was socially unacceptable to wear one, and when the police saw a nection-wearing person they would use any excuse to hassle the individual. But there were no specific laws against them.

When her grandchildren had told her that *they* wore headbands all the time, she had tried only briefly to dissuade them; she had spent more time listening to their descriptions of the headband's capabilities. Her grandchildren's descriptions sounded considerably different from the list of dangers usually described on the news.

The man who had saved her life watched her for several more seconds, then apparently made up his mind about something. "You really ought to get one yourself, you know. Do you realize how dangerous this mountain is? And it's getting more dangerous every year."

She started to tell him that she knew perfectly well how dangerous it was—then stopped, thinking back over the years, realizing that it *had*, by gradual degrees, grown worse every year.

"With my headband, I see things better," he explained. "I confess I don't understand why very well—I mean, it doesn't affect my eyesight. But I notice more things about what I see, and I can get a view of what the extra things mean—like how that piece of ice would fall, and more or less when."

She nodded her head, but her mind was distracted. The Mountain *was* changing! The Mountain *was* getting more dangerous! The rapid alternation of clear, sunny days with cool, misty days had become more vigorous over the course of the last fifty years, leading to more weak layers and ice faults. She had never really noticed until now.

Then the full impact of her savior's words struck her—she held her hands to her throat as she considered how her husband had died. She realized that, with a nection, his death could have been prevented.

She smiled at the man. They talked; she invited him to dinner at Alexander's.

When she returned home, she started searching through electronic equipment catalogs. If she bought one mail order and wore it only while hiking, there was no reason for any of her friends ever to know.

It was a simple white headband, soft absorbent cotton. She slipped it on her head, expecting to feel something special, but nothing happened. She started to clean the house, still waiting for something to happen. It never did. Eventually she sat down and read the instructions that had come with the headband.

The instructions told her to start with a simple request, and to visualize herself projecting the request at her forehead. She projected the request, "two times two?" just above her eyes. Nothing seemed to happen. She knew the answer was four.

She tried again, and this time she noticed a kind of echo—she knew the answer was four, but the thought of the answer came to her twice, in rapid succession.

The next time she tried it, she noticed that the echo seemed to come from her forehead.

Next she projected a request to divide 12345 by 6789. She didn't know the answer—but wait, of course she did, it was 1.81838. Of course she didn't know the answer to many decimal places—but as she thought about it, she realized the next digit was 2, the next was 6, then at an accelerating pace more digits roared from her memory—she shook her head, and the stream stopped. She took the headband off, shaking a little. She didn't try it again until the next day.

A week later, she hiked past Camp Schurman and peered up the slope. She projected her view of the slope through her forehead to study the patterns of snow and ice.

It did indeed look different as she looked at it this way. She had a sensation similar to that of looking at the edges of a cube on a sheet of paper: at one moment, the lines formed a cube with the top showing. The next moment it was an alternate cube with the bottom exposed. She could flip the cube, or at least the way she looked at it, at will.

In the same manner she could now see patterns of slippage in the layers of ice crystals; then she would flip the image and it was just snow, the beautiful work of nature that she had loved all her life.

For a moment she wished she could see it from above as well—and her heart skipped a beat as the wish came true. Suddenly she was looking down from a great height. She saw the long curves of shadows across the snow from high above, and she saw the shorter but distinctive shadow of a woman with a pack standing on the snow field. She threw the headband to the ground even as she realized what she had just seen: a view of the Mountain from a satellite passing by.

She stared at the white headband, almost invisible in the white snow, for a long time. She felt distaste, wonder, fear, and curiosity. Curiosity finally won out. She twisted the headband back on. She blinked her mind's eye, blinking from her own eyes to the satellite's eyes and back again, a moment's taste of the new sensation.

Vertigo struck her. Though the satellite was interesting, it was not comfortable. She would not look at the world from a satellite's height often, but it was yet another life-saving form of sight: From a distance, it was easy to spot a depression in the snow that might signal an underlying crevasse, even though the depression was too shallow to be seen close up. Such crevasses were invisible until one stepped through to a long fatal plunge to the Mountain's heart.

The headband was so clearly a life-saving tool; why were people so set against it? Why did some of her friends support laws proscribing it?

It didn't make any difference; she had no need of it except here on the Mountain.

Though the fight over the headband's legal status did not at first interest her, it became an increasing impediment to her life. The headband was quite useful in a number of ways; though each individual use was trivial, in sum they qualitatively affected her life. She stopped tracking her checkbook; it was all in her head, all the transactions, the current balance, and even the encumbrances. When she awoke in the morning she could turn on the coffee pot if she wanted to, without getting up.

She wore her headband while hiking, and while working around her house; but she dared not wear it to work. One day an ecologist asked her a question about the marmots that inhabited the park. She grew angry as she had to manually root through the computer systems trying to find the answer, for she knew that the answer was available for the mere thinking about it if she could wear her headband. That night she stopped at the drugstore and bought two more capsules.

She swallowed one. This capsule was nastier than the others she had taken in earlier years. Before, the nanomachines she had swallowed had gone through her body, fixing what was not right, then flushing themselves out again. But the machines in this one would build, just under her forehead, a subcutaneous nection.

The other capsule would dissolve the nection away if she decided she didn't like it.

When she awoke the next morning she was very hungry. She felt her forehead, but there wasn't anything there.

The next morning she felt her forehead again, and it was . . . different. She looked in the mirror; with the flickering double vision of her eyes and the analysis from her forehead, she could see on the one hand that she looked the same as always. Yet on the other hand, there were curves there she hadn't noticed before. When she went in to work, one man complimented her on her new hair color.

No one else commented until her boss arrived. When he entered the reception area and looked at her, his eyes lit up, and he laughed.

She looked at him with mild annoyance. Then she noticed, again with her double vision, that there were very shallow curves in *his* forehead.

He came up close, and put his finger to his lips. "Listen," he said.

She listened. As she concentrated, she heard soft murmurs in the background; as she focused on the murmurs, they grew louder, until she could hear that he was speaking—but not with his lips, not through her ears. She heard him through her forehead. "Welcome to the gang," he said. "Isn't it great fun, joining a rebellion? I haven't had this much fun since I was a teenager."

They both broke into laughter. Everyone else in the room wondered what the joke was about.

She talked to her children, and her children's children, more often now; though they were spread from Mars to Mercury, they were but a thought away. It surprised her to realize that the simple process of dialing the number, and the uncertainty of whether or not she would get through, had often put her off even though the cost of calling had plummeted in recent years till it was virtually free.

She became increasingly comfortable with her distant grandchildren. Through visual links like the one she had with the satellite, they took her on outings into the stunning naked beauty of their home planet Mars. When they asked her for the hundredth time to come for a visit, she agreed.

In her youth she had ridden trains across the country. She had expected the space trip to be the same, but it was not. The ship was far more comfortable than any other vehicle she had ridden; it was more comfortable than her own home, though she still did not quite like it as well.

When she arrived, she found she loved to hike across the plains and the canyons of an unknown planet. She walked amid forests of alien trees, related to the Earthly trees from which they had been shaped, yet different. Comparing the lands of Mars to the lands of Earth reminded her of watching the sun set two days in a row: though the outcome was the same, the process was nevertheless different. The strange wilderness yielded for her new kinds of solitude.

She came to know her grandchildren's children for the first time. Before, these children had represented an unspoken, uncomfortable complication in her thoughts of Mars. They were *different*. They were of her blood, but not in the manner of normal children. They had been genetically engineered.

Her grandchildren had designed them, giving them a parent's loving care long before they had ever been conceived. Only the best characteristics of her family had been passed on; she did not know how the other aspects of these radiantly happy children had been chosen. They were very different from her, but not quite alien. With time, she learned to love them as they loved her.

One day they went on a longview picnic. First they walked to the high edge of a deep canyon. She looked over the rim. The height was not great by comparison with the distances in space she had traveled to come here. Yet *this* distance impressed her. It impressed her because she could appreciate it: thousands of tiny twists and angles of rock acted as signposts, allowing her to mark off the immense distance in tiny steps. She shook her head, smiled, and stepped over the edge.

Together with her family, she descended gently on suspensors; their picnic basket and wine glasses descended with them, on suspensors of their own. They watched the planet come up to meet them as they dined and chatted.

The discussion turned to the family's upcoming expedition to Jupiter. They had asked her several times to come along, but she had refused. Now they asked her again. She watched the extraordinary scenery float past her and considered the question one last time. A trip to Jupiter would have been all right if it could have been like Mars. But it could not, and that was both the attraction and the horror.

Though humanity had made Mars Earth-like, they could not do the same for Jupiter. Jupiter's methane oceans simply were not amenable to terraforming. No one could go there in person.

To see Jupiter she would, in a sense, have to leave her body. Oh, she wouldn't have to leave it very far; indeed, in one sense she would stay with her body on Mars throughout the journey. But just as she had seen Rainier through the satellite's eyes rather than her own, just as she spoke to her friends with her headband rather than her voice, now she would have to use her headband for all her senses.

And the machine would not merely *replace* her sight, her hearing, her touch, her smell—it would *transform* them. Ordinary sight and sound did not work on Jupiter; for each of her old senses a new one would be substituted. She would see ultrasonic vibrations; she would smell ionic changes. For all intents and purposes, she would live as a being designed for the comforts of Jupiter's titanic gravity well.

Of course, she would not be marooned there: she could leave at any time.

The pleasure of her experience on Mars made her

confident; the quiet exhilaration of the longview picnic made her bold. She agreed to go along.

For a moment it was dark, a moment too short to launch the panic she held in a trip-wired readiness. Then there was light, a confusing light that seemed oddly related to the sounds that joined it. She held up her hands. They were metal, and she looked at them in alarm. She closed her eyes, and it was better.

The strange sounds took on rhythm. Instinctively she turned toward them, and her back feet rotated, propelling her closer. When she felt she was too close—she could smell the source of the sounds now, a tangy, pleasant odor—she opened her eyes. Studying the shape as it wavered before her, seemingly separated by shimmering air, she realized it was another robot like herself. Indeed, she recognized it: she was looking at her granddaughter.

She looked around and had a sudden overwhelming sensation of immensity.

The hugeness of space had seemed dwarfed by the height of the Martian canyon, for she had been able to comprehend it through the tiny weathered etchings of rock she could peer at in the distance. Here on Jupiter her comprehension was even greater, for her senses ranged distance with new clarity. The ultrasonic echoes told her how far it was to each whorl of current she could see; she could see to distances very great indeed. It made her think of the way she had felt as a child, looking across a vast Kansan plain for the first time. It seemed as if infinity was right *there*, within easy reach. She reveled in it for a moment, then stepped out.

She was back in her own body again, sitting on Mars.

She dipped back in for ten minutes and stepped out again. Next she went in for half an hour. Then an hour.

She had sworn that she would not stay on Jupiter for more than an hour at a time; a longer stay required mechanical operation of parts of her body while she was away. But once she became so absorbed in exploring the Jovian landscape, she stayed for an hour and a half. The maintenance machines disconnected themselves before she returned, and their intervention didn't seem to make a difference. So she stayed longer.

Jupiter, she found, was an astonishing world, truly alien from all she had experienced before. And the new senses she acquired through her new robot required extensive exploration of their own. It was all incredibly novel, and she realized she would need at least a year to explore.

The linkage between her mind on Mars and her robot body on Jupiter had delays; to have a completely satisfying experience, she would need a temporary residence that didn't require such a commute.

So a small cylinder, somewhat smaller than a Coke can, was launched at an asteroid that had been parked in orbit around Jupiter for this purpose. As the billions of robots from the cylinder swarmed across the asteroid, transforming it into a marvelous home, she boarded another ship. It seemed silly to spend any of her transit time stuck in the confines of her cabin; she went to Jupiter for the duration. She intended to return to her own body when it arrived in orbit.

But when it arrived, she was busy. She was learning about a new robot designed for the frozen world of Europa, with another whole new set of senses, new novelties to explore. She left her body in storage for a short time longer.

A year passed. And by then, it just didn't seem to matter.

A bubble hung poised on the edge of the solar system, a sphere pockmarked with thousands of holes, each hole the width of a pin. A bolt of light struck the sphere, a bolt powered by kilometers of molecular mirrors near the orbit of Mercury.

The bubble seemed to explode as thousands of needles leaped from their cradles, driven forth by tiny beams of laser light, slivers of the titanic bolt from the Sun. The needles accelerated away from the bubble for years, till their speed reached close to that of light. Thereafter they drifted ever outward.

Upon occasion, a needle approached a star. The needle would shift, to ensure a close passage. If planets or other items of note beckoned, the needle would swoop in, on a tight spiral to oblivion: its billions of nano-machines would break apart at the touch of an asteroid, and build anew. Where once there had been a needle, now there would be a bubble, and a molecular mirror, and thousands of needles that would explode out and travel forever.

But in addition, the nanomachines in that system would continue to build. They would build machines and living flesh well suited to the conditions of the planet. And then the nanomachines would come back together into a single structure—not a needle now, but a communication bubble. Through the bubble and its instantaneous communication she could live across space. She could dwell at home near Jupiter yet roam among the stars.

She was often one of the first humans Called to newly open planets. Her wisdom from Earth, her expertise from Jupiter, these made her invaluable as an explorer and a guide. As she had swam within the methane oceans, so now she swam in carbon dioxide atmospheres, or flew through liquid mercury. She imprinted herself upon organic synapses and silicon circuits light-years from home, and lived in many places.

Mentally she was bigger now than she had been at twenty-five. The meaning of complexity had changed for her; she understood the laws of physics with the same simple clarity with which she understood the rules of checkers. She could build a starship as easily as she could pitch a tent.

Her mind had grown and spilled from the confines of her original body. She could easily dedicate a part of her mind to each of several different tasks. Notably she could lead several different groups, touring several different planets, all at the same time.

But of all her new capacities, it was the boundless singing that filled her with wonder.

She was not an introspective person; she did not often think about her own past, and how strange she might have found her present. But when she did think such thoughts, the singing amazed her most of all.

When she was twenty-five she had liked vintage Fleet-wood Mac. At one-hundred-five, she had admitted her growing fondness for Beethoven. Pressing two hundred, she had fallen in love with Monteverdi. In later centuries she had come to appreciate the double beat of the Echoes of Saturn and the operas of Ro Biljaan. Patterns so subtle that the unaugmented human mind could not even sense them filled her with ecstasy.

She no longer listened to one or the other of these musical masters at rare opportunities. Rather, they all played, all the time, each in a different subliminal part of her mind. They gave to her a rippling sensation of love that never quite went away. The constant under-tone of the singing formed the theme that bound her mind together, no matter how many different things she might do at one time.

As the melodies suffused her mind they intermin-gled, sometimes playing upon one another in a concor-dance of point and counterpoint. Once, such a duet evoked from several masterpieces a harmony, which surged to drive the cadence of a grander euphony, that captured and empowered an even greater polyphony, filling her mind with a symphony of symphonies. And on a thousand planets, with a thousand bodies and a thousand voices, she leapt in the air and filled the sky with lilting laughter, a chorus of joy that spanned the arm of a galaxy.

Returning to ground on those scattered planets of distant stars, she felt surprised by her outburst. She marveled at herself. In her childhood she never would have laughed in such a way. She had once been so quiet it had been easy to think she was shy. The millen-nia had changed her, and she was delighted; how sad it would have been, never to express one's deepest joy!

Still, she was a woman of simple tastes. In earlier times some would have called her sturdy. Others might have called her childlike.

Yet these were not fair descriptions; better to think of her in the terms of ancient mythology. She was an elemental, almost a force of nature, with a core of simplicity that mocked overeager acceptance yet offered adaptability, that rejected panic yet always guaranteed caution.

Her elemental qualities were vital, humanity had come to realize. Though the needles traveling through space never found other intelligent beings, they had found scattered remains of what had once been intelligence. Other species had come up to Singularity and had died there.

Some had died in a frenzy, as the builders of new technologies indulged in an orgy of inventions, releasing just one that destroyed them all. Others had died in despair, as fear-filled leaders beat down the innovators, strangling them, putting the future beyond their grasp. The fear-ridden species settled into a long slide of despair that ended with degenerate descendants no longer able to dream.

Only those who knew caution without fear, only those marked by her elemental form of prudence, made it through. Only humanity had survived.

And humanity had not survived unscathed. Terrible mistakes had been made, many lives had been lost. Even millennia later there still remained a form of death—or perhaps not death, but a form of impenetrable isolation. The dreams could become too strong, so strong that the individual lived in dreams always, never reaching out to touch reality. Many of her friends from the early millennia had lost themselves to these enchanted infinities leading nowhere.

She did not fear such dream-bound death. Seeing the span and deep intensity of her own dreams, she could almost understand those who wrapped themselves within and disappeared. But the new things humanity found every day were just as wonderful. The volume of space touched by the needleships grew at a geometric pace, opening hundreds of star systems. Even on days when few strikingly new systems were found, there were new planets, constructed by artists, awaiting her exploration. And the new things she learned in the realm of the mind matched these treasures and more.

Someday, she believed she, too, would dream an

endless dream. She did not want to live forever. But the beginning of that dream was far away.

The new meaning of death was complemented by a new meaning of life. This new meaning was extremely complex, even for her; life dealt with wholes much greater than the sums of their parts. But she understood it intuitively—it was easy to distinguish an engineering intelligence, good only for manufacture, from a member of the community, even though that member might once have been just an engineering intelligence as well. New members of humanity usually came to life this way: an intelligence designed as a machine or an artwork expressed a special genius, a genius that deserved the ability to appreciate itself through self-awareness. When this happened, the psychological engineers would add those elements of the mind needed for life.

In this manner her great-great-grandchildren had been born. Her great-grandchildren had envisioned them, giving them a parent's loving care long before they had even been designed. Only the best characteristics of the minds of her family had been passed on to them. They were very different from her, but not quite alien. With time she learned to love them as they loved her.

The day came to say goodbye to her oldest friend. With her wonderful old Earth-born body, she returned to Earth to hike Rainier one last time: Rainier, whose surface lay so cold and eternal, was boiling within. With dawn, she knew, the boiling fury would break through, in the greatest volcanic event in Earthly centuries. She stood at the summit the day before the end and surveyed the horizon. Her feeling of appreciation grew till she thought she would burst. This was home in a sense few others could now understand.

She descended. A marmot met her on the way down; she swooped him into her arms and carried him to safety, though he fought her and cut her and it seemed her bleeding would never end. Still, the marmot could not prevent her from saving him.

She had considered saving the Mountain itself; she

could, she knew. She could lace the Mountain with billions of tiny tubes, capillaries so small no living thing would notice. She could extract the heat, cool the heart.

But to deny the Mountain its moment of brilliance seemed not right: perpetual sameness was never right, though change might often be wrong.

So the next day, she and the marmot watched the eruption from afar. It was as beautiful as she had expected. And though the aftermath was gray and dreary, she knew that in a very short time the marmot's children would return to the Mountain, and a new kind of beauty would grow there.

Nor was the Mountain truly lost. Even as her Earthborn body returned to her asteroid circling Jupiter, she built an exact replica of the Mountain: an image, molecule for molecule, of the Mountain's surface the day before it erupted. When her body returned, she joined the Mountain, to walk there forever, in another part of her eternal dream.

Haikku, her loyal companion, was long dead; but she traced the descendants of his descendants. She arranged a mating. A new pup was born with Haikku's genes, in the image of Haikku. And so Haikku2 came to join her on the slopes of Mt. Rainier, on the orbit of Jupiter.

One day two needleships met in space. This was not uncommon; needles from different launchers often crossed paths and were easy to spot, with the hundreds of kilometers of molecular sensor webs they spun.

But this meeting was special, for one of the needles had no link to a human. It belonged to aliens.

Aliens! Wild hopes and wilder fears rocked the human community. She watched the hysteria calmly, confident it would pass and wisdom would rule.

The needles passed one another, too fast to meet. They swerved in long, graceful arcs to a distant rendezvous.

A sense of calm, and prudence, returned to humanity. They selected a contact team to break off and meet the aliens.

The needles closed. In their last moments they danced

in a tight orbit about one another, a dance of creation: for though the needles died, a bubble formed where they met—a communications bubble.

The two communities, human and alien, reached out. They touched—but the touch was jarring. Bafflement ruled. The deadlock of confusion ensued.

She watched with interest. She felt sorrow that it was not going well, but her confidence remained.

Then from the contact team she received a Call. They needed her; they needed her elemental resilience and adaptability.

But in needing her elemental nature, they needed more than she had ever given before. They did not need the thoughts or calculations of her mind: they needed the basic traits of her personality, the very core of her being. To reinforce the team, she would have to expand her communication channels, open them so wide that what she thought, they would also think; there would be no filter protecting her internal thoughts. Far worse, what others thought, she would think; there would be no filter protecting her internal memories. It seemed to her it would be easy for her memories to get scrambled; she would rather die. And so for the first time in millennia, she was afraid. The team asked others of the community that held her special strength to come with them instead; they, too, were afraid.

Meanwhile humanity was failing. The anticipation, the yearning, the hope for contact with new beings developed a tinge of desperation.

They showed her how easy it was to open the channels of her mind—but more, they showed her again and again how easy it was to close them. They did not believe they would need her for long, thousands of milliseconds at most. They guaranteed she would be fine afterward. Reluctantly, she agreed.

She opened her mind; the shock of raw contact stunned her. A moment's near-panic like that of her first exploration of Jupiter returned.

And then she was moving, there within the team, and she grew accustomed. The sensation reminded her of jumping into a mountain lake—the cold plunge that blotted out all thought, the sluggish warmth of her muscles responding, the passing of the coldness from her awareness as she concentrated on the act of swimming. She swam among the members of her team.

Here she found many tasks to perform, the calming and soothing of a myriad of panicked souls as they plunged into the ice-cold lake of alien minds. She became the muscle that supplied the warmth, that allowed the awareness of the team to move beyond the cold, to swim.

As the team responded, the sensation of cold changed to one of warmth, a merry warmth, and she was a bubble floating on a wide, warm ocean, clinging and bouncing with the other bubbles, some friends, some human, some alien. Then they were bubbles of champagne, effervescent, expanding and floating away.

She floated to a greater distance; they no longer needed her; she was free to go. She closed the channels to her mind with slow grace, as would a woman walking from the sea through the sucking motions of the surf. She found herself alone again.

In those first moments of solitude, being alone seemed unnatural, as unnatural as the communion had seemed earlier; she felt the coldness that comes after a swim, when breeze strikes bare skin. She shuddered.

Was she still herself?

Of course you are. You are all you have ever been, and more.

The answer was her own, but it had once belonged to another person. For a moment she stumbled; perfect memory did not guarantee instantaneous memory, and she was seeking thoughts from her infancy. Then she remembered.

Jack!

She remembered, he had known that she'd remember.

What had happened to Jack?!

Could she have missed him all these years? She initiated a search of the community, but knew its futility even as it began; he could not, would not have remained hidden.

Yet her need to know him again grew stronger as she opened more of her long unbidden memories.

She searched swiftly back through the annals of history. Her search slowed suddenly to a crawl as she reached the early moments of Singularity: before the dawn of civilization, records had been crudely kept, with links insufficient to allow swift scanning. An analogy to cobwebs made her smile for a moment.

Only a handful of machines maintained this ancient knowledge, older machines in older places. Her search plunged to the surface of Earth. There, in a place once called California, all the remnants of prehistoric information had been collected. But it had not been collated. It would take much time to find Jack in this maze. But she had the time.

A salary report from a corporation of long ago . . . an article on accelerated technology's impact on the individual . . . a program design with its inventor's initials . . . and suddenly she found him, in a richly interconnected tiny tapestry within the sparsely connected morass. She read all of it, rapidly, as if she were inhaling fresh air after too long a stay in a stale room.

Jack had saved her life, she realized. The capsule she had taken so long ago to heal her backache, that first step on the road to the life she now knew, was his—he had designed the machine that designed the machine that designed that pill. It turned out that he had learned much from her on that day when they walked quietly amidst the lush green wilderness. And it had taken her all these millennia to learn what he had known even then.

From her, Jack had learned the importance of making technology's steps small, making its pieces bite-size. He had learned this as he watched, in her disbelieving eyes, her reaction to the world he had planned.

For those who loved technology and breathed of it deeply, small bite-size steps were not important. It would have been easy to callously cast off those who did not understand or who were afraid. But Jack had thought of her, and had not wanted her to die.

Reading these glimpses of his past, she grew to know

Jack better than she had ever known him in life. With her growing wisdom, she soon understood even the clarity of organization that encompassed this lone swatch of antiquity: the clarity, too, was of his making. He had believed in her. He had believed that one day she would search for him here. And he had known that, when she arrived, her expanded powers of perception would enable her to understand the message embodied in the clarity, and in all his work.

I loved you, you know, Jack told her across the millennia.

She wanted to answer. But there was no one to hear.

It hurt her to think of him lost forever, and she had not felt hurt for a very long time. Feverish, she worked to rebuild him. The Earth-bound computers gave her all the help they had to give, every memory of every moment of Jack they had ever recorded. She traced her own memories, perfect now, of every word he spoke, every phrase he uttered, every look he gave her in their long walks. She built a simulation of him, the best and most perfect simulation she could build with all her resources, resources far beyond those of a million biological human minds. It was illegal to build a simulation such as this, one of the few laws recognized by the community, but this did not deter her.

The simulation looked like Jack; it talked like Jack; it even laughed like Jack. But it was not Jack. She then understood why it was illegal to build such a simulation; she also understood why it was not a law that needed to be enforced: such simulations always failed.

Jack was gone.

What could she do?

What did she have to do? Suddenly she realized how silly the simulation had been: how could she have hoped to get closer to him, than to live his vision of the future?

Only one small action, one appropriate action, remained that she could perform. She could remember forever.

And so, just as a part of her lived forever on the Mountain, just as a part of her lived forever singing, so now she maintained a part of her that would spend all its moments remembering her earlier moments with him. She became in part a living memorial to the one who brought her here.

And though no one could hear, the essence of her memory would have been easy to express: *Jack, I love you.*

She turned her attention to the living members of humanity. There were many other places in the community, she realized, where the techniques she employed in contact with the aliens could help; there were many places where they needed her elemental force invested with the fullness of such expanded communion. She was eager to go. But still a question remained.

Would she still be herself?

The answer Jack had wrought so long ago welled up from within, her rightful inheritance of his understanding. Part of the answer, she knew, lay within another question:

Are you still yourself, even now? Were you still yourself, even when you were twenty-five?

She looked back with the vision that perfect memory brings. She remembered who she had been when she was twenty-five; she remembered who she had been when she was just ten. Amusingly, she also remembered how, at twenty-five, she had erroneously remembered her thoughts of age ten. The changes she had gone through during those fifteen years of dusty antiquity were vast, perhaps as vast as all the changes she had accepted in the millennia thereafter. Certainly, considering the scales involved, she had as much right today to think of herself as the same person as she had then. Expanded communion would not destroy her; she was her own bubble no matter how frothy the ocean might become.

At least, this first time she had remained her own bubble. Would it always be so?

She dipped into communion, and withdrew to ask the question. She found the answer, and it was good. She dipped again, for a longer time; and still the answer was good, perhaps better.

She dipped much longer still and asked one more time. This time she understood. The answer was so simple, so glorious, so joyful, that she did not ask the question again for a billion years.

And by then, it just didn't seem to matter.

Hypermedia and the Singularity

Hypermedia is one of the technologies that will take us into the future of "The Gentle Seduction."

I wrote this article about hypermedia just before writing "Seduction." I had come to realize about a year earlier that hypermedia was going to be a very important technology, and I had set out to make myself an expert in it. I went so far as to write a hypermedia version of one of my novels.

Despite this, I did not realize at the time just how central a role hypermedia would play in my own future. Xanadu, which gets a one-paragraph mention here, received financial backing from Autodesk (one of the quietest but biggest software companies in the world) the month after I completed "The Gentle Seduction." A month after that, I met the Xanadu team for the first time. This team was composed of some of the smartest, most talented people I had ever met. But though they were very bright, none of them had ever managed a software engineering project of this size to success.

I, however, had.

So from Xanadu I received a call. They made me an offer I could not refuse. So I moved to California, to build great software, to hurry my vision to fruition.

You see, I do not merely wish to write about Singularity. I wish to experience it.

I cut a number of passages from the final drafts of "The Gentle Seduction" because, in the end, there was no place to put them. One of those was the following, an observation she makes shortly before entering expanded communion:

"The population had stabilized at just a bit over a

trillion individuals. A trillion seemed about the right size for a community: large enough to allow some diversity, but small enough so that you could get to know each member of the community quite well."

With the right balance of enthusiasm and prudence there's no reason we can't be members of that community.

I hope to meet you all there, on the other side of Singularity. I'm looking forward to it. I hope you are, too.

Hypermedia and
the Singularity

-*A Child Dying of Adrenoleukodystrophy*
-*Sanskrit literary style*
-*Buttons to begin an Article on Hypermedia
  and the Singularity*
-*Flight in Information Space*
-*Definition of Hypermedia*
-*Road Map*
-*Definition of Singularity*
  *TO SEE ONE OF THESE SECTIONS, JUST POINT
AND CLICK*
*(oops—this is a paper document, not a computer
document).*

Road Map

This article is about the relationship of the technology of *hypermedia* to the approaching time of technological *Singularity*. There are a lot of ways we could start this discussion; up above, in italics, you see a list of the starting places that I considered before writing. The article, as it now stands, has the following layout:

1) *the list of buttons (the section in italics at the beginning of the article),*

2) *the road map (that's where we are now),*

3) *a major section to define hypermedia, with sidesteps to consider:*
   a. Sanskrit literary style

b. *flight in information space*
c. *hypermedia art, and*
d. *issues of hyperstyle*

This lengthy discussion of hypermedia is followed by:

4) *a shorter definition of the Singularity, and*

5) *a discussion of how the Singularity and hypermedia are interrelated. This discussion of interrelationships wraps up with an example of how hypermedia will accelerate our approach to Singularity: the story of the child with adrenoleukodystrophy.*

Finally, the article ends with:

6) *a discussion of the next steps in hypermedia development, who is taking those steps, and where it will lead.*

Definition Of Hypermedia

Hypermedia is much easier to use than to define. In one sense, you have already seen a definition of hypermedia in the early layout of this article, though in practice it's difficult to grasp without a computer-based example.

Hypermedia is the child of *hypertext*. Ted Nelson coined the term hypertext in the sixties and defined it simply as "nonlinear writing."[1]

Linear writing has been mankind's standard for millennia. One alphabetic character follows another, one word follows the next, building sequential sentences, paragraphs, and chapters. The writer designs his document for a reader who is *trapped*: the writer assumes that the reader only has the ability to go forward one step, or backward one step, but nowhere else.

Of course, we have had limited forms of nonlinear writing mixed in: the table of contents and the index are modern (though primitive) nonlinear writing tools—though slow, they do help the reader skip to the sections of the document of most interest to him.

Sanskrit Literary Style

Nonlinear writing goes back at least as far as Sanskrit. With one of the stylistic approaches used in Sanskrit, the document's opening passage was a series of one-line descriptions of what would follow. The next section contained a paragraph for each one-line description; the next section devoted a chapter to each paragraph description. This design encouraged the reader to skim only as far as he needed to go, reaching into the deep, extensive discussion only as a last resort. The article that you are reading now, with the list of items as its first paragraph, is organized in a way similar to those ancient Sanskrit documents.

Newspapers also encourage nonlinear reading—the headers for the different articles appear in a bolder, larger style, which the human eye can automatically pick out (the powerful perceptual computers behind our eyes that do this automatic selection are a major reason why people find Macintosh-like, icon-oriented software easier to use—using imagery, we can grasp many features without recourse to our conscious reading abilities). After the eye has picked out an interesting article, the first journalistic paragraph summarizes the whole article—only the most in-depth reader must go beyond that first paragraph.

But this is exactly where newspapers fail—the in-depth reader must page back and forth from the front to the far back just to read a whole article.

And while the newspaper frustrates the in-depth reader, the textbook with its index frustrates the skimming reader, who has no real way of perusing just the summaries. The nonlinear extensions to linear books fail because paper is inherently a linear medium. Enter the computer.

Modern desktop and laptop computers have grown powerful enough so that they can give us a truly nonlinear medium for document presentation. No longer must we ask the question "should I set my article up like a newspaper, for skimmers, or should I set it up like a book, for detailed readers?" Set it up for *both*.

With either Guide[2] or Hypercard™[3] (the two widely-accessible hypermedia tools at the time of this writing), the table of contents can be a series of one-line entries that are treated as *buttons*: when the reader points at the entry and clicks, the computer brings forth the detailed backup information in the twinkling of an eye. This detailed information can in turn contain other buttons.

Buttons do more than link a brief description with its detailed explanation. Buttons can link multiple, partially related items. A paragraph describing a disease might have a link to a separate paragraph about the cure, which might be linked to a list of related medicines, each of which is linked to a manufacturer, each of which is linked to a list of products, each of which is linked to a list of diseases for which that product is the cure. In this sense hypermedia offers instantaneous references, akin to the suggested reading lists tagged on to encyclopedia articles.

The elements of a hypermedia document do not all have to be text—they can also be pictures, sounds, and full-color videos and animations. For many documents, the table of contents should not be a list of chapter names, it should be a *picture*. A car repair manual, for example, might have a picture of the car as its first item. The mechanic would point to the part of the car he needed to know about, which would give him a closeup view and a short textual description of what it is and how it should work, with a few extra pictures (through other buttons) of typical forms of wear that would call for replacement. The mechanic would zoom in again and again until he found the specific part to replace—and he would then press the button that runs a short video sequence showing how to remove the old part and install the new one (for a simple example of zoom, see Figure 1). With these links interconnecting pictures, text, and video sequences, we have true hyper*media* (for the syntactically finicky, the word "hypermedia" is a singular group noun, unlike the word "media," which is the plural of medium).

The links inside a hypermedia database allow the

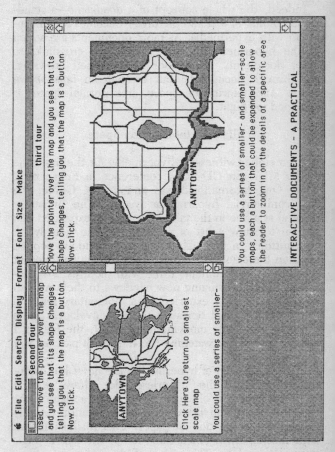

Figure 1. Zooming in on a map. Clicking on the major waterway in the small left-hand map pops the larger, detailed map at right. This shot was taken from the examples supplied with Guide, from Owl International.

hypermedia reader (a hyperreader?) to leap through a document as quickly as today's linear reader can turn a page.

Indeed, the whole concept of a *document*—a stand-alone volume of text and pictures—becomes less meaningful with hypermedia. As more documents are added to the hypermedia database, with rich crosslinks to other documents, the reader finds himself browsing, not through documents, but through an *information space*. And information space, like normal space, is designed for flight.

Flight In Information Space

I remember witnessing hypermedia for the first time at the Microsoft CD-ROM conference in February of 1987. Owl International was announcing Guide, the first commercial hypermedia system. The presenter pointed at a line in the table of contents, expanded that section to show a list of subsections, and quickly hit four buttons. In an eyeblink, four new windows popped open on the computer screen, each showing a different section of the document, three with pictures. He continued to click, bringing new windows to the fore with new information. I experienced a momentary sense of disorientation. That sensation quickly developed into a sense of breathless movement, of *flight*, the feeling I usually reserve for watching the stars flash past on Star Trek.

With the advent of hypermedia, the quiet but explosive revolution of the "paperless office" draws close at last. The paperless office received much acclaim years ago, but the vision faded as computerization actually *expanded* the creation of paper. This disillusionment with the paperless office came about through a tragic misunderstanding. The vision of the paperless office, however dim, was correct.

When a new technology is introduced, people's natural first reaction is to use the technology to do the same old tasks more quickly. Thus people first used computers to create paper—and they succeeded beyond their wildest nightmares. Computers have dramatically increased paper production—but they have not, by any current measure, increased productivity. This is about to change, and will change with ever greater speed for the next decade as we build tools that make computerized data more effective than paper counterparts.

Hypermedia is a key ingredient for creating that effectiveness (though other ingredients are still necessary to match the merits of paper, namely durability, portability, and resolution; these, too, will be solved, but that's another article). Once data is put into a hypermedia-based information space, it is easier to retrieve and easier to read than it would be on paper. People will not want to print hypermedia documents: the translations will lose so much value, writers will instead give readers access on the computer. As all the worker's data begins to show up in the same format, interlinked with all the other data so that he can toggle back and forth at the touch of a finger, productivity will start to rise.

Alas, in our modern society, improved productivity no longer guarantees improved performance. Bureaucrats can always increase the demand for paperwork (or computerwork) to negate any increase in productivity. Technological solutions to more classical problems have not faced such an unbounded obstacle. Not even the government will move a city ten times as far away from you just because your new car goes ten times as fast. Bureaucrats can, however, require ten times as much paperwork once you get there. Consider the effect of our recent tax simplification: it made bestsellers out of thick books about taxes. It seems clear that bureaucrats *will* require even more paperwork.

Hypermedia Art

Besides giving a big boost to the paperless office, hypermedia will give rise to a new form of art to stand beside painting, cinematography, and literature. Indeed, hypermedia may become the culmination of these separate lines of artistic expression, as it weaves the now-disparate genres into a stunning tapestry. In a hypermedia novel,

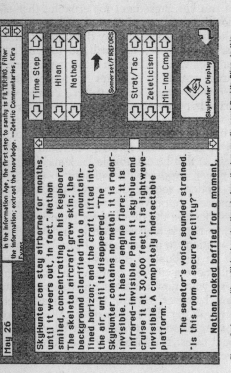

May 26

In the Information Age, the first step to sanity is FILTERING. Filter the information; extract the knowledge. --Zetetic Commentaries, Kira Evans

SkyHunter can stay airborne for months, until it wears out, in fact." Nathan smiled, concentrating on his keyboard. The skeletal aircraft grew skin; the background clarified into a mountain-lined horizon; and the craft lifted into the air, until it disappeared. "The SkyHunter contains no metal: it is radar-invisible. It has no engine flare: it is infrared-invisible. Paint it sky blue and cruise it at 30,000 feet: it is lightwave-invisible. A completely indetectable platform."

The senator's voice sounded strained. "Is this room a secure facility?"

Nathan looked baffled for a moment,

Figure 2. A scene with multiple character threads from the hypermedia novel David's Sling. In this scene, Nathan Pilstrom describes the Sling Project to Iilian Forstil. The reader can follow Iilian or Nathan through the story by pressing the arrow buttons (forward/backward) arrow buttons next to their names. By pressing the arrows labeled as Time Steps, the reader can read the story in pure chronological order (following the sequence of scenes found in the paperback version of David's Sling. Additional buttons allow the reader to skip to just those scenes that discuss Zetetic philosophy, or to scan discussions of America's military-industrial complex. The "SkyHunter Display" button takes the reader to an animation of the SkyHunter. The animation enacts the sentence, "The skeletal aircraft grew skin; the background clarified into a mountain-lined horizon; and the craft lifted into the air, until it disappeared." This novel was built in Hypercard™, from Apple Computer

the reader has much more control over which pieces he reads—he might choose to follow a single character through the course of the story one day, and a different character the next. *Winds Of War* by Herman Wouk might be much more readable in this fashion. *David's Sling*, the world's first hypermedia novel, allows the reader to follow not only characters but also subject topics through the period of time chronicled by the story (see Figure 2).[4]

Following multiple character threads in this manner opens up even more unusual possibilities. The reader may revel in reading a single scene from several different points of view—Roger Zelazny's *Amber* series offers some interesting hypermedia possibilities in this regard. And the reader would benefit from hypermedia when engaging Heinlein's future histories just because he could finally *find* things.

In SF novels in particular, hypermedia gives the writer a way of sharing his mountains of background material with the interested reader, without imposing on the tight construction of the plot. *David's Sling* has a separate section of Blueprints for those who desire more technical information about the Sling Hunters (see Figure 3). Indeed, in *David's Sling* a reader skilled in the arcane mysticisms of modern management can read the entire story with the Program Evaluation and Review Technique (PERT), in a series of PERT charts (see Figure 4). This is almost certainly the first time that management science has been intentionally used for artistic expression (though from what I have seen, management science is often used unintentionally to create works of fantasy).

Future hypermedia art will require ever more innovative intertwining of graphics with text and animation. The development of truly great hypermedia documents—whether they be pure art, pure information, or a weaving of the two—will require an array of skills that includes illustration, writing, cartoon creation, and cinematography. The most urgently needed skill will be a new one that might best be called *link architecture*: the design of sets of links that offers the reader intuitive flight

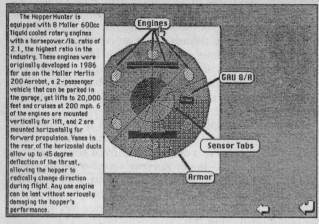

The HopperHunter is equipped with 8 Moller 600cc liquid cooled rotary engines with a horsepower/lb. ratio of 2.1, the highest ratio in the industry. These engines were originally developed in 1986 for use on the Moller Merlin 200 Aerobot, a 2-passenger vehicle that can be parked in the garage, yet lifts to 20,000 feet and cruises at 200 mph. 6 of the engines are mounted vertically for lift, and 2 are mounted horizontally for forward propulsion. Vanes in the rear of the horizontal ducts allow up to 45 degree deflection of the thrust, allowing the hopper to radically change direction during flight. Any one engine can be lost without seriously damaging the hopper's performance.

Figure 3. Part of the description of the HopperHunter from the Blueprints section of David's Sling. When the Engines button is pressed, as it is in this shot (the cursor is denoted by the small hand), an information box pops open to give a textual account of the engine components. In densely packed images, the clutter of the separate buttons could be avoided by making each component of the image "live". Just clicking in different regions of the image would pop information about the region or would zoom in on it. In such active-component pictures one major issue is guaranteeing that the reader recognizes all the buttons; existing conventions for denoting the presence of a button are inadequate.

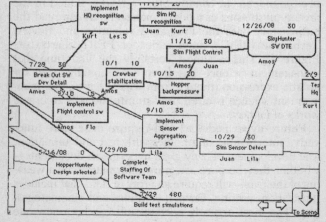

Figure 4 PERT chart view of the middle of the novel. Those familiar with PERT charts will recognize that Amos is a critical resource on the critical path. This dependency has grave consequences in the outcome of the story.

paths. Whereas modern writers only have to worry about the transition from one paragraph to the next paragraph, the hypermedia author will consider dozens, perhaps even hundreds, of such transitions. Part of skillful design will be to keep the number of transitions, the number of branches, small, while still guaranteeing fast and understandable traversal of the whole document.

Fortunately, these designers will have hypermedia style guidelines on-line to assist them.

Hyperstyle

Some discussion of hyperstyle here may help illuminate the meaning of hypermedia.

Hypermedia designers, just like ordinary writers, would do well to start with the *Elements Of Style* by Strunk and White. As Strunk would say, "Omit needless words. Omit needless words! OMIT NEEDLESS WORDS!"[5]

Items in hypermedia should generally omit even *more* words. In linear literature, one must occasionally summarize terms and ideas from other chapters to guarantee that the reader has the proper context for the current discussion. In hypermedia, however, the author would simply plunk down a button linked to the explanation, leaving the reader the choice of plunging ahead or getting a refresher.

Bold writing, another major thrust of *Elements of Style*, also becomes easier. In linear writing, how can one address complex problems that demand complex analysis? Throughout history, speakers who have strived for accuracy have labored at a disadvantage: Men of reason find that true statements require so many qualifiers that their sentences turn to quicksand—and their audiences turn to stone. Meanwhile the short-sighted sloganeer can stir the soul with his quick, simple, wrong answers.

Given hypermedia, reasonable men can make bold, powerful statements, slugging it out slogan for slogan with fanatics—with one telltale difference. Numerous buttons will surround the reasonable man's bold statement, allowing skeptics to branch to more careful supporting arguments.[6] Writers will thus discourse in a way similar to the way we teach physics to children. All of our early education, about little electron and proton spheres whirling around, *is a pack of lies*—but the lies are eminently satisfactory unless you need that deeper understanding, easily achieved in later courses.

This hypermedia approach to bold writing, incidentally, could create a new legal problem if widely used. We might want to consider laws prohibiting the paper printing of hypertext without the author's explicit permission: such printing, which would rip the bold statement from its supporting links, could supply the unscrupulous opponent with the ultimate tool for quoting out of context.

Critics repeatedly cite two fears of hypermedia. First, they fear that you won't be able to find things, i.e., that the information will be "hidden" someplace. A related fear is that you won't be able to find *yourself*, i.e., that you will become lost in the maze of buttons. The sense of disorientation I felt upon first witnessing hypermedia, that sense of "Star Trek Warp Speed," is only pleasant for people on a lighthearted romp; it is catastrophic for people trying to do their work.

The worries about hidden information are probably overblown. There are two causes for this fear. First, one can make legitimate complaints about hidden information in most of today's hypermedia documents. All of today's hypermedia authors are necessarily novices; they are still experimenting with what works and what doesn't. Hiding information behind concealed buttons is cute, fun, and alluring for the beginning writer; but those writers that respect their readers will quickly outgrow the urge to play games. Hidden buttons may have a place in hypermysteries, but nowhere else.

The second cause of hidden information phobia is that people compare hypermedia to a hypothetical *perfect* system, rather than to an everyday *paper* system. Even with hypermedia assistance you'll occasionally lose items. You'll know that a critical datum resides *somewhere* in that information space, but you'll know you'll never find it.

But you'll find it more often in information space than in paper space. In my office, with two huge filing cabinets bursting with linear paper, information loss occurs *every day* (my file cabinets are organized a lot like Heinlein's future history). If I could reduce the loss rate to once a month, it would transform my life (of course, people who organize their file cabinets more carefully have fewer problems in paper space. But people who arrange their buttons more carefully will also have fewer problems in information space; they will literally retrieve items in the blink of an eye).

The other oft-cited fear, of losing *yourself*, is considerably more serious. Disorientation is virtually universal for people encountering a hypermedia document for the first time. A key to successful hypermedia construction will be the creation of the *road map* that shows the reader how the pieces are interconnected. The road map will be the visual presentation of the link architecture mentioned earlier. A sample road map can be seen in Figure 5.

Novices in hypermedia design often predict that the road mapping problem will be solved automatically, that future hypermedia presentation systems will magically build the maps themselves. After all, the computer knows where all the links are, why not let the computer build a composite picture of them all? Of course, the computer *can* build such a picture, and automatic map-building will supply a useful tool to the developer of an information space. But there are thousands of possible map designs for a given information space, based on different graphic arrangements of the objects in the database. Only a human being with a talent for extracting order from chaos can draw an *understandable* map, with subject-oriented symbology, with straight paths for the "main highways" that readers will often take, and with meandering branches for the links that are less traveled.

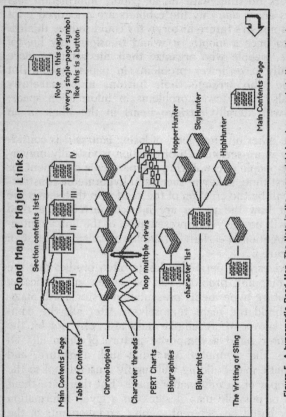

Figure 5. A hypermedia Road Map. The Note in the upper right-hand corner alerts the reader to the presence of buttons he might otherwise not recognize; these buttons support "teleportation", in that you can leap to other parts of the document through the map itself. The design of effective maps is a fine art that will see much evolution in the coming years.

In large information spaces, the maps themselves will have maps showing their interconnections, in a manner analogous to maps in an ordinary atlas. The best road maps will never be more than one button away, no matter where you are in the information space. They will always have a small dot inside, showing YOU ARE HERE. And these maps, unlike ordinary geographic maps, will support *teleportation*—if you see a place you'd like to go, just point, click, and prepare for landing.

These map buttons, and all the buttons binding the information space together, will give the reader unprecedented control over his own exploration. Because the reader will have choices of what to read next, hypermedia literature will be *interactive* in a way that no current form of art can equal (with the exception of computer games, which have not yet been recognized as art).

Earlier, I mentioned an analogy between hypermedia links and the suggested reading lists in the encyclopedia. Anyone who has run such a series of links knows that it can be fun, even with slow, finger-based indexing. But it can also be frustrating. Hypermedia will bring the fun back into learning again.

Definition Of Singularity

I hope I've succeeded in defining hypermedia. Our next topic, as you may recall from the road map at the beginning of this article, is the technological Singularity. "Singularity" is the term first used by Vernor Vinge[7] to describe the result of an exponential increase in technological sophistication. As the rate of technological advance rises beyond the point where normal human beings can comprehend it, mankind will encounter problems and solutions that cannot even be understood, much less described, in today's context. The people who enter the epoch of the Singularity will find all their material needs fulfilled. They will also be effectively immortal. Looking back from their present, they will consider the concerns of our generation (such as wars, environmental pollution, and bureaucracies) to be appalling yet quaint, just as we might view the concerns of stone-age hunters. By analogy, we, today, can understand the problems beyond Singularity to the same extent as the prehistoric hunter can understand our problems: how would you explain the idea of "cutting red tape" to a Cro-Magnon?

Those of you who have been reading *Analog*'s editorials and fact articles have encountered the idea of Singularity several times. One of the transformational upcoming developments is nanotechnology. With trillions of self-replicating nanorobots scattered through the solar system, we can build machines and products sufficient to fulfill all imaginable material desires (though we will surely imagine outrageous new material desires once nanotechnology starts pouring forth this cornucopia).

Alas, there's one little problem: there are limits to growth in the rate of improvement in technology. People who predict exponential growth for systems are almost always wrong. In practice, systems tend to follow S curves: after a period of exponential growth, some limiting factor intercedes and constricts the growth to asymptomatically approach an upper bound (See Figure 6).

For technological progress, the limiting factor is the human mind. As the velocity of change increases, we humans, who are developing that technology, spend increasingly more time just learning recent technology, leaving us less time to create even better technology (I myself read twenty or more magazines a month, but I churn out about four articles a year). As the complexity of the tasks increases, there will be fewer of us who can understand it well enough to make the next improvement.

A nanotechnology spaceship factory will require the careful orchestration of thousands of *kinds* of nanorobots in a harmonious collusion. This problem is tantamount to building a complete ecosystem of organisms, with the constraint that the ecosystem not only sustain itself but also create a complex machine. Who among us—what thousand-man team among us—has the requisite set of skills to set up this extraordinary symphony?

We know the answer in a vague way. "Computers," we wave our hands, "will augment our minds in con-

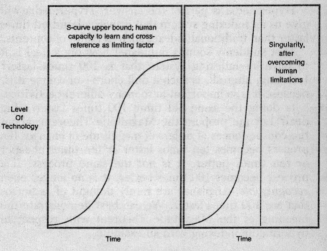

Figure 6. Exponentially growing systems generally encounter a limiting factor that tapers down the exponential behavior, causing the system growth to actually follow an S curve. Even if we overcome human limitations, the level of technology will eventually hit some kind of limiting factor--but not till long after we have altered our capabilities beyond current comprehension.

structing these systems." Yes, they will—but how? Word processors won't make the difference. Not even the sophisticated simulation tools used to design aircraft today can make the whole difference—we need to be able to design something worth simulating before we can check it out.

Relationship Of Hypermedia
and Singularity

Hypermedia is part of the answer. Hypermedia will give us an indexing system that is over a hundred times faster than traditional indexes such as tables of contents.

That suddenly sounds mundane: how big a deal is it to have an indexing system that is 100 times faster? Indexing, after all, is such a dull chore—of course it is, because it is so important to so many different activities.

Is doing the same old thing 100 times faster a big deal? Let me propose the Magnitude Theorem, about the consequences of orders of magnitude of change: If a process becomes ten times faster or ten times cheaper or ten times better, it is *not* the same process. If a process becomes 100 times better, it is no longer even *recognizable*. Airplanes are rarely thought of as horses that are 100 times faster. We can best demonstrate the meaning of the Magnitude Theorem with respect to hypermedia indexing with an example.

A Child Dying Of
Adrenoleukodystrophy

In November, 1987, *Newsweek* ran an article about a heroic couple. Their child had a very rare disease, adrenoleukodystrophy, known as ALD. The disease was characterized by the accumulation in the blood of very long-chain saturated fatty acids, known as VLCFAs. The VLCFAs attacked the nervous system, leading to death in a few years.

ALD had no known cure; the doctors threw up their hands and went on to assist others whom they knew how to treat. Most parents would have thrown up their hands at that point as well. But this couple did not surrender so easily.

They started their own research, and soon found that the scattered researchers on ALD had never met. So they convened a meeting of all the ALD researchers in the world. None of these men had any solutions either—at least, none that they could implement in less then ten years, using advanced genetic engineering. But one researcher had found, in test tube experiments, that monounsaturated fat, oleic acid, reduced VLCFA production.

So the couple gave up their jobs to pursue a cure for ALD. Their research became more intense, this time searching for a company that could produce oleic acid in a purified form.

After finding a company that could manufacture oleic acid, after testing it for toxicity, they started giving their son oleic acid. It reduced the levels of VLCFAs—but not enough. The couple realized that, to make further progress, they needed to understand *why* oleic acid helped, so they could develop something even better.

Again, research. With months of effort, including the finding of an article from a Polish medical journal, they developed a theory about oleic acid's success. Comparing and crosslinking accounts of animal experiment successes with the kinds of chemicals used in those experiments, it seemed that *monounsaturated* long-chain fatty acids monopolized the elongation process, blocking production of the toxic *saturated* VLCFAs.

Research! Now they needed the longest-chain monounsaturate they could identify—the longest one that was not toxic. Erucic acid, from rapeseed oil, was a long chain indeed. But it caused heart disease in animals. More research! Animals, they learned, metabolize erucic acid differently from humans; no heart disease or any other problem in humans had ever been identified.

And research. They had to find a company that could purify the oil sufficiently to make it useful. Again, after a long search, they found one.

When at last they could treat their son with erucic

acid, his VLCFA levels dropped to normal in three
weeks. Unfortunately, it had taken years for the couple
to complete the long search—the long cross-indexing of
existing information—to find the cure. Their son was
already in a coma. At the time of this writing, it was
unclear whether he could recover.

Is it obvious how hypermedia could have affected
this effort? If databases on ALD, biochemistry, molecular structures, chemical manufacturers, and ongoing research activities had been interlinked in a hypermedia
information space, the effort that took these people
years could have been completed in a few months (See
Figure 7 for a picture of a "Hypermall," where future
searches for such cures might begin).

Those parents could have saved the life of their child.
Even more incredibly, they could have saved the life of
their child *cheaply*—without sacrificing their own lives
to the effort. Their search for a cure could have been a
modest activity, rather than a heroic event.

With hypermedia information spaces, this could open
up a breathtaking alternative for those of us faced with
seemingly insurmountable problems: *if no one else has
a cure, OK, I'll invent one! If no one else has a device,
OK, I'll invent one!* With hypermedia information spaces
at our disposal, our ability to keep up with the technology explosion will itself explode.

Next Steps In
Hypermedia Development

Putting all the world's data into an information
space would be a huge undertaking—just digitizing it
would be an enormous task, and beyond that is the
effort of putting in the crosslinks, the hypermedia buttons. Putting the world's knowledge into hypermedia
might become the titanic yet vital project for the information age that the transcontinental railroad's development was for the industrial age. Building information
space will give us the same increase in speed and power
for information movement that the railroads gave us for
material goods.

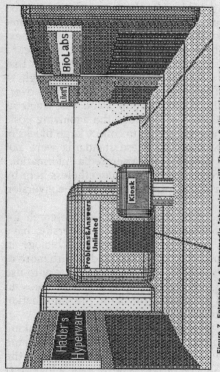

Figure 7. Entrance to a hypermedia "shopping mall". Though 2-dimensional road maps work well for many purposes, 3-dimensional metaphors offer the reader even more intuitive explorations of information space. This demonstration of tomorrow's hypermall was constructed using a 3-D design tool; it literally allows the designer to roam the corridors at will. Entering the Problems&Answers store (by clicking on the entranceway), the reader finds problems tacked on the bulletin board; one of those problems is a request for a cure for ALD. The reader can enter the Library to search for reference material, and use the Bio Labs to conduct experiments. If the reader needs services not available in this mall, he returns to the Problems&Answers store to post his own problems for outside assistance. He might, for example, ask for a chemical company that can refine oleic acid. In this manner the store acts as a connection to electronic networks and bulletin board services. The Kiosk, which has a map of the mall, doubles as a teleporter.

Several organizations are working toward the building of a global information space, albeit slowly. Apple Computer is probably the leader in the use of hypermedia on personal workstations, having introduced Hypercard, the most-raved-about hypermedia product in history. At its first public presentation, it received a standing ovation from the audience.

Both Apple and Microsoft, the two principal drivers of personal computer technology, have made major commitments to the optical storage devices needed to inexpensively store hypermedia databases. At last year's Comdex, Kodak displayed an optical disk juke box that could store half a *terabyte* of information, enough to store a century of *Scientific Americans*, 400 times over.

The rise of digital information standards, such as Postscript and SGML, will reduce the agonizing costs now incurred by anyone trying to collect large blocks of data from diverse sources. These standards were not designed as data formats for hypermedia information, but their widespread adoption will nonetheless help by creating a smaller set of formats from which conversion will be necessary.

Researchers at IRIS, the Institute for Research for Information and Scholarship at Brown University, have built curriculum materials for English and biology in their own hypermedia system, Intermedia, with more to follow. Key goals include the building of easy-to-use tools for creating information spaces (called webs in Intermedia), and to allow growth of the information spaces without bound (see figure 8).[8]

Perhaps the most visionary hypermedia undertaking is the Xanadu project, started by Ted Nelson (the same Ted Nelson who coined the term hypermedia in the first place).[9] The Xanadu project is developing a hypertext publishing network capable of interlinking millions of documents for thousands of users. Xanadu is also building several examples of front ends, or user interface software, to this information space for personal computers such as the Macintosh, and the IBM PC; their long term plan is to support third-party front end developers.

Xanadu incorporates many significant features beyond the basic hypermedia concept. Xanadu will maintain version control of all the documents in its information space. Links to one version of a document are also present in all other versions (as long as any of the linked data is still present). Thus the reader may trace the evolution of a concept. It also allows the original author to update and correct his work, based on the comments and criticisms others have leveled at his document (and which have been attached to his document by later readers).

The basic links in a Xanadu information space are two-way, i.e., when a link is installed, it puts a button at both ends, allowing the reader to go in either direction (which is considerably different from Hypercard and Guide). Thus when an author inserts backward references to earlier works, the system automatically creates *forward* references. This will fulfill the scholar's greatest fantasy, giving him a bibliography that lists not only material that predates an article, but also a bibliography of all the works created *later* (several years ago, *Analog* published a story about a thiotimoline-operated typewriter. This typewriter could print material from the future, offering a similar forward referencing capability; the idea was hysterically funny because it was so self-evidently impossible. I would have added a reference here to the issue of *Analog* that has the story—but the effort to find it is overwhelming, until we get *Analog* into hypermedia).

Xanadu even has a reasonable answer to the question, "How does the author get paid?" The creators of Xanadu database material (and anyone can be a creator here) will receive royalties based on the number of times their material is accessed; the reader will be charged based on the number of kilobytes of data he reads.

Even the Library of Congress is exploring the application of optical media in its quest for self-improvement. Anyone who has ever attempted to use the Library will appreciate their sense of urgency: the card catalog is not a boxful of index card racks, it is a series of rooms,

full of boxes full of index card racks. A subject such as
"Advertising" sprawls across half a dozen racks. Stoic is
the researcher who selects a handful of books from that
mammoth collection, necessarily at random, then waits
several hours for retrieval—only to find that these weren't
quite the books he had in mind.

As information spaces like the Library of Congress
get linked up, new commercial enterprises will arise
that blend a bit of the editor's role, the publisher's role,
and the reviewer's role. How will the average reader
separate the wheat from the chaff? Part of the answer
will be that respected reviewers and editors will con-
struct link-sets that point out all the documents that
they thought were excellent.

Other value-added retailers will build unique, cross-
pollinating link sets that highlight the interrelationships
between items with no visible connection. Harmonic
oscillators from physics have applications in fields from
molecular biology to cosmology; a unilateral pull-out of
Soviet forces from Europe several years ago, heralded
by some news people as an overture of peace, turned
out to be a preparatory step for the invasion of Afghani-
stan a few months later—long after everyone had forgotten the connection.

A link-set spanning just the history of the United
States might save us from the great danger to technology that I alluded to earlier: the danger that, as our
ability to process paper increases, bureaucrats will increase the amount of paper. One set of buttons that I
am personally eager to insert into an American history
information space is a set of links connecting govern-
mental regulations with the consequences of those
regulations—*all* of those consequences. In the early
days of railroads, short-haul passengers felt outrage that
the railroads charged almost as much for short local
runs as they charged to go the long distance from New
York to Chicago. These angry citizens put the railroads
under government regulation, and this fixed the problem: the long distance fares were increased. [10] This might
sound like a strange fluke—but the same thing happened when government took regulatory control of the

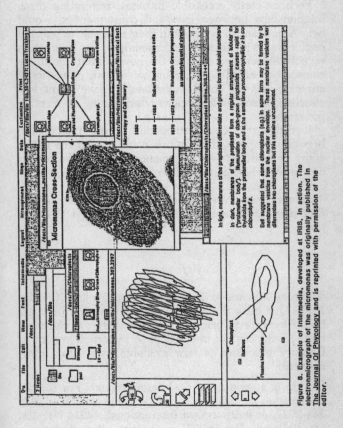

Figure 8. Example of Intermedia, in action. The electronmicrograph of the micromonas was originally published in The Journal Of Phycology and is reprinted with permission of the editor.

airlines. The future is all too predictable for those who remember the past—for those who have a rich set of interconnections showing the relations between those past events.

Perhaps easily accessible linkages, reiterating these relationships between laws and consequences, would help Americans to understand their vital role as cultural engineers. With such an understanding, our interaction with bureaucracies such as the government could become more rational. We could make institutions more effective—or we could *intentionally* make them less effective, based on a deeper understanding of effective government.

Just this one clear articulation of the relationship between people and institution could pay for the entire effort of building our information space. Who knows where we might go from there?

Author's Note: Needless to say, this document was first drafted in hypermedia, then translated to linear form.

References

[1]*Literary Machines*, Theodor Nelson, Project Xanadu, 1987. This book discusses hypertext from the perspective of hypertext's originator, and as such is as close to a bible as one can get in the field. A hypertext version of Literary Machines is now available from Owl International.

[2]Guide is a product of Owl International. For further information contact Ed Taylor or Jamie Welch at (800) 344-9737, or write to Owl International, 14218 NE 21st St., Bellevue, WA 98007.

[3]Hypercard is a trademark of Apple Computer, Inc.

[4]*David's Sling*, Marc Stiegler, Baen Books, 1988.

[5]*The Elements of Style*, Strunk and White, MacMillan Publishing Company, 1979.

[6]*Engines of Creation*, K. Eric Drexler, New York: Anchor/Doubleday, 1986. In addition to being the pre-eminent book of nanotechnology, this book discusses the possible impact of a Xanadu-style hypermedia system of the nature of debate and decision making.

[7]*Marooned In Real Time*, Vernor Vinge, *Analog*, May-August 1986; Baen Books, copyright 1986. This is, to my knowledge, the first time the term Singularity was used to describe the result of exponential advance in technology.

[8]"Iris Eyes," Roger Strukhoff, May 1988. Also see "Intermedia: The Concept And Construction Of a Seamless Information Environment," by Yankelovich, *et. al*, *IEEE Computer*, January, 1988. If you have further questions, you may write to IRIS Brown University Box 1946, Providence, RI, 02912.

[9]"Managing Immense Storage," Theodor Nelson, *Byte Magazine*, January 1988. This article describes the nuts and bolts behind Xanadu. For further information contact the Xanadu Operating Company, P.O. Box 7213, Menlo Park, CA 94026.

[10]*Free To Choose*, Milton and Rose Friedman, Avon Books, 1980.

A CHOICE OF DESTINIES: "Melissa Scott [is] one of science fiction's most talented newcomers. . . . The greatest delight of all is finding out how she managed to write a historical novel that could legitimately have spaceships on the cover . . . a marvelous gift for any fan."—*Baltimore Sun*   65563-9 • 320 pp. • $2.95

THE GAME BEYOND: "An exciting interstellar empire novel with a great deal of political intrigue and colorful interplanetary travel."—*Locus*
                                        55918-4 • 352 pp. • $2.95

THE TRUTH
BEHIND THE LEGEND!

FRED
SABERHAGEN

Once upon a time, King Minos of Crete angered the Sea God, Poseidon. And Poseidon in revenge, sent a monster to plague him. And that monster was— But everybody knows the story of the Minotaur, right? Wrong—not the true story! Here's an exciting new look at an ancient Greek myth—a look through a uniquely science fictional lens.

"Fred Saberhagen is one of the best writers in the business."—Lester Del Rey

The brilliant craftsman, Daedalus, and his young son, Icarus, haven't been at King Minos' glittering court very long when the realm is disturbed by strange visitors from the sea: a menacing man of bronze and an eerie, white-furred creature, half man, half bull. Little do the Cretans know that this minotaur, this White Bull, is no supernatural being sent by an angry Poseidon. Instead, he's actually an extraterrestrial, come to Earth with a thankless job: administer to the stubborn Greeks the principles of a liberal, high-tech education. But the Greeks aren't the best of students. Daedalus finds himself in the middle of things, trying to keep the peace between King Minos, hot-blooded Prince Theseus of Athens, and the White Bull. But the Minotaur himself must learn that it's not wise to meddle in the affairs of primitive peoples. After all, they just might take offense . . .

December 1988 • 69794-3 • $3.95
